Bermuda Triangle

By Jerry Allen

Published by Island Dog Publishing

Copyright © Gerald N. Allen
May, 2018

ISBN-13: 978-1987653960

ISBN-10: 1987653963

Also by Jerry Allen

Force of Habit
Winter of the Swan
Power Lies
Cast and Blast
Break a Bad Habit
Bad Habit
The Resort

This sailor's yarn is the result of an
overly active imagination. Any resemblance to people alive
or dead is purely coincidental.

For those searching
for freedom on the seas.

1

The ocean sparkled beneath a sprawling blue sky. *Frihet* plowed to the southeast, its heel constant in the steady wind. Blue sky and blue ocean stretched to eternity.

"We should see Bermuda soon," said George, scanning the sea ahead. White cumulous clouds were stacked on the horizon.

"Is the island causing those clouds?" asked Windy, wiping salt spray from her gold rimmed glasses.

"Yes. It's the heat rising off the land."

"It's only a little over two days since we left Cape Cod. We made great time."

"Who's hungry?" said Duncan, coming up the companionway and carrying a platter of sandwiches.

"I am," answered George.

"What a change since we crossed the Gulf Stream," said Windy, reaching for a sandwich. "It was cold when we left the Cape."

"It's November," said Duncan. "Anything can happen in November. I'm going to hate going back home."

"You are welcome to stay all the way," said George.

"I wish I could. But it's a busy time of year for me and I need to get back to work."

"It would only be another week."

"The people I caretake for on the Vineyard are fussy," said Duncan. "The only time I get to take off is usually in February. Besides, I have a wife and baby at home."

Nobody spoke while they ate. The sun felt warm and the humidity from the ocean thickened the air. For the past hour the VHF radio had been picking up Bermuda Harbor Radio talking to boats entering the island's waters. George had yet to contact them to announce their presence and he wondered if radar had spotted them yet.

Their fifty foot slope sailed on a close reach with the autopilot steering. The twelve knot breeze came in over the starboard side and for almost twenty-four hours the boat's knotmeter hovered close to eight knots.

"What's that over there?" said Windy, pointing to the east.

George saw nothing, but then something orange peaked above the waves. "I don't know." He reached for the binoculars.

Something orange floated, he could see that much, but it kept disappearing into the troughs between the waves.

"Let's go check it out," he said, stepping behind the portside wheel and shutting off the autopilot.

As he turned the boat, Duncan eased the genoa sheet while Windy let the traveler slide to port before easing the mainsheet further. On the new heading the apparent wind decreased dramatically and the humid air felt hot.

"This is bathing suit weather," said Windy, peeling off the windbreaker she had been wearing.

"The sun is strong," laughed George. "Don't burn up."

Since crossing the Gulf Stream they all had changed into shorts, but the breeze had been cool enough they felt more comfortable in jackets.

Duncan looked ahead through the binoculars. "I think it's a life raft."

"A life raft?" said George, peering around the corner of the headsail.

Windy stepped up onto the side deck and walked ahead to the shrouds to look.

The knotmeter still said over seven and a half knots, but the boat suddenly seemed slow.

"It is," said Duncan, adjusting the focus.

"Is there anyone in it?"

"I can't...there's something...there's something in it."

The raft grew closer and no longer hid between the waves. An arm or something draped over the side. Wrinkled piled fabric, which once been a hood or tent, had obviously collapsed.

"We'll douse the genoa when we get close," said George.

"It's a person," said Duncan. "That's an arm we're looking at."

A hundred and fifty feet from the raft they rolled the genoa around the furler on the headstay.

Windy moved to the portside amidships. George steered downwind of the raft and then turned sharply to come up alongside it.

"One person onboard," yelled Windy. "A woman."

The mainsail flogged as they coasted up alongside.

Duncan, a volunteer EMT back home, jumped down into the raft.

"Windy, drop the main," yelled George, hitting the engine start button. Underneath the raft an inch of brownish green growth waved and a half dozen small fish looked to be calling it home.

The freed halyard hissed and mainsail zipped down to pile up on the boom.

"That raft has been drifting awhile," said George, trying to get a look at the person onboard.

Duncan knelt beside her with his fingertips touching her neck. "She's alive," he yelled. Water inside the raft sloshed up over her waist.

"Windy," said George. "There's a big fucking shark under the raft."

Glancing downward, "Jesus!"

"Duncan, be careful," yelled George, turning the wheel to stay with the raft. "You got a big shark under you."

"A shark?" said Duncan, trying to look over the side.

"A big mother, a great white I think."

The sailboat nuzzled against the raft and Windy passed Duncan a line, which he used to secure the raft firmly alongside.

George shifted the transmission into neutral and went forward to help. Duncan easily lifted the limp woman up to the sailboat's gunwale, where George and Windy hoisted her aboard.

"She weighs like a doll," whispered Windy.

George carried her aft and down into the cabin, where he set her on a settee. She looked to be in her thirties and wore only the bottom of a soiled two piece bathing suit. The rusty red of her skin spoke of days roasting in the sun. Blisters lined her lips and matted kinky blonde hair lay plastered against her skull.

"Get a cool damp cloth," said George.

"What are we going to do with the raft," said Duncan, dropping down into the cabin.

"Cut it free," said George, stepping toward the nav station and reaching for the VHF radio. "First make sure the woman is all right."

"Bermuda Harbor Radio, Bermuda Harbor Radio," said George, "this is the sailing vessel *Frihet*."

"Sailing vessel Free Hit, this is Bermuda Harbor Radio. How do you spell your vessel's name?"

"F-r-i-h-e-t." answered George. "We are approximately ten miles north of North Rock, at 32 degrees 56 minutes north, 63 degrees forty-two west. We have just rescued a young woman from a life raft."

Duncan checked the woman's pulse as Windy stretched a cotton sheet up over her shoulders.

"We have you on radar," answered Bermuda Harbor Radio. "What is the woman's condition? Do you require assistance?"

Duncan shook his head and gave George a cautious thumbs up.

"One of our crewmembers is a trained Emergency Medical Technician. The woman is unconscious, but appears stable. We can be to St. George's Harbor in about an hour and a half, maybe less. Can you have an ambulance meet us at Ordinance Island?"

"Of course, Captain Attwood."

The operator manning the shoreside radio had recognized George's boat's name. Even in Bermuda people had followed his race the previous summer.

"*Frihet* clear," said George, putting the mic back.

Duncan wet a rag and let a drop of fresh water land on the woman's lips. Her tongue snaked it away. "She'll be okay," he said.

George headed up the companionway. "Windy, let's get this boat moving."

2

George watched the ambulance pull away and cross the bridge from Ordinance Island into King's Square, then disappear around the corner of a pale yellow stucco building. Windy and Duncan checked *Frihet*'s dock lines and put out fenders between the boat's slate blue hull and the cut granite bulkhead of Ordinance Island.

Standing next to George, a Bermuda Customs Agent said, "She'll be fine. We have an excellent hospital. It's in Paget Parish, just the other side of Hamilton. Maybe tomorrow you can go visit her."

"Can you come into our office and fill out a report," said a Bermuda Police officer.

"Sure," said George. "Let me clear in with customs first."

A half hour later he stepped back aboard *Frihet*. "Paper work is done," he said. "Who's up for a beer?"

"Sounds good," said Windy.

"I'm buying," said George. "The White Horse Tavern is right in the square. First I have to drop the two pistols I have onboard at the customs office."

"They take them?" said Duncan.

"I'll get them back when we leave," answered George.

"I wonder what her name is?" said Duncan, stepping ashore.

"The police sent a boat out to find the life raft," said George, following. "Maybe they can find it, but it's a big ocean and it wasn't floating very high. It might tell us something."

13

A herring gull picked at a French fry on the asphalt, while a second one squawked overhead. On the far side of St. George's Harbor an enormous blue motor yacht flew an American flag at the stern. More than a dozen sailboats rested along the quay, most carrying American flags, but Canadian and English flags were also present. Stepping around a herring gull, George said, "We'll go to the hospital to see the woman tomorrow."

"We were lucky there was room for us to tie up," said Windy, looking at all the boats rafted along the quay and between Ordinance Island and town. A person could walk across the hulls from *Frihet* to the town of St. George's Parish and skip using the bridge.

"It's not a coincidence," said George. "We were expected even before I called Bermuda Harbor Radio. Spring and fall a lot of boats migrate through here."

A silver haired man approached on a Vespa scooter, slowing to a stop in front of them. "Captain Attwood," said the man. "I am Frederic Fishwissle, the Harbor Master. Welcome to Bermuda." Between the man's feet sat a West Highland terrier who looked very happy.

"Thanks. It feels good to be here."

"I heard you had some bloody excitement on the way. That is terrible, but the young woman will receive the best care possible here." The dog remained sitting and appeared to grin.

"I'm sure of that," said George, anxious to get going. "We're heading to the tavern for a beer. Would you like to join us?"

"Another time maybe," he answered. "Tomorrow night you and your crew are invited to dinner at my home. Many people would like to meet you. Can we send a car to pick you up about seven?"

George glanced at Windy and Duncan. "Sure, we would love it."

With a wave, Frederic turned the scooter and motored away.

*

"How long will we be in Bermuda?" asked Captain Hauglund.

"Not long," said Bill Sanderlee, wondering about the captain's past. The man had only signed on three weeks before their leaving New York, but his resume' had been spotless. If he was as fastidious with running *A New Beginning* as he was with his uniform, the boat would be well taken care of. "How is the crew working out?"

"Fine, even though they are new to the boat, they are all experienced."

"Good," said Bill, looking across the harbor at Ordinance Island. There were eight crew, besides the captain. It seemed like a lot to keep his yacht running, but it was the first boat he had ever owned and he did not question the number Hauglund requested. Out on the foredeck, two young men polished the stainless on the windlass and anchor roller. Ahead of the bow the chain disappeared into the turquoise water. "I wish we could tie along the land."

The Captain glanced at Sanderlee, then across the harbor at the sailboats nestled against the bulkhead. It had been less than two years since he had last visited Bermuda and the place had always been a favorite. He had always looked forward to coming back, but Sanderlee was an unknown. "Only small boats can tie along the quay," he said. "If you wish to go ashore the crew can take you."

Hauglund had never worked for anyone that was new to yachting. The story he had heard was Sanderlee's wife ran off with the number two man of Sanderlee Computing, which apparently caught him completely by surprise. His company, which had grown into a multibillion dollar enterprise, was solely owned by himself, but he sold it quick and walked away when his wife sued for divorce. The yacht was a huge lifestyle change and shocked his family and friends. What was he searching for?

"Maybe I'll ask one of them," said Sanderlee.

Hauglund nodded, thinking it would be easy to dupe this guy.

*

"How was your trip?" asked the bartender, polishing a glass.

"Uneventful," replied George, "until Windy spotted the life raft."

Windy and Duncan sat to George's left at the bar, each of them with a Heineken and a bowl of fish chowder in front of them. The traditional decanters of sherry pepper sauce and black rum had been set on the bar, along with a basket of hot rolls.

"She's a lucky woman," said the bar tender, referring to the woman they had plucked from the sea.

"Hopefully she'll be fine," said George, reaching for the sherry pepper sauce.

"How long will you be in Bermuda?"

"Duncan here is flying back to the States on the first flight he can book," said George, laughing. "He's got a wife and kid that are waiting for him. Windy is helping me get to the Caribbean before she flies back. A young man named Varg Sundhal is flying in tomorrow or the next day to join us."

The bar tender smiled. "Where is Brigitta?"

George had been wondering when he would ask. Brigitta had designed the 112 foot sailing yacht he had captained the summer before for Harold Habit. Along the way, with her long blonde hair and bright smile, she had stolen the heart of almost every male sailor in the United States.

She and George were deeply in love, but then a head injury had turned Brigitta's life upside down. To rest and hopefully recover, she had gone home to Finland's Åland Islands to be with family while she recuperated. During that famous race, George drove Habit's expensive yacht into the side of the boat owned by the man who had caused Brigitta's injury, sending the man overboard. The press loved the story, making both George and Brigitta instantly famous.

"She's still in Åland with her family," said George. "She's going to fly to the Caribbean when I get there."

"The way she looks," he said, while polishing a glass, "I bet you can't wait."

The clicking of flip flops behind them meant someone had entered. A man wearing dark blue shorts and a white polo shirt slid onto a bar stool to George's right.

"You're George Attwood," he said, offering a hand. His accent came from New England somewhere, probably Boston.

"Yes," said George, shaking the man's hand and wondering how long this would go on. Would anonymity ever return?

"I'm Bill Sanderlee. I watched you race," he said, "on ESPN. What a finish."

George wasn't sure what to say. Reflexes, or lack of, caused the end of the race, not any intentional decision. "Thanks."

"Could you teach me to sail?"

George laughed. "Do you have a boat?"

"I own the big blue yacht anchored on the other side of the harbor."

"We saw it," said Duncan. "It's a big one."

"Two hundred and twenty feet," said Sanderlee, beaming. "It's my first boat."

"Really," said Windy, leaning to look around George. "Congratulations."

"I'm serious, I would love to learn to sail."

"We're just passing through," said George. "Where are you headed?"

"No place in particular," said Sanderlee. "My plans are flexible."

"If we cross paths again, we can talk about it," said George.

3

The taxi dropped George and Windy at the front of big boxy King Edward VII Memorial Hospital in Paget Parish. The woman at the front desk had expected them and mentioned Beth Weatherington's condition as greatly improved, then offered directions to her room.

George knocked and they entered. "Good morning," said George.

She looked like a different woman, cleaned up with her kinky blonde hair splayed on the pillow. "Hi," she replied. "You are the people that found me?" Her smile came with an English accent.

"Yes. You look a lot better than you did yesterday," said George.

"They've had me on fluids all night," she said, lifting her arm to show the attached tube. "I still feel weak."

"My name is George, and this is Windy, she's the one that spotted you first."

"My name is Beth," she said, trying again to smile. "Beth Weatherington."

"Can I ask what happened?"

"I was single handling, coming from Stonington, Connecticut, headed for the Caribbean." She turned to look out the window. "My boat hit something."

"Hit something?"

"Yes. Under the water."

"Do you know what?"

"A submarine."

"A submarine?"

Beth didn't look certain, but she said, "I am quite sure."

"Did you see it?"

"No, but I could hear it, a thump, thump, thump."

"Most subs are quite quiet."

"What else could it have been?" She appeared flustered.

"I don't know," said George. "Did you mention it to the police?"

"Yes, they were here earlier this morning."

A nurse entered and asked, "Is everything all right?" She looked at the monitors attached to Beth, then took her pulse.

"Fine," said George. "We were just visiting."

"Yes," said Beth.

"Don't stay too long," said the nurse, turning to leave. "She needs her rest."

"Can we do anything for you?" asked Windy.

"I lost everything," said Beth. "That boat was all I owned. My money and everything is gone. Now I have to start over."

"Where are you from?" asked George.

"Poole, England," she said. "I've been working on boats, doing varnishing or working as a stewardess, trying to save money to buy a boat of my own. Now *Orange Blossom* is on the bottom of the sea." Tears welled up in Beth's eyes.

"What kind of boat was she?"

"A Bristol Channel cutter. A good stout boat, not fast, made of wood, but strong. I spent a year fixing her up."

"You'll have another boat someday," said Windy, reaching to give Beth's hand a squeeze. "At least you're alive."

"When you get out there's a spare cabin on our boat, if you need a place to stay," said George. "We're staying here for a few days at least. After that we're heading to St. Thomas in the U.S. Virgin Islands."

"They may release me tomorrow," said Beth. "I might take you up on that."

"Here," said George, pressing a card into her hand. "My contact info is on that card. The boat is tied alongside Ordinance Island in St. George's."

"I have to get a new passport," said Beth. "And I have no money, nothing. There's a little money in a bank in the British Virgin Islands, that's all."

"Maybe you can have some wired here," said Windy.

"You've been to the BVI?" said George.

"I worked on charter boats there, as a stewardess. We were based in Tortola."

"We're heading that direction," offered George.

Beth looked out the window, then turned back and said, "Thanks, both of you."

"I'll check on you tomorrow morning," said George.

Stepping out of the hospital, the air felt hot, heavy, and humid. Somewhere a car horn honked and small automobiles and mopeds zipped by. Stopping next to a palm tree, the west wind rattled fronds overhead while they waited for a taxi.

Windy said, "I don't think she recognized you."

"I like that," said George.

Glancing at his watch, he added, "Duncan should be on the plane and waiting to take off."

*

"What needs to be done on the boat?" asked Windy, stepping from the taxi. Tourists poked through King's Square, probably from the enormous cruise ship tied along Penno's Warf to the west.

"We're in good shape," answered George, leading toward the bridge to Ordinance Island. "Maybe we'll pick up some groceries later."

"Mr. Attwood," said a man wearing a dark blue sports jacket, a blood red tie, and Bermuda shorts with black knee socks. "I am Officer Nord, with the Bermuda Marine Police." He fell into step with them. "Can I ask you a few questions?"

"Certainly," said George.

"We did find the raft that Beth Weatherington was found in," he said. "We have people looking at it right now. She claims to have collided with a submarine. Did you know that?"

"Yes." George stopped on the quay beside *Frihet*. "We were just visiting her."

"We thought it unlikely. A submerged container that fell off of a ship seemed a more likely scenario. Don't you agree?"

"She said she heard something, like a prop wash or engine."

"Did you see anything...unusual?"

"No. The raft was in tough shape. From the stuff growing on the bottom it looked like it was floating for days."

Officer Nord looked across the bay, then asked, "How long are you staying in Bermuda?"

"A few days, maybe a week."

"Don't leave the island without letting me know. Enjoy your stay." Officer Nord turned to walk toward the Marine Police Office at the end of Ordinance Island.

"What was that about?" asked Windy.

"There must be more to the story than we know," said George, stepping aboard. "What are you going to do?"

"How about I make us some lunch?"

"You're not paid help," laughed George. "You don't have to do that. I'll help you. After lunch I want to call Brigitta."

"You emailed her earlier," said Windy.

"Yes. I told her about finding the woman. We haven't talked for a couple of days."

"After lunch I'm going to go shopping to find a dress for tonight. I never thought we'd be invited out in Bermuda."

An hour later, after Windy had left, he sat at the nav station as Brigitta came on the screen.

"You look great," said George. Her eyes sparkled and her blonde hair was down onto her shoulders. "How are you feeling?"

"Good," she said.

They talked about things she had been doing, mostly visiting friends and a little sailing. The bouts of depression caused by the head injury had passed. She had been invited to be a guest lecturer at The Royal Institute of Technology in Stockholm, and planned to participate. Ian Stock, the chief naval architect at Harold Habit's marine design company Fast Habit Yachts, had been in touch, asking if she would be interested in doing some design work. She said something about other work too for Harold, but didn't offer details.

George mentioned the visit to Beth Weatherington at the hospital and recounted her story. When he told Brigitta about Beth's predicament, Brigitta said she hoped George offered her the spare cabin that became empty after Duncan left. He pointed out that Varg Sundhal would be arriving in two days and the cabin was supposed to be for him. She laughed and said Varg should sleep on the settee in the main cabin.

He then asked if she had heard anything about Harold Habit's yacht *Force of Habit*. Brigitta said it would be out of water at the Hinckley boat yard in Rhode Island for the winter. Repairs wouldn't start until January.

"The damage is not really that bad," she said. "Markov's boat is a mess. I heard it is hauled out at a yard in Fairhaven and they are considering scrapping it. *Force of Habit* nearly cut the boat in two."

Markov was the Russian who, in a failed kidnap attempt, caused Brigitta's head injury, with its resulting bouts of depression and mood changes. In the race in Nantucket Sound, when Markov's boat refused to give to George's right-of-way, George drove *Force of Habit* into its side, effectively ending the race for Markov's boat. While the two boats were tangled, a third boat owned by an Englishman sailed past them to win the race. *Force of Habit* did manage to finish with jury-rigged repairs.

"Are you going to do some work for Ian?" asked George.

"Yes. There are two projects I was working on before that still need to be finished. He said there are other interesting things coming up too."

She mentioned an America's Cup team that had been making inquiries and a boat for the Vendee Globe Challenge, plus two wealthy men had yachts they wanted designed. Eldridge Chapman, the owner of Tomorrow's Yachts and the builder of George's *Frihet*, had also been in touch, asking if she could design a smaller version of the TY50, maybe 45 feet long, as well as a larger boat, nearer 60 feet.

"You are becoming a workaholic," said George, laughing. "Don't forget we were planning to spend some time together in the Caribbean. *Frihet* means freedom, do not forget that."

She smiled. "I haven't forgotten. If the depression stays away, I should be with you before Christmas."

"I could visit you there," offered George.

She laughed. "Why would you want to do that? We have almost no sunshine this time of the year. The Caribbean sounds like a better idea."

A voice on the quay hailed George.

"Someone outside is calling me," said George.

"I should be going too. My father wants my help moving his boat into the barn."

"I love you," said George. "I can't wait to see you."

"I love you too."

*

Captain Hauglund looked at his watch. The boss, Bill Sanderlee, had been gone for most of the day. Where could he have gone? Sightseeing? It wouldn't have been a surprise. At the end of the hallway a large generator purred.

"The door has disappeared," said Olson, running his hand along the wall of the corridor.

"An excellent job," said Hauglund. "Nobody would guess there is a cabin behind the bulkhead."

Stepping into the bright white engine room, they both turned to the right. A red toolbox stood head-high and built against the wall. Olson opened one small drawer in its upper right corner and pushed a button. With a swish of compressed air, the box swung outward revealing a doorway. He stepped inside.

"Perfect," said Hauglund, following.

A leather couch, table, two teak chairs, and refrigerator sat in the small cabin. A doorway led to a head complete with shower and tub. On the wall hung a large TV and a second refrigerator sat in a corner next to a three burner stove. On the table, a small key board sat beside a mouse.

"The couch opens to a bed," said Olson. "The cabin isn't big, but someone staying in here shouldn't get claustrophobic."

"You have done good work," said Hauglund. "Sanderlee will never notice this. He has never stepped into the engine room since he bought the boat."

"Unless someone is looking for a secret room, it will go unnoticed," said the First Mate. "Without measuring the compartments on either side, the space will not be missed."

4

"There appear to be bullet holes in the raft that Beth Weatherington was found in," said Officer Nord.

"Bullet holes?" said George.

"Yes. We counted six holes and believe three bullets passed completely through. By their locations, the raft was fully inflated when someone shot at it."

"Someone wanted her to die?"

"It would appear so. Are you sure you noticed nothing more?"

Tourists clustered around the replica of the ship *Deliverance* in the center of the Ordinance Island, while others poked along looking at the sailboats tied to the quay.

"No," said George. "Have you asked her about it?"

"That is where I am heading next."

"Why did the raft still float?"

"It was built with multiple air chambers. One still had not been breached."

"That explains why the canopy had collapsed, the support must have lost its air."

"Definitely."

"I offered her a berth about *Frihet* if she needed a place to stay," said George. "I'm not getting myself into something, am I?"

Officer Nord's eyebrows went up. "Not that we know of, but bullet holes in a life raft is rather unusual. I am off to the hospital now, if I learn anything troubling I shall return. "

George walked over to stand with the tourists next to the plaque in front of *Deliverance*. What the hell was going on? He started to read.

Admiral Sir George Somers and his men became shipwrecked when their ship *Sea Venture* hit a reef near St. Georges in 1609. They had been in a fleet of nine ships heading towards Jamestown to create a new settlement. Unbelievably, all 150 on board made it ashore in the St. George's area. On the island, they found many hogs, which they could eat and then survive. Some think the hogs were left by passing Spanish vessels. During the next nine months the men built two ships, *Deliverance* and *Patience* to complete their journey.

George looked at the full size blocky replica and shook his head. Naval architecture had come a long ways.

*

"Captain Attwood," came a voice from the dock.

"Are you ready?" asked George, outside Windy's cabin.

The door opened and she stepped out in a pale blue halter top dress.

"You look beautiful," he said. Her thick strawberry blonde hair was pulled back, but still hung to her tanned bare shoulders. In her hand she carried high heeled sandals.

"You do too," she smiled. George had put on a blue blazer and khaki pants.

"Shall we," he said, offering an arm.

On the quay, Windy slipped into her shoes and they followed the driver to a silver Range Rover, where he held the door for them as they climbed into the back. He took a road west, passing over a bridge and by the airport. In the lights of the runway, a United Stated Coast Guard jet took off, climbing into the darkening southern sky. George watched its lights disappear as they drove across a long causeway. The road took them along the south coast and white breaking waves glowed along the reefs off of the shore. The driver made an abrupt turn between two ivory turrets and up a sloping drive. Several cars parked beside manicured flower gardens and a young man, wearing dark Bermuda shorts and a white button shirt, opened the car's door as they stopped.

"Welcome to Coral Conquest," he said.

"There is the guest of honor," announced Frederick Fishwissle, stepping from the front door to greet them. "I think there is someone inside you would like to see. Come."

George introduced Windy, then followed. Inside the door several people blocked the way. Waiters, in black pants and white shirts, offered trays of hor d'oeuvres. Fishwissle shuttled them through, smiling and shaking hands like a politician, often introducing George and Windy before taking them onward.

The room wasn't large, but beautifully furnished with couches, paintings, and a white marble fireplace. Beyond French doors, a lawn lit by torches reached out to an ocean view. Stepping outside, George noticed a pool to the right where a bar had been set up on the blue stone patio. His old boss, Harold Habit stood there talking to Sir Edmund Edge, the owner of the boat that had won the big race the previous summer.

"George," said Harold, putting an arm around George's shoulder. "Good to see you."

"George," said Edge, offering a hand. "Likewise."

They talked about George's trip down and his solo trip to Maine back in August and September. Frederick's wife offered to show Windy and Edge's wife around the house. A waiter appeared with a tumbler of 18 year old Macallan for George.

"What brings you to Bermuda?" asked George, facing Harold.

"My company built a facility here," he said. "I wanted to see the progress, and I guessed you would be here, too. Edmund has a home here and graciously offered me the use of his guest cottage."

"I wanted to be here when you passed through," said Edmund. "Many of my friends in Bermuda want to meet you."

"Have you heard from Brigitta?" asked Harold.

George smiled. "Daily. She sounds well."

"I know," said Harold. "You remember Ian Stock, the head of Fast Habit Yachts? He's desperate to have her come back to work for him. Customers will pay a premium to have her name on the design. And let's not forget how brilliant her ideas are."

"She wants to go sailing," said George, "not spend her days in some office."

Harold didn't reply, but the questioning look on his face gave George concern.

"Come," said Frederick, "let me show you around."

For the next hour George mingled and met dozens of people. The commodore of the Royal Bermuda Yacht Club insisted on George bringing *Frihet* to the club's docks as a guest. A neighbor of Frederick's offered George the use of a 1970 MGB roadster while staying there, but George insisted they didn't need it. Dinner came and went, the conversations rotated around sailing and yachts.

When people started to leave, George led Windy through the house to find Frederick and thank him for the evening. On the way to the front door he spotted Harold.

"How long are you here in Bermuda?" George asked.

"I'm leaving in the morning for Washington."

"Trouble still?"

"Things have quieted down. The American public has a short attention span."

"Well, good night," said George, and with a smile he added, "and don't be trying to steal Brigitta away from me."

Harold smiled and patted him on the shoulder. "Have a safe trip south."

The Range Rover waited near the front door. As George and Windy climbed in the back, he asked, "Did you have fun tonight?"

Windy smiled. "Yes. The people were very friendly."

"Yeah."

Traveling down the drive, George wondered about Harold's life. The man had been born brilliant, made billions writing software and creating a company that put satellites into space to spy on people, but was he really happy? Harold worked ferocious hours, constantly fought with politicians, and seldom took time for himself. Supposedly, he loved to sail, but George wondered if he ever found the time anymore.

"Are you all right?" asked Windy, reaching for his hand.

The darkness hid her face. "I'm fine," he said, "just thinking about Harold. I couldn't live his life."

"We each choose our own path." Her hand squeezed his and then released.

The white lights of the airport were on their right. "I keep trying to slow my life down," said George. "Harold's an alright guy to work for, he'll treat you right, but I'd had enough."

"I might not fly back," said Windy, "when we get to the Caribbean."

"You'll look for a job down there?"

"I'm thinking about it. Sailing on Harold's boat opened my eyes to a world I didn't know existed. Rather than wait for his boat to be fixed…I don't know what he would have me do all winter."

The car stopped in King's Square. "I'm not going to tell you what to do," said George.

Two couples still sat on little round tables outside The White Horse Tavern and music filtered out the door. Otherwise the square was empty.

"I'm going to change into shorts and pour a night cap," said George, walking towards the bridge and Ordinance Island. "You want to join me?" A young couple holding hands walked the other direction.

"Sure," said Windy. "It's a nice night."

Tiny ripples dimpled the surface of the harbor and the night sounds serenaded.

*

Captain Hauglund watched the screen. Jagged lines moved from left to right, one red the other blue. Touching the up and down arrows on a keyboard moved them and finally, with patience, the two entwined into one purple line. A smile formed on his lips. Glancing at his watch, he wondered how much longer Sanderlee would be ashore. Probably not much longer.

He shut off the computer and the overhead lights before stepping out of the cabin. With a swish of air the red toolbox closed the doorway behind him.

*

"Damn," said George, looking at his laptop.

"What is it?" asked Windy, stepping from her cabin.

"Varg isn't coming?"

"Why?" She had changed into a simple little halter dress and walked barefoot.

"He was offered a chance to sail on an eighty-five foot schooner in the South Pacific. I can't say I blame him for taking it. He sent along a picture of the boat, she's a beauty."

"We can sail *Frihet* with just the two of us," said Windy.

"I know," said George. "I was planning on taking her south by myself, but Brigitta insisted I have someone with me." He didn't say anything, but he also didn't think Brigitta would like him spending six or seven days alone at sea with someone as attractive as Windy. George knew he wouldn't like it if the table was turned…but maybe he trusted Brigitta more than he trusted himself.

"Are you going to call her tonight?"

"What was that?" He realized he hadn't been paying attention. "No, it's almost morning there. It's a six hour time difference."

"Your usual, scotch?"

"Yeah, with ice. Let's sit outside."

As they settled into the portside of the cockpit, Windy asked, "So what do you know about Harold's business? Or should I not ask?"

"I don't know if it matters," said George. "He owns satellites that can see people well enough to identify them from outer space...think about it. And they're tied in with security cameras all over the world, then he writes software that can keep track of billions of people at once. Someone said they thought Harold was working on software that would anticipate people's actions ahead of time. Governments and industry love him. Privacy is a thing of the past."

The subject stirred anger and he swirled the cubes in his glass. Lights from somewhere reflected in Windy's glasses. She smiled and his irritation eased.

"The National Security Agency is one of his biggest customers," continued George, "which is why he keeps flying out to Utah. His business has competition from drones now though."

Windy sipped her scotch. "Didn't he say something about his company having facilities here, in Bermuda?"

"Yes. I don't know what that is about."

Windy smiled. "Maybe Bermuda Harbor Radio uses his software to see boats approaching the island."

"That could be," said George, the thought washed away his sour mood. "Bermuda is very protective of her coral reefs." He tasted his whisky. "Somehow Harold knew I was on my way here. I never told him, so he must have been watching. That's why the harbormaster reserved a spot for *Frihet*."

From shore an insect made a ratcheting sound, accentuating the night's emptiness. The music had stopped at The White Horse Tavern and King's Square looked quite dark.

"Things will work out," she said, stretching her legs out to rest her feet against the folded cockpit table.

The pale blue of her dress contrasted with her tan and he noticed how little fabric it contained. Firm muscles toned her legs, legs that were at home on the deck of a sailboat. Sailors often have muscular shoulders, and hers looked like a tennis players. Windy certainly was easy to be around and easy on the eyes. Another sip of scotch tasted of honey and went down easily, intensifying its glow.

He said, "We should get some sleep."

5

"Brigitta, how are you?" said George.

Of course things were fine. They had talked the day before. Brigitta had been up since five in the morning, working on a project for Fast Habit Yachts, which surprised George. She rattled on about the details, but he understood little of it. The sun shined dimly that time of the year in the Åland Islands and Brigitta worked in the living room at her parents' home, wearing a tee shirt with a sailboat printed on the front and jeans. Through a window behind her, George could see the blue of the Baltic Sea.

"Where are your folks?" he asked.

"They are off to market," she said.

He asked about her sister.

"Tova is at work," said Brigitta. "She has her own apartment in Mariehamn."

"What do you have under that tee shirt?" teased George.

"You dirty old man," she laughed, then yanked her top up. "Take a good look."

"Ah," said George, as she pulled it back down. "I miss you."

He told her about Varg's change of plans. "Why don't you fly here to help sail *Frihet* south?"

"Oh…I wish I could. I have promised to have the engineering done on projects for Fast Habit Yachts."

"How long will that take?"

She looked troubled. "A month, maybe two."

"Two? Still done by Christmas?"

"Yes," she said, without conviction. "Then I can come to the Caribbean. They are paying me a ton of money, we will not have a worry."

"I'd rather be with you and be poor," said George.

After an awkward moment, she said, "I really should get back to work."

George glanced at his watch. It was almost ten. "Yes. Go back to work." He hit the off button.

Windy sat on the port side settee reading and didn't say a thing. George stood and walked to the sink where the breakfast dishes were piled.

"She can't make it?" asked Windy.

George started the hot water running. "She has work promised for Fast Habit Yachts."

"It can't wait?"

"Apparently not."

Windy went back to reading while George cleaned the plates.

From the dock came, "Hello. Anybody on board."

George recognized the English accent and stuck his head out of the companionway. Beth Weatherington stood on the quay, wearing shorts, a tank top, and a big smile. "Come aboard."

"What a boat," she said, stepping over the lifelines and carrying two large shopping bags. Her blonde hair looked like an explosion.

"You got out early," said George.

"I made sure of that," said Beth. She looked much healthier than the day before, with a grin and a sparkle in her blue eyes.

"Come on in," he said. "You remember Windy. The aft port cabin is yours for as long as you want it."

"I had a visitor late yesterday afternoon," said Beth, setting her bags down. "I believe he was your boss once, Mr. Harold Habit."

"Really? Coffee?"

"Yes, please. What a generous man. He knew of my predicament and gave me five thousand dollars, cash. Can you imagine that? Cash."

George handed her a mug. "I am not surprised."

"What is even more amazing, he asked what my boat cost me and offered to buy me another. Can you believe it?"

George sat and motioned for Beth too. It did sound a bit over the top, but he said, "He always has been generous."

"I wish I'd told him the boat cost me a million dollars," she laughed.

"Well, that certainly helps with your situation."

For the next several minutes she asked about *Frihet* and George answered her questions. Her life had revolved around boats, but she had never been aboard one like *Frihet*.

"We're short crew," said Windy. "Would you like a ride to St. Thomas?"

George shot Windy a cold glance, but she obviously missed it. He hated to go to sea with someone he didn't know really well, even if they had an extensive sailing resume`. The world was full of want-to-be sailors and three hundred miles from land wasn't the place to train them. Worse still was to be trapped on a boat with someone who was a plain old asshole.

"Are you serious?" said Beth. "Of course I would. I'll start looking for a boat to buy down there."

"Well, put your things in your cabin," said George. "We're staying here today and then moving to the yacht club tomorrow. We'll be in Bermuda for at least a few days. We'll keep an eye on the weather and try to pick a settled stretch, but I am in no hurry to leave."

"There's a million things I need, so I'd like to go shopping again," said Beth, turning to Windy. "Would you like to come with me?"

"That would be fun."

*

Three hundred and forty miles to the east of Bermuda four United States Navy sub chasers worked a grid over a five hundred square mile section of empty ocean. Eighty miles to the north, a one hundred and eighty foot long gray vessel shadowed them. The former Russian R/V *Aisberg* had been privately purchased, painted gray, outfitted with the latest in underwater surveillance equipment, and re-christened *Absent*.

Absent could run silently for days on huge banks of batteries that were charged by diesel engines. Aboard her were some of the brightest minds in the world of undersea communications. A half dozen crewmen managed the ship, while the scientists worked in one cavernous cabin below decks. Captain Jay Able had thousands of hours of sea time and had visited every continent during his career, but never was there an assignment like this one.

"Anything?" he asked, as the head scientist entered the bridge. For three days they maintained a stationary location north of the sub chasers. Before that they stayed in one location for eighteen days almost two hundred miles due north of Bermuda.

"Nothing," said Christine, looking out the windows toward the foredeck. "I needed to see sunlight." She smiled.

"Your team has incredible patience," said Able.

She looked like a scientist, with a round face, her hair pulled back into a ponytail, and dark rimmed glasses. Below decks it was hot, so she wore shorts and a tank top. Beads of perspiration glistened on her skin. "A breeze comes in the hatches," she said, "but it is awfully warm inside."

By keeping the bow into the wind and deck hatches open, air found its way through the vessel. Air conditioning made too much noise, hence disrupting their listening, and was seldom used. Able glanced at the depth sounder. The bottom lay almost two miles below them.

"How long will we be here?" asked the captain.

She filled a paper cup from a large glass water dispenser. "As long as the Navy is working that grid." Bubbles gurgled up inside as the water poured.

"Can I ask what they are looking for?"

Christine's eyebrows went up. "I can tell you the CIA has a large presence on those sub chasers."

"CIA?"

She nodded and took a drink. "Beneath the sea are some of the most powerful weapons ever created."

"Nuclear subs?"

"Yes. And there are people working very hard to make undersea drones, which will be able to search out submarines and follow them." She sipped from the cup. "Billion dollar submarines could become obsolete because of a hundred dozen inexpensive underwater drones."

The captain looked out through the windows at an empty sea. "What is our part in this?"

"Communicating with the drones is a difficulty many are trying to solve. So far the answer has been to make them autonomous, only communicating on the surface every three months or so. The problems have been tremendous, as you might imagine, and many remain unsolved."

Autonomous drones roaming the sea…it sounded unbelievable and a bit troubling. Christine faced into the breeze coming in the windows and plucked at the damp fabric of her top. He asked, "Are we listening for drones?"

"We are listening, hoping to hear someone communicating with a drone."

"What's our boss's part in all this?"

"He invented some of the early drones," said Christine. "His latest ones are over thirty-five meters long and can work autonomously for sixteen months."

"Sixteen months, that's incredible. How do they communicate with land?"

"Periodically they surface to charge batteries and can send information to his satellites."

"Does he share the information to the government?"

"So far, only periodically. The Defense Department is going to put undersea drone development out to bid. There are competitors…some are less than honest."

Captain Able looked out at the horizon. Somewhere beyond it, four sub chasers searched endlessly. "What is the urgency now?" he asked. "We've been at sea almost a month and searching continuously."

On a screen to the right of the helm a satellite view showed the four sub chasers on an empty section of dark blue sea.

"Harold Habit's lawyers have asked me to not say anything more than what I just told you."

*

George slid onto a bar stool in the nearly empty Wharf Tavern.

"Hey Mate," said a man to his left and offering a hand. "You're George Attwood, I've seen your picture, my friends call me Flake."

"You on a boat?" asked George, as the bar tender approached.

"Yeah, the black boat rafted ahead of yours, named *Raven*." He chuckled. "As in ravin' mad."

George laughed, then ordered a beer. The man looked a character, with a bandana tied around his head pirate-style, in a feeble attempt to contain his sun-bleached hair, and a heavy gold chain hanging around his neck. "You passing through?"

"No, not anymore. I signed on as a shore-side hand for the New Zealand America's Cup campaign. Work doesn't start for almost a month though."

"That should be interesting." The Cup boats were high tech catamarans that sailed atop foils at unbelievable speeds. For the first time ever the Cup races would be held in Bermuda.

"I'm not sure how long the Harbor Master will let me live on my boat," said Flake. "They might make me move ashore."

"See what happens," said George. Liveaboards weren't popular in many places, often seen as free loaders who paid no taxes.

"Did you see Her Majesty's warship?"

"Yeah," said George. Sometime during the morning it had entered St. George's Harbour and anchored not far from the large blue motor yacht.

"The U.S. Navy came in a few days ago for one night, four ships. They were doing something northeast of the islands, the fishermen have been seeing them. It's like they are looking for something."

"It's probably war games," offered George. "They have to spend our tax money somehow."

Flake swallowed the last of his beer. "Something's going on. Out the west end of the island there's a place surrounded by chain link fence with razor wire on the top. It wasn't there last year. There's even armed guards, and you never see guns in Bermuda. Something big is happening."

George laughed. "Yeah, the America's Cup Races."

Flake stood to leave and laughed too. "Even bigger than that, if that's possible."

George tasted his beer, wondering if the fenced in place could be the facility that Harold Habit had mentioned. His mind wandered to Brigitta and what project she might be working on. It seemed like she enjoyed the challenge of creating yachts more than the using of them. Had she changed her mind about a winter in the Caribbean? What about the life together they had talked about?

A tourist couple sat and on the way to them the bar tender asked if George wanted another beer.

He ordered a Macallan, neat.

6

"Dinner's on me tonight," said George. "I made a reservation at The White Horse Tavern for seven."

From among the shopping bags piled on the port settee, Beth held up a little sky-blue dress. "I knew there would be an occasion to wear this."

"I have a new dress too," said Windy, pawing through a bag.

"I'm going to hit the shower," said George, smiling. "There will be cocktails in the cockpit afterward."

An hour later Windy joined him in the cockpit, carrying a glass of wine. Beth still dried her hair inside her cabin.

"You look nice. How was your day?" asked George, putting down a magazine. She sat next to him wearing a short dark-blue print halter dress.

"Fun. Beth is a hoot. I think we went in every clothing store in Hamilton."

"Did she spend all five thousand dollars?"

"She's actually quite frugal. When she was a kid their family didn't have much money. Her father used to be the custodian at the Poole Yacht Club, that's how she got introduced to sailing."

George smiled. "Everyone with an English accent sounds wealthy to me."

"She isn't." After a sip of wine, she asked, "Have you heard from Brigitta?"

"No," said George. "I started to write an email, but then deleted it."

"She just has a few commitments," consoled Windy.

"She didn't have to take them on. After her head injury, the doctors said she needed to avoid stress and working too hard. Now she is back at it."

Windy set her hand on George's arm. "I think she loves what she does. For her it isn't work."

The hair dryer in Beth's cabin stopped.

"Beth, there's wine open," said Windy, sticking her head in the companionway.

"Scotch too," said George. "We have a well-stocked bar."

"Wine is fine," said Beth, stopping inside the companionway. "Does anybody need anything?"

"I love your hair," said Windy. The kinky blonde curls looked like a lion's mane hanging down onto her bare shoulders. "And the dress too."

"I hear you had fun shopping," said George.

"Yes," said Beth. "And we ate a lovely lunch at a place right on Hamilton Harbor." Her darkly tanned legs sat across from George. "We got a lot of girl-talk out of the way." Smiling coyly, she added, "Now I know all about you."

"There's not a lot to know," laughed George. "I'm just a simple sailor trying to get back to being simple. The last two years have been too crazy for me."

"You've achieved celebrity status in a sport that almost nobody pays attention too, sailboat racing."

"If you want to call what we did racing. It was a far cry from serious racing."

"Someone won and someone lost."

"You look amazing," said George, "considering we plucked you out of the ocean only two days ago."

"Well, thank you. But I am tired," said Beth. "It will be an early night for me."

"How long were you in the raft?"

"Sixteen days. There were rations for two weeks packed in the life raft." She laughed. "The food lasted twelve days. The water ran out two days before you found me."

"You didn't have an EPIRB?" asked Windy.

"I did, but when the boat crashed everything went topsy-turvy and I couldn't find it. I was lucky to launch the life raft."

"There's two EPIRBs on our boat, one in a locker and another in our raft," said George. "I like redundancy."

Beth smiled. "I do too, now." She sipped her wine. "I was mostly dehydrated when you found me, maybe hallucinating too." And she laughed, "And I lost twelve pounds. Of course I put more than half of that back on when they pumped fluids into me in the hospital.

"Do you remember what you were hallucinating about?" asked George.

"When you found me I was dreaming about my parents, which I haven't done in years, they both passed away a long time ago. Before that, well, maybe it wasn't hallucinations, the Marine Police say someone shot holes in my raft."

"What do you remember?" asked Windy.

"It seemed so bizarre, I thought my mind was playing tricks. It seemed so crazy that I started to laugh."

"Did you see the shooter?" asked George.

"The waves were big. When I would go up over one I could see a bright orange inflatable boat with two motors on the back. Then sometimes it wouldn't be there. There looked like two men in it."

"If someone were shooting at you, why would they have stopped?"

"I do not know." Beth looked suddenly tired and troubled.

"Let's go see if the hostess can seat us at the tavern," said George.

During dinner they talked about boats they had sailed on and places they had been. Beth had raced a lot growing up, finagling her way onto boats as crew, sometimes for the cranky captains that nobody else wanted to crew for. It had made her tough, she said, and also taught her a lot about diplomacy.

When they got back to the boat, they all retired to their own cabins.

*

Bill Sanderlee studied the bottles of wine. There were just too many choices. Thankfully the store was empty, except for one slender woman at the far end of the isle to his right. Outside the small store, tourists cluttered the streets, but soon they would be heading back toward the cruise ship. A large smiling Bermudian woman watched from behind a register and asked if he needed help. Shaking his head no, Sanderlee reached for a bottle of Sangiovese just as the slender woman did too.

"I'm sorry," he said, letting her go first.

"No, my mistake," she said, with a trace of an English accent.

"Do you like that wine?" he asked. There wasn't a wedding ring. She wore a skirt with button shirt, looking like a professional on her way home from work. Her wavy brown hair was pulled back and flowed onto her shoulders

"Yes, and it isn't too expensive." She took two bottles.

"Do you live here? In Bermuda?" asked Sanderlee.

"Yes, in Hamilton. I have an apartment."

"I'm Bill Sanderlee. I'm visiting, here on a boat in St. George's Harbor."

"I am Cynthia Campbell."

"You look like you are on your way home from work. What do you do?"

"I'm in financial planning, it's a small office with two of us." She smiled. "What do you do?"

"There's a little restaurant across the street, The Harbour Front, it's right on the water. Can I entice you into sharing a bottle of wine there?"

Cynthia glanced at her watch. "I was planning to...never mind, it all can wait. I would love to join you. I don't know if we need to split a bottle." When she smiled, he notice the dark blue of her eyes.

Over drinks he learned Cynthia grew up in London, but decided to stay in Bermuda after a vacation there. Like many island tourist destinations, the cost of living was high, but she had done quite well. She and her business partner planned to open a second office in the British Virgin Islands.

A platter of sushi arrived as Bill explained how he had started a software company that blossomed into a multi-billion dollar giant. About the time his wife ran off with the number two man of his organization, another company made an offer to buy him out. The actual day to day running of the business bored him and he walked away from it an incredibly rich man.

"So, how big is this boat you have?" said Cynthia. Flickering candlelight danced in her eyes.

"Two hundred and twenty feet," said Bill, refilling her glass. He laughed and added, "It's my first boat." The remainder of the bottle went into his glass.

"Really?"

"I have an excellent captain and crew. I'm learning."

"To boat?"

"To enjoy life. I used to work all the time. It was work I enjoyed, but it became my only focus. Now I can do anything I want. My plan is to have no plans."

Cynthia laughed. "Are you going to show me your boat sometime?"

"Tonight?"

"Not tonight," she smiled. "How about tomorrow? I have the day off."

"Excellent," said Bill. "We can make a day of it, go for a ride."

"What can I bring?"

"Bring? The boat has everything imaginable on it. Just bring yourself and a bathing suit. Maybe we can swim somewhere or use the boat's pool."

"Your boat has a pool?"

"It isn't big, but it's enough to cool off in and swim short laps. I'll send a driver to get you and then I will bring you back to Hamilton by boat. Can you be ready by nine?"

"Let me write my address on a napkin," she said.

*

"This is the cabin," said Captain Hauglund, stepping past the red tool box. "It isn't large, but I think you will find it comfortable." He knew the Chinese were tall, but Dai stood almost seven feet, yet thinner than a broom handle.

He nodded, "Are the divers done?"

"Yes," said the Captain. "The sensors are in place under the hull and working."

Dai set his duffle on the couch and sat by the computer keyboard. He typed a few strokes and the screen lit up.

"Can we bring you something to eat?" asked the Captain. "Our chef has been informed of your favorites."

Dai nodded.

The cell phone in Captain Hauglund's pocket vibrated. He looked at the text.

He is on the way back, leaving Hamilton now.

That was good. It would be thirty or forty minutes before he returned to the boat. Captain Hauglund turned to the First Mate, "See that Dai has something to eat, and anything else he wants."

*

Through the hatch over his berth George could see the stars. A faint breeze filtered through the boat and occasionally water gurgled along the side of the hull. No sound came from the land other than shoreside insects singing. Sleep seemed elusive.

What was Brigitta doing? He glanced at his watch, it was nearly three, which would make it nine o'clock her time. For a moment he thought about calling her. What would he say? Would she be working? Probably, that's the way she was in the past. It would be better to call her in the morning, when she would be expecting his call.

The boat moved. It wasn't much, but it heeled to port. Did someone step aboard? George didn't like tying along the quay, tourists could step onto your boat, but more likely cockroaches trotted down the dock lines.

He listened. Could it have been a breeze? Again the boat moved.

He slipped from the bed and pulled on shorts. Silently, on bare feet, he stepped through the cabin to peer out the companionway. Distant streetlights illuminated the empty cockpit. The boat moved again.

Cautiously, George stuck his head out. Windy sat on the cabin top with her back against the mast.

"Hey," said George, quietly. "You all right?"

She smiled. "Yes. I couldn't sleep."

"Would you like a glass of wine?"

"Sure."

A few minutes later George handed her a large long stem glass and sat beside her, holding a second glass for himself. "Wine always works for me, when I can't sleep."

"Me too," said Windy. She wore an oversize white tee shirt that said *Frihet* on it, with her strawberry blonde hair hanging loose down to her shoulders.

"Where did you get that shirt with my boat's name on it?" asked George.

"When your boat was being christened," she said. "Mr. Hardy, the head of Tomorrow's Yachts, was giving them away." Grinning, she added, "I took three."

He swallowed some of his wine. "Do you think Beth is going to work out as crew?"

"She's fine," said Windy. "I like her a lot. When we had lunch she told me all the places she'd sailed. She's done a lot."

"She's lucky to be alive."

"Yeah." Windy sipped her wine. "Have you heard from Brigitta?"

George took a gulp from his glass. "No. I'll call her in the morning." A loud insect on the land started to chatter.

To lighten the conversation, Windy asked, "So how are the Virgin Islands different from Bermuda?"

"Oh my God," said George, "the Caribbean is insane, compared to this place. In Bermuda everything is neat and orderly. In the Caribbean turmoil is the norm. You'll see."

"Turmoil?"

"The lack of order is part of the charm," said George. "Maybe that is the freedom of the place." He drank more of his wine. "One time, when I was riding a scooter in Bermuda, I stopped on a bluff to look at the ocean. On a tiny faraway beach, walled in by tall rock cliffs, a young couple was skinny dipping. Two Bermuda Police officers tried for almost an hour to find a way to get down to that beach to arrest them, or give them a ticket at least. It was impossible to get there unless you swam and they didn't want to get their uniforms wet, so they finally gave up. That sort of thing would never happen in the Caribbean. There nobody would care."

Windy laughed. "I can't wait to get there. This will be the first New England winter I have ever missed."

"It feels like I've been gone from the Caribbean for years, but it's only been one winter away."

"I emailed Harold and told him I wasn't coming back," said Windy. "I'll try to find work down there." She settled back against the mast and looked up at the starts.

"You'll enjoy the sail down," said George, looking up at the stars too. "Being offshore is about as free as a person can be on this planet. Everything we need is on the boat. You fall into the natural rhythms, noticing things like the stars at night and the clouds. You will feel the reality of traveling around the outside of a big blue sphere."

Land lights reflected on the glassy water.

"How long will it take to get there?"

"It will take about six days. The wind is often light this time of the year. At least it will be warm." Far away a car's horn honked. "Exactly how long it takes will depend on when we pick up the tradewinds. Sometimes you can almost see the islands before the tradewinds kick in."

Windy took another drink from her glass then set it on the cabin top. "Can I ask you something? Would Brigitta have been jealous, or worried, if just you and I sailed this boat to the Caribbean? I mean, it's silly, but unchaperoned?"

George tilted his head back and drank the last of his wine. "Should she be?"

Windy's hand slid next to his, her pinky finger touching his. "You tell me."

He wasn't sure what to say, he wanted Brigitta, but she seemed so distant. Hell, she was *so* distant, thousands of miles distant and engrossed in a project that she seemed to love more than him. Windy looked beautiful in the dim light. George brought the empty glass to his lips, hoping for one last sip. "We need to keep our relationship just friends," he said, glancing down at her hand, "for now, anyways."

"I shouldn't have asked that, I'm sorry," said Windy, moving her hand away and forcing a frown. "You are a man spoken for. It must be the wine talking."

George smiled and stood. "You are sweet. And beautiful, but I'm going back to bed, to sleep."

7

The computer screen blinked and Brigitta's face appeared.

"Hi," said George, "Where are you?" He recognized the painting of the J boat *Shamrock* on the wall behind her. It hung in Newport, Rhode Island.

She smiled. "At Fast Habit Yachts. Harold's jet flew me over."

"Why?"

"There is a project they need me to work on with them. It is important."

"Another one?"

"It will not take long. It should be done before Christmas. I'll skip some of the others they wanted me to do."

"This is a new one?"

"Yes. But I can't tell you what it is about. I'm promised Harold that."

"Harold? What's his part in this?" It all felt like a bad dream.

"It's for his company. That is all I can tell you. I'm only here today and maybe tomorrow, then I fly back to Åland to work from home."

A smiling head appeared behind Brigitta and waved. "Hi George." The woman looked like Brigitta's twin.

Brigitta smiled, "That's Tova, she flew over with me."

"Hi Tova," said George. With Brigitta's sister there he didn't want to get into an argument.

"Hi George," said Tova, again. "It is nice to finally meet you." She laughed. "You can always take me sailing if my sister is too busy."

Giggling, Brigitta pushed her sister aside.

"I am short crew," said George. "Varg had a change of plans and won't be joining us here. He's off to the South Pacific instead. Windy asked Beth to join us and I think she will."

"You will have a crew of beautiful women," teased Brigitta. "You won't miss me."

"I would trade them all for you," said George, feeling annoyed. "Sailing single handed still has an appeal."

"I don't want you disappearing at sea because something stupid happens," said Brigitta. She could see George wasn't happy.

"Where are you staying?" asked George.

"We're staying in a hotel in Newport," said Brigitta. "I should get back to work."

"Okay. I'll call you tomorrow, about the same time, if you are still there."

"Okay," said Brigitta. "I have much to do and Tova wants to go play tourist."

"I love you," said George.

"I love you too." The screen went blank.

In the galley, George poured himself a cup of coffee, then went on deck. Tourists loitered in King's Square and gulls picked at the asphalt. On the black sloop ahead of his, Flake applied varnish to a toe rail.

"Hey Cap," said Flake. "Where did your crew go? I saw them headed ashore."

"Probably to find croissants," said George. "They were talking about them earlier."

Flake put down his brush and can of varnish to walk aft. Beads of sweat shined on his darkly tanned shoulders and a bandana kept his hair back. George sauntered up to the bow to meet him. "You're a lucky bloke," said Flake. "I'd bed either of those two hotties in a heartbeat."

"They're both just friends," said George. "The one with the kinky blonde hair we just rescued from a life raft a couple of days ago."

"I heard about that," said Flake. "What a find."

"The other one, Windy, she used to work for me on a boat I was running up in New England."

"You got all the luck, man. The last woman I had on my boat split over a year ago."

George sipped his coffee, that didn't surprise him. "We're leaving here in a bit, heading to Hamilton. We've got an invitation to stay at the Yacht Club."

"Hey," said Flake. "If you need a hand moving your boat I can come along. I'll just catch a ride back here afterwards."

"No, we're all set. Here comes my crew now."

Windy and Beth walked across the bridge, talking and laughing about something. Beth carried a white paper bag.

A half hour later *Frihet* backed from its berth alongside Ordinance Island. Ahead of the bow, Flake stood by his stern rail to watch them leave. Clear of the Ordinance Island, George turned the wheel to point the bow out into the harbor. Windy handed him another cup of coffee, while Beth coiled dock lines.

"Did you get ahold of Brigitta?" asked Windy.

"Yes. She's in Newport, Rhode Island." They motored to the southwest, toward the airport on the far side of the harbor.

"Newport? Really?"

"Yes. Working."

"For how long?"

The breeze came from ahead, but only blew hard enough to raise ripples. A large white rigid inflatable, with a big white outboard on the back, pulled away from the outside of Ordinance Island. George noticed Bill Sanderlee sitting next to an attractive dark haired woman ahead of the helm. With their big smiles, they looked like a couple going on a picnic. A young crewmember dressed in white piloted the craft.

"Brigitta's going home tomorrow," said George, "or the day after. It's a new project for Harold Habit, something she can't talk about."

"You don't look happy."

"I'm not. She promised to have everything done by Christmas. I wouldn't bet any money on that."

Out in the harbor they hoisted the mainsail. Beth certainly knew her way around a boat, cleating the main with just the right amount of tension in the luff, then adjusting the mainsheet and traveler. The genoa barely filled in the light air. It would be hot sailing downwind.

On a beam reach, they ghosted east through the manmade passage known as Town Cut, with its cliff-like coral sides and Australian pines hanging in at the top. It didn't feel wide enough for the cruise ships that passed through it, but they did almost daily. Ahead stretched a sparkling blue horizon.

"Do you know the way?" asked Windy, as they cleared the Cut.

"We'll sail around the north side of the island. There's a channel to the northwest ahead, it's called The Narrows, then it divides into two channels to the west. We'll take South Channel. It's closer to the island."

He thought South Channel would be more interesting, with the island to look at. Beth stood next to the mast, watching the island slip by. She wore shorts and a polo shirt, over the slender body of an athlete. A breath of wind tugged at her wavy blonde hair.

"It's hot," said Windy. She pulled her tee shirt off, revealing a bikini top beneath.

"It will be cooler when we turn," said George. "The apparent wind will pick up."

"Would you like another coffee?"

"Sure."

Windy disappeared toward the galley. Ahead a sailboat beat into the light wind, heading into St. George's Harbour. It felt good to be on the water again. Far away, on the horizon to the north, a white sail headed toward Bermuda.

"Here," said Windy, passing him a mug. She had replaced her shorts with a bathing suit bottom.

"Thanks."

Beth stayed up near the mast and looked astern at the island's hillside, with its dozens of pastel colored houses scattered about. The pale blue of the water grew a shade darker as the depth increased.

"More coffee?" asked Windy.

Beth shook her head no, then turned to look ahead. A slice of wind found its way through the land cut and pushed a strand of her hair across her face. She pulled her tee shirt up and off, revealing two bare perky breasts, pulled her mane back to contain it with a stretchy tie, and then down went her shorts, uncovering one of the smallest bathing suit bottoms George had ever seen. With a big smile, she looked back at George and Windy, gave them a thumbs up, then sat on the cabin top, looking ahead with her back against the mast.

"She's certainly not shy," laughed George.

"I told you she was fun," said Windy.

*

Bill Sanderlee took Cynthia's hand as she stepped aboard his glistening yacht, *A New Beginning.* Her free hand carried a small dark blue duffle bag.

"Welcome to my home," he said, motioning toward curved stairs that led up from the teak boarding platform to the main deck.

"This is your only home?" she asked, ascending.

"I still have a house outside of Boston," he said. "It's for sale at the moment."

On the spacious aft deck, lounge chairs were arranged either side of a small table. A potted palm tree provided an insignificant bit of shade. At the back of the house, large glass doors had slid aside, creating a fifteen foot wide opening. The teak felt cool beneath Cynthia's bare feet.

"So you are starting your life over?" said Cynthia, peering inside.

Leather couches sat either side of a round cocktail table. Rows of books lined shelves beneath the windows on either side. Further in, a dining table with ten chairs sat before what looked like a well-stocked bar. A curved staircase led upward. Inside, a young woman misted and then wiped the large starboard side windows.

"Let's go this way," said Bill, motioning along the port side deck.

"This is much bigger than most people's homes," said Cynthia, looking in the windows.

"I am quite lucky. Have you done much boating?"

"Some, with friends," she answered. "Never on a yacht like this."

"This way." Bill stopped at the base of a set of stairs to let her lead the way up.

At the top of the stairs he guided her forward and into the wheel house. "This is Captain Hauglund," he said.

"Good day," said Hauglund.

"What a boat," she said, looking at the computer screens over the large windows. A young man sat on a stool in the corner, looking intently at another computer screen.

"This is my First Mate Olson," said Hauglund. "He is my right hand man and someday will captain his own vessel."

"As I mentioned earlier," said Bill, "we would like a leisurely sail to Hamilton."

"That is an easy task," said the captain. "I have notified the galley that there is a guest on board."

"We'll be back at the pool," said Bill.

Cynthia followed him aft along a side deck to a glass door just beyond the stairs they had come up. He opened the door and she passed through, continuing along the side deck.

"The doors assure privacy," he said. "If we need anything we can buzz the galley."

The deck opened up to an area the size of a tennis court, encircled by a four foot high wall topped with a wide teak rail. In the center of the far end, two teak steps surrounded an oval pool about twenty feet long. At the forward end of the deck a roof protruded aft about fifteen feet to provide shade. Lounge chairs were arranged both in the sun and in the shade, many with side tables containing flower arrangements or baskets of fruit. Those in the sun had little umbrellas. A circular small dining table, with two chairs, sat in the shade. At the aft end of the deck, at the far end of the pool, a canopy shaded a large square lounge piled with huge pillows.

"There is a bathroom and changing room through that teak door," said Bill, pointing toward the white wall at the forward end of the pool area. "We have complete privacy here. The crew will not arrive unannounced."

"I am impressed," said Cynthia. "This is the way to travel. How was the trip down? Did you get bored?"

"I must confess, I flew down. There was business to finish up, so I let Captain Hauglund take *A New Beginning* down and I flew to Bermuda after he arrived." He motioned toward the lounges in the shade. "Can I get you coffee, tea, or a cocktail?"

Cynthia settled into the further one. "How are your Bloody Marys?"

"I don't know," he laughed. "I've never had one on board." He pushed an intercom button on the side table and ordered two.

Pulling sunglasses from her bag, she asked, "Is it time for bathing suits?"

"If you'd like."

"I would love to catch some sun before it gets too strong." She stood and, carrying her bag, headed for the teak door.

*

Christine stepped out onto the small deck ahead of the bridge. "The air feels good out here." She undid her ponytail, letting her hair move in the wind.

"It does," said Captain Able. "How are things going?"

"We have picked up contacts, lots of them. Our team is trying to sort them out." Perspiration caused her jersey to stick to her skin. Rolling the bottom of it upward, she exposed the flesh of her stomach to the cooling breeze.

"Contacts?"

"Communications. We don't understand what a lot of them mean. We had been listening at the wrong frequencies and even mistook some of the sounds for sea life."

"So, it's sophisticated?"

"Very. The sub chasers have moved further south. We need to decide if we are going to follow."

"We, meaning you and me, or we, meaning you and your team."

She smiled. "Me and my team. This must be hard for you, all this waiting."

"I've been on more interesting assignments." There were only four women on board, all part of the scientific team. Christine was the team leader and certainly the most attractive. "How hot is it inside?"

"The thermometer says ninety-six degrees. It isn't bad when the breeze finds its way through."

"There's not much air today."

"No. It feels good to be up here on deck."

"My cabin is cool, the wind always blows through. Can I entice you into having dinner with me tonight? I think you are off by then."

Christine smiled. "I'd like that. My shift is over at four."

"My cabin has a private shower too, if you would like to use it."

She laughed. "That sounds great. There's twelve of us in the guest cabins trying to share one. Modesty went out the window after about a week at sea."

*

"George will be angry," said Tova.

"He will understand," said Brigitta. She took a bite of her sandwich. From the windows of Fast Habit Yachts, they could see the boats in Newport Harbor. The rest of the staff had gone to lunch.

"I am not so sure of that. He wants to go sailing with you." Tova sipped from a bottle of water. "And you are going to let him sail with a boat full of women? Are you crazy?"

"Tova, I have been asked to do something important."

"More important that George?"

"No." Brigitta set her sandwich down. "If I could tell him what it was he would understand."

"You cannot tell him?"

"I promised Harold."

They ate in silence, watching a schooner come alongside the end of Bannister's Wharf.

"Your English is much better," said Brigitta.

"I have been practicing. Even in my design work it is helpful. In your field, engineering, it is essential."

Crewmembers from the schooner cleated dock lines.

"You have always taken work too seriously," said Tova. "Even in school you put studies before everything."

"That is not true," said Brigitta. "After college I went to work as a stewardess on Harold Habit's boat for fun, rather than do engineering."

"And what did you do on his boat? You spent all your time designing another boat. I think you like working better than anything."

Brigitta smiled. "I do enjoy my work."

Tova nodded. "You are good at it."

"It is easy for me, I am lucky."

"Are you really going to be done before Christmas?"

"I do not know," said Brigitta. "There are big problems I must solve. Eldridge Hardy has put together a good team to work with me, but much of what we are doing has never been done before."

A woman amidships on the schooner adjusted a spring line while a man on the foredeck eased a dock line.

"Do you think George would let me sail to the Caribbean with him?" asked Tova.

"Are you serious?"

"I love to sail, you know that. It would be fun, I have never done an ocean passage."

"I can ask him."

Tova laughed. "I can keep an eye on George for you."

"Ha! You stole the first boy I ever liked," laughed Brigitta. "That was when I was only eight years old! Who will keep an eye on you?"

Tova teased, "I thought George was your first boyfriend, I do not remember others."

8

Passing a green can that marked the end of the channel known as The Narrows, George turned the boat due west. The apparent wind climbed to fourteen knots. Windy cranked in the genoa on the starboard side and Beth looked skyward as she trimmed the mainsail. The turquoise bottom passed beneath them at seven knots. Ahead, the water turned a darker shade of blue and its surface sparkled from the sun. George set the autopilot to hold the course and started to pull the pale-gray canvas bimini into place over the cockpit.

About six miles to the north, a gentle ground swell surged against the coral reefs that protected the island, creating a long white line along the horizon. Inside the reef, scattered coral heads poked upward in huge areas that were left uncharted, but ahead were several miles of relatively deep water over a sandy bottom. In twenty minutes they would tack to the south.

George settled against the starboard life lines to watch the mesmerizing water slipping along the hull. Both Beth and Windy soaked up sunshine on the foredeck, but soon the heat would send them back to the shade of the bimini. Far away to the north an outboard motor purred.

Was Brigitta really going to be done by Christmas, wondered George. She certainly liked to work and solve all kinds of technical problems. Maybe it was the difference in their ages. He tried to remember what he felt passionate about when he was sixteen years younger, but couldn't. Was it selfish of him to want her to stop?

Off to port a large tanker waited to unload. On shore, enormous white storage tanks waited for the fuel. To the north an anchored red boat flew the red and white diver's flag. Two white sails barely poked over the horizon, probably boats migrating from the States.

George tried to picture Brigitta on the boat with him, but it was pointless. The distance between them seemed to be more than miles. Patience had always been one of his strong points, but this...frustrating.

Windy and Beth came aft along the port deck, all smiles and complaining about the heat, both carrying towels. Ducking into the shade of the bimini, Windy asked if George wanted anything to drink. He answered water. The two disappeared down inside the boat and he could hear them laughing.

He wondered if they had put clothes back on...he hadn't even noticed.

*

For almost two hours they sat on lounges in the shade of umbrellas and talked, learning about each other's lives. They hardly noticed their passage through Town Cut and were oblivious to traveling east straight out into the open Atlantic Ocean. Captain Hauglund stopped *A New Beginning* three miles east of the island, where he kept the vessel stationary with her bow into the light wind. A half hour later they motored west to turn northward through The Narrows.

Bill had not dated since his wife left, instead throwing his energies into selling his business and more or less emotionally running away. At least that was how it sounded to Cynthia. Bill loved the way she listened to his stories, but, more than that, the way she looked in the tiny pale yellow bikini. A miniscule gold chain around her neck held a narrow slice of white coral that dangled between her breasts. Not staring was a challenge.

She told stories about college and the struggles of trying to start a business in Bermuda. He talked about growing his business from a one-man basement operation into a multibillion dollar corporation. Vodka tonics arrived with a slice of lime. They talked of their childhoods and families, cars they had once owned, and places vacationed.

With the alcohol loosened tongue, Bill confided that his wife was the first woman he had ever dated. Long before the word nerd came to being, he had been one, spending all his time in science and math classes.

"I wanted to catch some sun," said Cynthia, changing the subject.

"It is still shining," laughed Bill.

"The sun is strong now, it is too easy to burn."

"Shall we cool off in the pool? Or would you like some lunch?"

"Yes, let's take a dip," said Cynthia, getting up. "Then we'll need to get back into the shade."

She stood a few inches shorter than Bill, with the slender body of an active person. When he rose from the lounge he realized how quickly the alcohol had gone to his head. "I've only been in the pool once," he confided. "It was a couple of nights ago, the stars were fantastic."

"That must be fun," she said.

Leaving his empty glass on the table, he offered a hand and together they walked toward the pool.

"This is beautiful," she said, looking along the side deck toward the doors they had come through. "We have complete privacy."

"We do. The previous owner had it designed that way. And the wall around us not only provides privacy, but also breaks the wind, making it possible to use this space on days when the breeze is chilly."

"Brilliant." She looked at the land to the south. "Where are we?"

"That is Fort Saint Catherine. The captain said he planned to take North Channel. Have you ever looked at a chart?"

"No. They only confuse me." She smiled at her own joke. "Bermuda is beautiful, even from far away." He followed her up the two steps and together they settled into the pool. "This is heavenly," she said. "I would use this pool everyday if I could." Four breast strokes took her to the far end.

Bill sat on the ledge that created a seat all the way around inside the pool, which left his shoulders only an inch above the water. "It is relaxing, but it isn't big enough to really swim in."

"It's refreshing, that is what's important." She pushed to swim back, but stopped to stand in the middle where the water was inches below her chin. Laughing, she said, "At least you don't have to worry about people drowning."

*

Captain Hauglund stood in the bridge behind First Mate Olson, who sat in a leather chair in front of an array of computer screens. To his right, a second chair remained empty, but the screens there were also lit. Some displayed navigational information, others systems onboard the vessel, such as fluids in tanks and electrical usage. Behind Hauglund, a long padded white leather sofa sat elevated behind a tiny table centered on a post, so the owner or guests could look forward over the heads of the helmsman.

No wheel existed in what used to be called the wheel house. Instead, small toggles, switches, and buttons in front of Olson controlled the speed and heading.

Hauglund picked up what looked like an old fashioned black telephone and pushed a button. "Were you able to get what you needed?"

From down in the belly of the vessel, Dai said, "Partial."

The phone went dead.

Frustrated, Hauglund said, "That man doesn't say much."

*

Windy came up to the cockpit, wearing a snug tank top with a bikini bottom, and passed George an insulated glass of ice and water. "It feels good to be sailing again.

"Yes."

"You were thinking about Brigitta, weren't you?"

He nodded. The thin fabric of Windy's top left little to the imagination and he was glad dark glasses hid his eyes. Taking a deep breath, he tried to appreciate how lucky he was...on a beautiful boat, sailing somewhere warm, with two attractive women who he enjoyed the company of. It didn't work, the ache inside persisted.

"There's the big blue boat that was anchored in St. George's Harbour," she said, pointing behind them.

"What was his name, Bill something?"

"Yes, Bill Sanderlee," said Windy. "That's quite a yacht for a first boat. He said it's his home now."

"I wonder how long it will be before he is bored."

Windy put on her sunglasses. "Why do you say that?"

"I don't know," said George, realizing it sounded rather cynical. "He's used to running a large corporation and inventing things, this may seem anticlimactic."

Windy wondered if George realized what he had said. Could that be what had happened to Brigitta?

"Hey, lunch you two?" asked Beth from the companionway.

"You wore it!" said Windy. It was a little white halter dress of jersey that barely went below Beth's hips.

"You like?"

"It's cute. I should have bought the turquoise one like it."

The women slipped into a conversation about clothes. George looked aft at the big blue motor yacht, in wonder of how much thought women put into their appearance. He cared about his appearance, but could easily live with one suitcase of clothes, and it could be a pretty small suitcase in the lower latitudes. A smile snuck up on him...it was pretty darn nice that women liked to look their best.

*

"It must the sun and alcohol," said Bill, "certainly not the company. I feel like shutting my eyes for a couple of minutes."

Cynthia smiled. "Are you a napper?"

"I like a midday nap, always have." He grinned. "I'll make a confession, when I ran my business I used to take a five minute nap in my office chair, almost every day, right after lunch."

"I won't feel insulted," laughed Cynthia. "But can I work on my tan? I will risk the afternoon sun, because there's a few tan lines I would like to erase."

"Of course. But be careful, don't burn."

Cynthia smiled. "I won't. I might have to freshen my sunscreen."

The sun had slipped well past its zenith. Earlier, they lingered over lunch during a third round of drinks, then took another dip in the pool. Conversation never lagged, which surprised Bill. He never considered himself a social butterfly and small talk often could be difficult. Yet Cynthia fascinated him and talk came easily.

As Bill settled back in his chair, she spread a towel on a leather and teak lounge chair in the sun at the far side of the pool. With her back to him, Cynthia removed the top of her bathing suit and stretched out on her stomach. Bill was mesmerized. Feigning sleep behind his dark glasses, he couldn't take his eyes off her bare shoulders.

Cynthia wondered what sort of an impression she was making…Bill certainly didn't seem like one of the planet's movers and shakers. He seemed too timid to have run a giant corporation, and certainly not what she had expected.

There was no way to know, but she guessed he wasn't asleep. It didn't matter though, he soon would be awake. Hadn't he said he was a five-minute-napper?

The sun felt heavenly on her shoulders. It had turned into a relaxing day and her job was going to be an easy one. She wondered how much longer before they reached Hamilton. Not wanting to chance waiting too long, Cynthia rolled over.

From behind his sunglasses and still pretending to be asleep, Bill fought to control his smile. That was not his body's only reaction.

9

George adjusted the port stern line. Docking European style, also called stern-to among sailors, with an anchor keeping the bow out and the boat perpendicular with the dock, wasn't George's favorite way of docking. If the anchor slipped at all it was too easy to damage the boat's stern. Either side of *Frihet* other sailboats were docked the same way, so he assumed the holding ground for the anchor was good. Immediately to port, old dark coral rose up almost to the surface and made it impossible for a boat to tie up there. Crossed spring lines kept the *Frihet* from moving side to side, yet pulling on either of the dock lines moved the boat close enough to the dock to step ashore.

Windy cleated off the starboard spring line.

"Welcome to The Royal Bermuda Yacht Club," said a man wearing a blue blazer with Bermuda shorts and black knee socks.

"It is nice to be here," said George, trying to remember if he had met the man at the Harbor Master's party.

"If you need anything, just ask."

"We'll be fine.

"The Club is planning a meet and greet event tonight, at six and in your honor. I trust you will be there."

George hadn't expected more than dockage. "Of course we will, there are three of us."

"We know.

The three of them had spent the day sailing, venturing past Ireland Island at the west end of Bermuda, then beating down along the west coast, picking their way through numerous coral heads. Beth stayed at the bow, leaning against the headstay, watching for obstructions and signaling course changes when necessary. Some of the coral heads came up within inches of the surface.

George had hoped her lack of clothing wouldn't offend the locals. In two very shallow areas, channels were marked by posts and they had been forced to pass close by other boaters. Beth always waved back.

At Somerset Bay they had turned around, then sailed on a broad reach in light air. By the time they rounded the reefs off Commissioner's Point, at the western tip of Bermuda, the day had become unbearably hot. Close reaching on a starboard tack, the apparent wind climbed over ten knots, cooling them off, and, back in deeper water, Beth returned to the cockpit, where she slipped the new little dress back on over her head.

Earlier, while watching her at the bow, George had wondered if that was going to be the new normal dress code for the rest of their trip. Changes in latitude…what was that line? Or was it the freedom of the sea thing? Not that he minded, there wasn't anything he could think of he would rather look at than an attractive woman, although a classic sailboat with a nice shear came close.

During the afternoon, Windy had kept him company in the cockpit, staying in the shade and often reading to pass the time. He wondered what she thought of Beth's near nudity. The Windy he knew back on Cape Cod wouldn't have bought a miniscule thong like the one Beth wore. Or would she? The thought brought an involuntary smile.

After reaching across Grassy Bay, they had tacked south and then west toward Parson's Bay. The thumping of a helicopter landing caused them all to look at the shore. The racket came from the fenced in compound that the man named Flake had mentioned at the bar. George wondered if it had anything to do with things that Harold Habit had talked about.

Tacking to the south again had brought them into deeper water. Beth disappeared inside to come back out wearing a big floppy straw hat that caused her kinky hair to flair under it. Windy said something about that being a good idea and came out wearing a ball cap.

There had been little conversation, which suited George fine. Mindless chatter usually drove him crazy, which was why cocktail parties often made him nuts. A week at sea with these two wouldn't be bad at all. And it would take most of a week to reach the Virgin Islands. For a while he had wondered what Windy and Beth planned to do once they got to the Caribbean. And, as sailors have wondered for generations, how far south they would have to go to find the tradewinds.

"Are we using the showers ashore?" asked Windy, as the man from the Yacht Club walked away.

"It's up to you," said George. "Our tanks are full, the water maker topped them up today."

"I'll clean up onboard," said Beth. "Then let's go check this place out."

While the two aft showers ran, George checked his email. One, from Eldridge Hardy at Tomorrow's Yachts, mentioned a prospective buyer visiting the next morning at the club. George took a deep breath, sales wasn't exactly his forte, but it would pay the bills. His ability to purchase *Frihet* came about only with his promise to sell more boats like it. Tomorrow's Yachts more or less bought his famous name.

About to close his email, a new one from Brigitta popped up. His heart skipped a beat.

George,
I hope you are not mad at me. This work is something I must do. I know you will understand.

Tova would like to sail with you to the Virgin Islands. Would you mind taking her along? She is an excellent sailor and I think you will enjoy her company.

I will talk to you tomorrow. Still be in Newport for one more day.
Love,
Brigitta

George tried to remember what he knew about Tova. Brigitta said she worked as a graphic artist and designer. He knew she sailed, but hadn't Brigitta once complained that Tova used to party too much and didn't take life seriously enough. That probably meant back in her college days, and she was a year or two older than Brigitta. He had never even seen a picture of her until she popped up on the screen behind Brigitta earlier.

He typed, "Sure, she is welcome."

Hitting the send key, he shook his head and thought, "I must be nuts."

*

The phone beside Bill Sanderlee hummed. "Yes?"

"We'll be arriving in Hamilton in twenty minutes," said Captain Hauglund. "We will be tying along the outside of the dock at the Princes Marina."

"Thank you," said Bill.

Cynthia sat up to turn her back to him, then put on her bathing suit top.

"I hope that was okay," she said. "Do you mind?"

"I enjoyed it," said Bill, grinning at her proper English accent. "We will be docking in about twenty minutes. It must be the drinks, I never sleep that long."

She smiled and walked toward him. "I'm glad you slept. I must confess, it's always been a fantasy of mine to be tanned all over, with absolutely no tan lines what so ever."

"You should have spoken up earlier. I'm sure they would be almost gone by now."

Wearing a sly grin, she sat next to Bill. "So what are our plans? Can I take you to dinner?"

"Take me? I was planning to ask you."

"Ever optimistic, I brought a dress."

"Would you like to use the shower in the master cabin?"

She grinned. "Is that your cabin?"

"Yes, and I promise to be a gentleman."

The cabin was enormous, as wide as the boat, with Oriental rugs and curved dressers built against the forward curved wall. A king-size bed sat opposite a large television over the dressers and, at the port side of the cabin, a desk with a computer sat against the wall beneath curtained windows. In the starboard end, three stuffed chairs were arranged around a small round table beneath matching windows. At either end of the curved dresser along the forward side were doors. One led to a tiled bath with two vessel sinks before a mirrored wall. Against the aft wall a large shower stall stood next to a tub big enough for four or more. A television even hung on the wall above the tub. The other door led into a huge walk-in closet.

"My apartment isn't as big as this cabin," said Cynthia. "You live like a king."

"While you shower, I'll make us dinner reservations," said Bill.

Twenty minutes later, she emerged and said, "Your turn."

"You look lovely." She did, in a little black dress with her wavy hair down on bare shoulders.

"Do you mind if I take a stroll outside while you get ready?" she asked.

"Not at all."

She walked along the starboard deck, looking at the pink six story hotel on shore. Two young crewmembers wiped down the large windows along the sides of the boat's house. The marina appeared to be full, except for the outer part where they were docked. It was obvious the outer dock was the only place that a yacht as large as *A New Beginning* could fit. On the shore, between the marina and the hotel, people swam in a giant pool.

Cynthia went up the stairs they had gone up earlier, but instead of heading aft toward the private pool area, she went forward and stepped into the bridge.

Captain Hauglund smiled. "You look nice. How did it go today?"

"Fine. It will be easier than we thought. He is what the Americans call a geek, very smart about some things but not so much about others." Outside, forward of the bridge's massive windows, a crewmember scrubbed the teak deck with soapy water. On the starboard side of the bridge, First Mate Olson sat in front of a computer screen.

Hauglund said, "That is what I think too."

"He is too trusting. It did not surprise me when he said his wife had an affair for over a year before he found out. How did he survive in business?"

Hauglund shrugged. "It is not our concern. Dai needs more time away from land, there is too much noise near the harbors. And the divers have things that must be done under the boat again."

"What do you want me to do?"

"Can you get him to take the boat out again tomorrow? Offshore?"

She smiled. "That should be easy. When will the divers do the work under the boat?"

"Tonight. Keep him occupied."

"And we are copying all the data Dai is accumulating?"

"Olson," said Hauglund.

Olson looked away from his computer screen and answered, "Yes, and he is totally unaware."

*

Captain Able cleared their empty plates from the table. Through the window of his cabin the empty horizon stretched beneath a few cumulous clouds. The late day sun still illuminated their tops in shades of pale pink, but the bottoms had turned gray. Before sitting, he poured wine in Christine's glass.

"That is my limit for tonight," she said. "I have to go back to work in six hours." She slowly turned the glass's stem in her fingers. "Thanks for inviting me up. The change is nice."

"Even a big ship gets small after a while," said Able. She looked nice, all cleaned up and in a simple dress. Usually, when he saw her, she had been down inside the hot boat working for hours in sweaty tee shirts and shorts.

"We'll have to move tomorrow," she said. "The sub chasers are getting further south."

"Why do we have to follow them?"

"In case they find what we are looking for."

"I thought we were listening?"

"We are, but…" she cocked her head, "there is something we are looking for too. What do you know about communications with submarines?"

"That it is difficult," aid Able. "Don't they use low frequency acoustics?"

"That is true. There have been many experiments lately. Other systems have been tried. I told you before about the drones our country is developing. Other countries are working hard on it too, the competition is fierce."

"That still doesn't tell me what we are looking for. Drones?"

Christine sipped her wine. "I really can't tell you more."

"Would you like to watch a movie with me?"

She glanced across his little cabin. The wall mounted television hung beyond the foot of his bed. The only chairs in the room were the two hard ones they sat on. Grinning, she said, "From your bed?"

He laughed. "We'll prop up some pillows to make it like chairs."

"Okay," she said. "Do you have anything lighthearted?"

*

"Where's Beth?" asked George, walking on the dock back toward *Frihet*.

"She was talking to a man from Canada the last time I saw her," said Windy. "That was quite a party."

The Royal Bermuda Yacht Club hosted various elegant functions throughout the year. George's race the previous summer had attracted the attention of most of the sailing world, and the club had even showed the race on a giant screen in a function room. The owner of the winning boat, a man originally from England, visited Bermuda often enough that he was a non-resident yacht club member. It was his suggestion the club host the event when George visited the island.

"Yes," said George. There had been too many new faces and he knew he wouldn't remember any of their names the next day.

"Did you hear the man with the beard talking about two boats missing?"

"Someone else was talking about it too. Two sailboats. One of them got out a mayday, but the other just disappeared."

"Spooky," said Windy.

"Maybe that was why the Coast Guard jet was taking off from the airport, they stop here to refuel."

"There certainly haven't been any storms," said Windy.

"I know," said George. "I've been watching the weather. The winds over much of the Atlantic have been unusually light." He glanced at the Rolex on his wrist. "I'm having a night cap. Want to join me?"

She smiled, "If it's one of your single malts."

Stopping at their boat, George pulled on a dock line to bring the stern in, then they each stepped aboard. Lights glistened on the water. "It's a beautiful night."

Inside, Windy disappeared into her cabin while he poured a half inch of fifteen year old Dalwhinnie into two tumblers. Before carrying them back to the cockpit, he kicked off his shoes. It was a spectacular night, with a warm light westerly breeze. The hushed sounds of the city drifted from beyond the yacht club, but most of the partiers had gone home and the music had stopped. Lights showed from a few of the boats along the docks, but most were dark.

"What a night," said Windy, coming out of the cabin. She had left her shoes inside, too, and her hair looked freshly combed. "Thanks," she added reaching for the scotch as she sat beside George.

"Do you think Beth is coming back tonight?" asked George.

Windy smiled. "I don't know. She attracts a lot of attention."

"And you don't?" laughed George. "You both looked stunning tonight."

"Beth looks beautiful." George had noticed how Beth's off-white halter dress contrasted with her dark tan.

He smiled and slouched down to rest his feet on the folded-down leaf of the table in the center of the cockpit. "I love the way you look." Thin straps held Windy's pale blue dress in place, showing off firm shoulders and much of her back. "One of the things I love about the lower latitudes is the clothes that the women wear."

Windy glanced down at her own dress. "It is fun."

"We're going to have another crewmember," said George.

"Who?"

"Brigitta's sister, Tova."

"Ha!" laughed Windy. "She's sending Tova to keep an eye on you."

"No. That's not it."

"Men are so stupid. You don't think that is true?"

"Brigitta is not like that. Right now all she is thinking about is work."

"And not losing you?" Windy sipped her scotch. "I'd bet money on it."

George took a mouthful of the whisky. Maybe Windy was right. That would be a good sign. It would mean Brigitta still planned a future for them as a couple. "You think so?"

"Yes." An outboard motor hummed somewhere out beyond the harbor. "What do you know about Tova?"

"Not much. She sails. And she works as some sort of graphic artist or designer. Brigitta used to complain that Tova didn't take life seriously enough."

Windy smiled. "Isn't that pretty common among sailors, particularly the ones that live aboard their boats?

George grinned and held up his empty glass. "That may be. Would you like another dab of scotch?"

"That would be great."

George brought the bottle up from inside and sat beside Windy again. In the dim light it was difficult to judge how much he poured.

"Where's she going to sleep?" asked Windy. "With you?" Her face said she was kidding.

"On the settee in the main cabin."

"Those beds in our aft cabins are huge, if she wants to share a bunk with me I might consider it."

The smooth single malt tasted heavenly and George paused to savor it. "That's up to you. At sea the settee in the main cabin has the easiest motion and the lee cloth makes it pretty snug, so you won't roll out."

"What a trip you'll have," laughed Windy. "A boat full of women."

The whisky kicked in big time and George felt the glow. "Does Beth's...lack of clothing bother you?"

"I'm envious," said Windy, "really. I wish I felt that self-assured. She's beautiful."

"So are you." Windy had set her glasses aside and faraway lights reflected in her eyes. A thin gold rope around her neck glistened and pulled his eyes down to the top of the pale dress. Were there tan lines inside? A silky bare leg brushed along the side of his, causing his breath to catch.

Windy smiled. "She got lots of waves from boaters today."

"I noticed that," said George. "If you had been at the bow it would have been the same way."

"To be dressed like that I'd have to have been drunk," laughed Windy. He noticed the nearly empty glass in her hand.

And there wasn't a drop left in his tumbler. "Bermuda is a pretty conservative place," said George. "Topless, or even just wearing a bathing suit in town, is against the law." He considered refilling their glasses.

Windy swallowed the last of her scotch. "I don't think anyone cared today, out on the water like that."

"I enjoy your company," said George, picking up the bottle. "You're a good friend." She smelled of citrus and vanilla, and the side of her foot felt heavenly against his.

"That's the whisky talking," laughed Windy.

Smiling, George said, "I think we should go to sleep. We probably shouldn't drink so much like this, or we'll end up doing something we both regret."

"Ha! Maybe only one of us will regret it," joked Windy.

10

"What time is your customer showing up?" asked Windy, wiping down the cabin top.

"About ten, that gives us two hours to clean the boat up," said George, hosing down the cockpit. "I hope Beth is up by then. Did you hear her come in?"

"It was getting light out, probably five, maybe a little earlier. If she's not up soon, I'll get her up."

"I sent Brigitta an email and said I would call her later," said George. "I hope she isn't upset."

"She won't be," assured Windy, grinning. "Remember, she's the one sending her sister over to spy on you."

An hour later, Beth emerged from her cabin, looking rested, as if she had a full night's sleep. The three of them had the boat cleaned and the galley provisioned well before the potential customers showed up.

The possible buyers turned out to be a professional couple in their early fifties looking for a boat to do extensive cruising on when they retired, which they planned to do before they hit sixty. After a tour of the boat and demonstrations of the various systems, they left the dock for a sea trial. The perfect Bermuda weather helped make a favorable impression, and both the husband and wife took a turn at the helm. For years they had raced a Sabre 34 in club races, but wanted a larger performance yacht that two people could easily sail. The TY50 pretty much sold herself. Before four in the afternoon, *Frihet* docked European style at the Royal Bermuda Yacht Club again.

"Thanks, both of you," said George, watching the customers walk down the dock. "I think I've sold my first boat. Let me take you two out to dinner."

"George, please don't take it badly, but I made plans," said Beth.

"That's fine," said George. "It is your loss. Windy and I will go without you."

*

"Dinner was nice last night," said Cynthia, watching the distance between the dock of the Hamilton Princess Marina and the hull of *A New Beginning* increase. "I have never had tuna done like that."

"It was nice," agreed Bill.

From the pilot house deck they leaned on the railing and watched as side thrusters continued to push the big yacht sideways. Water hissed and roared as if boiling between the hull and the dock. Tourists up by the hotel's pool stood to watch the grumbling yacht. Below Cynthia and Bill, on the yacht's main deck, the crew coiled the heavy dock lines.

The night before they ate at a linen covered table on the terrace at the Crown and Anchor, lit by a lone candle inside a hurricane shade. Conversation again flowed easily and plans were made to go out on the boat for another cruise the next day. Bill had flinched, hoping nobody had overheard, when Cynthia mentioned tanning all over. Afterward, they slowly walked the three blocks to Cynthia's apartment, often lingering to look in store windows. At the door, she didn't invite him inside. She knew the power of want.

At nine in the morning he greeted her as she approached the boat and offered breakfast. She stowed a duffle in his cabin and, by the time they came back out on deck, the dock lines had been cast off.

"So where are we going?" she asked.

"Captain Hauglund suggested going out onto the open ocean. There are supposed to be whales migrating through. Perhaps we will be lucky and see one."

Bill took her hand to lead her aft to the pool area where breakfast waited beneath silver covers on a round table. An umbrella, the same shade of blue as *A New Beginning*'s hull, provided shade.

"I feel so naughty, just asking this," she said, glancing at the pool. "Have you ever skinny dipped in there."

He laughed. "I told you, I'd only used the pool once before yesterday. So no."

Coyly, she smiled, "Can we have more of those yummy Bloody Marys?"

"Of course," said Bill, reaching for the phone. Cynthia looked stunning in a summery low-cut cotton dress. Her hair was pulled back in a French braid and dangling ear rings accented her long neck. "I noticed you brought a bigger bag today."

She smiled. "I wasn't sure what to bring so I brought some of everything."

An hour later, breakfast was done and one of the crew cleared away the dishes. Picking up the last plate, she asked if they needed anything else. When both replied no she left.

Cynthia made a fuss about undressing, appearing hesitant, but then stretched out nude on a lounge in the sun. Bill stayed in the shade of an umbrella, unable to stop staring at her body from behind his dark glasses. He had never seen a woman naked outdoors, or anywhere else. Occasionally, he caught glimpses of his ex-wife, but nothing like what he was seeing of Cynthia.

His stare did not concern her. She dozed and enjoyed the sun's soft caress. It was easy to imagine him looking at her breasts, so she arched her back to press them skyward. Occasionally she would roll over, but Cynthia spent most of the time with her breasts pointed at the heavens. When the sun climbed higher, perspiration beaded up on her bare skin. It didn't go unnoticed.

A half hour before noon, she propped herself up on elbows and said, "Bill, I need to cool off. Will you join me in the pool?"

Hoping she wouldn't notice his arousal, he said, "In a minute."

*

Brigitta's face came on the screen. "Hi."

"Hi," said George. "You look nice." Her hair was pulled back into a thick ponytail and she wore a white wool sweater.

"Thanks. It's been a hectic day. I might be here for a few more days."

"Brigitta, remember your health," said George. "The doctors said to avoid stress."

"I know." She looked flustered. Changing the subject, she said, "Tova will be arriving in Bermuda tomorrow, the flight gets in at three."

"I'll meet her at the airport." George heard a hairdryer start in Windy's cabin. "

"Thanks. She's looking forward to this, and you'll enjoy her company."

"I am sure I will," said George. After an awkward lag, he asked, "Can you tell me what you're working on?"

She shook her head. "You know I can't."

"It's for Harold?"

She nodded her head. "Yes, and the government."

George didn't know what to say, finally blurting out, "Does your work mean more to you than our relationship?"

"George, how can you ask me that?"

"I've been trying to remember what felt important to me…years ago," he didn't want to say sixteen years ago and bring up the difference in their ages. "Things were different then. I was more idealistic."

"I like what I do," she said. "I can't help that. But you mean a lot to me. I love you."

"More than your work?"

"What kind of question is that?"

"Answer it."

"I can still do what I do and live with you."

"Really? I'm tired of being alone, sleeping in an empty bed. It's not what I want."

"George?"

"I'm sorry." He felt confused. "Can we talk about this tomorrow? It's been a long day."

"Sure," said Brigitta.

"I love you," he said, and then hit the exit button.

George realized she had never asked about the customer that had arrived earlier. The hum of the hairdryer stopped. He walked to the liquor cabinet to find the bottle of Dalwhinnie.

"I hear a bottle," came from Windy's cabin.

"Want to join me?" said George.

"You called Brigitta. It didn't go so well?"

He shrugged and reached for two tumblers. "I don't know."

She came out of her cabin wearing an oversize tank top, "Want to talk about it?"

"Not really," he said, pouring. "She may be staying in Newport for several more days."

"Is the job getting bigger?"

"I don't know. Tova will be arriving tomorrow afternoon." He sipped the scotch. "We have a reservation for seven."

"We don't have to go out. There's food on board."

"How about we get a pizza somewhere? I haven't had pizza in ages."

Windy smiled. "That would be perfect. Let me change."

An hour later they sat at a roadside table for two at a place called Portofino and ordered a large pizza. "Did Beth say where she was going?" asked George.

"I think she is seeing the Canadian again."

The waiter returned to set two glasses of red wine on their table. "She's liable to jump ship," said George.

"You never know," said Windy. "How soon were you thinking of leaving Bermuda?"

"I don't know. For years I've wished I'd spent more time here. Are you in a hurry?"

"Not really. I was here after a Marion to Bermuda Race a few years ago, but we went home almost immediately."

"Tova might have a schedule she needs to keep. I think she runs a business with a partner."

For an hour they talked and ate. Windy kept the conversation moving with stories about races she had been in, mostly along the New England coast and the one to Bermuda. When their wine glasses emptied, the waiter brought two more. With one piece of pizza remaining they quit. For the next fifteen minutes they relished the last of the wine and watched the tourists on the street.

"Back to the boat?" said George, digging out his wallet.

"Yes."

A short walk down Bermudiana Road took them to Front Street, where they started to cross toward the Royal Yacht Club property. An approaching Toyota caused George to grab Windy's hand to hurry her across. "What was that about?" she said, turning to look at the car speeding away.

"Just someone being an ass," said George, watching too. He realized his hand still held Windy's. "It's time for a night cap. Will you join me?"

"Yes."

With hands still entwined, he led her through the yacht club and down to the dock. Along the way they talked about what provisions were needed before leaving. There wouldn't be much, because the freezer on board was well stocked before they left the States. On reaching the boat, George let go of her hand to pull on a dock line, which brought the boat in closer so they both could board.

"There's not much left in that bottle of Dalwhinnie," said Windy, kicking off her sandals.

"I have another," said George, going down inside the cabin. He passed up the bottle and a full one too. "Ice?"

"Tonight, yes. The scotch hit me hard last night. Watering it down might be a good idea."

"Me too."

George settled into the cockpit next to Windy and handed her a tumbler of ice. "Nice shorts you have on." Into each glass he poured an inch.

"They look just like yours." They did, both were baggie, khaki, with oversized cargo pockets.

"You shirt looks better than mine." She had on a white tank top that had a picture of *Frihet* on the front. He wore a pale blue button shirt.

"I don't know about that," she laughed.

They clinked glassed together. "To our first successful sale," said George.

"Who made these?" asked Windy, looking down at her tank top.

"A screen printer in Falmouth on Cape Cod." The front of hers dipped enough to show the tops of her breasts. "I should have had them cut lower," he teased.

"You couldn't do that," she protested, laughing.

"Can I ask you something? When a woman wears a low cut top, is she aware where she is aiming her cleavage? I mean, I've had women wearing low cut tops bend down in front of me and it makes it almost impossible for a guy not to look."

Windy laughed and swallowed a gulp of her whisky. "I'll never tell."

"You're no help," laughed George.

"Okay, my turn. Why did you hold my hand all the way down the dock?" asked Windy, still grinning. "Are we just friends? Or is it more than that? You're sending mixed messages."

"Oh," said George. His smile faded. "I don't know what I'm doing. It felt right. I'm sending me mixed messages too." He wondered why the wine had hit him so hard.

"I'm sorry." She clasped his hand. "I liked it, it made me feel safe." Windy could see the confusion on his face. Changing the subject, she asked, "What do you suppose Harold Habit's connection with Bermuda is?"

"I don't know," said George. "That compound out by Parson's Bay, I keep wondering if that is his. It reminded me of the place he had in Rhode Island, with razor wire atop a chain link fence. If it is connected, you know it has to be something to do with spying. That man is into everybody's business."

"You sound angry."

"Maybe I am. It's not just Harold, it's the government. The NSA has wiped out privacy. At least we can escape to the ocean. But Harold's satellites can see us there too." He took a hurried sip from his tumbler. "Maybe he is trying to find a way to track submarines? That must drive him crazy, something he can't see."

His rambling made Windy smile. It must be the drinks, she decided, and at least George was passionate about certain things. She asked, "Would the government hire Harold to develop a way to find subs?"

George brought his scotch to his lips again and looked across the harbor where a jet settled toward the airport. "It could well be. He's been their ace for a long time." He went on to tell about Harold's collection of satellites that could see people on earth well enough to identify their faces. The whole system was tied into millions of security cameras and computers sorting out the data.

"That's impossible," said Windy, letting her hand rest against his leg.

"I'm sorry," said George. "I sometimes blame Harold for my losing Brigitta." He took another swallow. "But I think if she wasn't solving his problems, she would be solving somebody else's. She just likes the challenges."

"What could be her connection to this?"

"I don't know. It has to be something to do with boats. Underwater drones? Harold's business had trouble competing with flying drones. Brigitta seems to have a way with anything that moves through water."

"Are there really underwater drones?"

George shrugged. "Let me get my laptop."

A minute later, he sat beside her and googled "underwater drones". Silently, hip against hip, they read. Nations had been developing underwater drones to locate and shadow nuclear submarines. Relatively inexpensive drones could someday make multi-billion dollar submarines, with their multitude of nuclear weapons, obsolete. Problems with communication had hampered the development of drones, but some had been designed to operate autonomously for months at a time. A few of the ones developed by the United States were over a hundred and fifty feet long and could go for long periods of time between recharging of batteries. The article went on to describe various forms of undersea communication. Neither of their alcohol soaked brains could comprehend any of that.

"Wow," said Windy. "Maybe we hit it."

"It could be," said George. "Brigitta could design a submarine. She can make anything." He read again about undersea acoustic communication, but couldn't grasp any of it. "You ready for a refill?"

"One more, and then I'm going to bed."

"Me too," said George, opening the new bottle to pour. "Can you imagine that? An underwater drone three times as long as this boat?"

"It's scary that it operates on its own? And for months at a time?" She took a healthy swallow from her refilled glass.

George shut the laptop and took another drink too. "I sometimes wish I'd lived a hundred years ago."

"Hey, let's lighten the subject," said Windy, patting his leg. "Do you have any more potential customer's lined up?"

"Not really. Eldridge Hardy lines them up. I'll probably have to go back up the East Coast in the spring to sell boats."

George was very aware of their bare legs resting together and Windy's hand resting on his thigh. In the dim light, her eyes looked to be waiting. He glanced down, a nipple poked against the inside of her top and he wondered if she were aware of it. His hand moved on top hers.

To change the subject, he asked, "What would be your perfect job, when you get to the Caribbean?"

She smiled and settled against his side. "Working on a boat exactly like this one."

There wasn't another boat exactly like *Frihet*, at least not yet. Hull number two had been laid up, but wouldn't be ready for months. What Windy meant was obvious.

"I still have to see what Brigitta wants." He wanted desperately to kiss Windy.

Windy forced a smile, "I know. It's all right. I sent my name in to a crew placement agency on St. Thomas. There's a big ketch that will have an opening after the first of the year."

George gave her hand a squeeze.

Ashore, somewhere, a car honked its horn and a voice carried across the harbor. Water from a boat's wake lapped against the hull and a dock line creaked.

George said, "It's time to call it a night."

11

Cynthia stood outside the shower in Bill's cabin, letting the water to get hot. The day had turned out better than she had hoped.

After feigning shyness, working on an all-over tan in the soft morning sunlight had been delightful. Then she and Bill ate a leisurely lunch in the shady section of the pool area, followed by frozen mudslides as dessert. It was easy to see he was smitten. Again, conversation had never stopped. She got Bill talking about his childhood and parents, neither of which he sounded too happy about.

When the mud slides were gone, they cooled in the pool, and, after a great deal of coaxing, she even had Bill skinny dipping. It had taken almost an hour, but his self-consciousness finally succumbed to the alcohol. They then spent the rest of the afternoon between the pool and the shade, talking about things they would like to do someday. The entire notion of looking for whales had slipped away.

When the sun settled low in the western sky, *A New Beginning* passed back through Town Cut and into the St. George's Harbour.

"Where are we?" she had asked, knowing the answer. They were both leaning against the railing wearing only towels tied around their hips.

"In St. George's Harbour again," Bill had answered. "This is where we left from yesterday." She smiled, remembering how tightly he had tied his towel, as if it falling off could be fatal.

She had then expressed concern, "You're not bringing me back to Hamilton?"

"If you want to go back, I will get you a taxi," he answered. "I would prefer it if you spent the night. The chef has prepared a meal fit for royalty."

She remembered pressing her body against his and sharing their first real kiss. He moaned. It was too easy. That was exactly the reaction she wanted. They made love upon returning to the master cabin and his performance was better than she had hoped.

"Bill, why don't you shower with me?" she called out. "This shower is huge."

Wearing only a big grin, Bill walked in from the bedroom. He had never imagined a woman like Cynthia. His wife never had varied from the routine…it was twice a month and solely missionary position. Sometimes they even skipped a month…or two, or three, or more. The woman never tried to look sexy and somehow made sex feel dirty. Cynthia felt like a breath of fresh air.

He stepped into the shower with her. A half hour later he emerged, having experienced things he had never even dreamed of. As he dressed, he hummed along with her hair dryer.

"That was fun," she said, coming out of the bathroom wrapped in a towel. "I like life aboard a yacht."

Bill had put on black slacks and a white linen shirt. "You said something about wanting to open an office in the British Virgins," he said. "I could take you there, on this boat."

She tossed the towel aside and slid onto the bed. "Let me see…I could fly there in a couple of hours, after the turmoil of an airport and the inconvenience of airlines, or live in luxury, for maybe a week or so aboard this boat, and have the best sex of my life…which do you think I'll pick." She laid against the pillows and propped her head up on an elbow. "Why don't you take those clothes off and come here."

They didn't leave his cabin until the next morning.

*

Hauglund read the text and shook his head. "The man is crazy." Through the bridge's enormous windows, they could see the lights of St. George's across the harbor.

"A problem?" asked Olson.

"Dai wants more time at sea to tune the receivers, which means the divers may have to go under the boat again if things are not right." Hauglund shrugged his shoulders and stuffed the phone back in a pocket.

Olson watched a computer screen, a series of red numbers marched downward. "I hope our people can sort all of this out."

"I thought you understood these things?"

"Most of it, not all," said Olson, the dim red light illuminated his face. "How is Cynthia doing?"

Hauglund smiled. "Mr. Sanderlee is being trained like an American puppy, with little treats."

"Can I ask why the Chinese are going through all this trouble, to hide on a private yacht?"

Olson had been a model crewmember, following orders without questions. Of all the crew, he and the engineer were the only ones that knew about Dai in the secret cabin. Hauglund wondered what had changed. "This way arouses no suspicion, an American yacht with its owner on board. Our people knew Dai would be looking for a yacht to hide sensors on and that he didn't need a lot of room. They arranged for me to meet him one night in New York and to answer Sanderlee's ad about the same time. Dai thinks I am just a greedy old man, maybe a bit of a pirate. You've noticed that money is not a problem and gotten your share."

The numbers flowed silently down the screen.

"Has Dai eaten?" asked Hauglund.

"Not much. I bring him trays of food, but he hardly touches the stuff. Do you think any of our crewmembers are suspicious?"

"Of what? Our boss and Cynthia are creating quite a distraction. Nobody goes down to the engine room except you and the engineer. Dai is almost invisible."

"What did he say he would be doing?"

"Experiments with underwater communications, and I didn't need to know much more than that. The Chinese navy does have nuclear subs, everybody does these days. I guess they need to talk to them." Hauglund wondered how much to tell. "The United States Navy has been searching for over a month, looking for something east of here. Maybe a submarine has sunk. A research ship has been shadowing them, staying over the horizon to the north."

"It doesn't sound like routine activity."

"It is not. I think each side fears the other will make a breakthrough in undersea communication. Maybe one side is getting close." Hauglund watched the hypnotic cascade of numbers cross the screen. "Are you sure this is all getting back to Moscow?"

12

Three hundred miles to the southeast of Bermuda, a fourteen foot long shark known as AS-09 swam with its dorsal fin clear of the surface, absorbing Global Position Satellite information from satellites over twelve thousand miles above the earth. Swimming with its body barely beneath the surface, solar cells in its back gathered energy, helping to delay the depletion of stored electricity.

AS-09 swam a straight course, due east, at a leisurely four knots. It could swim faster, but that would wear the batteries down at an alarming rate. For a hundred hours the course and speed would not change, but the shark would slip beneath the surface for hours at a time. Beneath the sea, it listened for its prey.

South of Bermuda an identical shark known as AS-11 swam slowly, listening to the almost imperceptible sounds of a nuclear submarine hundreds of feet below it. Tiny silicone chips inside its head sifted through the noises, identifying it as the United States Los Angeles-class fast attack sub, the USS Asheville. The three hundred and sixty foot sub had moved little during the previous eight hours, as if it too were waiting for something. If the sub traveled at its maximum speed of over twenty knots, the shark would have been only be able to keep up for a few hours before its batteries would drain. Slowly, the shark's caudal fin moved side to side, propelling it forward.

From somewhere to the northeast of Bermuda, a third shark, AS-02, swam south, its batteries slipping toward twenty percent of capacity. It traveled toward its mother, the source of life. Sliding upward to expose its fin, the shark learned it was almost back to the nursery. Safely underwater again, it sent out a ping. The returning sonar confirmed the proximity of Mother.

Through the clear water of the open Atlantic, it visually recognized her from two hundred and seventy feet away. Beneath Mother's belly, eight other sharks nestled like remoras. AS-02 found an empty titanium nipple and swam up against it, latching on. For the next eight hours it would ride there, soaking up the energy needed while exchanging all it had learned.

Mother knew of every vessel, both floating and submerged, within a hundred thousand square mile area. Her two dozen sharks came and went, on her directions, to record locations and speed of everything they encountered. When their thirst for electrical power returned, they swam back to her. Not one single shark had been lost in Mother's many months at sea.

In the beginning, they had tracked only submerged vessels, but that became too easy. Mother had been programmed to be secretive and to learn from experience. For over six months she had eluded every attempt to find her and accumulated a vast amount of knowledge that she knew not what to do with. Accumulating information became an obsession. No better example of a self-learning artificial intelligence had ever been created.

Barely making headway, Mother continued south.

*

"You're up," said George, stepping back aboard.

"I could smell the coffee," said Windy, sitting in the cockpit reading something on a tablet. "You must have started it before you went ashore."

"I went looking for a newspaper, but I don't think anybody publishes a daily anymore. I'll have to read it online."

"You are old fashioned," she laughed. "I was reading about the missing boats. People are saying there's some sort of cover up."

"How's that?" He went inside to pour a cup.

"Two sailboats vanish, Beth's boat mysteriously sinks, and there hasn't been much in the press. The United States Navy has been searching for something, several fishing boats have seen them. We saw the Coast Guard jet leaving from the airport and it went over again this morning."

"I don't know," said George, sitting beside her. "Is Beth here?"

"Yes, she got back early last night, probably a half hour after we went in."

"I never heard a thing." He sipped his coffee and opened his laptop.

"Are you going to call Brigitta?" asked Windy. "She sent me an email, just chit chat really. It sounds like she's almost done in Newport."

"I'm supposed to call her in twenty minutes."

Windy went inside, but through the companionway asked, "What are we doing today?"

"I have to meet Tova at the airport at three," said George. "Other than that there are no plans. I might take a walk around Hamilton."

Alone in the cockpit, George called Brigitta on his laptop. Her smile came onto the screen. "Good morning," he said. "You look beautiful."

"I'm feeling good," she said. "The things that needed to be done here are complete. I fly home tomorrow morning."

"Good. I worry about you. The doctors said it would take a long time to get well. I think Caribbean sunshine would work wonders."

"I'm sure it will."

They talked about Harold and mutual friends. The design office had become a beehive of activity. Three more marine architects had joined the staff and personnel from the Naval War Offices in Newport had moved in too. Brigitta asked him not to spread that around, even if it wasn't classified.

"They have you privy to classified information?" asked George.

"Some. I needed it for the project."

"I don't like that. I hate the idea of someone hurting you again."

"I'll be fine, it wasn't really important things. I should be going. Give my sister a hug for me when she gets there."

"I'll shut my eyes and pretend she is you."

"Don't you get carried away," laughed Brigitta.

"You're still on schedule to come down before Christmas?" He noticed a flash of something in her eyes...worry, fear, what?

"Yes."

They ended with "I love you" and promised to talk the next morning.

"Good morning." Beth came up from inside carrying a mug of coffee. "Is that the mystery woman I've been hearing about?"

"Brigitta? Yes."

Beth sat across from George. "Windy says it's iffy, her showing up."

"I don't know. She has a lot on her plate."

"Well, I hope for your sake she does." She sipped her coffee. "What are we doing today? Selling another boat?"

George laughed. "I wish. Today is do whatever you want. I'm going to poke around Hamilton some. At three I have to meet Brigitta's sister, Tova, at the airport."

"Windy said we had one more crew coming. Aren't you a lucky guy," she teased. "A boat full of women."

He smiled. It would make a great story to tell someday.

Five hours later he stepped from a taxi and walked into the terminal at the L. F. Wade International Airport. At the British Airways terminal, he waited for Tova to clear customs. Stepping through the gate, she looked exactly like her sister.

"Welcome to Bermuda," said George, grabbing her duffle bag from her. "How was your flight?"

"Fine," she said, following his lead.

"You sound different than Brigitta. Her accent is almost British. You sound like you're from Sweden."

She laughed. "I am different from Brigitta in many ways."

"Your hair is a little darker, hers looks almost white sometimes."

"Most of the ways I am different are on the inside, not how I look." She laughed. "And I hope the tropical sun lightens my hair."

"Let's get that taxi."

On the way to Hamilton, George pointed out landmarks he knew and explained the things they had done the previous few days.

"When do we get to sail?" she asked, as they stopped in front of the Yacht Club.

"Tomorrow we'll bring the boat around to St. George's Harbour. It's a nice day sail. What is your schedule? Do you have to be home soon?"

"I brought a laptop with me. Much of my work can be done from anywhere. Brigitta told me the boat has a satellite connection to the Internet."

He smiled. "You are like your sister. She works all the time too."

"I know when to stop and have fun though. Brigitta thinks her work is fun, so never stops."

"I'm in no rush to leave Bermuda," said George. "We're stuck under a big high pressure area and the winds have been light. I'd like to see a front move in and bring some wind with it."

At the boat, introductions were made and cocktails served. About the time the sun kissed the horizon, Tova offered to take everyone out for dinner. They ate on the terrace at the Crown and Anchor, laughing, telling stories, and creating quite a stir. For a while the conversation focused on the missing boats and Beth's mishap, but then went back to lighter subjects.

The women attracted the attention of four sailors at a neighboring table and soon another round of drinks appeared, bought by the sailors. About eleven o'clock George stood to announce his departure. Beth followed suit, but Windy and Tova stayed behind with the newfound friends.

Walking out on the street, Beth said, "You are going to enjoy the peace and quiet when we all leave you."

He laughed. "The company is nice."

"You never met Tova before?"

"No. Her sister told me a little about her. She looks a lot like Brigitta." Few people walked on the sidewalks and the streets were near empty.

"Thank you for taking me in. I was at a loss for what to do," said Beth. "It is appreciated."

"It's nothing. Do for others, as you would want them to do for you, that's my motto. What sort of boat are you going to look for?"

"I don't know. My old boat was strong, but she was slow." Beth laughed. "Sailing on *Frihet* opened my eyes." They turned onto the yacht club property.

"Would you like a night cap?" asked George.

"I saw you the other night," confessed Beth, "in the cockpit with Windy. She likes you, I knew that from the moment I met her. When I saw the two of you in the cockpit, I hid, not wanting to interrupt what might be a special moment."

"We're just friends," said George, reaching down to grab a dock line.

"Sure you are," said Beth, stepping aboard.

"You never met Brigitta," he said, following. "She's beautiful and brilliant. Actually, she looks almost exactly like Tova, but she's a couple of years younger. Scotch or wine?"

"Wine. I'll sleep better." Beth sat while George went inside.

"I hope red will do, we're out of white," he said, coming back out. Taking out the cork, he said, "Brigitta is flying to the Caribbean before Christmas."

"Really? Windy said that was not definite."

He passed her a glass. "Maybe it isn't. Brigitta gets caught up in her work."

"And strings you along."

They clicked glasses together. "To smooth seas and fair winds," said George. After a sip, he added, "I don't know what to think."

"There are some things a woman can sense," said Beth, "and Windy likes you a lot. She is working very hard at being civil because she respects…you and Brigitta."

"She has a job lined up on a big ketch when we get to St. Thomas."

Beth smiled. "And she would like nothing better than to blow it off and go sailing with you."

George shook his head. "What about you? Are there any men in your life? You're an attractive woman,"

"I have no desire to settle down. The attention of a man is nice, but I have never found one to stay with for more than a day or two. Maybe someday. Men say the sea is their mistress," she laughed, "it's my gigolo." She took a swallow of her wine. "Tova has a twinkle in her eye too. Sisters…oh, the fights we had."

George shook his head. "Now where does that come from?"

Grinning, she said, "My sister and I always fought over the same boy. She was a year younger than me. When I left and to went sea, I think she celebrated for a week."

George refilled their glasses. "What do you remember about the day you lost your boat?"

"Not much. A jarring crash that stopped the boat as if it hit a wall. I can still see the water coming up over the cabin sole." She swallowed a gulp of wine. "What a nightmare. I jumped below to grab the EPIRB, but everything had flown out of the locker where I kept it. Water came up to my waist in no time. I scrambled out and launched the life raft. The boat sank like a stone."

"You were lucky."

"I know, another minute and I might not have been able to launch the raft." She smiled. "I keep having nightmares about treading water in the middle of the ocean."

"At least you survived."

"I'm glad there was food and water stored in the raft. Time completely became a blur. I slept a lot. Sometimes I wondered about hallucinations, particularly when I was being shot at. I really thought it was all in my mind. Even when the raft started to leak, I never believed somebody shot it."

"You don't remember much about the shooters?"

"Not really. I remember laughing, thinking my mind was going crazy. Sometimes I shut my eyes and can see it, an orange boat with two outboards and two men."

George had never heard of such a thing, at least not out in the middle of the ocean. Pirates were still a concern off the shores of a few troubled poverty-stricken countries, but not north of Bermuda.

"Here comes our crew," said Beth, looking where the marina joined the land. Windy and Tova walked down the ramp to the docks. She teased, "I knew they wouldn't be late. Each of them wants to keep an eye on you. They are afraid I might lure you to my bed."

George laughed. "I'm going to start locking my cabin door at night."

Beth grinned. "You may have to."

13

A hundred feet from the docks of The Royal Bermuda Yacht Club, George brought *Frihet's* bow into the wind. The mainsail shot upward and, as the luff drew taut, Windy sheeted it in and adjusted the traveler. *Frihet* flinched in the wind and leaned to starboard. Water gurgled along the hull.

With a grumble the genoa unfurled from the headstay and drew in snug along the starboard side. The boat surged ahead.

Windy looked to George and said, "We're leaving with style."

He grinned. Beth trimmed the genoa. Tova stood at the headstay, looking up at the sail. The breeze dragged a few strands of blonde hair across her face.

When George dressed earlier, he had put on khaki shorts with a polo shirt the slate-blue of *Frihet's* topsides. Over the left breast, *Frihet* was embroidered in gold letters. The women had all followed his example and dressed as he had. Later that morning, pictures of George, Windy, Beth, and Tova, with the boat under sail, would circulate around the Internet.

They sailed by the Princess Hotel Marina and out Two Rock Passage, between Mowbray and Lefroy Islands. A small sailboat tried to keep up, but they easily outpaced it. A motorboat came alongside with a man taking pictures. George gave them a wave, but wished they would leave.

"People are going to think Brigitta is back," said George, watching the motorboat. "Tova looks so much like her."

"Do you think so?" asked Windy.

"Yes. It will be online. I'd bet money on it. BRIGITTA SNEAKS BACK."

Out in Great Sound the motorboat dropped behind, then turned back for Hamilton. George looked at the sails, the trim looked perfect. He moved to the starboard helm and settled against the lifelines, steering the boat more northward. Beth eased the genoa while Windy slid the traveler over before easing the mainsail too. In the light air *Frihet* ghosted along at six knots. Tova walked aft along the port deck and stepped into the cockpit.

"Thanks everybody," said George. "We looked good leaving Hamilton. It's all free advertising for Fast Habit Yachts."

"I like our uniforms," said Tova.

"People are going to mistake you for your sister," said George, noticing how her eyes picked up the color of their shirts.

"It would not be the first time."

"Would anybody like something to drink?" asked Windy.

Sailing on a broad reach in the light air made the morning feel hot. Iced coffee sounded good to everyone.

"I'm putting a bathing suit on," said Tova. "I look white as a ghost compared to everyone else here."

"Don't burn," said George. "Use some sunscreen."

All three of the women disappeared inside the boat. George pulled his shirt off over his head. The faint breeze felt good on his skin. When the sun got stronger he would put on a pale-blue long sleeve shirt for sun protection.

Tova came out first in a little two piece, carrying a towel and an insulated glass of iced coffee.

"Don't forget the sunscreen," reminded George.

She smiled and awkwardly, held up a tube in the towel hand, then headed forward along the port deck.

A few minutes later, Beth came up wearing a tank top that went down over her hips and disappeared forward too. Windy came out carrying two iced coffees and handed one to George.

"You're not going to go up forward to cook in the sun?" said George.

"We get enough sun back here, even under the bimini. They won't last long, the sun will be cooking them up in less than an hour."

Crossing Great Sound, neither of them spoke. George hadn't realized how much Tova looked like Brigitta until he saw her at the airport. Seeing Tova in that little bathing suit, he realized they were almost identical in every way. The sight of her made him miss Brigitta even more. Maybe having her along wasn't such a good idea.

Approaching Irish Island, Windy brought out the binoculars to look at the fenced in compound they had spotted earlier. George looked too, but there was little to see other than armed guards looking out. Somebody certainly didn't want anyone to get inside. A black helicopter sat silent.

They held the course, passing the old naval base and the tip of the island, northward toward North Channel. Far to the east, a giant white cruise ship headed into the opposite end of North Channel and would pass close to port. George worried about what the two women up forward were wearing, or not wearing, and considered saying something.

But long before the channel turned eastward, Beth and Tova came back to the shade of the bimini, both dressed as they had left the cockpit earlier. Twenty minutes later, they sailed by the cruise ship and waved up at the dozens of people looking down on them.

Sailing east, the apparent wind increased and the day felt cooler. They reached The Narrows and turned toward Town Cut before noontime. A classic yawl, which George recognized as an early Herreshoff design, passed heading out to sea. He admired the mahogany cabin sides and the pinched mahogany transom as he waved to the two young men onboard. Glancing at the stern, he read *Gwen.* An hour later *Frihet's* anchor bit into the sandy bottom at the north end of Smith's Harbor, beside the tiny empty island named Peggy's Island.

"We're less than a half mile from St. George's," said George. Hen Island to the north blocked the view of it. "If anyone wants to go into town, I'll run them in with the inflatable. I'm not up for living in a fishbowl along the quay."

Everyone opted for lunch and a swim.

*

"George, we have company," said Beth.

He blinked his eyes open and glanced at his watch, almost five. A large white inflatable approached between the north end of Smith's Island and little Peggy's Island. Across the top of Peggy's Island scrub, he could see the blue stern of *A New Beginning*. A young man stood at the helm of the dingy, the only passenger on board.

"Good day," he said, coming along side to grab the toe rail. "Bill Sanderlee would like to invite you and your crew aboard *A New Beginning* for cocktails and a casual dinner."

George glanced at his crew, it was easy to see they would love to see the insides of a two hundred and twenty foot motor yacht. "What time would he like us?"

"Six, I can pick you up."

"That's okay. We would love to come over, but we'll use our own tender."

"See you then," said the young man, pushing his boat away.

The shower in Windy's cabin already ran. Beth had disappeared inside.

"When did *A New Beginning* anchor over there?" asked George.

"Maybe an hour ago," said Tova.

"You got some color today," said George. "I hope you didn't overdo it." She glowed pink.

"I am fine. I will put some lotion on before I go to sleep."

"Are you going to be okay sleeping in the main cabin?"

Tova nodded. "It is fine. I'm going to go change."

"You can use my shower if you want," said George. "I'll shower after you, it doesn't take me long."

"I will do that," she said, smiling.

She grabbed her bag and followed him to his cabin, where he pointed out the door to the shower and handed her a towel. While the water ran, he picked out a clean pair of shorts and a button shirt to wear. When Tova stepped out of the shower, wrapped in a towel, he stepped in.

A few minutes later, with a towel around the waist, he came out to find Tova wearing a little white dress while she dried her hair in his cabin. "I hope you don't mind," she said, pushing the blonde hair back.

"Not at all." The resemblance to Brigitta made him ache. "Take your time." He grabbed the clean shorts and stepped back into the head to slip them on.

*

At a minute before six, Cynthia looked down on the tender from *Frihet* as it came along the stern boarding platform of *A New Beginning*. A crewmember, dressed in white, took the offered dinghy's painter, then helped the women aboard. Bill Sanderlee walked down the steps to greet them.

There were handshakes and smiles.

Earlier, when *A New Beginning* returned to the anchorage, Bill recognized *Frihet* anchored off their stern and mentioned meeting George in a bar. She had suggested inviting him and his crew over for drinks, thinking it might be fun. While Bill showered, she googled George Attwood and learned enough about him to keep cocktail conversation lively.

George introduced the women to Bill. One, wearing a skirt with a halter top, Cynthia recognized as the woman rescued from the life raft. Her picture had been in the online news. A darker blonde, wearing gold rimmed glasses and a dress, she knew to be a regular crewmember of George's. Her picture had been in photos of the previous summer's famous race. An online news source said George's girlfriend, the famous designer of racing sailboats, had been spotted aboard his boat in Hamilton earlier that morning, and there she was, standing aboard *A New Beginning*.

Bill led the group up the steps to the main deck, where Cynthia greeted them. Again, introductions were made and she learned that it wasn't Brigitta that had boarded, but rather her sister, Tova.

In the center of the aft deck, a small fire flickered in a bronze bowl more than a meter across. Chairs had been arranged around the perimeter and a steward waited at an impromptu bar set up against the house. "What will it be?"

A blender hummed, turning out a batch of Bushwhackers, which both Beth and Tova accepted. Windy took a glass of Beaulieu Vineyard Georges de Latour, which Cynthia already sipped from a long stemmed glass. The only scotch was 18 year old Macallan, one of George's favorites. Bill stayed with an already poured drink that appeared to be either gin or vodka with tonic. They sat around the fire, watching the flames dance, as if it were a camp fire.

Bill told of going offshore that morning, looking for whales and spending the day at sea, then asked about their day. A stewardess appeared with a tray of stuffed tiny shrimp, and before she disappeared a second arrived with a platter of small cheese filled quiches. As their glasses emptied they were refilled as if by magic. One after another, trays of food marched in.

Cynthia sized up all of the guests, deciding Beth had a defiant streak, which was probably why she escaped to a life at sea. Beth told a few stories about slipping through customs in Canada that had everyone laughing. Windy had sat beside George and often glanced his way. It was easy to see her attraction to him.

Tova sat on George's other side. The soft glow of the firelight made her look angelic…and very sexy. Cynthia thought the woman must be able to get any man she wanted.

George appeared to be a content man. She wondered if he felt any attraction for any of the women sailing on his boat. How could he not? All of them were beautiful, each in a different way. Earlier, after she googled information about George, she read the story of Brigitta's head injury and how it affected her. It read like a tragic love story, their separating so she could live back home in familiar surroundings, with the hope she would get well again and return someday.

"How about a tour of my boat?" offered Bill.

They followed him through the main deck, then went up the stairs to the pilot house deck. First he took them forward, where he introduced them to Captain Hauglund and First Mate Olson, then led them aft, to where a second fire danced by the pool. Light softly wafted up from beneath the water's surface.

Bill leaned against the railing to look across at St. George's Town. "What a night. We are all truly blessed to live as we do."

"We are," said Windy, stopping next to him.

Cynthia stood next to George. He asked. "Where are you from?"

"Bermuda is my home," she answered. "I met Bill only a couple of days ago, and it has been like a dream. Never did I imagined spending time on a boat like this."

He asked about her job and she told him of Bill's offer to take her to the British Virgin Islands and her plans to open a second office in Road Town.

George grinned. "Flying would be faster."

Trying to look coy, she answered, "But not as much fun."

"I can only imagine."

A steward appeared with two more Bushwhackers, another tumbler of Macallan, and a glass of Beaulieu Vineyard Georges de Latour.

"When are you leaving?" asked George.

She put on an excited face. "Hopefully soon. Maybe the day after tomorrow."

"We may leave tomorrow," said George. "The winds have been light and I had hoped for a change, but that doesn't look like it is going to happen."

"The wind doesn't matter for this boat."

"Bill is going to get my crew drunk," said George, watching Tova suck on the straw in her glass. The thick drink didn't come up easily. "Those Bushwhackers are nothing but alcohol mixed with alcohol."

"They have been eating and those drinks are small," said Cynthia. "They will be fine. I noticed you have barely touched your drink."

George smiled. "Somebody has to stay sober enough to drive us home."

For a few minutes they talked about Bermuda, then Cynthia asked about Brigitta. He smiled at first, it was easy to see he like talking about her. But when asked about her return to sailing, she noticed his answers became evasive. She wondered if Brigitta might not ever come back.

A steward appeared, pushing a linen covered cart, atop which a platter of barbecued ribs still sizzled. A second steward and a stewardess started to set a round table for six, lit by four sculpted glass oil lamps. Another cart appeared with a wooden bowl of salad, baskets of bread, and assorted condiments.

Cynthia smiled, "You are not going to go home hungry."

"It smells good," said George.

"Would you excuse me a moment?" she said.

While everyone else watched the dinner preparation, Cynthia hurried along the starboard side to the pilot house, where she stepped inside. "How did it go?"

"Dai said perfect," said Hauglund. "He wants to go out tomorrow to confirm his test, and then leave soon after that."

"Good," said Cynthia. She walked back aft to the pool deck and the guests.

They dug into the mountain of ribs. Fingers became messy, but laughter and teasing accompanied the meal. Cynthia sat beside George and Windy sat on his opposite side. About mid-meal, Cynthia noticed Tova often glanced at Windy and George. She smiled to herself. Could Brigitta have sent Tova to keep an eye on George? Smiling inwardly, she thought what a soap opera this would make. Or maybe Tova had designs on George? Men were so stupid. They were always the last to pick up on romantic chemistry.

Damp hand towels appeared as the plates piled with bones were taken away. Petite bowls of ice cream piled with fat red strawberries were set in front of each of them.

Among protests over the volume of food, they enjoyed the desert. Windy placed her last strawberry in George's mouth, and Cynthia noticed the disapproving look on Tova's face.

Thinking it might provide great entertainment, watching the blossoming triangle, Cynthia said, "We should all go swimming."

"It's getting late," said George. "We should be going back to our boat." The faces of his crew expressed bewilderment.

"We have towels," she offered.

"We didn't bring bathing suits."

"You've never been skinny dipping? Don't be shy." She slapped his leg and leaned close. "Today I finally got Bill swimming in the skinny."

"Really," George laughed, "it would be fun, but we have a lot to do tomorrow. Maybe we'll meet again in the Virgin Islands."

14

Mother moved slowly, beneath her nine sharks suckled, recharging and sharing information they had gathered. She had found, in the warmer water of the southern latitudes, that communication with the sharks became easier as the water became less dense. Their coded messages now traveled many hundreds of miles. Simultaneously, mother could communicate with a dozen sharks, noting their position and vessels they had found. When the sharks nursed beneath her, they shared records of water temperatures, salinity, and densities, as well as marine life encountered and details of the vessels they had tracked. Mother knew everything about the ocean for hundreds of miles.

One shark, AS-11, less than a mile southeast of the entrance to St. George's Harbour, had encountered another vessel made of a mystery material. So far, every vessel of this material that the sharks had located had been small, slow moving, and difficult to detect. Mother feared there may be larger ones, or perhaps there would be a flotilla of them. Any unknown caused concern. An hour earlier, she had changed heading and accelerated to intercept the vessel.

It would take hours to reach the vessel, but AS-11 would shadow the vessel until she got there.

*

George cleated off the tender and stepped up to the deck. Beth already was pouring wine into tall glasses on the cockpit table. "Would you like one?" she said looking his way. The other women had gone inside.

"I might have a dab of scotch," he said.

Windy came back out wearing tee shirt that hung down over her hips and took one of the wine glasses. "That was quite a boat," she said.

"Lots of money," said George. "Every year he is probably going to spend what *Frihet* cost new, just to keep that boat up."

"At least," said Beth, picking up a glass. "Maybe more."

Heading for the liquor cabinet, George dropped down inside the cabin. On the port side Tova's bare backside was to him as she dug through her duffle bag. "I'm sorry," he said.

Glancing over her should, she smiled. "It is all right. Back home we do not care so much."

Even her butt glowed pink.

Rattled, George clunked the bottle of Dalwhinnie against a bottle of Mt Gay rum in the liquor cabinet, then almost dropped a tumbler.

Tova slipped into a tee shirt that hung a few inches below her hips. He motioned for her to go up the steep stairs first…they looked like Brigitta's legs. He turned away to avoid staring.

On the cockpit table a lone candle flickered.

Plans were made for the morning while the tiny flame wavered. A few groceries were needed, but not much else. Windy and Beth offered to get them at the little store near King's Square. Tova asked if there was time for a little clothes shopping in the morning, and all three of the women decided to take a taxi into Hamilton. George said they should plan on meeting at Ordinance Island at four to head back out to *Frihet*.

Then things would be stowed, dinner eaten, and they could leave before dark.

*

Gwen silently slipped through the night. Dennis stayed in the cockpit, mesmerized by the billions of stars overhead. It was the middle of the night and his watch wouldn't be over for two hours, but he felt wide awake. A glow in the northwestern sky indicated where Bermuda hid beyond the horizon. The light wind barely shaped the sails.

Inside the boat's narrow cabin, Russ slept in a snug pilot berth against the starboard hull. The lee board, which created a secure canyon to sleep in, was not needed. *Gwen* did not heel at all in the light night air.

The crash and upward jolt jarred Russ awake. *Gwen*'s cracking and groaning mahogany planks splintered around him. Oak frames shattered like cannons in a second crash. The noise swallowed his own screams. In the blackness, he fell into water on the port side.

Cushions, floorboards, and furniture floated about him. "Dennis!" he called, desperately trying to stand. Broken cabinets moved under his feet. He reached out to touch the nearly vertical cabin sole and tried desperately to see out the companionway.

The boat rolled further to port and dropped a foot or more. Water rushed in everywhere.

"Dennis!" he screamed.

Nearly chest deep water floated cabinet doors and broken pieces of wood. Russ pushed toward the companionway. Water washed in over the bridge deck and he knew soon they would sink. His hand slid across the bulkhead, searching for the Emergency Position Indicating Radio Beacon, only to find its bracket empty, the collision had jarred it free.

A flash lit the cabin. That meant its strobe worked. And hope.

The unit was designed to start automatically if it landed in water. On the second flash Russ saw the sideways cabin half full of water. The next blink showed the cockpit empty.

Russ took a step forward, trying to catch the floating EPIRB, but slipped and jammed his right foot into a crack behind a cabinet that had broken partially free from the hull.

He ducked under the water to try pry the pieces apart, but nothing would move. When he came up the sea was up to his chin.

Taking a gulp of air, he ducked down a second time and used every muscle in his body, but nothing would move, his foot was still trapped.

Standing again, the water was over his head.

*

Mother waited, then sent another sonar ping. The hull was indeed made of a material that was not familiar to her. She searched the memory banks again. Nothing, it was not steel, aluminum, titanium, or fiberglass. The vessel sunk downward into a thousand fathoms of water.

The danger had passed. The three sharks, which had been attached to her underside before she ordered them all away, returned to continue feeding.

One living thing still floated among the debris. A heat sensor indicated a porpoise or human, their body temperatures too close to differentiate. Neither were a threat, so mother turned south and proceeded slowly.

Dennis treaded water. Cushions and pieces of wood floated around him. Phosphorescence glowed about his hands and legs. He called out Russ's name, but held little hope. *Gwen* had disappeared too quickly.

He grabbed a cushion and a cooler-sized locker that had broken free. Jamming the cushion inside made the locker float higher. With his chest up on the locker and holding on, he tried to believe what he had just seen.

When the boat actually jumped upward, there was a submarine. Trying to stand as *Gwen* rolled, he had fallen into the water. Wide and long, unbelievably long, that was what he remembered. And the whump, whump, whump of what must have been a propeller's cavitation. Then it submerged and continued silently ahead, leaving a glowing trail of phosphorescence.

Dennis looked about, the debris had started to disperse. It would be days before anyone missed them. To the north the sky still glowed from the lights of Bermuda.

How long could he last, he wondered. At least the water felt warm.

The EPIRB popped to the surface within an arm's length.

15

Brigitta's face came on the screen. "Good morning," said George.

"Good morning." He could see something troubled her. "Did you see the news this morning?" she asked.

"About the boat?" Bermuda Marine Police, working in conjunction with the United States Coast Guard, had plucked a sailor out of the Atlantic a little before dawn. It happened only fifteen miles south of the eastern end of Bermuda.

"Yes," said Brigitta.

"You look upset."

She nodded. "They are flying me to San Diego today."

"Who? Harold?"

"No, the Navy. This project, they need me out there, just for a few days. There are computer people that need my help."

"What is so important?"

"They don't want it to happen again, what happened last night."

"What happened?" George felt confused.

"That boat sinking. It has to do with that. I can't tell you anymore."

George took a deep breath, finding it all incredible. "I'm coming up there."

"You can't, I'll be airborne in an hour. It's all top secret."

"Unbelievable," he said. He stood up and walked away, then came back to the computer. "Let me know when you are there, can you do that?"

"Of course. I'm not in any danger."

"Your doctors wouldn't agree with that. You were supposed to take it easy."

Brigitta tried to change the subject. "How is everyone?"

"Fine. I took the women ashore and they went by bus to Hamilton to do some shopping. There's maintenance I need to do on the boat. We're leaving after supper."

Brigitta forced a smile. "You'll have fun offshore with a boat full of beautiful women. Enjoy your quiet time today."

George was at a loss. "How long will you be on the West Coast?"

"A few days. Then it is home to Åland."

"It seems like every time we talk, something has changed. You'll still work from home?"

"Yes." She looked tired. "I really should go pack my things."

"Okay. I'll talk to you tomorrow morning."

"I love you," she said.

George thought the remark sounded mechanical, not from the heart, but answered, "I love you too."

The screen went blank.

He took a deep breath and climbed up to the cockpit. *A New Beginning* motored toward Town Cut, its blue hull gliding through the water. Captain Hauglund stood beside the bridge house, his white shirt glowing in the morning sun. Overhead, a long tailed tropic bird flew toward the northwest. They always looked so bright white and clean, thought George, like Hauglund's uniform.

Back inside the boat, he brought The Royal Gazette, Bermuda's online newspaper, up on the computer. There were several lead stories, one headline read 'Brigitta in Bermuda", but he opened one about the rescued sailor. It contained video of a recorded press conference.

Dennis Thorpe insisted a submarine had rammed their vessel, a very large submarine.

Could Brigitta be involved with submarines? George's cell phone rang.

"Officer Nord here," came the voice. "You must have seen the news? Thorpe's event adds a certain amount of credibility to Beth Weatherington's story. We would like to talk to her again."

"She's ashore right now," said George. "We are planning to leave, tonight, for the Virgin Islands."

"How can I get in touch with her?"

"I'm supposed to pick her and my other two crewmembers up at Ordinance Island at four."

"I will meet you there," said Nord, ending the call.

George clicked on the headline about Brigitta. Several photos showed *Frihet* leaving Hamilton Harbor and it did look like Brigitta standing at the bow. Funny, he thought, he could never remember Brigitta standing at the bow. She preferred to be in front of the computer down in the nav station, working with numbers and trying to solve some engineering problem. Tova had been enjoying the moment.

The boat did look sharp, and again he was glad the women had worn the crew uniforms. There were even aerial shots that must have been taken from a drone. At least it hadn't caught the women sunning on the foredeck.

He brought up *Frihet's* maintenance schedule on the screen. Work needed to be done.

At three-thirty he headed across St. George's Harbour for Ordinance Island. The women weren't there, but, after tying off the dinghy, he found them sitting in the shade of an awning at a round table outside the front of The White Horse Tavern. A half dozen colorful bags were piled on the fourth chair, along with two bags he guessed contained groceries.

"A successful day" he asked, bringing a fifth chair to the table.

"Yes," said Tova. "It's fun to shop someplace different."

"Officer Nord wants to talk to you, Beth," said George. "You must have heard about the young guy they plucked out of the ocean last night. Nord says the man's story adds credibility to yours."

She smiled, "I knew they never really believed me. Even with the bullet holes in my raft."

"Nord is supposed to meet us at four."

"Isn't that him?" said Windy, pointing at a man headed their direction.

"Good day," said Officer Nord.

"Join us," said George, offering his seat and dragging another to the table.

"Thank you," he said. "Beth, the gentleman that was rescued this morning, Dennis Thorpe, believes his vessel was rammed by a submarine. He is very lucky, having floated next to an EPIRB for only a few hours before being picked up."

"We heard about it today," said Beth.

Turning to face George, Nord said, "We would appreciate it if you could delay your departure a day. When Mr. Thorpe was brought in, he was taken directly to the hospital. An hour ago he was released, but, as you imagine, he is quite exhausted. The Princess Hotel offered a room and I believe he is asleep as we sit here."

Turning to Beth, he continued, "We would like you and Mr. Thorpe to compare notes, so to speak. Perhaps together you can remember something that might help us."

George waited for Beth's reaction, when she glanced questioningly at him, he said, "Of course we can stay an extra day."

"Thank you," said Officer Nord. "It would be good if you could sit in on the conversation too. You were there for her rescue. I will speak to the manager here. We can use a table inside in the corner, I am sure. Would one o'clock work for you?" He stood and smiled. "It will be a late lunch on the department's tab."

As he walked away, Beth said, "I'm sorry about the delay."

"That is fine," said Windy. "We can see more of Bermuda."

George glanced at his watch. "It's not even quarter past four yet. Let's bring the boat in to the empty spot inside Ordinance Island, then have dinner out, my treat here. It's the last chance for a night out before putting to sea."

Twenty minutes later they clambered aboard *Frihet*. Ten minutes after that the windlass brought the anchor up into its chocks. Crossing the harbor, the groceries and new clothes were stowed. At five-thirty the boat floated securely alongside the stone bulkhead of Ordinance Island.

Sitting in the cockpit, George listened to the hum of hair dryers inside the boat and smiled. What a comedy, he thought, a man goes to sea with three gorgeous women. Tourists loitered on the dock, so he sat with his back to them. Soon they would disappear toward the cruise ship on Penno's Warf.

Windy stepped up the companionway ladder first wearing a short tropical print dress he had never seen before. "A drink before we go eat?" she asked. The neckline dipped daringly between her breasts.

"Sure," said George, trying to contain a grin. "My usual." As she turned, there were bare shoulders as the dress vanished down to her waist. Changes in latitudes…he doubted Windy would have worn that dress back on Martha's Vineyard or Cape Cod.

Beth came out wearing a new skirt and halter top and Tova followed in a short blue dress. Windy passed up two glasses of wine, then came out carrying a wine and George's scotch.

"It's a good thing we're going out tonight," teased George, "so you could all wear your new outfits. You all look lovely."

"Who's up for going into town after dinner?" said Beth. "I looked it up. The last bus leaves Hamilton to come back at eleven forty-five."

"Not me," said George. "You all go."

Beth looked at Windy, then Tova. "It will be fun. There's a place called The Spinning Wheel where the locals go. There's music and dancing."

"All right," said Tova, looking at Windy. "Come with us."

"Maybe," said Windy. "Let me think about it."

They talked about the Dennis Thorpe and how lucky the man was, then speculated on why submarines might be colliding with sailboats. None if it made sense. Submarines were supposed to be very aware of everything in their environment. Could it be a poorly run submarine from some third world country? But the odds of it colliding with one sailboat were astronomical, and more than that extremely unlikely. When their glasses emptied they went ashore for dinner.

The hostess sat them at a round table with a red linen tablecloth in the far corner of the waterside terrace. A bottle of 2013 Lake Sonoma Winery Cabernet Sauvignon was ordered for the table and George also ordered a Macallan neat.

After they placed their orders, he said, "There's a few boat rules when we are offshore. I want everybody serious for a moment. Tova, I don't know if you've ever done an offshore jaunt.

"We'll do four hour watches," he continued, "starting at six, ten, and two, then repeat, with all of us in the mix, which means you'll have twelve hours off between watches and never have the same watch twice in a row."

He sipped his scotch. "We'll keep it simple and do it alphabetically, with Beth starting the first watch at six, then me, then Tova, and last Windy. That's pretty simple isn't it?"

"Offshore, cocktail hour is at five in the evening, but only if there are no reefs in the main. If there is enough wind for a reef, we don't drink, period. Nobody's to get out of the cockpit without a harness when they're outside alone, or any time after dark, even if everybody is up. If you fall overboard you are dead, remember that."

George expected wise ass remarks, but the women took it all seriously. A male crew would not have been like that. He continued, "Meals are every six hours, at six and twelve, if you are on watch, find something to prepare, and cook enough for everybody. There's all sorts of easy things, like stews in the freezer, but don't be afraid to be creative. You'll be popular.

"And be ready ten minutes before your watch is supposed to start. If your replacement isn't up ten minutes before you are supposed to be done, wake them up. Nobody wants their watch to drag on while waiting. It is acceptable to just watch the radar screen over the nav station, you are more likely to see a faraway ship there than when you are outside. The dim red lights inside the cabin will let you read, but won't destroy your night vision. I keep the intruder alarm on the radar set at three miles when offshore. A buzzer beeps if a ship comes closer. You can move that out further if you want.

"I think that's it," he said, ending.

"Thank goodness," said Beth. "You made it sound so serious I was expecting a dress code."

Everybody laughed.

"I worked on a boat owned by a Scot," said Beth, grinning. "He paid miserably, but worse were all his bloody rules. He made such a fuss about wearing shoes with the proper soles. One day I came up on deck wearing nothing else."

"What happened?" asked Windy.

"He fired me. It was for the best."

"There's no dress code," laughed George. "Offshore is the last place we can be free, but we want to stay safe. That Scot probably had a boat with slippery decks. *Frihet* has excellent non-skid surfaces."

Their waiter started to place salads on the table.

"Can you really sleep in the forward cabin at sea?" asked Beth.

"It has to be calm," answered George. "Sailing alone across the Gulf of Maine, last September, I slept in an aft cabin. The motion there is mild. Tova's been sleeping in the best spot to sleep offshore, the settee in the main cabin."

"Oh good," smiled Beth. "If the ocean gets rough we can take turns sleeping with Tova. She's beautiful."

Again, laughter, as Tova stuck her tongue out at Beth.

"Bring us another bottle of wine," said George. "We're celebrating our departure."

Over salads, they talked about meals to make offshore. Everyone had an idea. Beth sounded like the best cook and the one with the most experience cooking in a galley, having worked on charter boats. By the time the main course arrived, they talked about possible desserts. Tova liked to bake and promised things for the sweet tooth.

"I'm stuffed," said Beth. "There will be no dessert for me."

"Me either," said George. "I'm calling it a night."

Beth looked at Tova. "Are you ready to go to town?"

"Yes."

They both turned to Windy.

"I'm bowing out," she said. "If I go into town, I'll regret it in the morning."

"Suit yourself," said Beth, rising from the table. "Thank you George for the meal. I hate to rush, but the bus will be leaving the square in less than five minutes."

Tova hesitated.

"Come, Tova. It will be fun."

The two left, headed for the square. The waiter set the check in front of George.

"You really don't want to go?" asked George.

"No. I ate too much. I might go for a walk."

"Want to go up the hill? There's an old fort up there."

"Sure."

George left cash and then they ambled across the square, heading north, then turning east.

"It's this way," said George, leading her up Government Hill Road.

Small homes in pastel colors lined the sides of the road. Unseen Coki frogs screamed their shrill song. Where the road forked, he stopped. "Look at that," he said, pointing ahead.

Silhouetted against the night sky were the blocky sections of an unfinished church. The dark gables poked against the sky, but stars shined through where the roof should have been.

"The church was made of cut coral," said George. "It never was finished. In the daylight it looks sad, at night it is spooky."

"Come on," he said, walking on.

The road climbed and soon no houses lined the sides, only a vast lawn that ran off into the night. Before the road started to descend the far side of the hill, George touched Windy's bare arm and said, "This way." She followed him to the top of a small knoll.

There, they looked back at St. George's Harbour and the airport beyond. To the southwest ran the lights of Bermuda. North and east the ocean looked dark and empty. A few distant red and green lights blinked atop buoys marking the channels. Further up the hill, the shape of an old fort stood against the night sky.

"What a spot," said Windy.

"I've been here before," said George. "A long time ago."

Windy smiled. "With a woman?"

"Yeah. She's a vague memory now. Life goes on."

Neither spoke for a minute, but then Windy asked, "Did you talk to Brigitta today?"

He nodded. "Today she went to San Diego to work on some secret project for the government. Supposedly, it will only be a few days and then she flies to Åland to work from home."

"You sound skeptical."

"Everything constantly changes lately. I don't want to get my heart set on anything."

"It will sort out."

Together they watched the lights of an airplane sink into the cluttered illumination of the airport. A nearby cricket ratcheted out a drum roll, then became silent. A faint warm breeze wafted across the island, carrying the scent of unseen frangipani blossoms.

He took her hand, "Thank you for being a friend. I mean it."

She gave his fingers a squeeze. "I care about you and don't like to see you sad. Any time you need to talk…."

He put his arms around her and his hands found the bare skin of her back. He savored the feeling, the closeness, but his conscience caused the moment to feel awkward. George eased his hold and asked, "Can you find the North Star?"

Windy didn't want the intimacy to end, so turned inside his arms. It looked like a trillion stars poked through the night sky.

"There's the big dipper," she said, pointing, but leaving her right hand clasping his arms across her chest.

George inhaled her scent. His heart pounded.

"And the North Star?"

"There." Her hand rested on top of his.

He felt their fingers entwine. Her breaths timed with his. She brought his hand up to place it over a breast.

"Can we live in the moment?" she asked, pressing his hand against soft flesh, still looking at the heavens.

He held her tight, the soft hair of her head against his cheek. Life in the moment…he shut his eyes, cherishing the instant.

Windy's hand slid his through the low cut front of her dress, onto bare flesh.

Smooth and soft.

George's instant arousal surprised him. He tried to ignore it, hoping Windy hadn't noticed, but wanted....

A voice calling out shattered the moment.

Windy flinched, "Are there people up here?"

"No. It's probably somebody trying to find their dog." He took a deep breath, sliding his hands down to her hips. "We should be going."

Windy clasped his hand, not wanting to let him go.

"I'm sorry," he said. "I probably shouldn't have done that. You are beautiful."

"Don't be sorry. Remember, I asked you to live in the moment. It was my fault."

He slipped his arms back around her and they kissed.

16

Captain Jay Able picked up the bottle of wine, but Christine raised her hand.

"I've had enough," she said, "My shift starts in two hours." The candle light reflected in her eyes. "Thank you for inviting me to have dinner with you again."

"It truly is my pleasure," said Able. "Eating alone gets old in a hurry and I enjoy your company."

She smiled. "My staff is fine to spend time with, but, when you are in management, there is always this wall."

"I know," said the captain. He noticed worry creep into Christine's eyes.

She asked, "Do you have weapons onboard?"

"There are two rifles and two handguns locked in a cabinet on the bridge, and I also have a handgun in my cabin. Why?"

"There are two members of my staff that give me a bad feeling. I don't trust either of them."

"Weren't they vetted?"

"Yes, but they both claim to come from Eastern European countries where records are hard to access. We hired them separately, but I suspect they knew each other before boarding." She sipped a little of the wine remaining in her glass. "They spend a lot of time together, and at first I suspected they were gay, but it's something else. Emil sometimes carries a gun, I saw it in an open bag when they boarded one of the workboats."

"Who was with him?"

"Patrik."

"Maybe he doesn't trust Patrik. What do you think they have been doing?"

"I talked to the boss this morning and he cleared me telling you this. We are looking for an autonomous underwater drone that has gone rogue, or we hope it has. There are competing companies trying to develop drones for the military and also several non-friendly countries are in the game. Possibly someone else has control of the drone."

"Did Harold Habit's company make this drone?"

"I am not supposed to answer that, but I think the answer is obvious. He bought this ship and his people sign our paychecks.

"The drones are being developed to locate and track nuclear submarines," she continued. "Some are exceptional, and the missing one is years ahead of its competition. We are hoping to pick up its communications, which we have occasionally, but most of the time it is meaningless gibberish, at least to us. We send it on to the NSA and they have people trying to see if it is a code."

"Who would it be communicating with?"

"Maybe nobody, it could be totally malfunctioning. Or possibly somebody else has taken control and it's talking with them. Or it could be one of the sharks." She looked bewildered. "There's a lot we don't know."

"Sharks?" It sounded ridiculous.

"To expand the range of operation, the large drone works with smaller drones less than five meters long. The team that developed them actually made them look like sharks, at least the shape. Since the beginning they've been called Autonomous Sharks, or AS. There were eighteen assigned to Mother."

"Mother?"

"Yes, Mother Shark, which the team has been referring to as just Mother. She generates power and recharges the batteries of the sharks. They attach to nipples on her underside, recharge, and share information with her. Mother's processor was programmed to learn on its own and something has gone wrong. She didn't show up for her schedule rendezvous with our boat off of Cape Cod."

"Why do you think it is heading south?"

"Underwater communication is difficult. Some things work better in the warmer water of the lower latitudes. We think she is seeking this out, to keep better track of her sharks."

It sounded like bad science fiction to Captain Able. "You think Emil and Patrik are working for someone else?"

"I have been monitoring their computers. Possibly they are. Every time we need one of the workboats to do something, they volunteer. So far I haven't wanted to be a bad ass and tell someone else they have to go when those two are so willing. They could be communicating somehow when they are away from the ship."

"You mentioned Habit's lawyers once, what do lawyers have to do with all this?"

"I'm not supposed to talk with anyone about that." She looked uneasy.

"How big is Mother?"

"Two hundred and thirteen feet long, thirty-two feet wide, and only fifteen feet top to bottom. That is all top secret. Nobody else on board knows that."

"She is a big mother," said Able. He poured the last of the wine in his glass. "What would you like me to do?"

"The next time we need a work boat, can one of your men go with them? Just say it is your rules, or better yet, insurance company rules. Everybody hates insurance companies."

"Of course," said Able, smiling. "On the condition you have dinner with me again tomorrow."

"I'd like that," she said, smiling. "It gives me something to look forward to. I'm working all day tomorrow, so I won't have to leave so soon."

Captain Able reached across the table to give her hand a squeeze. "I'll look forward to it."

17

George watched the daylight creep into his cabin, trying to remember the details of the night before.

That hilltop kiss certainly hadn't been planned, but he had put himself in the situation. Did he want Windy? Of course he did, she was beautiful, but did he want a relationship with her? Was he ready to end the one with Brigitta? It had felt heavenly to hold Windy in his arms, and even to just be able to talk with her. That's what he missed, someone to be close to, emotionally.

George had lived long enough to know his style wasn't well thought out planning, but rather to go with the flow and maybe steer events a little bit. Was he taking the path of least resistance? They had held hands all the way back to the boat. He wondered if something more might have happened, if the possibility of Tova and Beth coming back hadn't been there. His will power had vanished by the time they had reached the boat. He pondered the possibility, but guilt washed over him. Could he be falling out of love with Brigitta?

There had been one more kiss inside the boat, a long passionate one, and then hesitation on ending the embrace. She walked into her cabin, gave him a smile, and then shut the door. He remembered the ache.

Tova and Beth had come back not long after he had climbed into bed. They tried to be quiet, but giggled about something. Sleep had come slowly for George.

He wondered where Brigitta was. San Diego? How did she end up connected to a United States Naval project? It had to be something to do with design. Much of the technology she brought into sailboat racing was applicable for marine and aeronautical uses.

Coffee, he could smell coffee. He slipped from the bed, pulled on shorts, and walked into the main cabin. Tova still slept on the port settee, breathing deeply with sheets draped over her midsection, leaving pink bare shoulders and legs exposed. He poured a coffee and climbed out to the cockpit, where Windy sat at the aft end.

"Thanks for making coffee," he said.

"I needed it," she answered.

"About last night," started George, sitting beside her. "I'm sorry I…"

She lightly slapped his leg. "Quit saying that, we were living in the moment. That's all. Today we are friends again, just friends."

George sipped his coffee, not sure what to say. "I really enjoy your company, I find you easy to talk to."

"I'm glad,' she said, in a hushed voice. "I like you a lot and feel the same way. But you have things you need to sort out. Maybe after we get to the Caribbean we need to have a long talk, or spend some time together, alone. Until then, let's keep things simple and just stay friends."

George took a deep breath. In a couple of hours he would call Brigitta. Life wasn't getting any simpler.

"Okay," he said. "You look nice." She had showered and combed her wet hair out in the cockpit, rather than risk waking Beth or Tova with the hair dryer. A snug tee shirt reached not quite down to her shorts.

"Thanks." She smiled.

"I need to stretch my legs. There's a neat church not fat from here, do you want to come along?"

"Sure. I didn't know you were religious," she said, standing, then added, "Let me put another shirt on over this."

"I'm not," said George, watching her pull on a button shirt. "I was in that church years ago, it's beautiful inside. There are big beams inside made of Bermuda cedar. The front of the church is over four hundred years old."

When they returned to the boat an hour later, Beth and Tova sipped coffee in the cockpit.

"If it was not for the full coffee pot," joked Beth, "we would have thought you two stayed out all night."

"Far from it," said George, wondering if either of them guessed anything. "We just walked up to the St. Peter's Church. You should go see the wood inside, it's beautiful."

A different cruise ship had tied along Penno's Warf during the night. Soon the square would be full of meandering sightseers. Tova went back to reading a tourist magazine and Windy disappeared into the boat to refill coffee cups and ditch the second shirt.

"Do you know that guy?" asked Beth.

George turned around. A black sailboat inched alongside. "Hey mate," said the man at the wheel. "Do you mind me rafting *Raven* alongside you?"

"Hi Flake, of course not," said George, not meaning it. "Let us help you."

He, Beth, and Tova held the boats separated while Flake sorted out lines and fenders. When Tova, wearing a low cut tank top, leaned over to grip the lifelines of *Raven* Flake stopped beside her to uncoil a rope. George wondered where his eyes were aimed behind his chrome aviator glasses. When the boats finally rested together, Flake thanked them.

"Would you like a cup of coffee?" asked Beth.

"That would be greatly appreciated," said Flake, stepping aboard *Frihet*. The big gold ring hanging from his left ear lobe hadn't been there the other day in the bar, nor the chrome sunglasses, but the same bandana fought to contain his wavy sun-bleached hair.

"We're leaving later today," said George.

"Me too mate, today or maybe tomorrow."

"I thought you had a job working for one of the America Cup campaigns?" said George.

"Hi," said Flake, turning to Tova. "We haven't officially met."

She smiled. "I am Tova."

Flake's face wrinkled. "You look like Brigitta. Her picture was on the news yesterday."

"That was me," beamed Tova. "She's my sister."

"This is Beth carrying your coffee," said George, "and that's Windy behind her. You may remember her. What happened to your job?"

Flake took the coffee and sat, then pulled a flask from a pocket and said, "Any takers? Black rum." When everyone shook their heads, he poured a healthy dab into his coffee. "It improves anything, coffee, tea, fish chowder. Anything," he repeated. "Now, about my job. It gets too cold here come January. I prefer temperatures where the women can wear miniscule bathing suits all day long and every day of the week." He smiled, revealing a gold tooth.

George guessed Flake had been fired even before he started. "So where are you heading?"

"I don't know, St. Thomas, the BVIs, Saint Martin, one of them islands. I've done the day sail gig before and will probably do it again. It's easy money."

George had done enough day sail charters to know it wasn't easy money, you were cook, host, entertainer, and, after the guests left, just a janitor in shorts. He said, "Good luck."

"I'll be looking for some help," said Flake, looking at Tova, then Windy and Beth. "If any of you are interested."

"Thanks, but I am just staying until we get to the Caribbean," said Tova, laughing. It was hard to take Flake seriously. "I have a design business in Stockholm."

"I already have a job lined up," said Windy, laughing too. "It's on a big ketch."

"I'm looking to buy a boat to sail around the world," said Beth.

"Sail around the world?" said Flake. "You'll need money to do that. A winter working on my boat should set you pretty."

"I'm all set," she insisted.

Trying to politely escape the uninvited guest, George said, "We were just about to walk up to St, Peter's Church. Would you like to come along? It's the oldest Anglican church outside of the British Isles, and the oldest protestant church that has been in continuous use in the New World."

"No thanks," said Flake. "The last time I walked out of a church I had gotten myself married. Churches give me the willies."

"I have to go change," said Tova.

"Me too," said Beth, following Tova into the boat.

"Thanks for the coffee, mate," said Flake, standing and giving George a pat on the shoulder. "I'll probably be seeing you later."

"Could be," said George, hoping it wouldn't happen.

Dropping inside the boat, George found Tova and Beth laughing. "Would it have been impolite to not let him raft alongside us?" asked Beth.

George nodded his head. "You never know when we'll want to tie up and not be able to find room."

"There's a space over near The Wharf Tavern," said Beth. "I could see it."

George laughed. "If you weren't all so beautiful, I'm sure he would have gone there to be nearer the bar."

The four of them left the boat and started across the bridge toward the square.

"Excuse me," said a smiling young man, in a strong British accent. "Can I ask Brigitta a few questions?" Another man, with a shoulder mounted camera, stood behind him.

"I am not Brigitta," said Tova. "She is my sister."

The man's face expressed surprise. "Can I ask you a few questions then? Perhaps we can sit at a table." He motioned toward The White Horse Tavern.

For a half hour Tova and the rest of the crew chatted with the reporter. The man with the camera shot video from several different angles. George noticed Flake lock up his boat then walk along the shore toward the cruise ship dock. When the reporter left, Beth and Tova continued to the church while George and Windy went back to *Frihet*.

"Is there anything you want to do before we leave?" asked George, following her inside.

Windy shook her head. "No. It will be good to get underway. How long do you think Officer Nord will take?"

"I have no idea," said George, feeling awkward. Their friendship had changed, there was unfinished business. Windy's snug tee shirt appeared painted on and the curves he had touched the night before called to him. Tova and Beth would be gone for quite a while….

He glanced at his watch.

"Are you going to call Brigitta?" Windy's eyes searched his face.

"Yes."

"I'm going to walk to the stores, I'll be back before lunch."

George slid into the nav station and turned on the computer. Brigitta wasn't online yet. It was still before five in the morning in California, so he checked for email. The second email down came from her.

George,

I am sorry, but I will be in meetings all morning, starting early. We have an emergency that I cannot talk about. Talk to you soon. I hope all is well. Say hi to the girls for me.

Love, Brigitta

He read it a second time, then turned to a weather website, chiding himself for not keeping a better eye on the weather.

A cold front came across the North American continent, causing the development a low pressure area off the Carolina's coast. Strong southwest winds were forecast for Bermuda, with cooler temperatures.

"At least it is a change," he said to no one. With luck they would be south of the low before it got strong.

Shortly after noon, the women came back carrying bags. Windy had met Beth and Tova coming back from the church, which led to mimosas at The Wharf Tavern and then poking around a few of the tourist shops about the square. George continued to read a novel, while they laughed and told stories while stowing things away.

At one o'clock they met Officer Nord at The White Horse Tavern. He introduced Dennis Thorpe, a wiry man in his early twenties, who looked very tired. A second officer accompanied Nord, a woman named Sylvia. They had made arrangements to use a round table at the back of the inside dining area.

Dennis Thorpe told the group everything he remembered about the night his boat sank, then Beth told him what she recalled of losing her boat. Officer Sylvia recorded the conversations and Nord took notes.

George's phone vibrated in his pocket and he looked to see who called. Harold Habit.

"Excuse me a moment," he said, then headed for the door.

"What's up?"

"George, I am coming to Bermuda. It's about the sinking of *Gwen*. We need to talk to the young man who was rescued."

"Who's we?"

"There's a man from the Navy with me. I'll be there late this afternoon. Can you make certain he is still on the island? And I would like to see you afterward."

"I'm at a meeting with him now," said George. "I'll tell him. He is staying at The Princess Hotel in Hamilton. We're tied alongside Ordinance Island in St. George's."

"I'll call you."

"What's up with Brigitta?" asked George, changing the subject. "You sent her to the West Coast?"

"She volunteered," said Harold.

"Volunteered?" said George.

"Yes. It is important work she is doing. I was worried she might be overdoing it, but she didn't think so. The Navy is happy to have her assistance."

"I worry about her," said George.

"She is a very capable woman," said Harold. "She knows what she is doing."

George stuffed his phone back into a pocket, then sat on a bench. What was that woman doing? Could she be purposely trying to destroy their relationship?

By the time George went back inside the tape recorder had been turned off and they were placing meal orders. He told them about the phone call, which brought a round of questions that he didn't have answers for.

When they returned to the boat, he checked the weather again. Wind gusts to fifty were possible south of Bermuda, starting before daybreak.

"We're staying right here for another day," said George. He explained about the forecast and how Ordinance Island offered protection from the wind and waves that would whip across the harbor. "Maybe we should double up some of the lines, he suggested.

Before they called it quits, Windy and Beth helped push the rigid bottom inflatable into the garage pocket that Brigitta had designed into the transom of *Frihet*. It was a tight fit, but the tender would be safe.

18

"We will let the storm pass by," said Hauglund. "I have been watching the front come across the United States for days, it is a strong one. The sea will take a day to calm after it passes. Then we will leave." He wished they had left days earlier, to be well south before the front passed, but Dai keep requesting additional testing and Hauglund had to invent excuses not to leave.

Bill Sanderlee looked out the windows of the pilot house. White puffy clouds still lingered over the island, but the forecast called for cooler weather. Several sailboats that had been tied along the seawall had moved out into the anchorage. That he did not understand, somehow tying to land seemed safer to him. With the wind shift, the bow swung to point almost due south.

Would it get too cold to use the pool? The water stayed a constant eighty-two degrees, thanks to a heater, but Cynthia might not want to sit in the sun. During the last two days her tan lines had faded into oblivion. He smiled. The previous few days were the most fun he'd had in his whole life.

Cynthia had gone to town to shop, brought ashore by one of the crewmembers. Bill insisted on her taking his credit card and she had. He wondered what things she might come back with. From her last shopping trip she came back with what she called a C string bikini, which was something he had never even heard of.

*

"Will we make it?" asked Christine.

"Easily," said Captain Able. "We'll be anchored before dark. Your people can go ashore tonight, if they want. We'll shuttle them in with the work boat. If it blows hard tomorrow, we may not want the work boats in the water."

"Would we have been safe at sea?"

"Of course, this is a large vessel, but it would have been a terribly uncomfortable." He smiled. "Your listening devices probably would have heard a lot of crashing waves."

"It will be nice to walk on land," said Christine.

"Can I take you to dinner ashore?"

She smiled. "I would like that."

*

"Dai is getting impatient," said Olson.

"He has to wait," said Hauglund. "Did Cynthia return?"

"Yes, one of our crew brought her back out a half hour ago. She is in Mr. Sanderlee's cabin."

"Good. If it blows fifty knots tomorrow, they probably will not leave Mr. Sanderlee's cabin." He smiled and shook his head. "That is a lucky man."

"What shall I tell Dai?"

"Has he not seen the weather forecast? We are staying right here for tonight and probably all day tomorrow." Looking out the pilot house window, he added, "Those boats that are anchored to the southwest may drag anchor into us during the night. Have three men on watch at all times. If they tangle with us, cut them free and let them wash ashore somewhere."

"Yes sir."

*

George's phone vibrated. "Harold." He glanced at his watch, almost seven-thirty.

"I'm on my way, I'll be there in fifteen minutes."

"See you then."

Fifteen minutes later George felt the boat move, someone had stepped aboard. "Harold?"

"Yes." He came down the companionway, accompanied by a man wearing a dark blue sports jacket and tie. "Where are the girls?"

"At The White Horse Tavern."

"Good. I hoped to talk in private. This is Admiral Hanssen. " They both sat.

"Anything to drink?"

Harold smiled, "Scotch."

"Same," said Hanssen. "This is quite the boat you have here. I heard Brigitta Eriksson designed it."

"That's true," said George.

Harold continued, "As you know, two boats and crews are missing and two more crews claim to have collided with a submarine before sinking."

"Claimed to have?" interrupted George. "You still don't believe them?"

"We believe them," said the Admiral. "There is an out of control sea drone on the loose. We believe that is the source of the collisions"

"What are the odds on that?" asked George. "Unless it was doing it on purpose."

"The drone is designed to operate autonomously for months at a time. It failed to return to our boat off of Cape Cod," said Harold. "The drone works in conjunction with smaller drones that incorporate technology developed by Brigitta. It is supposed to communicate with our satellites when it surfaces periodically."

"It was your company that built it?"

"It is not just an it, it is a them. The big drone has eighteen smaller drones working with it. We call the small drones sharks."

"Every boat sunk was built of wood," said the Admiral. "We believe the drone is hunting wood boats."

"That's ridiculous," said George.

"Russia and China are building undersea drones, and several companies are trying to get the same government contract I am," said Harold. "Maybe somebody has messed with our drone. Maybe it has malfunctioned. We need to find it."

"Did you talk to Thorpe?"

"He saw it well enough to identify it in a photograph as our drone."

"What do you want me to do?" asked George.

"For one thing," said Harold, "give Brigitta some slack. Her part in this isn't the problem, the problem belongs to the programmers, but we need her help with other parts of this project. We don't want the Russians or Chinese to get their hands on the technology she developed."

"Our sub chasers are working this whole section of the Atlantic," said the Admiral, "from Bermuda south to the Caribbean. If we can't find the sub during the next week, my plan is to use a wood sailboat as bait."

George downed his scotch to pour another. "It all sounds bizarre. An unmanned sub searching out and sinking wooden sailboats?"

"We think it can't identify them," said Harold. "It recognizes metals or laminates like fiberglass, but wood was never programmed in as a boat material. For some reason it must see wood boats as a threat."

"And then your sub attacks?"

"It was never programmed to," said Harold, "but it has the ability to learn. Or possibly someone has learned how to hack into it and done something to it. There is a lot we don't know about Artificial Intelligence."

"The drone seems to be working its way south," said the Admiral. "We pick up bits of its communications with the sharks, or we think we do. Some of the things we are hearing are hard to identify, so there is little we are sure of. Coast Guard aircraft have been searching for wood boats and trying to keep track of them. This morning a decision was made to actually warn wooden boats that they are in danger."

Harold said, "George, would you to sail a wooden boat to lure the drone in for us?"

"Where?"

"Near the Virgin Islands, in United States waters," said the Admiral, "that is the direction the thing seems to be headed. It will take us a week to set things up. You'll be there about then. With Navy and Coast Guard all around you, there will be little danger for you or your crew."

George glanced at Harold and shrugged his shoulders in disbelief. "Why not. I've never been rammed by a submarine before."

The Admiral smiled. "Not many people have, and we want to keep it that way."

"Of course, all of this must be kept secret," said Harold. "We don't want anyone else trying the same trick."

George took a large swallow from his tumbler. It all sounded insane. A drone attacking wooden boats? He looked out a port at sailboats anchored in the harbor, none were made of wood. Finally, he said, "Would you like to go over to the tavern and meet Brigitta's sister?"

Fifteen minutes later George found Tova, Windy, and Beth at an inside table in a corner. Introductions were made, followed by talk of sailing.

Looking around the room, Harold spotted Captain Able having dinner with the leader of his underwater communications team, Christine. Excusing himself, he walked to their table.

"Well, look who I have found," he said. "What are you doing here?"

Captain Able stood up nervously, "I brought the ship into the harbor to ride out the weather."

"I guessed that," said Harold. "Sit." He pulled a chair over to sit with them. "I meant here, having dinner together."

Christine attempted to explain the highlights of what they had learned during the previous month, realizing it didn't sound like much. Harold asked how the ship was. Both Christine and Able talked about how hot it was inside the boat, and how little could be done about that. The two work boats had proven invaluable, setting underwater antennas and retrieving acoustic buoys.

"The two names you sent me," said Harold, "did you mention them to Captain Able?"

"Yes," said Christine. "Were you able to find anything more about them?"

"Their lack of a history before 1997 is a red flag," said Harold, "but both are experts in their field, establishing exemplary reputations the last few years. Keep an eye on them. That is all I can suggest at the moment. I should be going."

"The rest of my team is dining at those two tables over there," said Christine, motioning toward the other end of the room. "If you want to say hi."

"Of course."

Harold stopped and chatted with them for ten minutes, before returning to George and his crew. Five minutes later, Harold and the Admiral left.

George walked over and introduced himself to Captain Able and Christine. "Harold said you are on the research ship anchored in the harbor."

"That's right," said Christine. "We study underwater communication." She looked attractive, with a round face and her hair pulled back. She wore a pale green dress that left her shoulders bare, but the dark rimmed glasses made her look like a scientist.

"And you work for Harold?" asked George, guessing it had something to do with the missing drones.

"Yes," said the Captain. "Aren't you the one that captained his boat in the big race last summer?"

"I was. I've resigned now and I'm selling boats for a living," laughed George.

"I recognized Brigitta at your table before I recognized you," said Able.

"That's Brigitta's sister," said George, grinning. "Brigitta's still recovering from her head injury. She sent her sister along as a stand in." He guessed that was a safe story.

"She sure looks like Brigitta."

"Are you sitting out the weather?" asked George.

"Yes, we'll go to sea after it blows over."

"Good luck," said George, watching Beth, Windy, and Tova get up to leave. "I have to be going."

19

George woke. The wind hissed through the boat's shrouds and stays. During gusts it whistled around the mast.

A blast caused the boat to list to starboard, then she settled back. A halyard on a nearby sailboat started to ping against its mast like a drummer beating on a metal can. George hoped somebody would tie the damn thing off. Again the boat leaned, then she settled back onto her lines.

The night felt much colder than when he had gone to bed.

He wondered if the dock lines were all right. Sometimes fenders squeak between the dock and the hull, but he heard none. *Frihet* jerked against a line and eased back. George pulled on his shorts and slipped silently through the main cabin. Streetlights leaked into the main cabin and he could see Tova curled up in a sheet.

He stepped up to the cockpit and onto the side deck. Scattered drops of rain pelted his face, but the streetlights showed no puddles. The dock lines looked fine, but he shortened one spring line. A blast of wind swept cold across his bare shoulders, but the southwest breeze actually kept the boat away from the bulkhead. A half a mile away, on the far side of the harbor, two large boats had all their bright white deck lights on, illuminating more than a dozen anchored sailboats riding out the weather.

On *Frihet*'s starboard side he checked Flake's lines. *Raven* appeared to be behaving nicely and, again, the wind kept the boats separated. A light inside glowed, but George didn't try to raise anyone.

Stepping back into the cockpit, George found Beth sitting in the shelter of the dodger.

"You walked right past me," she said, smiling.

He grinned. "The shadows hid you. I was checking the lines."

"I know." She held up a glass of wine. "I couldn't sleep and I thought this might help."

"Can I join you?"

A minute later, he returned carrying a tumbler of Dalwhinnie and wearing a long sleeve shirt. "It's chilly tonight."

"Bloody cold I'd call it," she laughed, holding her glass up, waiting for a toast.

He clicked his against hers. "To a safe voyage." She wore an oversized heavy flannel shirt and sat with her knees up inside it like a poncho.

They talked about how quickly the storm might pass and the sea calm down. Beth mentioned the anemometer read sixty-seven knots in one gust, which was more than had been forecast. They stopped talking when the wind screamed, waiting for it to quiet. The boat flinched to starboard and jerked against the dock lines. Droplets of rain sounded like someone bombarded the plastic window in the front of the dodger with BBs. Beth mentioned she had once seen fifty knot winds offshore and hoped to never see them again.

The conversation hit a snag and, after a minute of listening to just the wind howl, Beth said, "It really isn't fair what Brigitta is doing to you." She smiled. "I know, it is none of my business."

George sipped his scotch while the wind screamed. It sure felt that way, but he had tried to be patient and see things from her prospective. He offered, "She's busy."

Beth shook her head. "Men are so slow. Her priorities have changed. Windy wants to jump your bones, but she respects you too much to pry her way in. And I'm not sure what Tova is doing here. Maybe she's supposed to keep an eye on you for her sister, or maybe she is trying to steal you away for a vacation fling." Beth grinned and sipped her wine. "It's going to be an interesting sail to the Caribbean, I wouldn't miss it for anything."

The wind howled ashore, rattling palm fronds and rocking the trees. George wanted to change the subject, so said, "Do you think we'll be able to get out of here tomorrow?"

Beth listened to the storm. "I don't know, maybe late in the afternoon."

The boat tilted to starboard again as another blast pressed against the side of the mast.

"Have you seen any sign of our neighbor, Flake?"

She laughed. "If he comes up on deck I am going to hide in my cabin."

"Hi." It was Tova standing in the companionway with a sheet wrapped around her shoulders like a shawl. "It's cold."

She looked very sleepy. "Would you like to borrow a warm shirt," said George. "And I have a blanket somewhere."

Tova made a sleepy smile. "Ja det skulle vara trevligt."

The spoken Swedish caused George to smile, remembering how Brigitta used to do that. He climbed back inside to dig a heavy chamois shirt out of a locker. Taking the shirt, she dropped the sheet, revealing a tiny shear tank top and lace panties.

"No wonder you're cold," laughed George. "You need to dress better than that."

"I didn't bring warm clothes," she said, pulling on the heavy shirt and tugging her long blonde hair out from the shirt's collar.

From another locker he grabbed a blanket and tossed it to her. "Get some sleep," he said.

Back in the cockpit, he said, "I'm going to try and get some sleep."

Beth smiled. "Tova is hoping you dream of her."

George grinned and shook his head. "You're nuts." He swallowed the last of the scotch, then went inside.

Passing the nav station, he turned on the computer…no email from Brigitta.

*

Cynthia listened to Bill Sanderlee's breathing. The man slept like a rock after sex. Outside the wind howled, but the boat moved very little in the protection of the shore.

Earlier, they ate fresh tuna for dinner, followed by crème brulee for desert, then retired to his cabin to watch a movie. She had suggested mild porn and soon they were watching a television over the Jacuzzi, on which a tanned couple copulated on a tropical beach. Bill had opened a bottle of Veuve Clicquot, an excellent champagne she wasn't familiar with.

Cynthia smiled. It hadn't been a bad assignment at all.

*

Captain Hauglund stepped into the pilot house. Outside, the boat's bright lights illuminated the world around them. The waves on the dark water were not large, but the wind lifted sheets of foamy froth into the air. Only two sailboats had anchored upwind of *A New Beginning* and with luck they would stay put. The research ship that had come in just before dark had anchored off the starboard aft quarter and posed no threat.

The three crewmembers standing watch looked bored. The senior officer had the engines idling in case power was needed to maneuver. Hauglund offered encouragement, then departed, heading down two decks. Walking toward the engine room, he met Olson.

"How's Dai?" asked Hauglund.

"Weird," said Olson, shaking his head. "The man's face never changes, he might as well wear a mask. He's sitting at his computer working, which is what he's always doing."

Hauglund grinned. "His people pay well, we can put up with his peculiarities. You and me, we split his cash. Then we send Dai's secrets to our country, which makes our people happy."

"Dai doesn't eat much," said Olson, shaking his head. "I don't think he has changed out of the same pair of shorts since he came on board, and most of the time he hasn't been wearing a shirt. Tonight it's colder, so he put one on."

"Leave him be, go get some rest. It will rain hard soon."

*

Captain Able listened to the wind. His best officer stood watch, so he wasn't concerned. There had been dozens of nights like that one in the past. In the darkness, he slid his hand across the bed to find Christine's. She gave his a squeeze.

"You awake?" he said, softly.

"Mmm. It's the wind."

"We're fine, it's just noisy."

"I know." Moving closer to him, she said, "I feel safe here."

"You are." His arm slipped under her bare shoulders. It had been a long time since he had felt the warmth of a woman.

"Dinner was lovely," she said. "I had fun. I haven't been on a date in ages."

"Me too." Christine's presence felt delightful.

*

Rain roared like Niagara Falls. George sat up and pulled on his shorts, trying to remember if any of the hatches had been left open at all. A boat can get stuffy quickly if shut up tight, and he guessed a hatch or two might be open a wee bit.

In the main cabin, he found Windy already shutting the companionway hatch. Tova sat up watching, still blinking the sleep from her eyes. An overhead hatch in the starboard aft head dripped. George dogged it down tight. Wind rocked the boat. The door to Beth's cabin opened and she stepped out.

A crash of wind brought another torrent of rain. Nobody even tried to talk over the ruckus. The early twilight created a watery mosaic on the windows.

Windy started to make coffee. She had put on jeans and a heavy sweat shirt, which made her the warmest dressed on the boat.

"We do have heat," said George, looking at the thermometer over the nav station. It read sixty-one degrees. He started to fiddle with the thermostat.

"The rain was blowing back into the companionway," said Windy. Beth wiped the water off the stairs with a towel.

The wind howled through the rigging and the boat shivered and rocked.

"What a night," said Tova, looking up at the overhead.

"It will blow through," said George. "Bad weather seldom lasts twenty-four hours."

Beth laughed. "Where does that come from?"

"That's an old sailor's axiom," said George, grinning. "It's true."

"I'll cook eggs, if anybody wants some," said Beth, digging a frying pan out of a locker.

"I'll help," offered Tova.

George turned on his computer to read the weather forecast. "It's supposed to blow through by late afternoon. The heaviest rain is this morning. Winds will shift to southeasterly."

Hesitantly, he clicked on email. The top one came from Brigitta.

Call me when you can. Love, Brigitta

He picked up his laptop and walked forward into his cabin, shutting the door.

A few minutes later, Brigitta's face came on the screen. "Good morning," said George.

In Swedish, Brigitta said, "God Morgon, hur mår du."

"I'm fine," said George, smiling. "You look great."

"Thanks. We completed a lot in San Diego and I slept well last night."

"Where are you?" He didn't recognize the map covered wall behind her.

"New London, Connecticut, at the Naval base. We flew cross country last night."

"And you slept?"

"Like a baby. I'll be here for a week, maybe two."

The comment made his heart sink, but he noticed the worry in her eyes. "I thought you were going home to Åland."

"Me too," she said. "We are working on something I cannot talk about."

"Brigitta, are you going to stay up there? Is this going to go on forever? What happened to our plans?" George felt frustrated.

"It will be over soon."

"Your work or our relationship?"

"George, be patient. The work here must be done and I will join you in the Caribbean. I love you."

She looked frustrated too. Was it with him or the work? "I love you too," said George. "I miss waking up beside you."

Brigitta looked about to cry. "I miss you too."

Wind rocked the boat, driving rain onto the deck and generating a train-like roar. Thunder reverberated like a cannon in a canyon.

"We're having quite a storm here," said George. "We're all safe in St. George's Harbour, but I should go."

"I saw you were having weather," said Brigitta. "I love you. Stay safe."

"Love you too." George shut off the computer and listened to the rain.

127

20

"Who's up for leaving tonight?" asked George.

The wind had let up mid-morning and the rain quit a little after noon. "We can have supper here and then go. The ocean will have quieted down some and the wind will be blowing in the teens out of the east. It will be a bumpy ride, but we'll click off some miles before morning. After that the wind is supposed to go light again from the northwest." He glanced at the women. "What do you think?"

Wind hissed through the rigging, but it was nothing like the howl of earlier.

"It sounds good to me," said Beth, looking at the sky out the open companionway. Patches of blue peaked between sooty clouds.

"Me too," said Windy. '

"I will make supper," said Tova, looking up from the book she had been reading. "You are all the experts at offshore sailing, so I will leave the decision to you."

"Good," said George. "Let's eat a little early, say in three hours, at five. I'm anxious to get going. The rain has stopped, so if you want anything ashore, now is the time to get it." He stood and went out into the cockpit.

Water dripped from the mast and shrouds, but no more fell from the sky. White caps still littered the harbor and two sailboats had washed up on the downwind beach. The research ship and *A New Beginning* still hung on their anchors. George wondered how long they would stay in the harbor, deciding probably until the next day. In a heavy sea, sailboats had the advantage of a steadying sail. Motor yachts would roll mercilessly at the whim of the waves.

Beth and Tova came up on deck to head ashore. George ducked back down inside again.

"You're not going ashore?" he asked.

Windy shook her head. "There is nothing I need." She cleaned up what was left of lunch. "Is there anything that needs to be done?"

"No, everything is ready," he said, putting clean plates back in a locker.

Windy wiped out the sink, making a point of scrubbing one corner. "Have you heard from Brigitta?"

"Yeah. She's in New London, Connecticut now, at the submarine base. She'll be there for a couple of weeks."

Windy stopped cleaning to look at George. "Doing what?"

"More of the same, stuff for the Navy."

"I feel so bad for you," said Windy. She put down the sponge to give George a hug.

He didn't resist, but felt as if he were sinking. Breaking it off, he said, "Hey, just friends, remember?"

She smiled. "That was a friendly hug, okay?"

"Yeah. I'm going to straighten out my cabin," said George.

Inside, he shut the door and stretched out on his bed. After the mostly sleepless night and without the scream of the wind and rumble of the rain, he dozed off. The women's laughter woke him. His watch said quarter of five and it smelled like something cooking.

He showered quick, put on clean shorts, then went into the main cabin,

The women were all in high spirits. Tova and Beth had made lasagna, salad, brought home fresh bread, and bought ice cream for desert.

By a little after six they had cleared out of customs, retrieved George's hand guns, and slipped their dock lines. Flake stood on the deck of *Raven,* watching them back away. As George put the transmission into forward, Flake offered a wave. Beth laughed and blew him a kiss.

The sky had cleared and a northerly blew about eighteen knots. Away from Ordinance Island, they put up the mainsail, tucking in one reef, and unfurled the genoa. With the transmission in neutral, they bore off the wind to head for Town Cut. The air felt dry and cool.

"I'll take us through the cut," said George. "After that it is Beth's watch until ten. Then I'll be on."

Under an expansive blue sky, the stiff breeze hurried them through. The pines on the tops of the coral cliffs that formed the cut shushed and waved in the wind. Where the land ended on the port side, the cannons of Gates Fort pointed to sea.

Beyond, confused eight foot waves tumbled into whitecaps and bowled over the shallow shoals and reefs. George ignored the churning water, instead focusing on the channel that led to deeper water ahead.

Passing by Can 2, they turned to just south of east. Windy eased the genoa, while Beth let the traveler slide all the way to starboard. Waves slid up under the transom, swaying it from side to side.

"We'll head due south in a couple of miles," said George. "The motion will be better then." He started the autopilot and turned to Beth. "It's all yours. If you have any questions, please come and get me."

Sitting with his back against the cabin, he looked back at the hills of Bermuda. The colors were already muting as the shadows grew. Windy sat on the far side of the cockpit, the wind stretching a strand of her hair across her glasses. Beth stayed aft behind the port wheel, but let the autopilot do the steering. Tova plopped down beside to him.

"Pretty, isn't it," said George.

"Ja," said Tova.

Windy ducked inside to come back out wearing a wind breaker with her jeans. She carried a second jacket she offered to Beth.

"Are you warm enough?" asked George.

Tova smiled. "Yes, thank you for asking." Her hand reached for his and gave it a squeeze, then released.

He wonder if anyone had seen that. "Don't forget to get some rest," he said. "Your watch starts at two."

"Ja." She smiled. "It is early still and I like to look at the island."

George knew that soon an empty ocean would surround them, but he always had found fascinating things to look at. There would be the pelagic birds, clouds of every configuration, and millions of stars and satellites at night. On most nights the moon kept company for a while, often with spectacular entrances or moon sets. On two occasions, on nights with showers, he had seen moon bows, something most never see one of in a life time.

Plus, there was time to use frivolously without feeling guilty. He would cook, read, write, play a guitar, and sometimes just sit to watch a shearwater glide over the water or a cloud drift away. Offshore felt like the last free place on earth.

"George, sleep in my bunk," said Beth. "The motion up forward will be awful."

"I might," said George, knowing she would wake him because his watch came after hers.

Hot bunking was what sailors called it. George had done it delivering a Bermuda 40 with one other crew member, years before. There had been only one bunk on board that it was possible to sleep in when the weather became bad, so whoever was off watch used it.

Four miles east of Bermuda they jibed toward due south. George thought about shaking out the reef, but decided to leave it in until morning. He put on a harness, snapped onto a jack line that ran along the port deck, and went forward to set a preventer on the boom. In a following sea, he did not want to accidentally jibe the boom at night and break something. Back in the cockpit, he took off the harness. With the change of heading, the apparent wind dropped and the night didn't feel as cold. The waves slid in under the stern, lifting the boat and causing it to yaw to one side and then the other, but the autopilot easily corrected.

"I'm going to get some sleep," said George. "Don't be afraid to wake me if you have any questions."

Beth smiled. "I'm all set." She looked comfortable nestled in the corner of the stern pulpit. The flannel-lined collar of her jacket was turned up against the wind and she had snapped the tether of her safety harness to a deadeye at the aft end of the cockpit.

"I'm going to try and get some sleep too," said Windy.

"Me too," said Tova.

George stopped at the nav station and wedged himself into the seat. He read wind 353° at 16 knots and boat speed 7.35 from the instruments. Water gurgled along the side of the hull. Waiting for the computer to start, he fought to ignore the boat's motion. There were no new emails from Brigitta. The weather forecast hadn't changed, tomorrow the wind would grow light and remain northerly.

Windy disappeared into the dark of her cabin, but left the door open. Closed up cabins get stuffy with hatches shut at sea.

Tova wiggled out of her jeans, but she still kept on George's heavy chamois shirt. She straightened out the sheet on the port settee, then stretched and grabbed the blanket.

"Let me put up the lee cloth," said George. "You don't want to roll out of bed during the night,"

She smiled. "I will be all right."

"No. I insist. Offshore is no place for an accident."

The lee cloth was stowed under her cushion, so she helped him get it out. Lines attached the canvas to handrails on the overhead, securing it in place. "There you go," said George. "It's like sleeping in a canyon."

"Thank you," she said, touching his hand. Her smile was Brigitta's smile.

"You are welcome," said George, wondering if that many buttons had been undone on the chamois shirt earlier.

After crawling in behind the lee cloth, she pulled the blanket up and gave him a little wave.

George went back to the nav station. At times he had slept in the seat in the nav station, but the motion of the boat was too much. He slipped into Beth's cabin and stretched out on her bed.

It felt like seconds later that she stuck her head in to say, "George, you're on watch in ten minutes."

He found her back in the cockpit sitting in the shelter of the dodger. "How's it going?"

"Fine," she said. "The wind is backing and dropping."

George looked up, she had trimmed both the main and genoa, and both drew perfectly. "It doesn't feel as cold."

"I'm chilled," said Beth. "I hope you left the bed nice and warm for me."

George smiled. "Have you seen any ships?"

"One, far to the east. Just a white light. The radar was set on three mile range and didn't get an echo."

George stepped behind the starboard helm and glanced at the compass, 165° magnetic, which was pretty close to due south true.

"I'm turning in," said Beth

George went inside too, stopping at the nav station. He checked the radar's intruder alarm and made certain it was set for three miles. In the galley, he dug a gallon container of stew out of the refrigerator to let it warm. An hour or so before midnight, it would go on the stove to simmer for hours. George knew a well fed crew was a happy crew.

In the nav station he wrote in a log book their position, speed, and heading. If anything happened to the electrical system on board, he wanted to know where they were when he dug out the sextant. Nautical almanacs sat on a shelf under the nav station.

Outside in the cockpit, he sat in the protection of the dodger and listened to the sounds of the sea. George loved nights like that, with the boat moving well and the stars bright overhead. Brigitta was supposed to be there, just the two of them sailing south. They had talked about it so often the summer before. Why did she let herself get wrapped up in all these projects? Did she enjoy the work so much she wouldn't be able to walk away from it? Was the passion of their relationship dying already? Flustered, he went back to the galley, where he found a box of double dark chocolate brownie mix. They would make a treat later.

Later, after eating stew, he settled back in the cockpit to read on a dimly lit tablet.

"Hi." It was Tova.

"Hi." George glanced at his watch. "You're not on for another hour."

"I know. I was hungry and the stew smelled good." She set a bowl up onto the bridge deck. "Would you like some?"

"I had some already, but you can put a little more in my bowl. It's by the sink."

A minute later she came up the companionway steps carrying his stew. "It doesn't feel as cold." She had pulled her jeans back on and slipped a wind breaker over the heavy shirt. Her blonde hair was back in a thick ponytail.

"It isn't. And the wind has let up some."

She sat close to George and they both ate. "Have you seen anything?"

"Beth saw a ship, it was far away," he said, noticing that Tova still had most of buttons undone on the shirt. No wonder she was chilled. "We've trimmed the sails some because the wind is backing. Other than that, it's pretty quiet." He smiled. "Some would say it is boring."

"It's beautiful out here. Look at all the stars."

"If you work at it," said George, looking up, "you can almost always see a dozen or more satellites in the sky at any one time. There's hundreds of them up there."

Tova scraped the last of her stew from the bowl. "Have you heard from my sister today?"

"She's up in New London, Connecticut, doing something for the Navy." George tried to not sound disgusted. "Every couple of days her plans seem to change."

Tova shook her head. "Brigitta has been like that all her life. In school, she would put her studies ahead of everything."

George set his bowl aside. "I miss her."

"She is too wrapped up in her work. It consumes her. Brigitta would forget those around her. Our parents encouraged hobbies, hoping she would do something beside school work. The only interest she ever took was sailing. She always loved boats. Now she has found a way to combine boats with mathematics and physics."

George said nothing.

They both listened to the water pass along the side of the hull. Stars glowed overhead, but there was no moon. Soft red light leaked out the companionway. Occasional white caps still boiled on the tops of the waves, but the sea was quieting.

George finally spoke. "I can't keep doing this, whatever it is she and I are doing."

Tova reached for his hand, "Things will work out, as they were meant to."

"I'm going to get some sleep," said George. "Are you alright? Put on a harness and stay attached to the boat when you're outside. And stay warm."

She nodded. "Use my bunk if you want. It is still too rough to sleep up forward."

"I might, thanks." He went down the companionway and stopped long enough at the nav station to check for emails. There were none.

He kicked off his shoes and slid into Tova's bunk.

The sheets smelled like Brigitta. He tried to imagine her there.

*

Voices woke George. He looked at his watch, quarter of seven. Windy and Tova stood in the galley. He slipped from the berth. As his bare feet hit the cool cabin sole, he said, "Good morning."

"Good morning," said Windy.

"God morgon," said Tova.

Daylight streamed in the windows and he tried to look out. The boat's motion had calmed, yet water still babbled along the hull. Steadying himself, George said, "What's for breakfast?"

"Eggs," said Windy, leaning against a countertop to maintain her balance in the moving cabin.

He smiled. "Can I have a side of bacon?"

"Of course," said Tova, grinning. George noticed dimples identical to her sister's.

Through the companionway the sky outside looked clear. The instruments in the nav station said wind 320° at 9 knots, boat's heading 165°

magnetic, speed 3.94 knots. "Things certainly calmed down during the night," he said.

"Yes," said Tova. "It warmed up as the night went on."

George tried to blink the sleepiness away. Had he dreamt about Brigitta? Or was it Tova? When she stepped away from the galley it looked like Tova had undone another button on the shirt. What was there…still one buttoned? Windy had put on shorts and a bathing suit top, obviously optimistic about the weather. He ran his fingers back through is hair, hoping to wipe away the cobwebs of sleep. Through the doorway to Beth's cabin, he could see her sitting up on her bunk.

"Coffee?" he asked.

Tova handed him a mug.

Up on deck, a blue empty ocean surrounded them. He sipped the coffee, this was life at sea as he remembered it…quiet and serene. But this time he shared the boat with three women. He had only been on an ocean passage once before with woman on board and she had been a paid stewardess on one of his employer's boat. George swallowed a gulp of coffee.

"George," said Tova, "you like your eggs over easy, right?"

He cringed, had Brigitta told her that or had she guessed? "Yes, but any way at all is fine."

A few clouds lingered to the north, but the rest of the sky looked eternally blue. He walked forward to lean against the mast. Private moments were few on a boat at sea and there he could only hear the water against the hull. The air smelled clean and of the sea. His eyes searched for pelagic birds, but found none. The world was empty except for *Frihet*.

Beth had come out to the cockpit, so he asked her to ease the traveler way over and then he shook out the reef. The early sunlight hitting his shoulders made the flannel shirt feel warm. Windy had guessed right, it would be a warm day with little wind.

*

The anchor chain clunked upward over the windlass. A young member of the crew leaned over the bow railing to hose mud off the chain before it came over deck. Captain Hauglund watched impatiently through the pilot house windows. A few high clouds lingered to the north, in an otherwise bright blue sky.

The research ship that had spent the night anchored behind them left shortly after sunrise. Dai messaged Hauglund, sounding angry, and wanted to know why they had not left yet.

"He is an odd one," said Olson, looking at something on the computer screen in front of him.

"Can you tell what he is doing?"

Olson hit a couple keys and rows of numbers came up on the pilot house computer. "He is listening and sending the information to his people."

"Are our people getting it too?"

"Of course."

"He probably heard the research ship leave." Hauglund smiled. "He probably listens to our boss and Cynthia going at it. Sanderlee's cabin isn't that far from him."

"Have you ever wondered if he listens to us?"

"All his sensors are under the boat. I don't think he hears Sanderlee in his cabin and we are another deck above that. We should keep our guard up though."

"Do we have any weapons?"

Hauglund wondered if he should trust Olson, but then said. "There is a handgun in the top drawer," said Hauglund, pointing to a stack of drawers beneath the instrument panel. "Pull it all the way out, there is a second compartment in the back."

*

Captain Able told the helmsman to set the course for 165° magnetic. The sky looked clear ahead and the white caps had disappeared from the ocean. A screen overhead showed satellite images of the U.S. Navy sub chasers three hundred miles to the south east.

He sat back in a leather chair and put his feet up. Two nights in a row Christine had slept in his bed and for the previous twenty-four hours they had been inseparable. It had been a long time since he had courted a woman and he found himself enjoying it. She was smart, beautiful, and laughed easily. Already he missed her.

Bermuda had slipped over the western horizon before they turned south. The island had always been a favorite place to stay, but this past stay was the best one yet.

Christine's shift started when they passed through Town Cut into the ocean. In twelve hours she would shower in his cabin again, have dinner with him, and then….

He couldn't control his smile.

21

They ate in the cockpit, savoring the early morning sun. Silently, the autopilot tweaked their course with minute movements of the helm. Afterward, while Windy and Beth unfolded the canvas bimini to stretch it back over the cockpit and provide some shade, George and Tova carried the soiled plates inside.

"I'll take care of these," he said. "Your watch is over. Get some rest."

"I am not tired," she said, setting plates in the sink.

Braced against the cabinets to steady himself in the rocking boat, George started washing the dishes. Reaching to set the clean ones in a locker, he glanced across the cabin. Tova wiggled her jeans down with her back to him. His heavy shirt already lay on the settee next to the lee cloth.

God Lord, he thought, she is identical to her sister. George turned away, trying to concentrate on cleaning the silverware, but the image of bare shoulders and blonde hair stayed in his head. When he looked again she had disappeared outside.

In the nav station, George made entries in the log book, noting position, heading, speed, and wind direction again. He checked email, finding mostly junk and one from Brigitta. She would be tied up all day with meetings and asked him to call that night.

George wrote Brigitta back, saying where they were and all was fine. He had no way of knowing if she would read it during the day, but it felt good to be writing her.

He changed into clean canvas shorts and a button short-sleeve shirt. Clean clothes always felt good at sea. In the cockpit, he found Windy sitting against the stern pulpit reading a book.

"Where's our crew?" he asked, knowing the answer.

"Up forward, soaking up the sun," said Windy, shutting her book.

"Seen anything?"

"Just a couple of clouds. The world is empty except for us."

George pointed, "There's a shearwater." The grey and white bird swooped low across the water, its wings frozen, gliding like a rocket for great distances and often disappearing behind the crests of waves. It seemed like it could sail forever without flapping its wings. "I think that's a Corey's shearwater."

They both watched for a minute, then George settled against the stern life lines beside her.

"Your watch is almost over," he said, "What are you reading?"

She held up the book for him to read the title, but it wasn't anything he recognized. "It's all right," she said. "Did you check the weather forecast?"

"Light winds and nice weather," said George. "Boring, which is what I like at sea."

For a moment they listened to the water gurgling along the hull. He enjoyed the breeze on his skin.

"Did you hear from Brigitta?"

"Just an email," said George, thinking Windy sounded troubled. "She wants me to call her tonight. Thanks for asking." He wondered what Windy's eyes expressed behind her sunglasses.

Beth walked aft along the port deck, carrying a towel and a paperback.

"My watch starts in five minutes," she said, stepping under the bimini and into the cockpit.

"Nice outfit," teased George. She wore only a thong and sunglasses.

"Freedom of the sea," laughed Beth. "I listened to your boat rules carefully. Remember?"

He nodded and smiled. "I am not complaining. Keep an eye on Tova. She's not used to this strong sun and will likely burn."

"She won't be up there much longer, it's getting hot."

"I'm going to go bake something," said Windy. "Maybe we'll have hot cookies for dessert after lunch."

As Windy headed below, George offered to help her find anything she needed in the galley, but she insisted she didn't need his help, ending with, "I'm okay."

"How are we doing?" asked Beth, sitting where Windy had been.

"The boat? Fine. We're not moving too fast, but we're in no hurry. The ocean will continue to calm down all day. Maybe tomorrow we'll have a little more wind."

"I meant you? Have you heard from Brigitta?"

Beth's accent sounded stronger than he remembered it. Did that mean something? "I'm fine," he answered. "She emailed me and asked me to call her tonight."

"Windy is frustrated, anxious. Don't you notice?" With a huff, she added, "Men, you are all a bit dim."

"We are just friends. And I have to keep it that way."

"She is working very hard at being your friend. Be careful. At some point she will become angry with you."

George wondered what Beth's stake was in this. Why did she care? Was she just being a concerned friend? A friend of his or Windy's? Or a pain-in-the-ass busybody. George shook his head, trying to empty it, realizing he was way over thinking things.

Tova stood up on the foredeck with her back to them and paused to gain her balance. Walking to the bow, she bent over the pulpit to look down at the water splitting as *Frihet* knifed through it.

"Of course there is that one too," said Beth. "I still haven't figured her out."

Watching Tova in her almost invisible bikini bottom, George smiled. "That must be where the inspiration for all those bare breasted figureheads on the bows of old sailing ships came from."

Tova took a couple of shaky steps aft, bent down, and came up with a towel, which she draped around her neck to hang over her chest in a lousy attempt at modesty.

"She looks so much like her sister," said George.

"Tova isn't Brigitta, she likes to have fun and, unlike Brigitta, doesn't work all the time," teased Beth, patting his leg. "Remember that. This soap opera is the best entertainment I have seen in ages. Try to keep it interesting."

Tova sat in the shade at the far end of the cockpit, with the towel still draped precisely in place. "It was hot up there."

"We didn't think you would last much longer," said Beth.

"You're a little pink," said George, "be careful."

She looked at her arms. "I am all right."

"That's not where you are pink," laughed George.

"Oh." Tova peaked under the towel, then folded her arms across her chest. "Can I take a shower?"

"Of course," said George. "It might be easier showering outside. The shower on the stern platform has a long hose. You can shower at the back of the cockpit, then rinse everything off. It's easier than cleaning up the showers inside."

"That sounds good," said Tova.

"I might shower too," said Beth.

With a smile, George said, "I'll go inside to give you some privacy."

"Don't go on my account," said Beth. "I've found that once you get past the modesty thing, a boat feels a whole lot bigger. I'm sure you have seen naked women before."

"I have things to do," he said, chuckling and heading inside.

He sat at the nav station and thought about the days when he ran a day charter boat in the Caribbean. The woman who worked for him as mate, Kim, had a knack for getting the most prudish customers disrobed. Her spiel sounded like a recording to him, but they fell for the "closeness to nature" and "spiritual experience of snorkeling naked" lines every time. Again, it was that changes in latitudes brings changes in attitudes thing. More than once, he had sailed home a boatload of burned buns. Life had felt so simple in those days.

Windy vigorously mixed something in a large stainless bowl in the galley. The instruments said boat speed 4.06 knots, heading 165° magnetic, and wind 6.7 knots from the northwest. Life felt pretty good.

"George," came from an anxious voice in the cockpit.

He stood and looked out the companionway. Two dripping naked women stood, looking over the stern. "What do you have?" he asked.

Over her shoulder, Beth said, "Come, you have to look at this."

A large shark swam behind the boat, maybe eight feet below the surface and fifteen feet back.

"It was up near the surface and further back, with its fin out of the water," said Beth. "Look at the white on the sides. It's a great white shark."

George had heard old sailor's stories about sharks following boats to eat the garbage thrown over the side. but he had never heard of one following a modern sailing yacht. It appeared to match their speed with ease. "Well, I'll be," said George, "I have never seen a shark follow a boat before. It must be fourteen or fifteen feet long."

"I was thinking about sitting on the platform to stick my feet in the water," said Beth. "I am glad I didn't."

"Will it follow us long?" asked Tova.

"I have no idea," said George. Something about the shark's head didn't look right. "Can you see its eyes?"

With a quiver of its tail, the shark disappeared into the deep blue below them.

"It's gone," said Tova.

"Keep your feet out of the water," said George, turning to go back inside.

At the nav station he typed an email.

Harold,

Tell me more about your shark drones. We just had what looked like a fifteen foot long great white shark following the boat. It didn't look like it had eyes.

George

It had swum like a fish, with a swaying body and tail. Almost every manmade thing that moved through the water had a propeller.

During development of the boat that he had raced the previous summer, *Force of Habit,* Brigitta incorporated newly developed technology that involved nano cellular and micro cellular plastics, which had been magnetized using other recently developed technology. By applying blue and green light, the polarity could be reversed, expanding or contracting the plastic, much like a muscle. In the past, laboratories only made it work in temperatures several hundred degrees below zero Fahrenheit, but somehow she and her team made it work at much higher temperatures.

On *Force of Habit,* using the bendable plastics, Brigitta created a keel that could change its foil shape as well as bend from side to side. Could the same plastics make a drone that swims like a fish?

He typed a second email to Brigitta.

Brigitta,

    Harold told me something of your underwater drones. He mentioned some called sharks, did you have a part in designing them? What looked like a great white shark followed *Frihet* for a short while today. It had no eyes. Could it have been one of your drones?

    George

    Windy put something in the oven and the door shut with a thump. He slipped from the nav station and looked out the companionway. Beth and Tova each sat in the aft end of the cockpit, wearing only towels tied around their hips and talking about something. Both of them frequently looked back over the stern. Tova started to pull a comb through her hair.

    Ah, life upon the sea, thought George.

22

"We received a message from Harold," said Christine. "We had been trying to find communications between the missing drone and satellites or surface ships, but now he wants us to just find the thing."

"What do we do differently?" asked Captain Able.

"The drone appears to be moving south. Let's set up a position about two hundred miles south of here and let the team listen. We've picked up its sounds before, but it was only the drone's communications we were hoping to capture. Now we need to pinpoint it. Possibly we can triangulate with the Navy."

"Anything knew with Emil and Patrik?"

"No. If we get into position soon and the ocean isn't rough, I may try to put out the big antenna again. Our team can still try to find the drone while the computers possibly intercept ELF radio waves."

ELF, extremely low frequency, radio waves required a giant antenna. To set one up, the ship's two inflatable workboats set off in opposite directions, stretching a copper wire encased in a protective plastic coating, each boat traveling sixteen miles to create a thirty-two mile long antenna. Getting it setup and functioning took hours, but they could retrieve it from the ship while underway if necessary.

"You think the drone communicates with ELF frequencies?" asked the captain.

"Possibly. The problem in the past has been the slow speed of message delivery, which meant very short messages. But I read recently there has been work done by the Russians where they encrypted larger bits of information into a simpler language that then is expanded when received.

It is very complicated, but if we can record a transmission, maybe someone in the defense department has the ability to unravel it."

"You think Emil and Patrik will volunteer to go out on the work boats?"

Christine nodded her head. "I would bet money on it."

"And you want one of my crew to go with them?"

"I had a better idea. This morning, from a cell phone camera I made a tiny device that can video them while they are away. When they get back we can see everything they did from an SD card." Her eyes showed excitement. "They may be transmitting something while away from the ship."

Captain Able looked out at the blank ocean ahead of them. The waves had calmed down and there wasn't any place he would rather be. Christine's smile had seemed brighter than ever the last few days.

"When is your shift over?" he asked.

"Not until six tomorrow morning. Can we have breakfast together?"

He smiled. "Of course."

"Then we'll put the video recorder in place."

*

Olson walked down the starboard side deck, headed aft. At the back of the house, Dai stepped out of the door that led down to the engine room. His thick dark hair was pushed back behind his ears and he only wore the same wrinkled gray shorts he had worn since boarding.

"What are you doing up here?" asked Olson.

Dai stepped past him and walked forward, then went up the stairs toward the pilot house. Olson followed.

A young man in his twenties sat at the helm and a second man sat to the port side in front of a computer screen that displayed navigation information. Both of their faces expressed shock at the seven foot tall Oriental man that had suddenly appeared in the middle of the ocean.

"Where is Hauglund?" asked Dai, turning to Olson.

"He's in his cabin," answered Olson.

"Get him."

Olson picked up a phone and buzzed the captain's cabin.

"Yeah," said Hauglund.

"It's Olson here. Dai is in the pilot house and wants to speak to you."

"The pilot house?"

"Yes."

"I'll be right there."

Captain Hauglund contemplated bringing the pistol that he kept in a drawer near his bunk, but in the lightweight clothing of a warm climate, hiding it was problematic. He hurried up the pilot house.

"To what do we owe this honor?" said Hauglund.

Dai nodded toward the two young crewmen.

"We need to talk in private," said Hauglund. "Take a break." The two disappeared out the port side door.

Turning to Dai, Hauglund said, "How am I going to explain you to the rest of the crew?"

"They need to know nothing," said Dai. From his pocket he pulled a piece of paper. "Take me to this location, fast."

Hauglund read 29° 24' N, 64° 07' W. "That's over three hundred miles from here."

"Twelve hours at top speed," said Dai.

"And what am I to tell Sanderlee?"

"The woman you hired can keep him distracted. If not, we do not need him anymore. The Bermuda part of the trip is done. There is no more going in and out of a harbor to set up and test my listening devices. We are through dealing with customs and immigration officials." Dai's eyes looked as black as coal. "He can go over the side. When we are just north of the Virgin Islands, we will set the yacht afire and let it sink."

"What about the rest of the crew?"

Without emotion, Dai said, "They are expendable."

*

Bill Sanderlee and Cynthia sat in a lounge chairs, both of them drying in the shade after a lengthy dip in the pool. A lone long tail tropic bird glided overhead, but neither of them noticed it. Around *A New Beginning* the empty ocean stretched outward in every direction. High above, the contrails of two jets ran almost parallel to the northwest and a few clouds lingered in the northern sky.

"Would you like another drink?" asked Bill, reaching over to give Cynthia's hand a squeeze.

"Only if you do," she answered.

Bill reached for the intercom and ordered two more rum punches.

"The fruit juice is good for us," he smiled.

"Of course it is," said Cynthia.

Keeping Bill enthralled and distracted had been easy. They had left Bermuda not long after sunrise, while she and Bill still snuggled in bed.

When they came on deck, blue sky and an empty ocean surrounded them. They ate breakfast up by the pool, took a swim, made love on the cushions beside the pool, and then talked while they dried in the gentle morning sun. Conversation with him had been exceedingly easy.

After a light lunch, accompanied by gin and tonics, they lingered in the water. The sun had climbed high by then, so they sought the shade of canopied lounges.

A young stewardess with bouncing auburn hair arrived carrying two sweating glasses on a tray. Smiling, she set coasters on the side table before carefully placing the glasses. "Is there anything else I can get you?" she beamed.

Wearing only a subtle smile, Cynthia watched from behind her dark glasses.

Bill grinned and said, "That is all Betsy. We're set for a while."

They both watched the young woman disappear along the side deck.

"You've come a long way," said Cynthia, reaching to touch Bill's arm. "A few days ago you would have jumped up to put on something besides your sunglasses."

Bill laughed. "I'm going to get rid of my tan lines too."

Cynthia grinned, the guy was starting to be fun.

23

George rinsed the soap off and grabbed a towel. Glancing over his shoulder, he couldn't see any of the women. Tova and Beth probably napped inside. Windy had slept for a while right after lunch, but had been answering emails in the nav station the last time he had looked.

With the towel around his hips, he went inside to his cabin to pull on his shorts. In the light wind, they had opened several of the overhead hatches and a cool breeze funneled through the boat. Through the open cabin doors, he could see Beth asleep in her cabin and Tova in Windy's. In the galley, he pulled pork chops out of the freezer to thaw. The cookies that Windy made earlier sat on the counter and he stole one.

"I saw that," said Windy, shutting her book.

"They're good, want one?"

She shook her head then slid from the settee to follow George out to the cockpit.

"Have you seen the shark again?" she asked.

"No. I haven't really been looking."

"Look at that," she said, pointing aft.

Behind them an enormous aircraft flew in their direction a few hundred feet above the water. The orange stripe on the fuselage indicated it belonged to the U. S. Coast Guard.

"That's a HC-130 Hercules," said George. "They are used for search and rescue."

The VHF radio in the nav station barked, "Blue hulled sailing vessel, blue hulled sailing vessel, this is the United States Coast Guard. We are looking for a missing research submarine. Have you seen anything unusual?" The plane started to bank into a wide turn in front of them.

George picked up the microphone, "United Stated Coast Guard, this is the sailing vessel *Frihet*, we have seen nothing unusual. Sorry."

"Sailing vessel *Frihet*, this is the United States Coast Guard. If you see anything, please report it. Have a good evening, Captain Attwood. United Stated Coast Guard clear."

George smiled. Even the young men in the Coast Guard knew the name of his boat.

"What was that about?" asked Beth, coming out of her cabin.

George explained as Tova came out of her cabin, too.

"A research sub?" said Beth.

George shrugged his shoulders, not sure how much Brigitta would want him to tell. "I'll send an email to Harold, maybe he's heard something about it."

"Isn't it cocktail time?" said Beth. "The sea doesn't get much calmer than this."

The women opened a bottle of Sangiovese. George poured a half inch of Dalwhinnie in a tumbler. Conversation centered around the Coast Guard while George started dinner with Tova's help, then they ate in the cockpit while the sun sank below the horizon. Afterward, Windy and Beth cleaned things up in the galley.

George stopped at the nav station to find a new email from Brigitta.

George,

The shark drones use the same technology we used to make the movable keel on *Force of Habit*. They are painted to look like great white sharks. Call me around nine.

Brigitta

He glanced at boat speed, 4.4 knots, wind northwest, 11 knots, heading 164°. Not much had changed. Neatly, he recorded the information, along with their position, in the log. Boat speed had hardly wavered and they certainly weren't setting any speed records.

Tova went out to the cockpit, it was her watch. Both Beth and Windy disappeared into their cabins to try and catch some sleep. George climbed up to the cockpit.

"Are you going to keep me company?" asked Tova.

"For a while," said George. "I'm supposed to call your sister at nine. You can talk to her too, if you want."

"That would be fun," said Tova. She raised both arms while pushing her hair back into a ponytail.

George couldn't help but notice the nipples pressing against the inside of her top. Did Tova do that on purpose? Of course she did, he chided himself.

"The day will cool quickly," said George, "now that the sun has set."

"I feel it. Under the dodger it is fine, but can I still borrow your warm shirt later?"

"Of course." He liked that she wore it, in a small way it made him feel good…sort of rescuing the damsel in distress. "You really do look like your sister's twin."

"She is beautiful, so I guess that is a compliment," said Tova. "We are so different though."

"How?"

"I would love to spend the whole winter in the Caribbean. She is torn between the work she loves and a man." In the dim evening light, Tova's hair blazed, making it appear even more like her sister's. "I never found work I could love."

George smiled. "Have you loved a man?"

"More than one," she laughed, "but they all turned out to be boys."

"You could find work easily, if you wanted to stay in the Caribbean."

Tova beamed, "I have been thinking about it. Windy told me about the job she has lined up."

They talked about the Caribbean islands. George tried to explain how each was unique and very different from Bermuda. Soon it was time to call Brigitta. George brought his laptop out to the cockpit. A dozen key strokes later, they had Brigitta's face on the screen.

She appeared to be reading something and was unaware George and her sister could see her. Brigitta's face expressed seriousness. Behind her a man's waist appeared. He passed her a piece of paper and she smiled, said something that George couldn't hear, then thanked him. Turning back, Brigitta noticed George on her computer screen.

A smile. "Hi. How are you?"

"Good," said George. "Tova is here with me."

"You are in the dark," said Brigitta.

George reached up to turn on a dim red light in the frame of the dodger. "Is that better?"

"Yes. Where's Tova?"

She slid close to George. "I'm right here. How are you?"

"Busy," said Brigitta. "It is nice to see you. Are you having fun?"

"Yes, the boat is beautiful and George is a nice captain." Tova giggled.

"George, did you tell Tova?"

"I didn't know if you wanted anyone to know."

"Tova, that shark that was behind the boat was an underwater drone. It uses technology we developed last year for the keel on Harold Habit's racing boat. Engineers have taken the technology much further than we did. I am working on refining the shape, making it move more easily through the water. These drones can swim hundreds of miles and use very little energy."

"How is the work going?" asked George.

Brigitta's smile faded. "Slow. The fluid studies take time. We have a tank to test in, but it takes days to make minor shape changes."

"Have they had any luck finding the rogue drone?"

"No. I am out of the loop on that, but it appears they haven't found the mother drone."

"Mother drone?" said Tova.

"It is a larger drone that charges the batteries in the smaller shark-like drones," said Brigitta. "It also coordinates their movements and is supposed to transmit gathered information to satellites. The thing is designed to function autonomously for months at a time, but it has disappeared."

"I emailed Harold," said George, "but haven't heard from him."

"He is in Utah at the NSA," said Brigitta. "You may not hear from him. He is too busy for his own good."

"Are you still on schedule to get away?" asked George.

"I hope so," said Brigitta, with a forced smile. "There is a team using the magnetized nano cellular plastics to create artificial birds. With carbon fiber skeletons, they will fly better than real birds."

"Are you involved in that?" asked George.

Brigitta shook her head. "Tell me about sailing."

George recounted the trip since Bermuda, with Tova filling in details. Tova added stories of shopping in Bermuda and spending time with Windy and Beth. Finally, Brigitta apologized and said she needed sleep.

"Good night," said George, "I love you."

"I love you too," said Brigitta.

"Good night my sister," laughed Tova. "I love you too."

"Take good care of George."

"I will."

The screen went blank.

George stood and walked to the starboard wheel. Behind the boat phosphorescence swirled in their wake. The horizon looked dark, but overhead a trillion stars punctured the darkness.

"Are you all right?" asked Tova, coming up behind him.

"Yeah." He felt her hand on his waist. "What do you think? Is she going to be up there forever?"

"I think she wants to be involved in the artificial bird project. Maybe she is already. That is why she changed the subject."

George turned around. Tova looked like Brigitta, a perfect doll-like blonde with an oval face that produced the cutest dimples when she smiled. Tova's blue eyes expressed concern though, or maybe a desire to help. He slipped his arms around Tova's waist and held her close. "I think so too."

After a minute, he broke it off. "Thanks, I should get some sleep."

Tova smiled. "Before you go, can you rub some lotion on my shoulders? I did get too much sun today."

George made a feeble smile, the temptation was the last thing he wanted, but said, "I would love to."

Tova produced a tube of lotion from somewhere in the front of the cockpit. While he squeezed some onto the palm of his hand, she sat and worked the back of her tank top up to her neck.

The skin felt silky, maybe slightly more muscular than Brigitta. His hands coasted across the flesh, enjoying the touch as much as she did. His hands stopped moving to massage her shoulders, which brought a contented moan, then slipped down along her ribs. He found himself relaxing too.

Tova leaned back against his chest, which forced his hands around her stomach. "That's nice," she said, clasping his hands in place.

She smelled of honey and silky hair rested against the side of his face. Tova duplicated Brigitta in size and felt just like her in his arms.

"It is," he said, inhaling deeply. His heart thumped like a drum.

Tova's face turned toward his. Without thought, George's lips searched for hers. His slippery fingers coasted upward over her curves.

George's head spun. His willpower spiraled downward. Was he kissing Brigitta? Tova? Did he care?

"Whoa," said George. "What are we doing?"

Tova straightened up, grinning and pulling her top back into place. "You tell me."

"We can't be doing this, not now."

"Because of Brigitta?"

"Yes. And…."

"Were you kissing me or Brigitta? Just then, in your mind?"

"I'm not sure."

Tova laughed. "You could imagine I am Brigitta and make love to me. I would not mind."

"I hope you are kidding," said George.

"I might be. Or maybe I would like to make love with you."

"We can't."

"I know my sister," said Tova. "She is in love with her work."

"Still, it would be weird. And with Beth and Windy on the boat?" Confusion overwhelmed George. "We can't do that."

Tova asked, "Do you like Windy?"

"We are friends," George realized he sounded defensive. "Just friends. When she agreed to help get this boat to the Caribbean, she was going to fly back to the States afterward."

"And now she wants to stay in the Caribbean," said Tova. "It's because she wants to be on your boat."

George took a deep breath. "Her watch starts in less than ten minutes. I should wake her up."

Tova reached for his hand to give it a squeeze. "Are we okay? I didn't mean to make things awkward. I was being a naughty tease." Her eyes searched his face. "Are we still friends?"

He nodded, "Yes, still friends."

"A good night kiss?"

Temptation, but he shook his head and said, "No."

George went down the companionway, fighting the urge to look back at Tova. Turning the light on in Windy's cabin woke her. George walked forward to attempt sleep in his own cabin.

The ache lingered. Tova's scent stayed in his head. He longed to hold her…or was it Brigitta? Sleep came slowly.

"George." Someone shook his shoulder. "George." It was Windy.

"What's up?"

"There's four ships out there."

"Four?" George couldn't ever remember seeing three ships at once on the open ocean, day or night. He stood and followed Windy back to the cockpit.

To the east the starboard running lights of four ships glowed. George looked at the radar over the nav station. The range was only set for four miles and the ships had to be just beyond that. The air had cooled considerably and he wished he had pulled on a shirt.

"I've been watching them for a while," said Windy. "They seem to be getting closer."

George went back inside and set the radar's range to twelve miles. The closest ship showed up 4.07 miles to the east. Their course would intercept *Frihet's* in eight miles."

"They are moving in unison," said George, going back into the cockpit. "Maybe they are military. What time is it?"

"Almost one."

"Let's turn the autopilot to southeast, 120° magnetic, for a half hour, then back to 165° at one thirty," said George. "The ships should pass well ahead of us before then."

"Thanks," said Windy. "I hated to wake you up."

George forced a smile. "It's all right, I sleep better knowing everyone isn't afraid to wake me up. Are you warm enough?" Windy still wore only shorts and a tee shirt.

"I've been sitting under that blanket," she said, pointing at one piled in the port corner under the dodger. "It's a beautiful night."

"I'm off to bed then, if there isn't anything you need."

She smiled. "I'm fine."

The always reliable Windy, thought George, ready to lend a hand while trying to remain unobtrusive. Why couldn't more people be like her?

"Come here," he said, wrapping his arms around her in a hug. "Thanks for helping me move the boat south. I'll see you in the morning."

Breaking it off, George felt awkward. Windy's hands lingered on his.

"That hug felt good," she said.

"It did, I needed it," said George.

A fleck of red light escaping from inside the boat reflected on the gold frames of Windy's glasses. "Me too."

"Good night," he said, then turned to go inside.

At the nav station, he recorded the course changes in the log. The wind speed had dropped to 6.2 knots and the boat speed to 3.6.

In his cabin, sleep came instantly.

24

The research ship *Absent* sat stationary at 30° 27' N, 64° 50 W. In every direction the world looked empty.

"We couldn't ask for better weather," said Captain Able, watching the crane swing the second orange 33 foot work boat out over the water.

"Emil and Patrik are more than a mile away already," said Christine, pointing to the west.

"The video recorder is working?"

"Yes. And the GPS tracker too. Shall we watch from the pilot house?"

The captain let her lead the way. Inside, a young man stood watch. The radar screen showed no other boats within twenty miles. Captain Able dismissed the young man and Christine took his seat in front of a computer screen.

Stepping out of the wheel house, Able could see the second boat in the water. The two men climbed down into it. Soon it would head due east.

In each of the workboats a spool contained 16 miles of wire. The weight of the wire and gear totaled nearly two tons, but the deep V rigid bottom inflatable boats, pushed by two three hundred and fifty horse diesel outboards, could easily make twenty knots in the almost flat sea.

Each boat would unspool the wire, one heading east and, the one with Emil and Patrik onboard, heading west. In the center, the wires connected aboard *Absent* to create a thirty-two mile long antenna. Every five and a half miles, tethers attached to buoys kept the wire from sinking beyond the sixty foot length of the tethers. Radar reflectors sat on the top of a six foot pole above each buoy.

Emil and Patrik's boat stopped five and a half miles away. There they would attach the tether to the wire and a buoy, then toss the buoy over the side before continuing on. The scenario would repeat at the eleven mile mark. Not far beyond that the low work boat would disappear from the radar, having traveled far enough beyond the curve of the Earth. It would be four hours before both boats returned to the research ship.

Retrieving the antenna could be done from *Absent*, so the work boats would again be put back on deck, cleaned, and refueled. The sun would be almost setting by then.

*

Captain Hauglund checked their position. A current set them north, not fast, but enough that Dai would not be happy. There was nothing he could do about it without starting the engine, but that would annoy Dai even more. Silence was the order. Dai didn't even want Sanderlee and Cynthia to play music up by the pool. Hauglund shook his head.

"What is it?" asked Olson.

"Dai. What he asked for is unreasonable."

"If he learns something of the American's drone, then we will learn it too."

"True. I hope we do not have to kill the American." Hauglund shrugged his shoulders and smiled. "I think Cynthia has grown fond of him."

"What are they doing?"

"They are by the pool. Cynthia is probably sucking his cock. Sanderlee told me she did not want the voyage to get over too quickly, so he actually asked me to slow the boat down. I did them one better and stopped the boat. As long as he doesn't suddenly ask us to hurry someplace, he can stay alive."

"How long does Dai want to stay here?"

Captain Hauglund shook his head. "I have no idea."

*

George sat back against the starboard corner of the stern pulpit. Ahead of him the helm made minute course corrections, directed by the circuitry of the autopilot. Overhead, white puffy cumulous clouds littered the sky and provided moments of shade. The wind had shifted to just south of west and blew near steady at ten knots. *Frihet* moved along at 6.18 knots, the best speed of the trip so far.

Earlier, about the time the sun peaked over the horizon, the smell of coffee had woken him. The gray light of dawn had filtered in the windows as Beth greeted him in the main cabin. Soon, both Tova and Windy were up too and they all ate breakfast in the cockpit.

A little over two hours into his watch the day started to get warm. On deck the breeze cooled, but in the shelter behind the dodger it felt hot. He had peeled off his shirt and sought out the shade of the bimini. The breeze blew cleanly through the back corner of the cockpit and George enjoyed it as he read a novel.

Tova and Windy had both disappeared to the foredeck, nearly naked and carrying towels and sunscreen. After breakfast, Beth had gone to her cabin and had not come out. George guessed she slept. A nap sounded like a good idea when his watch was over.

"Hi." It was Beth looking out the companionway. Her kinky blonde hair looked like an explosion.

"You're up," said George. "I thought you would sleep later."

"This is the best part of the day, before it gets too hot." Beth stopped at the top of the companionway to look over the dodger at the two women on the foredeck. She wore only what looked like a string around her waist and a pair of sunglasses.

"It is going to be a hot one," said George, watching her sit against the stern pulpit on the port side. "How did your watch go?"

"Okay. I saw a ship on the western horizon, but the radar said it was eight miles away. Other than that, I saw nothing. About four I started to get sleepy, so I made coffee. " She seemed completely comfortable with the casual near-nudity.

George worked hard at not staring. "The smell of it woke me up."

"I did not mean to wake any one up." She looked off at the eastern horizon. "What happened with you and Tova last night?"

"Nothing. What do you mean?"

Beth shrugged a shoulder and smiled. "At breakfast there felt like this electricity between you two."

"You're imaging things," laughed George.

"Maybe." She opened a paperback and started to read.

Looking from behind his dark glasses, George wondered about Beth. She looked like an athlete, with small breasts, like a runner or swimmer, and not the large chiseled muscles of a weight lifter. Something about her attitude and the way she carried herself displayed confidence. She certainly had a knack for interpreting relationships between people. Back in

Bermuda she had dressed nicely, but here at sea clothing meant nothing. He felt certain that if he wasn't there even the thong would have been discarded too.

He tried to read, but found himself glancing her way. What did she notice about Tova? Nothing seemed out of the ordinary to him. Did Windy pick up on it too? Women…how do they notice these things…no wonder some of them were accused of witchcraft in days gone by.

Tova came aft to the cockpit first. George tried not to look, but caved. She wore only sunglasses and smile, but carried the towel in front of her hips. "Hi," she said. "My watch starts in a few minutes."

She disappeared down the companionway.

Beth shut her book and, with a big teasing smile, said, "I'll leave you two alone. Have fun." She stood and walked forward along the port deck.

A minute or two later, Tova reappeared wearing a tiny blue sarong wrapped around her hips, sunglasses, and nothing more. She sat next to George at the back of the cockpit.

"Hi," she said, beaming. "Has anything been happening?"

"Not a thing," said George, fighting to control where his eyes aimed. "The wind has shifted some to the south, but it hasn't increased." He gave up and relied on his sunglasses to hide his gaze.

"It was getting hot up on the foredeck," said Tova. "The shade feels nice."

"It's starting to get hot here too. I'm going to take a nap inside. If you need me come and get me."

"Am I making you uncomfortable?" asked Tova, setting her hand on his thigh so he wouldn't leave.

"Maybe a little."

"I can put more clothes on."

"No, don't. I'm actually enjoying this, maybe too much. That may be what's bothering me."

She smiled. "The freedom of it is fun, dressing as we want, or not dressing. There are nude beaches in Sweden, but I have never been. You were the one that said offshore was the last free place on Earth."

"You are right. Don't put more clothes on. Please, I insist." He laughed. "Someone as beautiful as you should never wear clothes."

Tova grinned. "Thanks."

"I'm off to catch some sleep."

When he reached the bottom of the companionway, he turned for one last look. Tova had moved to the sunny side of the cockpit. Her long blonde hair had been pulled up in a knot behind her head and she looked a Norse goddess. The breeze flicked a stray golden strand that danced behind her head. The sarong lay folded on the seat beside her.

*

Captain Able and Christine sat in the privacy of his cabin and watched the video recorded earlier by the hidden camera on Emil's and Patrik's workboat. The workboat's two engines drowned out the audio while underway. The lens had been placed just aft of the center console, near deck level and aimed up. Captain Able fast forwarded until Emil and Patrik stopped to put out the first buoy.

"Emil is the blond one with the crew cut," said Christine. "Patrik is the dark one." George thought he looked Middle Eastern.

"Hey, what a day," said Emil, over the rumble of the idling engines.

"Yeah," said Patrik, pulling his tee shirt off over his head.

Emil did the same, while Patrik attached a buoy's tether to the antenna wire where it came off the spool. A moment later they were on their way again. Captain Able fast forwarded.

At the next stop the scene repeated.

"Can you see the ship?" asked Emil, as he tossed the buoy overboard.

"No, we are too far away."

"They will still be watching us on radar," said Emil, setting a duffle bag on the seat. From the bag he pulled a tube of sunscreen. "Would you do my back?"

Patrik smiled. "Of course." He squeezed lotion onto his hand and smeared it over Emil's shoulders. "We are at the edge of where the radar can see us. From here we are on our own."

"Thanks," said Emil, turning. The two men embraced in a kiss.

"I was right, they are gay," said Christine.

Captain Able looked away, he had never seen two men kiss before and found it troubling.

Emil returned the favor and rubbed sunscreen on Patrik's shoulders.

With eleven miles of wire overboard and the boat lightened by over a thousand pounds, Emil and Patrik raced at top speed toward the last buoy drop. Captain Able fast forwarded the video again.

When the workboat came to rest, Emil shut off the engines then stooped to set a small cooler on the seat. Opening it, he offered a beer to Patrik.

"Where did they get that?" asked Captain Able.

"I don't know. The cook gave them water and sandwiches in that cooler" said Christine. "They must have hidden the beer in the duffle bag."

Patrik dealt with the buoy, then tossed it into the sea. Emil stripped off his shorts and dove bare-ass over the side, disappearing from the video. Patrik did the same. Soon the two of them climbed back aboard unseen, probably over the outboard motors. Still dripping wet, they sat at the helm and sipped the beers and made small talk. Patrik retrieved a round canister from the duffle bag. It looked like a thermos, but he unscrewed what looked like the base end to extract a small antenna.

"Can you see what he is doing?" asked Christine.

"No," said Able. "His back is in the way."

Patrik tossed it side arm overboard, then drank the last of his beer.

The two men talked quietly, so Christine and the captain couldn't hear what was said, then Emil took Patrik's hand to lead him forward and out of sight.

"What do you think they are doing?" asked George, realizing instantly it was a stupid question.

Christine's eyebrows went up. "Do you want me to explain it to you?"

"No thanks."

Several minutes later Emil appeared in the video again. Laughing, he tossed his beer bottle into the sea and pulled a small pistol from the duffle bag. Alternating turns, they shot at the bottle until a round of laughter indicated it broke. They then threw the second one out for a target, but quickly ran out of bullets.

Captain Able recognized the pistol as a Walther PPK. "We could search their bag when they come back and take it from them," he suggested.

"I would rather not let them know we are onto them," said Christine.

"It's up to you," said the captain.

25

"George," said Beth, leaning in through the open doorway of his cabin. "We are opening a bottle of wine."

He glanced at his watch, it was almost five. Much of the day he had spent hiding in his cabin, reading and napping, only going on deck to eat lunch with the crew. Twice in the afternoon he had ventured as far as the nav station to check their progress and make notes in the log, but he always returned to his cabin. An hour still remained of Windy's watch.

"I'll be right there," he answered.

He didn't bother with a shirt, the day still felt warm. Something simmered on the stove, which made the main cabin feel even warmer. On bare feet he walked up to the cockpit.

"Have you seen anything?" asked George, hiding behind sunglasses.

"The navy made an appearance," said Windy.

"It was cool," said Tova.

"It looked like moose antlers poking above the horizon," said Windy, "and then the rest of the ship came up, headed straight at us. There were four of them all together, identical."

"It may be the same ships we saw on radar last night," said George.

"They came straight towards us, but when they were four miles away the ships made a ninety degree turn to port and sailed due south. I tried to raise them on the VHF, but they wouldn't answer."

Tova filled three glasses with wine while George excused himself to find a tumbler into which he could pour a dab of Macallan. Back out in the cockpit, he settled back against the back of the cabin with the tumbler half full.

"Our boat speed is better," offered George. "Can I make a toast to that?"

Everyone brought their glass up. "To more miles tomorrow than today," said George. "And even more the day after that."

The women slipped into talk about food. George leaned back against the cabin and sipped the scotch. What a trip, he thought. Beth still wore only the almost invisible bottom that she had on in the morning, and Tova had tied on the little sarong again. What a pair, or pairs…he fought back a grin. Right after he woke up, Windy changed into shorts and a shear halter top that clung like a coat of paint. George smiled, he would be telling stories about this trip for the rest of his life.

A rumble off the port side made them all look.

"That's a Seahawk helicopter," said George. "The thing on the cable below it is used to locate submarines." The aircraft flew straight to the north. "It probably came off of one of the boats you saw earlier," he continued. "We are too far at sea for it to have come from land."

"Is the United States Navy always out here like this?" asked Tova.

"No," said George. He then told them everything that he knew about Harold Habit's missing drone and Brigitta's involvement in it, even the part about it appearing to hunt boats made of wood. He left out the part about volunteering to be bait when they got to the Caribbean.

After a moment of quiet, Beth said, "That is something."

"It is," said George.

"That explains why he felt the need to pay me for the loss of my boat," said Beth, sounding angry.

"Are we safe?" asked Tova.

"I think so," said George. "Harold said the drone had been programmed to identify vessels of metals and composites, like fiberglass or carbon fiber."

Beth poured the last of the wine between the glasses. "So who's looking for it?" she asked.

"The U. S. Navy," said George. "And Harold bought an old research ship, leftover from the old Soviet Union days, and he has a team aboard it out here looking for it too."

"I need to tend to dinner," said Tova, swallowing the last of her wine.

"I'll help," said Windy. "My watch is about over." The two of them disappeared down inside.

"I am pissed," said Beth. "I could have died."

"You didn't," said George. "I am sure it weighs heavily on Habit's mind."

Beth looked about to say something, but didn't, then said, "There's light wind tonight and the weather is settled. Can I open a second bottle of wine?"

George smiled, glad she had asked rather than just opening one. For hours the wind had blown a little over ten knots and the forecast was for more of the same. "Sure, go ahead."

A minute later she reappeared in the cockpit, having put on a lightweight halter top and carrying a wine bottle.

They ate dinner in the cockpit, while the sun sunk into the horizon. After things were cleaned up, Windy retired to her cabin and Tova joined George and Beth in the cockpit. Little was said as they watched the western sky fade to gray.

A little before nine, George dropped down into the boat to call Brigitta from the computer in the nav station.

"Good evening," he said, when she appeared on the screen.

"Hi." She looked lovely, just like Tova, her blonde hair pulled back and wearing a top the blue of her eyes. "How was your day?"

George went through the highlights, then asked about hers. It sounded like the same things she had said the day before.

"Have they gotten any further with the flying bird-like drones?" asked George.

Brigitta's eyes light up. "You wouldn't believe what they can do. When the air currents are right, they soar and can stay aloft for hours, maybe days, without using any energy at all. Think of the possibilities. One might possibly circle the Earth."

George could see the excitement in her face. He said, "You really want to be part of developing them, don't you?"

The enthusiasm in Brigitta's face faded, but she nodded. "They are fascinating."

"Well, then do it. A chance like that may only come along once in a lifetime."

Brigitta looked about to cry. "What about us?"

"I can't be there," said George. "My heart is elsewhere. I want to sail and be free. The world's problems are not my problems."

Brigitta said nothing, and George had nothing more to add. It felt as though a weight had been lifted.

Finally, Brigitta said, "Can you call me tomorrow night?"

"Of course," said George.

"Good, thanks. I'll talk to you tomorrow," she said, then the screen went dark.

George sat for a moment…there wasn't an "I love you" at the end, or even a lingering goodbye. It hurt. It hurt bad. He found his tumbler and was about to pour scotch, but then thought better of it. Glancing at the clock, his watch started in a little over an hour.

Tova came down the stairs. "Are you all right?"

He nodded. "I just talked to your sister."

Tova touched his hand. "I hate to see this. She always has been that way. Work and studies before everything…or any one."

George looked at her little fingers resting on his, then said, "I'm going to get some rest. My watch starts soon."

Tova smile, "Wake me if you need someone to talk to."

George wondered why she wasn't cold, still wearing only the sarong. The sun had long ago set and the night air felt cooler. She walked to the far side of the cabin, with her back to him untied the knot that held the sarong in place, set it neatly on the settee, then stretched out on top of the sheets.

George ached to wrap his arms around her, or anyone, to just feel a woman's touch. For a moment he contemplated just a half inch of scotch, he knew sleep would come hard. Instead, he put the bottle back in a locker and he went up the steps to the cockpit.

"You look like your dog died," said Beth. "Have you been talking to Brigitta?" She sat with her back against the cabin just to port of the companionway.

Sitting to starboard, he said, "Yeah. I think it's over."

"That is tough. I swore off relationships until I am thirty-two." Low in the sky off the stern, the lights of an aircraft blinked in the sky. Beth added, "About then I plan to look for a guy and maybe settle down. Until that time, men are just an amusement."

"I'm slow on the settling down part," said George, forcing a feeble smile. A second airplane appeared a little higher and headed in the opposite direction. "So, how long until you settle down then?"

"Three more years. Losing my boat might have set that back a bit."

In the dark beyond the transom, a barely visible Wilson's storm petrel flittered over the boat's wake.

"Having Tova onboard doesn't help," said Beth, quietly. "She looks just like her sister, which has to be a constant reminder." She smiled. "And she's naked half the time. You must have excellent self-control."

George forced a grin. "I try not to notice."

"Right." Beth reached across the companionway to pat his thigh. "I pick up on some sort of chemistry between the two of you. Tova wants you, and maybe you only want her because she reminds you of Brigitta." Beth laughed. "This voyage is an incredible soap opera. Windy is trying to get up the courage to make a play too."

Talking made him feel better. Beth always found a way to lighten any subject. He tried to see the storm petrel, but only caught sooty flashes in the darkness. Phosphorescence danced in their wake.

"I'm not going to sleep," said George. "If you want to go in I'll finish your watch for you."

"I'll take you up on that." She turned around to sit with her legs in the companionway. "Are you sure you're all right?"

He nodded. "Yeah. Talking helped, thanks."

She slid closer to give him a hug, ending with, "You look like you needed that."

"I did."

Her eyes darted over his face. George went to put his arms around her shoulders for a second embrace, but she brought her mouth to his. His head swam…warm moist lips, smooth muscular skin under the fingers, soft hands kneading his flesh.

"Wasn't that nice?" she said, her arms still around his neck.

"Yeah. It was. I needed that." They breathed in unison.

"No strings, don't even think about it. It was fun, but I am not coming onto you." Beth smiled and gave him another quick kiss, and added, "You have two beautiful women onboard that both want you. Now, I am going to bed, and in the morning I want to watch more of this ongoing drama."

After she disappeared inside, George stood to look at the night around them. Overhead, billions of white stars turned the black sky blotches of gray. Water gurgled along the hull and to the east the moon had risen from the sea, creating white slashes on the wave tops beneath it.

He did feel better. Was it the talking with Beth? Or the silly making out like teenagers? George grinned. That woman was special. No, a decision had been made about Brigitta, he realized, and that had swept away much of the agony. There had been a promise to call her the next day and he wondered if he would. A call might only rekindle the anguish. You yank a band aid off, not remove it slowly to lengthen the grief.

26

Christine's phone chirped. She plucked it from the night table and read the text.

Relocate 100 miles south, at 1200 hours have Emil and Patrik repeat antenna setting. Navy will be watching and retrieve whatever they drop in the water.

Harold

"Jay," said Christine, shaking Captain Able's shoulder. "Jay, we have the go ahead."
"Hmm," he moaned. The bed felt too nice. "Where?"
"A hundred miles south of our present position, in twelve hours."
"Did the Navy try to locate whatever Patrik threw in the water?"
"Yes, but it was hours before they got there. They couldn't find anything."
"We should get going then." He propped himself up on an elbow. "We can't go over ten knots while retrieving the antenna. That doesn't give us much extra time. I'll roust a couple of crew."
"I'll have to get some of my team up, too. I'll make up some story about the drone having been located about a hundred miles south of here."
*
George sat in the cockpit eating leftover chicken stew. For quite a while he had watched a white light on the western horizon, but it finally

disappeared. Earlier, a little before midnight, he had made log entries while the food warmed. Since then, the clouds around the moon had kept him entertained.

"Hi." It was Tova coming up the companionway.

"You are up early. Your watch doesn't start for almost an hour." She again wore George's heavy chamois shirt. "Want some stew? There's plenty more."

"Maybe later," she said.

He told her about the light to the west. Together they looked westward and for a moment thought they saw it, but decided it was only a bright star sitting at the horizon.

"How are you doing?" she asked, settling down next to him.

"Better, actually," he answered. "I guess there was some closure, in a way."

"Well, if you need to talk I am a good listener. Relationships can be tough. My sister gets one thing in her head and obsesses on it to the exclusion of everything or everyone around her."

They talked about the missing drone. Tova wondered if the shark drone had been back. It could easily come and go without ever being noticed. Seldom did anyone look down into the water. Somehow the conversation drifted to whales and then satellites, but then stopped. Silently they searched for satellites overhead, pointing when they spotted one.

After several minutes, Tova said, "The other night, when we were alone in the cockpit, it felt special to me."

Tova's hair looked almost white in the starlight and a sparkle caught in her eyes. Only two lower buttons of the chamois shirt were fastened and her bare legs rested along the side to his…tempting.

"Me too," said George. "But I have a lot of confusing emotions right now." He caught the scent of jasmine. "I need some time."

"I know you do." She reached to squeeze his hand. "I'll take the rest of your watch if you want, there isn't much left."

"Thanks."

*

"It doesn't feel like we are moving," said Bill Sanderlee.

"I'm sure we are," said Cynthia. "The ocean is so calm the boat doesn't rock at all."

They were in his cabin in bed and had watched a movie.

"Do we have any more of that champagne?"

"Of course," said Bill. "Let me open another bottle."

As she watched his bare backside walk to the paneled door of the small refrigerator, she asked, "Are you up to watching a little porn?"

He grinned. "You pick it this time."

*

Captain Hauglund looked at his watch. Dai had not been seen or heard from for over twelve hours. Olson had tried to bring him food, but found the door to the secret cabin locked on the inside.

"Can you see anything?" asked Hauglund.

Olson looked from the computer screen. "It appears he is sending information to someone via satellite, but I am not so sure. Maybe he is making it look that way and sending the information another way."

"What other way?"

"Under sea," shrugged Olson. "Isn't Dai supposed to be an expert on that?" He typed a few key strokes and the images on the screen changed. "We haven't heard anything from Moscow about his information we are passing along to them. Either we are stealing real information or he is feeding us excellent gibberish."

*

George woke to the smell of bacon. The clock said Tova had another half hour on watch. In the galley, Windy stood by the stove, watching the bacon sizzle. On his way through the main cabin, he checked the instruments at the nav station. Boat speed was down to 1.2 knots, wind 2.1.

"I'm going to start the engine," he said, before going up to the cockpit.

"We are not moving very fast," said Tova.

In the light air, the genoa barely held its shape. The telltales on the back of the main sagged.

George pushed the engine start button and it leapt to life. "We'll get things moving."

The engine made hardly a sound, except for the occasional swish of its exhaust water. Slowly, the boat speed crept up to 7.2 knots. To push it higher burned an excessive amount of fuel and there was no need to hurry. He checked the autopilot, still 165° magnetic. Gentle restless rolls disrupted the glassy surface of the ocean. Tova pushed the button that hydraulically rolled up the genoa.

"Have you seen anything?" asked George. To the east, clumps of Sargasso weed appeared bright yellow. Currents kept them in a loose line that created a yellow road across the sea.

"No," said Tova. "It has been quiet." She looked hot in the heavy shirt.

The day already felt warm and the sun hung only a few degrees above the horizon. Scattered clouds blotted out parts of the hazy sky. To the east a Wilson's storm petrel danced on the surface near the Sargasso grass, attempting to catch its breakfast.

"You look sleepy," said George.

Tova smiled. "I am okay."

Beth's head appeared in the companionway. "How is everybody this morning?"

"We are fine," said Tova.

"Breakfast in five minutes," said Windy, from the galley.

"I'll set up the table," said George.

Beth came up the companionway carrying fistfuls of silverware. George looked twice to see if she wore anything at all. Nope.

In the center of the cockpit a table ran fore and aft. With its leafs down it stood only ten inches wide, but opened it became a table for eight. Soon plates of bacon, eggs, and toast were being passed up from the galley.

Afterward, everyone helped with the cleanup and Windy started her watch. George settled into the nav station with a third cup of coffee, where he made entries in the log and checked email. Nobody of importance wanted anything from him, which made him smile. The world finally was leaving him alone. He plotted their position on a chart. If they motorsailed all day they would be halfway by nightfall.

He grabbed a book and went up to the cockpit. Windy sat at the back, resting against the starboard corner of the stern pulpit. The other two women were missing and he guessed up on the foredeck.

"You look comfortable," said George, putting his sunglasses on. She wore a little white tank top and bikini bottom.

"I am," she said. "It's a beautiful morning. Look at the clouds to the west."

They looked like bright white cauliflower. He sat next to her. "It's going to be hot."

"It is already."

"You're not bored, with this offshore sailing?" asked George

"I have heard the joke, offshore sailing is days of boredom interrupted by moments of terror. That is not true, particularly with today's weather forecasting." Windy smiled. "It feels relaxing and free, I love it."

"How long do you think the sun worshipers on the foredeck will last?" asked George.

She smiled. "Not long."

George peeled his tee shirt off over his head. "Oh, there's a little air moving, mostly from the boat moving. It feels good." He tossed the shirt against the back of the cabin, then teased. "You can take your top off too, I won't mind."

"I feel funny about it," said Windy. "It doesn't seem to bother Tova and Beth. They are both beautiful."

"Don't feel funny about it on my account," said George. "And you are easily as beautiful as either of them, I think even more so." He went on to tell stories about the woman who worked as mate for him when he ran a daysail boat in the Virgin Islands, ending with, "She would get the most straight laced people skinny dipping by noontime."

"I'll think about it," she said.

George laughed, "I promise not to stare."

Windy wrinkled up her nose at him then yanked her top over her head. She took a deep breath. "It does feel nice."

"You are beautiful."

"Thanks, I might get used to this."

"The wind on the skin," said George. "You'll learn to sell it to the tourists." He smiled and added, "And you are very nice to look at."

*

"We've been sitting still long enough," said Sanderlee. "Let's get this boat moving."

"We have a problem with the engine cooling system," lied Hauglund. "It is not serious, but the engineer has it all apart. By this evening we will be underway again.

"This is ridiculous," said Sanderlee. "What if the weather turned bad? We would be at the mercy of the sea."

Cynthia stood behind him, looking exasperated. Captain Hauglund gave her a glare, but, unseen to Sanderlee, she shrugged her shoulders.

"I am sorry for the delay," said Hauglund, "if we can get things together sooner, we will.

Sanderlee and Cynthia disappeared out the pilot house's door.

"Have you heard anything from our man in hiding?" asked Hauglund, turning to Olson.

"No, the door is still locked on the inside."

"If we don't hear from him soon, we will bust down the door. We have played this game long enough."

Hauglund stuck his head out the door to look aft along the starboard side. "Cynthia is taking him to the pool deck. Let's hope she keeps him entertained for the day."

"There's an email for you," said Olson. "It's from Moscow." He printed it out and handed it to Hauglund.

Captain Hauglund. Dai must know we are intercepting his transmissions. What you are forwarding to us is false information. Deal with him as you wish.
GRU

Hauglund smiled. "The Intelligence Agency says we can do with him as we like. Do you suppose he has more cash with him?"

Olson wondered if Hauglund's allegiance was to Russia or his bank account. "We can look," he said.

"Later, let's see how long he stays in there. If he isn't out by tonight, the engineer designed that door so even when locked on the inside there is a way to unlock it. We want his hard drives intact. It must have the real data that he collected."

*

By George's watch the wind had dropped to nothing and the ocean had taken on a glassy oily look. Even the sea birds had disappeared. *Frihet* slipped through the water, pushed by her engine, with her mainsail up, but it offered almost no assistance. Small clumps of Sargasso grass slipped along the side of the hull and long streaks of it created trails in the sea. The only breeze came from the boat moving through the humid warm air. Frequently, they took turns using the anchor wash hose on the foredeck or the shower aft to cool off, but wet skin and the shade of the cockpit awning offered temporary relief.

"I'm making iced coffee," said Tova. "Would anybody like one?"

She had three takers, and disappeared inside.

Beth sat at the back of the cockpit, reading with ear buds in and listening to music. Windy's tablet rested on the cockpit table, where she read something. George had his back against the stern pulpit, aft of the starboard wheel, with a closed book resting on the deck beside him. He tried desperately to sort out his emotions. The biggest question was did he miss Brigitta?

If he could only back up time, way back, to before he ever met Harold Habit. Life used to be so simple, squeezing out a living doing day sails down in the islands. One day at a time, that was the way his life used to be.

Everything changed when he met Brigitta, no woman had ever touched his heart the way she did. Did he want her because she was so rare? She often talked about projects and scientific things that he could barely grasp. He had never met anyone so smart. Was it her brains that he found so…sexy? There he was, with three nearly naked women on a boat in the middle of the ocean, and he couldn't get a woman over a thousand miles away out of his mind.

Tova set two tall iced coffees on the bridge deck. Windy grabbed them and passed one to Beth. Tova came up carrying two more.

"You look lost in thought," she said, sitting next to George.

"I'm sorry," he said. "I'm just trying to sort things out."

"Things tend to work out as they were meant to be," she offered.

He smiled, thinking that was rather simplistic and she had said that before, and sipped his iced coffee. "I don't believe in pre-destiny."

She grinned, which tucked little dimples into her cheeks. "It is not predestined. It is just things tend to sort themselves out. That does not mean you are helpless to guide the way things happen."

Wondering if Beth listened in on their conversation and what her take on all of it was, George also tried to grasp what Tova meant. The iced coffee tasted delicious. From behind his sunglasses, he glanced across at Beth. A smile had spread across her lips…at least she found all this entertaining.

The radar's intruder alarm started to beep.

George stood. No boats were in sight. He dropped into the cabin. The radar screen showed an echo a half mile to the west. He climbed back to the deck.

To the west, a small black triangular shark fin sliced through the water.

"Do you think it's a drone?" asked Tova.

"Could be," said George. "Probably."

"Would a real shark fin send back an echo?" asked Beth.

"Birds do sometimes," said George, "so I think a shark fin would."

The fin stayed on a parallel course.

"I wonder how long it has been there," said Windy.

The fin disappeared below the surface.

27

The Navy helicopter flew low over the water. On a computer screen in Captain Able's cabin, Christine and the captain watched the image, captured by one of Harold Habit's satellites. The orange inflatable work boat had left a half hour before, heading back to the research ship and the two men onboard would never see the low flying aircraft.

Hovering over the last buoy that Patrik and Emil had thrown out, a man wearing a wet suit dropped into the water. Immediately his hand came up with a canister in it.

"Super," said Christine.

A second man proceeded down on a wire, then the two men rode back up together.

"It's amazing what our military can do," said the captain. "I wonder where their ship is."

"We should know soon if that canister is some sort of transmitter. The trick will be finding out who they are transmitting to."

The helicopter rose up from the water and started to the west. On the screen, the image shifted to the work boat speeding back to the ship.

"We'll have to thank Harold for his help," said Christine.

*

First Mate Olson walked along the dimly lit starboard side deck, heading toward the stairs that led to the lower deck. Reaching for the door handle, it swung open so quickly he never reacted to a machete swung at his neck.

Olson fell against the railing and Dai pushed, rolling the body over into the sea. It all happened so quickly that almost no blood fell onto the boat.

Dai walked forward and up the stairs, then proceeded to the pilot house. As he stepped in, Hauglund's eyes bulged when he noticed the bloody machete. Hauglund turned toward the drawer where the pistol hid, but the sharp blade caught him in the throat. A young man, who had been sitting at the helm, bolted out the door on the far side of the pilot house.

Dai engaged the engines, set the speed at ten knots, and turned the yacht due south. After locking on the autopilot, he looked at the radar. No other vessels were within its twenty-five mile range. At the computer to port of the helm, Dai typed a message and hit enter.

He stepped out the pilot house door to look over the railing, then dragged Hauglund's body out. A bloody smudge trailed from the puddle on the pilothouse floor. Dai hoisted the body up to roll it over the railing. It disappeared into the sea.

Walking through the pilot house and along the deck, he found none of the other crew members. He dropped down to the main deck and searched cabins, starting at the stern and working forward. All of the crew had disappeared, probably warned by the man who escaped from the pilot house.

In the galley, he broke two legs off of a table, then went outside and forward on the port side. When he reached the owner's cabin, Dai wedged a leg between the deck's toe rail and the corner of the cabin's door, preventing it from swinging outward to open. On the starboard side he did the same.

Dropping down to the lower deck, he found the door closed that led to the crew's quarters and guessed they all had to be hiding on the other side. The stout door had been built to be watertight and part of a watertight bulkhead, which was designed to control the intrusion of water in the event of a hull breach. The crew presented no problem if they stayed on the other side. To be certain, he walked aft to the engine room, where he found a screw driver. Back at the watertight door, he jammed the tip of the screwdriver into the mechanism that secured the door. Nothing would open the door while that screwdriver remained in place.

From a locker, he found a bucket, which he filled with water. Grabbing a mop, he walked back up to the pilot house. Twenty minutes later the last traces of the blood were gone.

Two decks down, Dai headed for the hidden cabin. Entering the engine room, the door on the far end opened and the engineer, who had been napping in the storage area, stepped in. The engineer thought it unusual for Dai to be outside the secret cabin, for he knew nothing of what had happened. When Dai smiled and nodded, the engineer noticed the blood on Dai's clothes.

Dai grabbed a large wrench from the tool box outside of his cabin and struck the engineer in the temple. The man collapsed. Dai tried to find a pulse, but the engineer had none.

Dai retrieved his things from his cabin and carried them up to the captain's. There, he dragged the captains things and tossed them over the side, then showered and changed into clean clothes.

Back in the galley again, he found cold chicken and vegetables in the refrigerator. Carrying the food and a bottle of wine, he climbed back to the pilothouse. On a world band receiver over the windows he found classical music. Sitting on the white leather couch at the back of the wheel house, he picked up the phone and buzzed the owner's cabin.

"Hello," came a sleepy male voice.

"Mr. Sanderlee, my name is Dai. You are now my prisoner. Captain Hauglund has taken leave, as well as the crew. Stay in your cabin and you will stay alive. In a few days we will reach the British Virgin Islands where I will depart and you and your lady friend can go free."

He shut off the phone and poured wine in a glass.

The printer next to the computer to port of the helm started to print.

Dai knew it would be the latitude and longitude of the meeting. When he finished eating, he would put the coordinates into the autopilot.

*

Christine's cell phone rang. Captain Able cursed the Wi-Fi that made it possible for phones to work out in the middle of the ocean.

As she listened, her smile faded.

"What's up?" asked the captain.

"The helicopter never made it back."

"What?"

"It just disappeared. They had it on radar and then it was gone. A second helicopter went up to look for it, but couldn't find a thing. It was dark."

"A bomb? Or a missile?"

"Nobody knows, at this point. They'll look for wreckage in the morning."

"Maybe we should have a talk with Emil and Patrik."

28

The rest of *Frihet's* crew had all gone inside to sleep. Tova sat on the port side, watching the ribbons of orange in the western sky. George tried to read a novel on a tablet, but his mind kept wandering.

Earlier, inspired by the unusually hot weather, they made up a batch of George's favorite hot weather drink, gin and tonics, for the five o'clock cocktail hour. Everyone had showered earlier, and the women had actually dressed up in summery clothes they had bought in Bermuda. While the sun settled in the western sky, they ate and the conversation drifted between drones and submarines and whether tuna fish or sharks were more aerodynamic. After the galley was cleaned up and things put away, Beth retired to her cabin. Windy read in the cockpit for a while, but didn't last long, leaving Tova and George alone.

"I'm supposed to call your sister," said George, after a long stretch of silence. The western sky still glowed dark pink and purple streaks.

"Oh," said Tova, teasing with, "I thought you were staying up because you finally wanted to keep me company."

The levity made George smile. "I enjoy your company." She looked nice in a short shear dress that George thought looked like a nightie. In the fading daylight her hair almost smoldered and her eyes looked a dark blue, nearly the color of the sea. Tova's skin had taken on a bronze warmth from days in the sun and with the daylight slipping away it looked brown.

"Are you going to call her?"

"Last night it didn't end well, it sounded like we were done." He looked out into the night. "But, in a way it felt good, like a weight had been lifted. It was better than the uncertainty."

Tova moved to sit beside him. "There is no one making you call her. Let it go."

"Aren't you afraid your sister will be hurt if I don't call?"

"I know my sister. Her interests come first. And right now I think it is her work."

"If I do that, don't call, am I going to spend the rest of my life wondering...what if?"

Tova smiled. "You waffle too much. Make a decision. Or flip a coin. Whatever you choose, you can always wonder if you made the right choice."

George knew she was right. Why was life so hard sometimes?

"Let her chase you for a while," offered Tova.

"Maybe she won't."

She shrugged a bare shoulder. "Then you will know."

A breath of air moved against the side of George's face. "I think we have some wind coming."

"That would be nice. The engine is not loud, but I am tired of hearing it."

"We are just over half way to the Virgin Islands," said George.

Tova sighed. "I do not want this trip to end. It is fun out here on the ocean."

George smiled. "You've acquired quite a tan." It boldly contrasted with the pale yellow of her dress.

She glanced at her arms. "Thanks, it has been fun, sunning on the foredeck." With a big smile she asked, "Can I get you to put more lotion on my back?"

He took a deep breath. "I would love to."

From the cabin top beneath the dodger, Tova produced the tube of lotion again. With her back to him, she peeled her dress up over her head.

"Whoa," said George, as he squeezed lotion onto his hand. "What are you doing?"

"Making it easy for you," she laughed.

"Easy to do what?"

"I will put it back on after you are done." she promised.

Her shoulders felt silky under his hands. Leaning close, he asked, "Done doing what?"

"Hmm, that feels good." She held her hair out of the way. "What would you like to do?"

"We have others onboard, and it's Windy's watch in a half hour, maybe less." It had to be the alcohol talking. He squeezed more lotion onto his hands, then slid them down her back. "We have to behave." His fingertips flowed over the curve of bare hips.

"You have too much self-control," laughed Tova, "or I am not all that attractive."

"Believe me, tonight I wish we could."

She turned to face him. "Me too." Her hand slid up the inside of his thigh. "You do want me."

He nodded. "Very much, but we can't. We shouldn't even be doing this. Windy could come out here any minute."

"I know."

Feeling flustered, George watched Tova slip her dress back on.

"You leave a woman very frustrated," she said.

George couldn't tell whether she was angry or kidding. "I feel the same way."

"Go to bed," said Tova. "I need to calm down before Windy gets up."

In his bunk, George realized he hadn't called Brigitta. The thought had slipped his mind.

*

Bill Sanderlee repeated the phone conversation to Cynthia, then tried to open one of the cabin doors. Neither would budge.

"What could he have done with Captain Hauglund?" he asked.

"This is bizarre," said Cynthia, dressing.

"We're prisoners here. Where did this guy come from?" He tried the other door. "Do you think he put the crew in a life raft?"

"I don't know." Cynthia had been involved with the Russian intelligence agencies long enough to know Hauglund was probably dead. As Bill pulled on shorts, she said, "I have something to tell you."

He sat at the foot of the bed.

"I have not been honest with you. People paid me to keep you occupied while your boat was used to gather information on undersea drones. You were not what I expected. I like you a lot."

Bill stood. "It's all been a lie?"

"No. Not at all. I care what happens to you. We are in great danger. I doubt Dai spared Hauglund or any of the crew."

Bill started to pace. "We have to get out of here."

"Let's see if we can secure the doors from this side," said Cynthia. "We are safer then. There's enough drinks and food in the refrigerator behind the bar to last for days."

Bill sat on the foot of the bed, then stood and started to pace again. "What do you know about Dai?"

"He works for the Chinese government and paid Hauglund to build a work space for him down next to the engine room. He has been hiding there since before we left Bermuda."

It sounded unbelievable. Bill asked, "What was he doing?"

"Listening mostly. We were not sure to what or why."

"We?"

"Hauglund, Olson, the engineer, and myself work for the GRU, the Russian intelligence agency. The rest of the crew knew nothing about what was going on. We hoped Dai would think Hauglund was just a captain who could be bought, but somehow he figured out Hauglund was working for the Russians or Americans and stealing his information. He started to feed Hauglund false data."

Stunned, Bill plopped down on the end of the bed again. "What changed?"

"I do not know."

"I mean about us, how you feel about me?"

"I expected you to be a bossy business man with a big ego, but you are a really nice man." Cynthia sat beside him. "It surprised me. I fell for you. Hauglund noticed it."

"I've enjoyed your company," said Bill, reaching for her hand.

"Dai may think I am an expensive hooker that Hauglund hired to keep you busy. That would be better than him thinking I am a GRU agent."

Bill glanced over at his laptop on the desk. "We will get out of this."

*

"This afternoon, while you returned from setting out the antenna, a United States Navy helicopter deployed from a ship to your last buoy drop," said Captain Able. "There they retrieved a canister you dropped into the sea. Somewhere on its trip back the aircraft disappeared."

Emil and Patrik sat on the opposite side of a bare wooden table, their hands secured with plastic wire ties. Overhead, one recessed light lit the small cabin. The senior member of Captain Able's crew and Christine were the only other people in the room.

Emil looked nervous and wouldn't make eye contact. Able guessed he was the weaker of the two and had been firing questions at him, but got no answers.

Patrik spit on the floor. "You can do nothing to us. We have rights."

Able leaned on the table. "You are not American citizens, you are outside of the United States, on my boat, and I am the Captain. I am the law here. If I decide to hang you, I will. Or maybe I will cut you so you bleed and then feed you to the sharks. Those men who died in that helicopter had families back home. I would love to rip your throats out."

"We did nothing," pleaded Emil. "We are here to work."

Christine described everything that she and Captain Able had seen on the video the day before. The faces of both men fell, but neither cooperated. Captain Able asked his senior crewmember to lock Emil and Patrik in their cabin and to post a guard outside the door.

"What are we going to do?" asked Christine.

"I'm going to contact the Navy to see if we can transfer the two of them over to one of their ships. I don't like having them onboard."

29

    Mother slowed to almost a standstill. A mile to the west one of her sharks, AS-12, hovered thirty feet beneath the surface of the ocean, directly over a Type-093 Chinese submarine two hundred feet below it. The sub moved slowly to the south, nearly silent.
    A mile beyond, another of her sharks, AS-08, trailed an Oscar-II class Russian submarine. Never had Mother come across two subs so close together.
    Both of the submerged vessels worked southward. In her most silent mode, Mother followed. She knew if any of them heard her it could mean the end. The sharks moved easily without sound, using what were effectively plastic muscles pushing their tails. Mother's speed, created by a propeller, would be limited by the need for silence.
    More than a dozen United Stated Navy ships patrolled within a hundred miles of her. Information in her memory chips identified them easily. The individual identity of foreign ships proved more difficult. Never had she seen so much activity within a small area. To be hunted by so many created demands on her computers that consumed unusually large amounts of stored electricity.
    Mother received a message from AS-11. Another boat of the mystery material had been found far to the west. That shark desperately needed to suckle because its energy levels were dangerously low and would return to mother with details of the boat.

*

The boat heeled a little to port, then settled back, waking George. With his eyes still shut he listened and waited. The engine still hummed and water gurgled along the hull, but the boat didn't tilt again. A locker door clicked shut in the main cabin, it probably was Beth. It had to be her watch.

He slid his hand across the sheet. Empty. He breathed a sigh of relief. Could it have been a dream? Or did Tova really share his bed for a while during the night?

George clearly remembered how badly he wanted her. What a tease she had been, having him rub lotion on her naked body. Down in his cabin, sleep had been elusive. He had ached to hold Tova, but eventually the hum of the engine had sung him to sleep.

And then warm flesh slid between the sheets and soft lips pressed against his. He recognized the scent, it was Tova. She felt just like Brigitta in his arms, with the same curves and silky hair and....

It had to have been a dream. He took a deep breath. Did her fragrance linger? Bringing his fingers up, he sniffed, catching the smell of the sun tan lotion.

What a dream, he thought, it seemed so real.

"George." It was Beth's voice on the other side of the door

"What?" He wondered why the door was closed.

"We have two boats on the radar directly ahead of us," said Beth. "I don't see any lights."

He sat up. "You can come in. How far off are they?"

The door opened. "Two miles. Shall I change course to the east?"

George realized his shorts were on the floor. "Yes, I'll be right there. Head due east. What time is it?"

"A little after three-thirty."

He pulled on the shorts and followed her to the cockpit. Ahead, the night looked black. A warm breeze blew from the southwest and humid haze muted the starts. Beth made the course corrections while he eased the traveler all the way over.

"We have some wind," said George. "I'll put out the genoa and you can shut off the engine."

The boat speed dropped to 5.2 knots on a broad reach, but the silence felt nice. Behind the boat, swirls of phosphorescence the size of dinner plates twirled before breaking apart and disappearing. Tweaking the sails, they brought the speed up to 5.7 knots.

"The air is sticky, but it feels cooler now," said Beth. "I was reading under the dodger."

George glanced her way. "Are you wearing anything?" he laughed. "You almost never wear anything at all."

"I never would, if I could get away with it."

Looking to the south, he said, "I wonder what is going on out there."

Neither said anything, but savored the boat coming alive beneath their feet. The air smelled of moisture. George dropped down inside to the nav station to look at the radar. Whatever the two blips were, neither of them were moving.

"There's soup if you want some," said Beth.

"I'm not hungry," he said, going back outside. "In a half hour we'll head south again."

Beth smiled. "When I saw your cabin door closed I thought you had Tova in there with you."

George shook his head. "No." He smiled and almost let the comment die there, but then added, "But I dreamt she was in there, or maybe it was Brigitta. In a dream I can't tell them apart."

"Maybe it wasn't a dream."

"It had to have been."

"The engine is not loud, but its sound could hide a person sneaking about during the night."

George tried to read Beth's face, but in the dark he couldn't.

"I'm not on for over an hour. Keep an eye on the radar and wake me if there's anything strange."

A few minutes later, Beth would check the radar and one of the blips would have disappeared.

*

Dai could barely make out the black silhouette of the submarine in the dark. His phone vibrated.

"Yes."

"Commander Fang and the team are on the water. There in less than five."

He shut off the phone and walked down to the stern boarding platform. Bow and stern side thrusters kept the vessel bow into the wind. Soon he could see four faces in the darkness.

As the inflatable came along the platform, one of the team grabbed the edge and another scrambled aboard. A second followed, then the third. Several duffels were passed aboard along with automatic weapons. Every bit of clothing, the inflatable boat, storage bags, and weapons were all matt black.

A slender member of the team pulled off a knit hat, revealing shoulder length black hair. Offering a hand, she said, "I am Commander Fang."

"Your name makes me smile," said Dai, taking her hand. "To the Americans you are a wolf, but in Chinese it means fragrant." He bowed slightly and motioned toward the stairs that led to the main deck.

Fang went up, then Dai, followed by the others. At the top introductions were made. Two were People's Liberation Army Special Forces, and the third a computer expert named Jun. One of the Special Forces men pulled the inflatable up the stairs to the deck, where they tied it off.

"Can you show me around the boat?" said Fang. "Jun will need a place to work. He has been following your work since you left Bermuda."

"Of course. The large cabin on this deck is wired for access to everything."

"Where is the drone now?" asked Fang.

"Not far from here," said Dai.

He told her about the crew who had locked themselves in the forward part of the lower deck and about Bill Sanderlee.

"He is locked in his cabin with a whore who Hauglund hired to keep him amused," said Dai. "There are guest quarters, enough for you and your men, we can leave him locked there."

Fang's face showed no emotion. "I have no problem with that."

*

The one hundred and ten foot sailing vessel *Rose Blossom* pushed through the water headed south east. She had left Beaufort, North Carolina as the storm pounded Bermuda, hoping to catch a favorable wind on the back of the low pressure area.

Onboard, the owner and captain, William Moore, hoped for one more profitable season doing charters in the Caribbean. Each of the proceeding eight years he had hoped the same thing, and every spring he headed north to yard bills that chewed up whatever money he had made. It wasn't easy keeping a one hundred and five year old boat in compliance with the United Stated Coast Guard regulations.

Twelve college-age young people worked as crew, most signing on for only free passage to the islands. Two older members had worked for him before and, as the sailors say, knew the ropes.

A west wind moved them along briskly, the old hull plowing through the sea at over eight knots. The bilge pumps cycled every three or four minutes, but easily kept up with the little water that leaked in.

Captain Moore looked up at the old soiled sails. Hopefully they would make it through the winter. He smiled, remembering how he one time convinced paying passengers to hand stitch his sails. People were funny, give them a little rum and tell a few stories, they would do almost anything on vacation.

The old boat creaked, but seemed to love the sea.

*

Nancy Atherson listened to Christine's story, then asked, "When is the Navy taking them?"

"In the morning," said Christine. "It is too dangerous in the dark. Have you ever noticed them doing anything unusual?"

"They were an odd couple. I always thought they were gay. It never crossed my mind they might be working for someone else, let alone a foreign government."

"Tomorrow we will adjust the schedule to make up for two missing members," said Christine. "We have to keep searching for the drone. I have asked for replacements for Emil and Patrik, because I have no idea how long we will be at this."

Captain Able listened silently. He hoped Atherson would leave soon and Christine would stay. The two talked about possible ways to better locate the missing drone, only parts of which he understood. Finally, Nancy Atherson left.

"How long can you stay?" asked Able.

Christine smiled, "Until morning."

Atherson went down a flight of stairs and then aft to her cabin. Each of the researcher's cabins contained a pair of bunk beds. With four women on board, they slept two to a cabin. She had shared a cabin with her supervisor, Christine, but lately Christine never came back at night.

Opening her laptop, she started to type. Hopefully the message would get through.

30

George poured himself a coffee and looked outside. The helm continued to make tiny course adjustments guided by the autopilot. The tilt of the boat felt close hauled and the instruments over the nav station said they charged along at 7.56 knots. Water whispered along the outside of the hull.

He climbed up to the cockpit, expecting to find Beth, but found the seats empty. Standing on the bridge deck, he looked forward. Beth sat with her back against the mast. She wore a safety harness, which George had asked anyone on deck alone to wear if they left the cockpit.

Beth must have sensed his presence, she turned and motioned for him to join her. He slipped on a safety harness too, snapped onto the starboard jack line, and walked forward along the side deck.

"What a morning," he said, sitting beside her.

"It is."

Ahead, sunlight poked through tattered dark clouds. To the east, gray streaks indicated rain beneath one large sooty cloud. The warm southwest wind tasted of moistness and the sea.

"Seen anything?"

"Just a few shearwaters," said Beth. The wind tugged at her bouncy blonde curls.

"I'm glad to see you wore the harness," smiled George. It was the only thing she wore.

Beth smiled. "You told us the rules."

He set his coffee on the cabin top. The crests of some waves tumbled, creating the first whitecaps they had seen since soon after leaving Bermuda.

"Want to canoodle again?" said Beth.

She laughed, "Oh, your face was priceless. I wanted to see your reaction." She patted his thigh. "I would though, I could use a romp right now. Maybe I am not going to like sailing single handed as much as I thought. The ocean does things to me."

George felt flustered. Beth's bluntness, yet the temptation…to kiss soft lips and touch a bare breast, and it wouldn't stop there. He said, "If we were alone…I don't think I could resist."

Beth laughed. "Ha! At least I am still desirable." She sipped her coffee and they watched a shearwater drift across in front of them. Finally, she asked, "Did you have fun last night with Tova?"

George still wasn't sure if Tova had been in his cabin or if it had been a dream. What did Beth know? "We talked, she sees her sister differently than I do."

"Your perspective is tempered by lust," said Beth. "That will blur your judgement, as the smell of rum tempts a recovering alcoholic. They look so much alike, you must want Tova sometimes."

"I do," confessed George. "And she can be a tease."

"I know," laughed Beth, "I have been watching." A wave slapped the side of the hull and they watched the spray sparkle and then float into the sea. "No one would know if she snuck into your cabin."

Except you, thought George. "I can't do that."

"It might ease some of your frustration."

"I'm not sure she's my type. She might think sailing is fun for a week, but I don't want to get involved with someone who's going to try and make me change my lifestyle. It would just make a mess of everything."

"You over think everything," smiled Beth. "Just have a fling with her. Or maybe Windy is more your type."

A wave smacked the bow again, which sent glittering droplets blowing back onto them.

"It's time to move back to the cockpit," said Beth, rising.

"God morgan," said Tova, as they stepped into the cockpit. "Vi seglar äntligen, I love it."

"What did she say?" said Beth, looking at George.

"Good morning. We are sailing, finally," he laughed. "I don't know much more Swedish than that."

"Your watch is up," said George, heading for the nav station. "Get some rest Beth."

"It doesn't look like we will be sunning on the foredeck," she said.

Tova and Beth pulled out a frying pan and eggs. George checked he emails. The first came from Brigitta.

George,

I am sorry I missed your call last night. My afternoon meetings turned into late night meetings. We didn't finish until midnight. Call me tonight at nine. Brigitta.

The next came from Harold.

George,

A large wooden topsail schooner left Beaufort, North Carolina two days ago headed for the Virgin Islands. The Coast Guard has been trying to locate it, but the cloud cover from the recent storm has kept it hidden. If you should see it, ask them to contact the Coast Guard immediately. They are in great danger. Cloud cover even blocks my satellite images.

The drone is still missing. Our plan still remains a go.

The instruments said boat speed 8.26, wind 16.9 knots 245°, course 165°. He went back up on deck, if the wind increased another knot it would be time to tuck a reef.

Life looked pretty good, except the clean break with Brigitta hadn't happened. The way it stood, he could still go back. But there wasn't an "I love you" or any other affection in the email, just empty excuses.

*

Nancy Atherson knew Emil and Patrik's computers were temporarily stored in a locker next to the lunch room. Christine had asked her to put them there and said together they would see what the hard drives contained. Gray morning light seeped in the window of her cabin and she knew it would be almost two hours before Christine showed up.

She attached her computer to both of them and started to simultaneously copy the stored files to hers. It would take at least twenty minutes. The idea of keeping her true identity secret from Emil and Patrik had been hers, and it proved to be the right one. Everything they had learned would have been transmitted to Moscow the day before, if the Navy hadn't picked up the transmitter within twenty minutes of it hitting the water, but she wanted to duplicate it to be certain. Those two men may have been brilliant, but they were reckless playboys as far as Nancy was concerned. Too often they took unnecessary chances.

As far as she knew, neither Emil nor Patrik had learned to communicate with the drone, or even how to locate it reliably. Nancy had worked at it too, but weeks of work had proved futile. Possibly the Chinese computer hacker aboard the American yacht had learned something.

After the files were transferred, she would lock their computers away. Later she would take them out with Christine and spend the rest of the day exploring the hard drives.

Checking again, there was no response from Captain Hauglund.

*

Commander Fang settled into a couch in the main cabin. The computer wizards, Jun and Dai, had set up gear on the dining table at the forward end of the room. Wires ran like snakes and hard drives hummed. One of the Special Forces team came aft with a platter of meats and vegetables.

"Would you like some?" he asked.

"Yes. You are Jin, correct? See that the others get something to eat too. Where is Lok?"

"There is plenty of food. Lok is in the pilot house."

"Good, take turns. I gave you the coordinates of our destination."

As he left, she pushed down the black jeans, opened a duffle bag, and pulled out a pair of shorts. The black jersey came over her head, and she slid on a white tank top. For a few minutes she ate, then walked forward. A hallway led to the galley. The refrigerators were well stocked, and a temperature controlled wine cabinet appeared full.

Fang took a bottle of chardonnay, a wine glass, and an opener, then walked back through the cabin and up the stairs. In the pilot house she found Lok fiddling with the navigation instruments.

"Have you figured them out?" she asked.

He grinned and nodded. "They are simple." Lok had already taken off his shirt and stripped down to his underwear.

Fang walked aft and through the door to the pool deck. This is nice, she thought, looking at the water. In one of the chairs beneath a canopy, she opened the bottle of wine. In a half hour she would check on the computer wizards.

A gust of wind carried pellets of rain under the canopy, so she moved forward to the shelter of a roof that came out from the back of the pilot house.

*

George sat in the shelter of the dodger, listening to the spat of scattered raindrops hitting the clear plastic of the dodger's front. Tova sat on the opposite side, her watch had just started. Beth had disappeared into her cabin and Windy sat in the nav station typing emails to friends.

"You look tired," said George.

Tova smiled. "I didn't get enough sleep last night." She slid across to his side. With a smile, she said, "You left me so frustrated." She wore a little sarong around her hips with a gauzy little tank top that could have passed for mosquito netting. He wondered if it felt as soft as it looked.

"I'm sorry, but I think you were the one that started it." He smiled. "You had me going too."

"You never called Brigitta. Did you forget?"

He shook his head. "I was distracted. When I got to my cabin I remembered, but then thought to hell with it."

"So, you two really are done?"

"You don't look sad," said George. "Shouldn't you be? At least a little?"

"Maybe I am not." She slid closer to set her hand on this thigh.

Her fingers toying with the hem of his shorts. "What are you doing?" he asked.

"Did you dream about me last night?" When he said nothing, she added, "I dreamt I snuck into your cabin. I did not care if you thought I was my sister. I wanted you."

A picket fence of lightning jolted down from beneath a dark cloud a mile or more to the east. A gust of wind swallowed any thunder and *Frihet* heeled to the west.

"I dreamt something similar," he said.

"We shut the door and made love quietly." Her fingers slid up inside the cuff. "Can we do it again?"

A blast of wind howled in the rigging and the boat tilted to starboard. "It's time to tuck a reef," said George, standing. "Do you want to help me?" The gust felt relentless.

He eased the traveler, then they both snapped on harnesses and worked forward along the windward deck. When they eased the halyard the rain poured down. Tova giggled as they muscled the luff down and hooked the reef cringle. The rain became a waterfall. By the time they had the luff taut again, they were soaked. Hair lay matted and clothes clung. Tova's gauzy top had become nearly invisible. She laughed and thrust out her chest to make sure George noticed.

She said something that the wind swallowed.

George laughed, "Beautiful." Thunder cracked overhead.

Climbing back into the cockpit, he said, "Get into dry clothes, you'll catch a cold."

He folded up the bimini and secured it against the twin backstays. By then Windy had come out to help. Drenched, they ducked into the shelter of the dodger. The torrent continued.

"What a storm," said Windy, over the roar of the rain. Her eyes were wide. "I haven't seen it rain like this in years, maybe ever."

"It will calm the waves down," said George. The wind had already lightened. "We may go through squalls like this all day long. We're sailing down a stalled front. Get some dry clothes on."

She ducked inside as Tova came out in dry shorts and shirt.

"I'm going to dry off," said George, leaving Tova in the shelter of the dodger. The rainfall had let up considerably.

Coming out of his cabin, he looked into the open door of Beth's cabin to see her asleep. He wondered how she slept through the ruckus. He headed for the companionway, but Windy stepped out of her cabin to take his hand and lead him back inside.

"There is something I need to ask you?" she said. Her eyes darted about his face. "Did you and Brigitta break up?"

He nodded. "I think so." Windy's damp hair was pushed back behind her ears and she had changed into shorts with a bathing suit top. George wondered what had she heard. Had she been talking to Beth?

"Think so?"

"We haven't talked in a couple of days."

"Are you okay?"

"It feels good, actually. The uncertainty was grinding me down."

"If you need to talk, I'm a good listener."

He smiled, "I know you are." His arms slid around her shoulders in a hug. "Thanks. You've been a good friend."

"A rainbow," came Tova's voice from the cockpit. "You have to see it."

"We should go outside," said George.

"And there's an airplane out here," said Tova. "A big one."

George scurried up the companionway. A large gray jet flew south overhead. "That's a P-8 Poseidon, they are used to locate submarines," said George. "They drop sonar buoys and then listen for sounds."

"There's another shower coming," said Windy.

George went inside to the nav station. The knot meter read 7.35, wind SW 13.0, heading 165° Magnetic. The radar showed the next shower a mile ahead. He wrote the information in the log along with their position. There were four emails, all junk, and a fifth one from Harold Habit.

George,

My satellites have located S/V *Rose Blossom* to the west of you. Storm clouds had her hidden. If you slow to 4 knots they will catch up with you about 4 PM Atlantic Time. Watch for them on radar and we will keep you posted on her position. The Coast Guard has warned them about the rogue drone. Please escort the *Rose Blossom*. I am trying to get Navy or Coast Guard to assist.

Harold.

Great, thought George, we finally have some wind and Harold wants us to slow down. In the cockpit he explained the message to Windy and Tova.

"We might be rescuing a dozen or more people if the drone attacks that old ship," said George. "Our boat will feel mighty small then."

31

Bill still sat at the desk with his laptop open, just as he had since shortly after they learned they were prisoners. The boat's connection to the Internet had been severed, but he had hacked into the vessel's security system and into the files containing information on the boat.

Cynthia toyed with her phone, which had a satellite link, but didn't dare try to contact anyone. That would be a last resort. If their kidnappers intercepted a call to her GRU contacts, it would probably be her death sentence. First, she would see if Bill could do anything.

"The boat was built with a security system," said Bill, standing for the first time in hours. "The previous owner had children and wanted to be able to keep track of where they were on board. Of course, it was also used for security. Wealthy people with kids are always worried about kidnapping. When I bought the boat I shut it down, except the motion detectors on the main deck. Now I have a lot of it back up and running." He ran his fingers back through his hair. "We have five people on boat who weren't part of the crew."

"Where is the crew?"

"It appears they have locked themselves in the forward section of the lower deck, that's where their cabins are. They are directly below us.

"I did get a visual from the pilot house," continued Bill. "The intruders appear to be Chinese, or Oriental anyway. One is a woman."

"Can you tell where we are heading?"

Bill sat at the desk again. "I got into the navigation instruments, we are heading south at about ten knots. I tried to get a destination from the GPS, but can't. Possibly they didn't put in any coordinates."

Bill's performance impressed Cynthia. "What are they doing?" she asked.

"In the main cabin they have set up computers and looks like they are trying to communicate with an underwater vessel."

"It must be one of the drones. Hauglund never told me the details, just that Dai was doing something with drones. Governments are developing them as an inexpensive way to shadow submarines."

"I can hack into the boat's computers easy enough," said Bill, wondering if she told the truth, "but that doesn't get us out of here. And there are five of them and just two of us. They probably have weapons."

"I have a gun," said Cynthia. "It's in the bottom of my makeup bag."

Bill smiled. "The nightstand, on my side of the bed, has a false bottom in the drawer. There's a Glock 9mm in there."

"We've stopped, you can't feel the engines," said Bill, as walked to a window to peek around a curtain. "It's raining outside. Most underwater communication is some form of acoustics. Maybe they are listening."

The boat felt eerily still.

"I miss our time at the pool," said Cynthia.

Bill smiled. "Me too. I need a break, let's take a shower."

*

Nancy Atherson listened to the helicopter leave. Again she checked her email, but there was no response from Hauglund. Could there be technical difficulties? She could not imagine anything else. Soon Christine would return and they would continue going through the contents of Emil's and Patrik's hard drives. So far they had only found odd bits of undersea sounds, the static like clicking that amplification exposed. Might some of it be a code?

Nancy wondered if Emil or Patrik would talk. Probably, she decided. They were crazy young people, only interested in computer wizardry and hedonistic play. She shook her head, while glancing at files scrolling down the screen on Patrik's computer.

A particularly large file she opened. Graphics displayed a repeated series of sounds, then a break, followed by a different set repeated. Patrik had used an algorithm program to sort the sounds and broke them into alphabetical patterns. Nancy made a note of the path to the file, then deleted it from Patrik's computer. Later, she would open the transferred version on her own laptop. Maybe the encryption programs she had there could make sense of it.

*

Fang sat at the table with Jun and Dai, thinking what a contrast. Jun wasn't tall, the top of his head not even as high as Dai's shoulders. The two of them stared at their computers, occasionally punched a few keys, and made short cryptic notes on scraps of paper.

A New Beginning sat dead in the water. She wondered how long they would want silence. Dai's face never showed any emotion, but once in a while Jun smiled, as if he learned something new. At least that felt encouraging.

The rain had stopped and the sun poked between the clouds. To the north, dark clouds flashed with blue and white streaks of lightning, but moved slowly away and to the east.

"I am going up on deck," she said, rising from the table. "If you need me use the intercom. When you want to head south, call the pilot house."

Climbing the stairs, Fang met Lok coming down. "Is everything all right?" she asked. He stood four inches taller than her and his black jersey stretched across the broadest shoulders she had ever seen on a Chinese man.

"Yes. It is Jin's turn in the pilot house. I was starting my break."

"I am going to sit by the pool for a while," said Fang. "Would you like to join me? There are cold drinks."

Lok smiled, female company would be fun, plus Fang outranked him and he would never wish to insult her. "Of course. Can I bring us something to eat?"

"That is an excellent idea."

"I will be right back."

*

Captain William Moore watched the Coast Guard jet crossing the sky to the east of *Rose Blossom*. The day before the plane had contacted him by radio and explained the danger caused by the rogue drone. Since then, he spoke to the crew, double checked the life rafts, and made certain the abandon boat bags were ready. The crew had slept on deck, rather than risk being trapped inside should the drone ram them. There was little else Captain Moore could do.

Rain showers had interrupted the day, but bits of sunshine kept everyone's spirit's up. Most of the crew had put on bathing suits to wash up in the rain, amid lots of laughter and bantering. In the center of the boat, a large awning over a table provided protection from the sun and rain. Someone had placed a bowl of fruit on the table.

The big airplane, with the United States Coast Guard's orange stripe on its side, banked to the right, making a giant circle around them. Captain Moore had been promised that somewhere ahead a sailboat would wait to escort them. He hoped to make it at least that far. The young crew seemed oblivious to the danger. Oh, to have the invincibility of youth, he thought.

"How long before we turn?" asked the young man at the helm.

"We sail southeast until the butter melts," said Moore, with a growl, "then we head due south." He loved playing the part of a crusty old sea captain.

For the first time ever, *Rose Blossom* had an equal number of young men and women sign on for the migration south. Usually the boys outnumbered the girls by two to one or more. For Captain Moore, being over twice their age, it was easy to think of college age kids as boys and girls. Two of the young men had accompanied Captain Moore as paid crew on several trips offshore, and he relied on them to keep things orderly. One of the women, Lilly, made the trip north two years before, and now returned, heading for the island of St. John. The rest had little sailing experience, if any.

Up near the foremast, one of his seasoned sailors chatted with a new sailor, a red head dressed in a bikini top and short shorts, with glowing pink skin. The sailor laughed as she handed him a tube of lotion. Wearing a big grin, he smeared the creamy liquid on the red head's shoulders.

Moore smiled, wishing he were that age again.

*

Captain Able said, "Harold has asked us to sail southwest. There's an old wooden schooner coming down from the States and he's afraid the drone might attack it."

Christine nodded, still looking at her computer's screen. "Is the Coast Guard going too?"

"I don't think so. But Harold is convinced the drone has gone to war on wooden boats."

"That's why his lawyers are involved. He's afraid he'll be sued."

"I'm sure he has a good legal team," said Captain Able. "Anyone with as much money as he does must always have somebody trying to get some of it." He looked out the window of his cabin. "Harold said George Attwood's boat is going to meet the schooner too, to escort it south."

Christine, staring at the screen, tapped a dozen keys on the key board. "There is at least one file missing," she said. "I'm sorry, I wasn't really listening. Are we escorting the boat all the way to the islands too?"

"Harold didn't say. Unless we come up with something more important to do, I bet he asks us to."

32

George looked at his watch and then gazed at the horizon. They should see *Rose Blossom* soon. He wondered if the ship had a radar reflector up in the rigging. The wooden spars on the old boat might not show an echo and she could remain invisible on their radar until the hull was above the horizon.

The clouds had broken up a little after noon and the wind grew light out of the west. For a while a long tailed tropic bird fluttered around the masthead, but then disappeared to the north. By midafternoon the day felt warm again and clothing came off. A small yellow warbler landed on the boat when Windy went on watch and it moved occasionally between the lifelines and the cabin top. George guessed the storm had blown the bird far from land and it probably was doomed.

Beth sat up forward with her back against the mast reading a book. She had put on an oversized cotton button shirt, which George guessed was to minimize exposer to the sun. Tova sat on the cabin top, just ahead of the dodger in the shade of the mainsail, reading a magazine. She wore only a bikini bottom and her thick hair was back in a fat ponytail. Her tan had evened out to a golden bronze.

Windy stood on a cockpit seat and scanned the western horizon through binoculars. "Nothing," she said.

"I'll try to raise them on the VHF again," said George, heading for the nav station.

A minute later he came back out. "They are a little late, we'll probably catch them about supper time," said George. "The captain is William Moore. He seems to be taking everything in stride and says his crew thinks this is a great adventure."

Windy scanned the horizon again.

George sat against the stern pulpit, then added, "There was an email from Harold too. The research vessel *Absent* is supposed to catch up with us soon, in case something happens to *Rose Blossom*."

Windy put down the binoculars and sat next to George.

"Good, I was afraid we would end up with all of *Rose Blossom*'s crew on this boat."

"Let's hope nothing happens to them."

Windy peeled her tank top off over her head and shook her hair back.

George laughed. "You've gotten over your shyness."

"It's your fault," she giggled. "You got me started."

"I'm not complaining."

"The sun feels good." She shrugged a shoulder. "I love the freedom."

"If you get too much sun I'm an expert at putting on lotion," offered George, grinning.

"I'll take you up on that," said Windy. She disappeared inside and came out with a tube. "I can't reach the middle of my back."

George squeezed lotion onto his hands and then massaged it into Windy's shoulders. "Nice shoulders."

"That feels great," she said. "Get the middle between my shoulder blades."

Glancing forward, George noticed Tova's glare, but then she turned away.

At five they debated whether to have a cocktail, but George pulled rank and said no. If anything happened during the night, he wanted clear heads all around. By then the day had cooled and shirts or sweatshirts came out. *Rose Blossom*'s sails grew closer.

"She'll turn to run parallel with us," said George. "We can roll out the rest of the genoa and make better time. She should be faster than we've been going."

"Look," said Windy, pointing to the east. "Is that *Absent*?"

"It must be."

George went inside to call *Absent* on the VHF. Captain Able asked to motor ahead of *Rose Blossom* and *Frihet* and then run in his vessel's silent mode. He explained his vessel had originally been designed to do research on whales and to listen to them. *Absent* could run silently for hours at a time, but not at the usual cruising speed. His plan was to get ahead, listen in the silent mode as *Rose Blossom* and *Frihet* caught up and passed, then to motor ahead again, leap frogging south. Possibly they could hear the submersed drone before it struck.

*

Three hundred feet below and a mile to the east, Mother moved slowly toward the little armada. Sensors told her two surface vessels accompanied the third ship made of the mystery material. Concerning her more, a submarine, which she identified as a Russian Delta III, had been shadowing her for eleven hours, sometimes getting within 500 meters.

Mother sent off the four sharks that had been nursing, fearing something might happen to them.

*

Captain Able shut off the diesel engines and shifted the silent electric motors into gear. On the radar screen over the pilot house windows, he could see *Frihet* and *Rose Blossom* three miles behind. His vessel would travel at three knots while the two trailing boats would catch up at a little over twice that speed. He planned to let them catch up and get ahead. When they were three miles ahead of him he would start the diesels to get ahead again.

"We have a contact," said Christine's voice over the intercom.

"What do you have?"

"We're trying to determine…" she answered. "It's a sub of some kind. Let me get a message off to Harold.'

Captain Able waited. The boats behind were not catching up very fast. It would be a long night of leap frog. He asked one of his crew to fetch him a coffee.

"I talked to Harold, the Navy has a P-3 Orion up and in the area. We should see it soon."

"Can you identify the sub?"

"We think it is the drone. The P-3 has sophisticated gear that will let us know for sure. I have a team attempting to communicate with it too. If it is the drone, maybe we can get it to surface."

"Yeah," said the captain. It sounded unlikely to him, but he didn't say anything more. He glanced at his watch, waiting seemed to be what he did the most of lately.

Ten minutes later the P-3 appeared to the east. With *Absent* running in the silent mode, the grumble of the plane's engines could easily be heard. From the back of the aircraft an object dropped and a parachute opened, settling the sonar buoy gently into the sea. It landed about thousand yards ahead and a little to the east. The aircraft banked around to make a large circle and dropped a second buoy just to the west.

"Harold has authorized the Navy to destroy the drone if they identify it," said Christine. "Of course he would prefer it if we can get the thing to surface."

"How would they destroy it?"

"I don't know. Maybe torpedoes launched from that airplane. They have ships not that far from here too."

Captain Able knew that would bring the search to a close and possibly end his time with Christine. Waiting wasn't so bad, he decided, and he hoped it wasn't the drone.

*

Nancy Atherson wanted desperately to go back to her cabin and the laptop she left there. Christine had asked her and the team to search for the drone though, and, if possible, communicate with it. If they could correct the software flaws, the drone might be saved.

A few hours earlier, she learned from the hard drive that Patrik had successfully contacted the drone and possibly made changes in the drone's programming. It looked like much of the drone's current erratic behavior could be his fault. If his work had gone a little further, they might have taken complete control of the drone.

"We have a second contact," said one of her coworkers.

"Another?"

"Yes. Further to the east."

Nancy walked to the large desk at the front of the room. "Christine, something I ate isn't agreeing with me. I'll be working back in my cabin for a while."

Christine smiled. "Do what you must. That sort of thing usually passes quickly."

Nancy wondered what the second contact was. A Russian sub? She felt helpless, not being able to reach out to her comrades.

On the way to her cabin she passed the one Emil and Patrik shared. It had been searched thoroughly and their weapons and contact cylinders had been found. They might have another hiding place on board, but she couldn't imagine where. Captain Able had his Chief Engineer and a second crewmember looking through the vessel, but it would take days to poke through every possible niche and corner.

She shut the door to her cabin and opened her laptop.

*

Commander Fang sat silently and watched. Neither Jun nor Dai had left their seat in hours. It felt like the most boring assignment she had ever been involved with, but she reminded herself that fulfilling one's commitments to the People's Revolution could often be difficult. At least Lok had provided a few moments of diversion up by the pool.

"Commander," said Jun, "we have two vessels below us to the east. One is a Russian submarine, the other the drone owned by Harold Habit. Dai has been deciphering Mr. Habit's drone's communications with its smaller drones." He stood up from the table. "Would it be possible to get something to eat?"

Fang snapped her fingers and Jin left for the galley.

"To the west three surface vessels are traveling together," continued Jun. "One is the research vessel chartered by Mr. Habit. Their distance from us exceeds radar range, but not by a great deal. Communications between the large drone and the small drones leads us to believe the large drone is about to attack the surface vessels."

"Good, you are learning its language." Fang stood and asked, "Is there any indication why it would attack?"

"The drone is afraid of what it does not know, and it does not understand one of the vessels. Every few minutes it sends out some sort of sonar that we are not familiar with. We think it is a test probe, possibly to determine the vessel's structure."

Fang walked to a window to look out. It had been hours since either Dai or Jun spoke and she focused her thoughts. She asked, "What are the Russians doing?"

"It appears they are following Mr. Habit's drone."

"I imagine they would love to steal it," she said.

"If I may," said Dai, rising from the table. "For days, someone aboard the vessel chartered by Mr. Habit has attempted communication with the big drone, the Mother as some call it. That has stopped. Mr. Habit's vessel's primary purpose appears to have been to locate the drone. I believe a person on board hacked into the operating system of the drone, unbeknownst to the rest of Mr. Habit's crew, attempting to steal it. Possibly he was working with the Russian submarine. He has not succeeded, has possibly damaged the operating system of the drone, and has never gained control of it. I believe Mr. Habit has a spy onboard, a Russian hacker. Why the man has stopped I cannot say."

Jin returned carrying a platter of chicken and vegetables.

"Eat," said Fang, motioning toward the food. "Then take a break. You have been working hard. Let us see what happens with the surface vessels. We can do nothing in the meantime."

*

"I have the schematics up," said Bill Sanderlee, looking at his computer screen.

The boat's manufacturer, a builder of aluminum mega-yachts in New Zealand, had supplied the previous owner with a digital version of an owner's manual. Bill had never opened it, but he at least knew where it was, on a thumb drive in his desk.

"Under the vanity in the head is a panel that accesses a passageway used to run wires and plumbing."

"Can we fit through it?" asked Cynthia.

"It looks like we might," he said, walking toward the head.

Under the vanity, what looked like marble panels were actually the fronts of touch-open drawers. Bill touched the center one and it popped out three inches. Pulled to its maximum extension, he felt around beneath it to find a compressible lever on each side. Pressing those, the drawer slid out further and dropped to the floor.

Looking in, he said, "What do we have that might work as a Philips head screwdriver? There's a panel in the back."

"There are scissors in a drawer," said Cynthia. "And a nail file."

Fifteen minutes later, Bill had the plate off, revealing the inside of a metal duct.

"Can we fit?"

"I think so," he said. "According to the plans, it goes forward to another main duct that runs below this deck all the way back to the engine room. Wiring and plumbing for the crew cabins all connect through the main one too. Maybe we can find the crew."

"Do you want me to follow you?"

"No. If I get stuck I may need you to help get me out. Let me get the flashlight that's in the nightstand beside the bed."

His shoulders easily fit into the duct, but the low top prevented him from lifting his head. Twenty feet ahead, light came up through a grate. Worming along, he started to perspire. The air tasted metallic and of dust. Reaching the grate, he looked down. It was the hallway that the crew cabins were off, but no one was in sight.

33

In the dimly lit cabin, George stopped at the nav station to look at the radar. *Rose Blossom* sailed a parallel course a mile to the west. A quarter mile beyond, *Absent* traveled silently, keeping up easily using battery power alone. The wind speed had been dropping since dinner time and *Frihet's* boat speed had dropped to 3.3 knots, about the same as the old wood boat.

George checked for emails, but found only one from Christine aboard *Absent*. He tried to remember how long it had been since he heard from Brigitta. At least the ache of missing her had faded. Hearing nothing was good, and he hoped it would stay that way.

The email from Christine said her team and the Navy had lost contact with the drone. It disappeared when it dove to a depth greater than a thousand feet.

Hoping that meant the likelihood of an attack had decreased, he climbed back up in the cockpit. The running lights of *Rose Blossom* and *Absent* glowed to the west. He wondered what the old sailing ship had for an auxiliary and how slow they would sail before Captain Moore started it. Settling down in the back of the cockpit, a shooting star caught his eye.

"It is a beautiful night," said Tova, coming out the companionway.

"What are you doing up?" said George. "Your watch isn't for over two hours." In the dim light her blonde hair almost blazed and her eyes sparkled. She wore the button shirt that he recognized as one of his.

"I could not sleep. Can I keep you company?"

"Of course." As she sat beside him, he told her about the email from Christine.

"Let us hope that means everyone is safe."

Tova had pulled her hair back into a loose fat braid. He hadn't seen it like that before, and commented, "Your hair looks nice."

She smiled. "If I braid it tight my hair gets wavy, until I wash it again." She pulled it over her shoulder, then touched his arm. "How are you doing? I haven't heard anything from Brigitta."

Her fingers felt electric. "Me either. I went all day without thinking about her, until I checked my email."

"Did she write?"

"No. I didn't expect she would."

Tova slid closer. "The night is not as warm as I thought it would be."

George smiled and took the hint, slipping an arm around her shoulders. "You could put more clothes on," he teased. "Or do up a few more of the buttons." It was easy to see she wore nothing beneath the cotton shirt.

She grinned. "I was hoping to get your attention."

"You have."

"We are alone. They are both sleeping hard," said Tova. Eyes the color of the Caribbean Sea darted over his face.

He slid a hand along a silky thigh. "We shouldn't. Beth is a light sleeper." The skin felt warm as the tropical sun and she smelled of frangipani, his favorite tropical flower.

"That feels nice," she purred. "Are you going to get me aroused and then leave me again?" When she turned to face him, her shirt hung open to the waist.

"Beth or Windy could come out here any minute."

Tova grinned and undid the only two fastened buttons on the front of the shirt, then slipped it off. "They are both snoring." She glanced at her own chest. "What do you think of my tan?"

She looked like Brigitta, the same curves and size, yet there was a sassiness that Brigitta didn't have and he found it fun. "It is perfect."

Tova laughed. "I hoped you would think so." Her fingers wrapped around his wrist to slide his hand along her thigh. "Now don't leave me wanting."

George tasted the Caribbean Sea.

*

Even at only three knots, the abrupt stop caused two crewmembers to fall. The snap of the massive eighteen inch wide by three foot deep keel timber reverberated like a cannon shot.

Instantly, *Rose Blossom's* slumbering crew became wide awake.

Amidst screams, Captain Moore ordered the life rafts launched and his paid crew passed out life jackets. A second crash bulged the deck upward and pushed in the port topside. Chainplates ripped from the hill and the top of the aft mast fell to starboard. Water could be heard rushing in.

The captain dashed to his cabin to collect a few personal items and the ship's log. Water already splashed around his feet.

*

"Commander Fang," said Jun. "It appears the drone has crashed into the wood sailing ship."

Fang tried to force the sleep from her head. How long had she slept? Outside the windows it still looked dark. Her watch said a little after midnight.

"What?" It did not make sense.

Jun repeated the information. "It then dove beyond three hundred meters and we lost contact again. Apparently it wanted to sink the ship."

Fang walked to the open doors at the aft end of the cabin. Neither the ocean nor wind made any sound. A million stars peppered the sky, yet she easily picked out a moving satellite. Failure would not be acceptable. She turned around and walked back to her team.

"Jun and Dai, work in shifts and keep trying to locate the sub. We will keep traveling south, the drone had been moving almost due south at four knots. Perhaps we will intercept it again."

"We will try," said Jun, looking skeptical. "It is a big ocean."

"Dai's listening devices are the best ever made," she said. "Much better than anything the Americans or Russians have."

"The Russian sub went east," said Jun. "We no longer hear it."

*

What sounded like the boom of thunder woke Beth and Windy. Together they dashed up to the deck as George started the auxiliary. Windy rolled up the genoa while Tova and Beth doused the mainsail. By the time they reached *Rose Blossom* the workboats from *Absent* were there plucking the crew out of the water.

Beth stood at the bow, leaning against the furled genoa, sweeping the surface with a floodlight. Tova stood at the starboard shrouds, peering into the dark. The sea washed over the old ship's deck and her broken masts floated among tangled lines in the water. Life jackets, cushions, and chunks of wood drifted everywhere. Windy stayed in the cockpit with George, where they both tried to see into the night. Flood lights from *Absent* sent earie shadows across the wreckage.

George picked up the VHF radio. "Captain Able, do you have everybody?"

"We think so. "When we get them all aboard *Absen*t we'll do a head count."

"Roger," said George. "We'll make one more pass around to make sure there's nobody still in the water."

"Good idea. If we have everyone, we're heading for St. Thomas. There is one possible broken arm here and two others with minor injuries. Saint T is the closest hospital and airport."

"Any news on the drone?"

"It disappeared again. So did the Russian sub."

With the engine idling, *Frihet* completed another slow circle. Pieces of wood floated all over the place. Empty life jackets drifted slowly in the light wind. A small teak door bobbed beside a plastic bucket. Cushions from inside the boat were tangled among broken chunks of the hull.

"Beth, can you grab that with the boat hook?" asked George, pointing at a life ring that said *Rose Blossom* on it.

"Of course."

He picked up the radio again. "*Absent,* this is *Frihet.* We are going to hang here overnight to see what is left in daylight."

"That's probably a good idea," said Captain Able. "We have the entire crew accounted for, so we are heading south."

"Have a safe trip. Hopefully we will see you in the islands."

Beth came aft along the side deck carrying the life ring.

"I bet Captain Moore will want that," said George. "We're staying here for the night. Who feels like a drink, besides me?"

"I thought you would never ask," laughed Beth. "Wine?"

"Whatever you want," said George.

"I'll have a scotch," said Windy, turning to George. "Your usual?"

"Of course," said George, feeling the tension slip away. "What a night. We were all very lucky. It could have been blowing a gale."

Beth came out carrying a bottle of Gibbs 2010 Obsidian Block Reserve Cabernet Sauvignon and George's Dalwhinnie. "Who wants a wine glass?"

"I'll try the scotch," said Tova. "If George doesn't mind sharing."

"Be my guest," he laughed, noticing she had buttoned her shirt crooked. Downwind of the sinking ship, he shut off the engine. "We don't want to get too close. There may be lines trailing in the water and we don't need to get one wrapped around our propeller."

The night felt deathly quiet. Someone turned on music as Beth poured an inch of scotch into three tumblers, then nearly filled a wineglass with the cabernet.

"To safe sailing," said George, raising his glass before taking a sip. Everyone took a swallow.

Tova coughed. "Aj! Som är stark."

The crew laughed at the Swedish. "Sip it, go easy," said Windy. "It is a bit of an acquired taste."

*

"What did you find?" asked Cynthia.

"I made it all the way to the engine room," said Bill. "The main air passage is bigger and easier to crawl through than this one."

"We can get out then?"

"Let's see where our captors are first," he said, walking toward his computer. A minute later he said, "There are four in the main cabin and one in the pilot house. They have two computers on. I can't tell what they are doing."

He hit a few keys, stared at the screen, and then typed still more. "Ah, they have listening devices somewhere. They are listening for something."

"It is an undersea drone, built by an American. My country would love to steal it, so would the Chinese. Everyone has been searching for weeks."

She went on to explain how drones were used to track submarines, then asked, "Can we sneak to the pilot house?"

"What do you want to do?"

"Kill the one there."

The idea shocked Bill. She asked, "Have you ever killed a man?" He shook his head.

"I have. It is not so difficult. Once we get him, we will wait to kill another, taking them one at a time. It is safe to assume they have automatic weapons."

"What is that?" he asked, pointing at her gun on the bed. "A silencer?"

"That is what your American movies call it. We call it a suppressor, it quiets the gun. No firearm is silent." She picked up the gun. "Shall we go?"

Bill crawled into the duct first, squirming along. Cynthia followed, but in the confined space he couldn't look back to see her. They crossed the air vent over the hallway, where they could hear music playing, then made a left into a larger passageway. Wires and piping ran along the right hand wall.

Bill sat up, waiting for Cynthia to catch up. On hands and knees, they continued, finally reaching a vent over the engine room. Bill turned four clips, then carefully lifted the grate up into the duct. A generator directly below them offered a place to step down to. The air felt warm and thick, and further aft the main engines purred.

Bill peeked out the engine room door, then said, "This way."

He led her to stairs that climbed up to the starboard deck. Opening the door a crack, he could only see aft. Light leaked out of the main cabin's large windows, but nobody appeared to be around.

They darted out and up the stairs to the pilot house deck. Turning left at the top, they slipped through the pool area to approach the pilot house from the port side.

Cynthia grabbed Bill's wrist to stop him and held a finger to her lips. Holding her pistol aimed upward, she worked along the side of the cabin, stopping just aft of the open pilot house door.

In one fluid move she stepped to the door and aimed with two hands. The shot sounded like a stifled sneeze.

*

George checked the radar and instruments. The wind speed read 0.2 knots and twitched from northwest to east, boat speed zero. The one scotch he consumed earlier had gone to his head and sleep would come easy. Tova sat alone in the cockpit and he hoped she could stay awake, but there was little danger if she nodded off with the radar's intruder alarm set for three miles. He had asked her to shine a light on *Rose Blossom's* bow periodically to make sure they didn't lose track of it during the night. Only the bow remained above the sea.

Beth had closed the door to her cabin and he could hear heavy breathing on the other side. Through the open door of Windy's cabin he could see her sleeping in the clothes she had on earlier. How much did they drink?

He climbed up to the cockpit. "Are you all right?" he asked. "I'm going to get some sleep."

She smiled and motioned for him to sit beside her. "Keep me company for a few minutes."

"I should get some sleep."

"Please."

"Are you going to behave yourself?" he laughed, sitting.

"Of course," she grinned. "I owe you a favor."

"What for?"

Little dimples tucked into her smile. "In Swedish I would say du njöt sexuellt av mig."

"I don't know what that means," said George, worried by the look on Tova's face.

"You made me very happy, just as the drone hit the ship." She giggled. "I thought the boom was...the word is the same in English as Swedish, my orgasm."

"How much did you have to drink? I really should go to bed," protested George, without moving.

Tova unfastened the buttons of her shirt again. "Jag vill sexuellt tacka dig," she teased. "It is the favor I owe you. Just enjoy it."

34

George woke to the smell of bacon cooking, Amber light trickled into the cabin and the boat slipped through the ocean silently. He stared up at the overhead. Laughter and voices in the main cabin told him Beth and Windy were in the galley. Tova's watch would end shortly and he wondered if any of *Rose Blossom* remained above the sea.

He took a deep breath, hoping to clear away some of the cobwebs. Their impromptu celebration the night before had turned into quite a party, with the crew having more than one drink to celebrate. He had stopped after the first, wanting to keep a clear head, but that first one was a healthy pour. They laughed and told stories for almost an hour before Beth and Windy finally decided to get some sleep.

He remembered Tova's silliness in the cockpit. What was he thinking, going along with that? They had taken a stupid chance and could easily have been caught by...Windy. He realized Windy was the one he didn't want to find him with Tova. Beth would have been unfazed and only have laughed.

Why? He had known Windy for quite a while and always liked her. The way she moved around a boat and worked hard impressed him. And she certainly was attractive. He remembered having long talks with her and the genuine concern she expressed about Brigitta's head injury.

The aroma of coffee filtered into the cabin. He rolled in the bed and sat up, his bare feet finding the cabin sole cool.

The door was closed and he almost never closed it. Tova had followed him down to the cabin after their little escapade in the cockpit. She insisted on kissing him goodnight. It was a good thing he stopped after one scotch or he might have pulled her into the bed. He knew she wouldn't have resisted. Was it all a big joke to her?

He pulled on shorts, grabbed a towel, and stepped into the main cabin.

"Our captain is up," said Beth, standing at the stove and wearing only an apron.

"Don't let that bacon splatter," said George, squinting from the light and trying to sound serious.

"We were going to let you sleep in," said Windy, pouring him a cup of coffee.

"How many eggs do you want?" asked Beth. "Four?"

"Two," said George, heading for the companionway.

"Here," said Windy, handing him the mug.

"You look nice this morning," he said. She wore a loose little halter top made of an open weave webbing and a bikini bottom that looked like gold coins stitched together. Trying not to stare, he added, "You could be on the cover of some swim suit magazine."

She smiled. "I bought this in Bermuda."

"I can see right through it, you'd get arrested wearing that there."

"I bought a blue one like it," said Tova, out in the cockpit.

Windy laughed. "Freedom of the sea, isn't that what you call it?"

He nodded and climbed up the steps. "How's Tova this morning?" She had changed into a long tropical print sarong that hung loosely from her neck.

"Fine," she smiled. "Did you sleep okay?"

"Like a baby," he said.

"*Rose Blossom* disappeared about an hour ago," said Tova. "Right after it disappeared, you should have heard the bubbles coming up. It sounded like a storm."

In every direction, chunks of wood and debris littered the glassy ocean. To the west, high clouds painted gray streaks in the sky. The air felt heavy with humidity and the sun, even though still low, already felt hot.

"It looks like we have the entire planet to ourselves," said George. "I'm going for a swim before we start."

He stepped down to the swim platform and kicked the swim ladder overboard, then dropped his shorts and dove in. The water felt cool and cleared his head. After three underwater frog-like strokes he popped to the surface thirty feet from the boat. A few feet ahead a piece of mahogany floated in the water. He swam to it to hold on and turned to look back.

Beth dove in. On the swim platform, Tova untied her sarong and tossed it aside, then jumped cannonball style into the water. George did a breaststroke back toward the boat. Windy came up to the cockpit, saw what was going on, then undressed to dive off the aft starboard quarter.

Skinny dipping hundreds of miles from land with three gorgeous women, thought George, my friends will never believe this.

"Our captain has finally gotten over his shyness," yelled Beth, starting to swim in his direction.

"It's about time," laughed Tova.

George ducked under and swam beneath the surface toward the boat. In the clear water he could see the rudders and keel of *Frihet* reaching down from the hull. He popped up next to the swim ladder and started up.

"He is shy," yelled Tova, treading water.

"I didn't think Americans were that way," joked Beth. "An Englishman wouldn't miss the chance to swim in the skinny with three naked women."

"The water feels heavenly," said Windy. "You are missing your chance, George."

With his back to the women, George dried himself off.

"Turn around," teased Beth. "Let us see what you've got."

"Ja," said Tova. "Låt oss se hur stor det är."

George did not know what Tova said and knew he probably didn't want to know. He pulled on his shorts. Turning around, he picked up his coffee and asked, "Does anyone want more coffee?"

The women laughed.

"How long before we sail, Captain?" said Beth.

George put on his sunglasses. "There's no hurry. I love to watch naked women swimming."

Beth struck the surface of the water with the heel of her hand, splashing spray up at George. "You are a dirty old man," she laughed.

"We'll be to the Virgin Islands in about thirty-six hours," he said. "The sooner we leave the sooner we'll get there."

Tova steadied on the swim ladder to float on her back. Her blonde hair flowed outward around her head like a giant sunflower.

"I'm not getting out of the water then," said Tova. "I want to stay here forever."

George laughed. "We'll run out of food in a couple of weeks."

When he first started doing day charters in the islands, two women broke his heart. One, the first year he was in business, and another a few months later. Both proclaimed to love him and the islands, promising to move there and start a life with him. Neither returned after flying back to the States, and only the first one had the decency to write and say she wasn't coming back. Vacation flings, that's what he learned to call them. After that he hardened his heart, only entering relationships with women who already lived in the Caribbean.

Watching Tova float in the water, George guessed he was her vacation fling.

*

Up on the roof of the pilot house, Bill and Cynthia waited. The sun felt hot and the movement of the boat created the only cooling breeze. For almost three hours the autopilot steered the boat south at a lowly four knots.

Bill wondered if they had cleaned up all of the blood in the pilot house. It had been done quickly with limited resources. First, they had carried the dead man down to the main deck where they silently dropped him over the side. The thought that someone might hear them had scared him more than anything had during his whole life.

Then, back in the pilot house, they wiped up the floor with a shirt someone had left on a hook inside the door. The sticky blood had already started to dry and came off the floor with difficulty, but they tossed the mess overboard. In a locker under the seats at the back of the pilot house, Bill had found a roll of paper towels and a bottle of Windex. It had been all he could do to keep from retching, but Cynthia appeared unfazed.

Footsteps coming up the starboard stairs brought him back to the present. Cynthia moved to peek over the edge of the house top, then looked back at Bill. She held up one finger and mouthed "one man".

"Lok?" came from the pilot house.

In a fluid move, Cynthia rolled off the roof and landed on her feet just outside the pilot house door. Her pistol came up and spit a bullet into the man's face.

"Let's get him out of here." she said, coldly.

*

George climbed up to the cockpit carrying a cup of coffee. Beth had just started her watch, Tova slept inside on the port settee and Windy in her cabin. The auxiliary pushed *Frihet* south at 7.2 knots on a glassy sea. Occasional clumps of golden Sargasso grass broke up the endless blue. To the west, high thin clouds hinted of a stalled weather system and the humid air felt of the tropics. All of the boat's topside hatches were open to let air flow through.

"I wanted to talk to you alone," said Beth, sitting at the aft end of the cockpit.

George sat beside her. "What's up?"

"Last night, the inflatable workboats from *Absent* were the same as the boat that shot at me."

"Are you sure?"

Beth smiled. "Before the bullet holes were found in my life raft, I thought it was all a hallucination. I am not sure about anything."

"Harold Habit owns *Absent*. His people wouldn't shoot at you."

"The boats were the same as I remember."

George looked away, then said, "I'll email him, we'll see what he says."

A flying fish skittered out of the water beside the boat, only to splash into the sea a few feet ahead. Another did the same, then a half dozen smaller ones followed erratically.

"I wonder what is chasing them?" said George.

Beth leaned back and smiled. "So, what happened last night?"

George cringed.

"Ha, the look on your face," laughed Beth.

"What do you mean? *Rose Blossom* sunk."

"I know that." Leaning close, she teased, "But Tova was hurrying to put her shirt back on when I came out into the cockpit. Am I right?"

"God morgon," said Tova in sleepy Swedish, coming up the companionway. She had haphazardly tied on a sarong around her hips and carried a towel in her hand. She smiled and gave them a little wave, then stepped to the side deck to go forward.

"Flygande fisk" she said, pointing off to port.

"We saw them," said George, understanding the little bit of Swedish.

"Something is chasing them," said Beth. Tova beamed and continued forward to nap in the sun on the foredeck.

Beth leaned close to George. "You are the flying fish and Tova is the wahoo. Did she catch you?" She barely contained her laugh.

"I don't know what you are talking about?" George fought back a smile.

"Really?"

"It was the alcohol," said George.

"Always blame the alcohol." Beth smiled and patted his leg. "You are a guy and she is a beautiful woman. Not many men could resist. This soap opera is getting steamy."

George asked, "Have you found any boats for sale online?"

"Are you trying to change the subject?" laughed Beth. "I think Windy saw Tova dressing too. I am surprised she let you out of her sight."

"I'm going to email Harold about the workboats," said George, standing and heading for the companionway.

*

"Jin? Lok?" came a voice from the main deck.

Bill Sanderlee waited, stretched out on his side, His heart pounded. Beside him, Cynthia listened at the edge of the pilot house top. Her nonchalance he found troubling.

A voice from directly below them said something in Chinese, which meant someone had climbed the stairs without a sound.

Perspiration trickled down Bill's side. He heard footsteps hurry along the side deck aft.

With an almost imperceptible buzz a platter-size four-rotor drone hovered over Bill, dropped a phone, then disappeared into the sky.

Cynthia sat up with a questioning look.

Bill picked up the phone and immediately its face glowed with a message.

United States Navy SEALs are landing aboard your vessel in one minute.

35

George sent his email on the way, wondering how long it would be before Harold replied. The man often took on more than any one man should, so it could be a long time. He poured another coffee and looked at the clock in the nav station. His watch started in a half hour. The boat speed, wind, and heading had been the same for hours.

Through the companionway he could see Beth sitting against the stern pulpit and reading a book. She looked like a Greek statue, with an unbroken golden tan covered her slender muscular body. Sunglasses and a thin gold chain around her neck were the only things she wore. A few minutes earlier he had been sitting and talking to her, not even noticing the lack of clothing. The novelty had worn off about a day after leaving Bermuda. Her nipples looked the color of chocolate and he wondered if the sun had darkened them too. What an unbelievable trip it had been.

The door to Windy's cabin opened. "Good morning," she said.

"Good morning," replied George. "You look nice this morning." She wore a button shirt made of what looked like fish net over a bikini bottom, something the Windy would never have worn back home on Cape Cod.

She beamed. "I bought this in Hamilton."

"Coffee?"

"Do we have enough ice for iced coffee?"

"Of course," said George, reaching for an insulated glass. "Maybe I'll have an iced coffee too."

"What a night," said Windy. "*Rose Blossom's* crew was very lucky." She opened the freezer. "Still no wind?"

"None," said George. "The ocean looks like the prairie. Hopefully we'll find the tradewinds soon."

Windy filled two glasses with ice, then handed one to George. "Is this our last full day at sea?"

"We should make landfall sometime tomorrow night," said George, starting to pour, "so there'll be one more. *Absent* will be there by tonight."

Windy pushed her wavy hair back. "Will you put some sunscreen on my back? I want to catch some sun before we return to the real world."

"Of course. Tova is up on the foredeck," said George.

Windy's smile flickered, but she forced it back. "Why don't you come up there with me?"

"I don't sit in the sun," said George. "Enough filters in under the bimini."

"You're probably right." Windy grinned. "I think you are the only one onboard with tan lines."

George laughed. "It's going to stay that way.

Windy took a sip of her coffee, then looked out the companionway.

"What did you and Tova talk about last night?" asked Windy. Her smile looked frozen, artificial.

"Nothing important," fumbled George. "Her sister some, and how we all are different."

Tears edged Windy's eyes. "Should I ask her?"

"Windy...." George felt like a total ass.

"I was going to try and ignore it, but I know what happened, or at least can guess. When I heard the crash, I jumped out of my bunk and saw her dressing" Windy looked away and wiped an wayward tear. "You said we would have a talk when we got to the islands, maybe spend some time together."

"Windy, I like you a lot, very much. You are beautiful and love to sail and you are so easy to talk to. What more could I want?"

"Apparently a carbon copy of your old girlfriend. Do you love her?"

"Who?" George wished he hadn't said it quite like that.

"Tova? Brigitta? Both of them?"

"Nobody," said George. Things were spiraling beyond reason. He hoped neither Beth nor Tova could hear. "It was just a physical thing, a reaction to circumstances." Through the companionway he could see Beth pretending to read, but struggling to contain a smile.

"I am going to pretend what I saw never happened," said Windy. "But I'd like to spend some time with you today. I think we could be good for each other."

"I think so too," said George. He reached to embrace, but she turned her back.

*

Something crinkled and popped overhead. Bill looked up at an almost transparent parafoil a few hundred feet above the boat. A second and then a third unfolded, followed by several more. They swooped down like birds of prey.

An automatic weapon on the main deck fired several shots. From the sky above a string of shots rained downward.

"It is the drone," said Cynthia. "It is armed."

Someone ran down the steps on the starboard side.

"Come," she said, rolling off the pilot house roof.

Bill looked over the edge. She stood with both arms out and two hands holding her weapon, first aimed into the pilot house and then swiveling to look down the stairway. A gunshot made her duck back behind the railing. She leaned out and fired three times. A string of shots rained down from above.

The first SEAL landed on the foredeck with his weapon ready. Two more set down a second later. Shots came from aft. The drone swooped down to stop behind the house, streaming bullets onto the aft deck. Gunfire from the deck sent it tumbling into the sea.

Bill slid over the side of the pilot house. A SEAL already stood beside Cynthia in the pilot house. Four more worked down the starboard deck, while three cleared the port side.

"Where did you guys come from?" asked Bill.

"We came from the carrier USS Harry Truman. I am Lieutenant Richards. Intercepted communications alerted the government of your situation twenty-eight hours ago. Satellites confirmed it and set this operation into motion."

"There were two more of them," said Cynthia. "We got lucky and killed them."

"There were five total," said Bill. "They killed my captain and two of his crew."

"That was what we believed," said Richards. "You should have your vessel back soon."

"The rest of the crew is locked below decks," said Bill.

"When we have secured the vessel you can let them out."

"How was their communication intercepted?" asked Cynthia.

"There has been a lot of activity in this part of the ocean, looking for a missing undersea drone," said Richards. "The Navy has a carrier group and several submarine hunters here. The Russians and Chinese are in the area too, looking for the same drone. Our people intercepted sonar pings from your vessel, something that is unusual for a yacht, so they zeroed in on it."

A string of gunshots at the stern interrupted. More gunfire and flashes followed.

Bill glanced at Cynthia. "Why are the Russians interested?"

Richards said something into a microphone on his collar, then listened through an ear piece.

"The drone represents serious technology. Russia and China would love to steal it.

"My team," he continued, "think they have the boat cleared. They will do a once-through, and then you are free to do as you please. If you would like professional help to reach your destination, it can be provided."

"We'll be fine," said Bill. "And I'll ask the crew. If any want to leave, can you take them with you?"

"Of course. What is your destination?"

"The United States Virgin Islands."

"When you arrive, there will be people that will want to talk to you. Is that all right with you?"

"Yes," said Bill, nodding. He looked at Cynthia. "One other thing, could you take Cynthia Campbell with you?"

"Bill, I would like to stay."

He shook his head. "No, I need you to go."

A young man appeared at the doorway. "All clear. Our team is all safe. There are three bodies aft."

"Our ride is on the way," said Richards. "We'll take the bodies with us. A Navy destroyer is on the way and will have a smaller boat alongside within an hour." He disappeared down the stairs.

"Bill, can we talk about it?" said Cynthia.

"No. I'll never be able to trust you," said Bill. "I won't tell them who you really are. That secret is safe. Just get your things and go. I'm going to let the crew out."

She stepped out of the pilot house and disappeared down the stairs toward the owner's cabin.

*

Sitting aft of the port helm in the shade of the bimini, George listened to Windy's stories about sailing with her father on Buzzards Bay. She certainly loved sailing and her infectious enthusiasm had carried her through several summers as a sailing instructor. After a few seasons as a regular crewmember in the Wednesday night races out of Marion, Massachusetts, she had sailed a handful of offshore races, including the one to Bermuda. With his eyes safely hidden behind dark glasses, he watched the way her breasts moved inside her nearly transparent top. She certainly wasn't the conservative New England woman he remembered from Cape Cod. He really wanted to wrap his arms around her.

Beth sat at in the shade at the front of the cockpit with the table leaf up, making jewelry she would sell to tourists down in the islands. The breeze, caused only by the boat moving, triggered glitter to escape and stick to everything, particularly her bare skin. Tova had returned from the foredeck just before lunchtime and read in the shade of the bimini with her back against the cabin.

"Well, this isn't really sailing," said George. "We need wind if we are going to sail."

"It will come," said Windy. "Look at the cumulous clouds peeking over the horizon to the south. When we get there the tradewinds will kick in."

"Do you think so?" laughed George.

"I would bet money on it."

Tova undid the knot holding her sarong in place, then stood, letting it drop, and kicked it aside. Looking out at the ocean to the west, she pushed her hair back with both hands, forcing it into a ponytail that she twisted into a knot to keep it up off her neck. The episode forced her breasts upward, obviously to gain his attention.

He tried very hard not to look.

"That's better," she announced, sitting in the middle of the cockpit and away from the cabin. "The air feels cooler on my skin."

"It is humid," said Beth.

"That's why I wore this," said Windy. "I like the way the air feels."

"Beth, you are all glitter," said George.

Tova laughed. "It makes you look magical."

"Maybe I am," she answered. "George, how about an afternoon beer brake? We couldn't have a calmer ocean to sail on."

"Sure, I'll have one too. You want one Windy?"

"Yes, I'll get them." Windy disappeared inside.

Tova stole a pinch of the glitter and sprinkled it over her breasts. "I'll have to remember this look."

"You really sell those bracelets?" asked George, watching Beth's hands pour glitter into a tiny clear plastic tube, then push the tube's ends together over a short piece of wooden dowel, creating a sparkling wrist-size ring.

"It takes about a minute and cost me about ten cents to make one of these, and I sell them for eighteen dollars. Tourists have bought thousands of these bracelets. They paid for a big chunk of my first boat."

Windy came up the companionway carrying four Heinekens, sans clothing.

"Good Lord," said George.

"Freedom of the sea," laughed Windy, setting a bottle on the table in front of Beth. A tiny gold chain hung around her waist.

Beth chuckled, and sounding quite British said, "I see I have started a trend. George, you are the only one still dressed, why is that?"

"That's not going to change," he said, taking an offered beer. "I'm shy, remember?"

"When we get to the islands, we'll get you liquored up a bit," said Beth. "Then maybe you'll loosen up a little." Turning to Windy, she added, "Take a pinch of the sparkles, it will look good on you."

Windy smiled and snatched a bit, then sifted it between her fingers over her head.

"I'm surrounded by glittering angels," laughed George.

The conversation turned to Caribbean daydreams and places to see, sail, and swim. Beth talked about two listings for boats in the United States Virgin Islands that she wanted to see, and one in the British Virgins. Windy had been reading about different anchorages in the Virgin Islands and asked George about several of them. Tova wanted to know about the beaches and where she could find a deserted one. When five o'clock arrived Windy ducked inside to fetch four more Heinekens, coming out dressed in a little halter dress.

"Did those steaks thaw out?" asked George, as his watch ended at six. "I'll start to cook."

"If there is any lettuce left I'll make a salad," offered Windy, standing.

"We have asparagus and potatoes too," said George.

"What's that over there?" said Tova, pointing to the southeast.

36

Bill Sanderlee stood on the aft deck, watching two divers pack up their gear. A large black inflatable boat sat tied along the stern boarding platform. Near the back of the house, Lieutenant Richards talked to someone via a handheld radio and two technicians packed away the electronics left behind by the Chinese boarders. A hundred yards to the west, the United States Naval destroyer the USS Carney sat ominously. For two hours both boats had remained motionless.

Lieutenant Richards approached. "The divers have removed all of the listening devices from the bottom of the hull. We will be leaving soon."

"Thank you," said Bill. "I have five crewmembers agreeing to stay with me."

"We will take those that want to leave back," said Richards. "Cynthia Campbell too."

A woman with long brown hair approached. "Hi, I'm Betsy, remember? I checked the food supply, we still have a freezer full of stuff."

"Thanks," said Bill. "Is Randall up in the pilot house?"

"Yes, he's figuring out the electronics."

"I'll leave you two alone," said Richards. "When we are ready to leave I will tell you. The sailing vessel *Frihet* is approaching from the north. I am sure they will be contacting you soon."

"Thanks," said Bill. "Betsy, can you arrange a meeting of the crew in a half hour? Let's do it up in the pilot house."

"Of course," she beamed, happy with the new authority. "Is there anything else?"

"Not right now." Bill started for the stairs.

Stepping into the pilot house, he said, "Can you run this boat?"

"Of course," said Randall. "I have the radar up and running, with an intruder alarm set for five miles. We have a vessel approaching from the north, I am guessing a sailboat because of its slow speed. The autopilot is programmed for a point just north of the island of Tortola. Craig is down checking the engine, but everything appears to be in order."

"Good. Set up a watch schedule, whatever you think is best. You can include me in the rotation if you want. I want to learn to run this boat too."

Randall smiled. "Yes sir. The boat almost sails itself though, so you may not be needed."

"You are the acting captain."

"If you look, you can see the approaching boat," said Randall, pointing out the starboard door.

*

George stood beside Windy and Tova in the cockpit, looking at the stationary motor yacht and the United States Naval destroyer ahead. Beth remained in the galley cleaning up the last of the dinner dishes.

"That's *A New Beginning*," said George. "The boat we had dinner aboard in Bermuda."

""I thought so," said Windy. "What are they doing?"

"I don't know," said George.

The destroyer started to move, but the yacht remained motionless.

George picked up the microphone, "*A New Beginning, A New Beginning,* this is the sailing vessel *Frihet,* come in please."

"George, Bill here. It's good to see you guys."

"It's a surprise to see you. Are you all right?"

"We had a little incident here, but the Navy helped us straighten things out. We're all set now."

"Good," answered George, not sure what to make of the story. "Are you on your way soon?"

"Shortly. We'll see you in the Virgin Islands."

George adjusted the autopilot back to 165° magnetic and *Frihet* turned a little to starboard. "We'll arrive tomorrow night sometime. I'll look for you there."

"We'll be there before you," said Bill. "Have a safe trip."

"You too," said George.

In western sky purple clouds made long streaks that reflected on the glassy sea. "The air feels cooler, maybe drier," said George.

"I thought so too," said Tova. She had put on an oversize tank top that fit like a dress. The thin fabric hid little. "Maybe it is because I had too much sun."

"Dress warm," said George. "I'm going to get some sleep. Windy's watch doesn't start for almost three hours."

Tova smiled. "Can you stay up with me a while?"

"He needs some sleep," said Windy.

"I do," said George, suddenly feeling very tired.

He dropped down into the cabin. The galley looked spotless and Beth had gone into her cabin to read. In his own cabin he shut the door, dropped his shorts, and stepped into the shower. Motoring on a flat sea sure made life aboard easier, but he wished to be sailing again. It had been a long day, but his next watch wasn't until six in the morning. George hoped for a good night's sleep.

The warm water washed away some of the sleepiness. As he scraped away his whiskers, he looked at the man in the mirror with the sun-bleached hair. Was he having fun? Yeah, the women were fun, and he loved their lack of clothing. He wondered if Windy was still in the cockpit with Tova. What would they be talking about?

The sheets felt cool when he slipped between them.

*

Nancy Atherson stood on the port deck of *Absent* and watched the lights of Tortola grow closer. The rescued crew from *Rose Blossom* sang and partied up on the foredeck, but she felt far from festive. When her cell phone showed two bars, she transferred the files from Emil's and Patrik's computers to Moscow. In the darkness she waited. If anyone had intercepted the communication she would likely be arrested.

"It's a nice evening," said Captain Moore, approaching. "The kids are happy to be here."

"They are," said Nancy. "I suppose most will only stay for the winter and then head north in the spring."

"Probably. What about you? Do you have plans after this assignment is over?"

She smiled. "I should be asking you what your plans are, now that you have lost *Rose Blossom*."

"I don't know. That old ship was my life. All I ever did was work on her or sail her. Finding another like her would probably be impossible."

"Was she insured?"

"Yes, but not for full replacement value. I doubt it will pay half what she was worth."

Music started up forward and a rousing cheer sounded on the foredeck, for what they couldn't see.

"Captain Able has been nice enough to offer me a bottle of wine," said Moore. "Would you like to share it with me?"

Nancy smiled. "That would be delightful. Can we get away from all the noise?"

"There's a bench on the aft deck, how about I meet you there in ten minutes?"

"Perfect."

*

Bill Sanderlee leaned against the open doorway of the pilot house and listened to Randall. The young man appeared to be a natural leader, with the rest of the crew listening attentively. In the dim red lights of the wheel house, they looked almost like a satanic cult. Randall ran through the basics of reading the radar and the operation of the boat. One person at a time would stand watch in the pilot house, but, at any time of concern, Randall was to be called. Trish volunteered to stand in as the cook, so she wouldn't be required to be part of the watch rotation. Everyone else would take three hour turns. It sounded like they were starting out on a journey around the world, not a hundred miles or so.

"We should be in St. Thomas tomorrow afternoon," said Randall, in closing. "Thank you all for staying aboard."

"One more thing," said Bill. "I too want to thank you all for staying. Tomorrow night we'll be in St. Thomas and we'll celebrate big time. I really appreciate this. There will be bonuses in your next paychecks."

Bill turned to walk aft, passing by the stairs that led down to the main deck, instead continuing to the pool area aft of the pilot house. From a temperature controlled locker he took a bottle of wine and a glass, then wrestled with the bottle's cork. After stripping off his clothes, he flicked on the underwater lights and settled into the pool. What a day, he thought, as he poured the wine. Never in his life had he experienced anything like the previous few days.

He settled back, floating weightless, remembering Cynthia's company. She had been fun, but he knew he should have suspected something. A wealthy man is always at risk of being taken advantage of, but being used to hide an espionage operation? Great sex can make a man do some mighty stupid things, and she was off the charts in that department. It seemed unbelievable that she worked for the Russians, and Hauglund too. Why had he been so gullible? They certainly had fooled him. He wondered if Cynthia would think of him as she flew back to Moscow.

"Mr. Sanderlee." It was Betsy, standing at the forward end of the pool deck. "Can I get you anything?" Weak white lights, inches above the edges of the deck and designed to illuminate the walking area, softly lit her face.

"Betsy," laughed Bill. "Call me Bill, please. You caught me...undressed. I apologize. And no, I do not need anything."

Betsy smiled. "The other day I brought you cold drinks when you and Cynthia were both naked. You don't shock me." She giggled. "How is the water?"

"Delightful," said Bill, sitting up straight in the far end. Her smile looked as bright as the morning sun. "How old are you Betsy?"

She laughed. "I don't think an employer is supposed to ask that, these days. But I'm twenty-three years old, if you really want to know."

He smiled, she was nineteen years younger than him. Company was what he needed, someone to talk to. Bill hesitated, then asked, "Would you like to share a bottle of wine and join me in a swim?"

"Naked?" The big smile never faded.

"You can go get a bathing suit, and I'll put mine on if it makes you feel better."

"Oh hell," she said, walking toward the pool and undoing the buttons of her white button uniform shirt.

37

At the touch, George flinched.

"Shhhh."

He blinked open his eyes. Almost no light found its way into his cabin. "Windy?"

"Quiet," she whispered.

He looked, but couldn't see the door, it had to be closed. "What are you doing?"

She brought her index finger to his lips, signaling silence. "Tova is asleep, snoring. Beth is on watch. It's a little after two."

"Beth will know what we are doing."

Windy smiled. "This was her idea. I told you she was fun. She thought it would be good for both of us."

"That figures." George slid back, making room on the bed, yet said "We can't."

Windy lifted the sheet and slipped into the empty space. "Why?"

She felt warm against is side. He blurted, "We agreed to talk when we got to the islands." Even in the dark he could see her smile.

"Actions speak louder than words."

What had Beth said to her? This certainly wasn't the reserved Windy he remembered from New England. Changes in latitude....

*

"Where are we?" asked Nancy Atherson, standing on the starboard deck and looking at the black outline of a mountain that rose above the sea.

The air smelled of tropical plants and waves swished against an unseen beach. To the west another island glistened like a Christmas tree. Each of them still held a glass of wine.

"Here comes the captain and Christine," said Captain Moore. "Let's ask them."

"It's a beautiful night," said Captain Able. Beside him Christine held his hand.

"It feels good to have arrived," said Moore. "Where exactly are we?"

"We're anchored off Lind Point, on the west end of the island of St. John. We'll clear in with customs in the morning." The thousand coki frogs shrieked on the shore. "Christine and I are going to open a bottle of champagne to celebrate arriving. Would you two like to join us up in the pilot house?"

Captain Moore glanced at Nancy. "We'd love that."

"I'd like to go back to my cabin for a minute," said Nancy. "I'll meet you there."

"Can I walk with you?" asked Moore.

"I'll only be a minute," she said, shaking her head.

Nancy walked to the door on the port side, went down one deck, and then aft to the cabin she shared with Christine. Inside she grabbed her laptop, carried it back up to the deck, and dropped if over the side.

*

The boat heeled to starboard, not much, but enough to wake George. Through the overhead hatch he saw sooty clouds and the genoa. The door to his cabin was hooked open and he heard someone come down the companionway. A puff of wind snaked in the open hatch and a drop of rain landed against his face.

He started to rise, but Beth appeared wearing a red Henry Lloyd rain jacket.

"It's starting to rain, just a squall," she said reaching up to close the hatch. "It will be over in a minute. I didn't want it to wake you."

George flopped back into the bed. Over him, Beth wore nothing inside the open jacket front and, in his half-awake state, he found her lean body erotically enticing. Hoping to get his mind elsewhere, he said, "How long have we been sailing?"

"Just a few minutes." She dogged down the final latch. "I'm not dripping on you, am I?" she laughed. "It got a wee bit wet outside."

"No. I was just admiring the view," he teased.

"I see the crew is at attention," she said, reaching to grip him through the sheet. "It's just like a tiller."

"Good God, Beth!" he squirmed away. "It's not my fault, it's on autopilot."

She let go and chuckled. "I'll take it as a compliment. When we get someplace I am going to make some good looking sailor think he's been caught in a hurricane. If it weren't for the other two on this boat you wouldn't be getting out of that bunk all day."

"That'll be a lucky guy," laughed George, wishing he'd worn something to bed.

"You were snoring up a storm last night. I think you were out for eight hours. You dreamed something too, and said things in your sleep."

"Said things?"

Smugly, Beth answered, "Yeah, it sounded like you called Windy's name. I suppose it could have been the weather you were dreaming about."

"I don't remember," lied George.

Rain started to pelt the cabin top.

"Your watch isn't for another half hour," said Beth, pinching his cheek as if he were a child. "Don't hurry to get up."

He watched the mosaic of rain on the hatch. Was Windy's visit all a dream? The details were fuzzy...he remembered trying to push her away and his willpower folding. It could have been a dream, he had dreamt almost the same things about Tova. Yet maybe it was real and Beth was playing games with him. Didn't Windy say her visit was Beth's idea? Beth loved to tease...he wouldn't put anything past her.

Rain pelted the boat and *Frihet* heeled to starboard. Water gurgled along the hull and he felt the acceleration.

George wished to be sailing alone, which would have been so peaceful. Or one woman would be okay. It wouldn't matter which, but with three on board and with two of them shuffling for his attention, there was too much potential for conflict. Shutting his eyes, he could still see Beth reaching for the hatch over his bed. George decided he needed to find something for a diversion.

He slipped from the sheets and pulled on his shorts. The air felt warm and humid. In the main cabin, Tova still wore a very thin jersey that had soaked in the rain. "How is our captain this morning?" she asked, smiling. Next to her the coffee pot gurgled.

"Sleepy," said George, trying hard to look somewhere else. Through the door of Windy's cabin he could see her sleeping peacefully among tussled sheets.

He dropped into the seat at the nav station to check the instruments, hoping to get his head back into sailing. Wind speed 14.5 knots 45° magnetic, boat speed 7.02 knots, heading 165° magnetic. The rain had let up, but still spattered the boat.

Opening his laptop, he waited for it to start up. Beth came down the companionway ladder still wearing the foul weather jacket. Her usually bouncy curls were wet and hung against her head.

"The captain is up," she said. "The rain is stopping, but I can see another squall ahead."

George said nothing, but checked his emails. The first email came from Brigitta.

George,
I am sorry for not getting back to you sooner. Work has been insane. Please forgive me.

I am in the Virgin Islands aboard a yacht leased by Harold. We are working with the Navy to trap or destroy the rogue drone. I understand Harold mentioned our plan to you while he was in Bermuda. When you arrive here we can go over the details.

On personal matters, you and I need to talk, to figure out if we have a life together. I am not happy doing what I am doing, I want to back up and start the last few months over. You are very important to me.

Love,
Brigitta

Ps – Has my sister made a pass at you yet? Just kidding, but she has a history of stealing the men in my life. Beware.

George shut the laptop, then climbed the companionway. Behind *Frihet* rain streaked down beneath a dark low cloud. Far ahead, another squall looked to be moving westerly.

"Coffee George?" asked Tova.

"Sure."

Beth came up carrying two mugs. "Are you all right?"

George wondered what showed on his face. "Something unexpected."

"An email from Brigitta?" guessed Beth. Sunlight peeked between the clouds, only to disappear a moment later.

He nodded. "I'm going up on the foredeck for a bit."

"Want company?"

George hesitated, Beth might be a jokester, but she was easy to talk to. Sulking never turned out well and usually it led to depression. He nodded. "Sure."

They stopped at the mast. "Everything is wet," said George.

Beth slipped off her jacket and dropped it ahead of the mast, inside out. They sat on it, each with a shoulder leaning against the mast. Flying fish skittered across the surface and foamy water swished away as the hull split the surface. Far to the east a Cory's shearwater coasted low over the wave tops.

"If it wasn't for the haze, we could probably see the islands by now," said George. "The haze is dust that blows from the Sahara Desert."

"I know that," said Beth, squinting. "Sometimes things are hard to see." She took a sip of her coffee. "Does she want to start over?"

"Wants to talk."

The sun peeked through another break in the clouds, creating sum beams that angled down to the sea.

"How do you feel about it?"

George toyed with his coffee cup. "The aching had passed. I was starting to move on."

A dozen boat lengths ahead, another shearwater swooped low far in front of the boat, clearing the wave tops by inches.

"My opinion, whether you want it or not, is she is not being fair. She has treated you badly. This is the second time, is it not? Or is it more? Didn't she run off with a man in Rhode Island a year ago? The woman clearly does not know what she wants." Her English accent sounded stern.

They watched a large flying fish leap from the water and glide away to port. George sipped his coffee, wondering how Beth knew about the man in Rhode Island.

"Did you talk Windy into sneaking into my cabin last night?" he asked.

Beth lightly slapped his thigh. "Would I do that?"

"She said you did."

"You must have dreamt it. We talked about how loud you were snoring." Beth laughed. "Did you enjoy the dream?"

George nodded. "Yes, I don't remember the details. I had a similar dream about Tova a couple of nights ago." Had Beth avoided answering him?

"You poor boy, sailing with two beautiful women who are nearly naked all the time. It must almost be torture at times."

"I count three beautiful women," said George. "And one of which *is* naked all the time."

"I don't consider myself beautiful," said Beth. "Average maybe. But thank you."

"I'll argue with you on that, but the other two women are trouble."

From aft came Tova's voice, "Do either of you two want eggs for breakfast?"

George shook his head, "None for me."

"Me either," said Beth.

Turning back to George, she asked, "What are you going to do?"

38

"Did you check the galley?" asked Captain Able.

"Yes," said Christine. "Maybe she is in Captain Moore's cabin."

"I knocked on his door and woke him. He walked Nancy back to her cabin after we finished the champagne, and then went to his own cabin."

"I'll walk through the boat again," said Christine. "Her laptop was missing from her cabin too. Where could she be?"

Captain Able glanced at his watch, almost seven. He had planned to be on the way to the United Stated Customs office by then. Harold Habit would be expecting them before noon.

Earlier, he woke to the chatter of his computer's printer. An email said the NSA had intercepted an encrypted cell phone call from a phone registered to Nancy Atherson. His instructions were to detain Miss Atherson until the Department of Homeland Security could talk to her.

*

Bill Sanderlee stood in the pilot house, looking at the purplish gray outline of Tortola far ahead. A few miles closer, and not nearly as tall, Jost Van Dyke hid over the horizon. One of the crew, Craig, sat at the helm. The autopilot did the actual steering, but Craig kept an eye on the instruments and radar.

"How is everything?" asked Randall, as he stepped into the pilot house.

Bill said, "Fine. We're still a long ways off, but it is nice to see the islands."

Randall looked at the instruments. "Mr. Sanderlee, you'll be needing a new captain," he said. "Someone with papers. I'll be taking the test the end of the month."

Bill nodded. "I will keep that in mind."

Betsy stepped into the pilot house. "Trish made home fried potatoes and has eggs and bacon cooking. Who wants some?"

They placed their orders and she left.

The computer next to the helm beeped and spit out a printed page.

"Mr. Sanderlee," said Randall, handing him the page.

Mr. Sanderlee,

The United States Navy would like to ask you a few questions. After clearing customs into the United States Virgin Islands, please travel to the anchorage in the northern part of Magen's Bay. There will be several vessels anchored there, further instructions to follow.

Captain Winston L. Olson
United States Navy

Bill folded the paper and stuffed it in his pocket. "What time do you think we will be there?"

"The U. S. islands? We'll be there about dark," said Randall. "I am not sure what the hours are for the United States Customs on St. John, but we can anchor off and clear in the morning."

"What about the British islands?"

"We can make the customs office on Jost Van Dyke before it closes," said Randall.

"Let's shoot for that," said Bill. "Is there anywhere to go ashore for dinner?"

"Foxy's," said Randall. "Probably the most famous beach bar in the world. We can get dinner ashore there."

"Let's plan on it."

Bill stepped out the door and went aft, and then down one deck. He almost collided with Betsy coming out of a door and carrying a tray of dinner plates.

"I am sorry," said Bill.

"No, it is my fault," said Betsy. "I should watch where I am going." Her smile seemed perpetual.

"About yesterday, last night," fumbled Bill. "I enjoyed talking to you. It was exactly what I needed."

Betsy beamed. "Me too. We'd been through a lot."

"I don't want you to get the wrong idea."

"We didn't do anything," laughed Betsy. "Just sat around naked in a swimming pool, talking about life and drinking some very fine wine. What is unusual about that?"

Her laughter made Bill feel better. "Nothing, I suppose. It was fun. Tonight we'll be anchored at the island of Jost Van Dyke. Will you have dinner ashore with me?"

Betsy grinned. "I would love that."

*

Nancy Atherson pushed her wet clothes into a plastic bag and then the bag into her backpack. Dressed in her dry clothes, she looked like any of the progressive eco-friendly tourists that visit the island of St. John, with Birkenstock sandals, baggy cotton shorts, and wire rimmed glasses. A tropical print scarf tied around her neck added a dash of color. A path along the shore took her behind a house sticking out on a point and then along a beach toward the lights of The Resort.

Earlier, after slipping silently off the boarding platform of *Absent*, the swim ashore in the dark had been uneventful. There, amongst the trees behind the soft sand of Solomon's Beach, she changed into dry clothes that she had brought ashore in a plastic garbage bag.

A fist full of American hundred dollar bills in her pack gave her a sense of security. It would be easy to stay undetected on an island bustling with tourists, and in a sailor's bar somewhere she would meet a boater who would take her offshore to a designated pair of coordinates. There, a Russian submarine would take her home.

In the lower latitudes, the sailors tended to be a shifty lot and she counted on that.

*

George sat against the railing at the back of the cockpit, with *Frihet* charging along at 8.25 knots in the fifteen knot tradewinds. Once he thought he saw the peak of Tortola poking over the horizon ahead, but eventually decided it was his imagination. For a few seconds a dolphin appeared to windward, where it did a flip and danced beside the boat, only to disappear as fast as it arrived and before he could say something so the women could see it too.

Around *Frihet* the empty sea sparkled. Had the dolphin been his imagination too? Stories were often told of shorthanded sailors hallucinating from lack of sleep. What was real?

Soon they would be back in civilization and the freedom of the sea would be over. It had been quite a trip that he would remember the rest of his life. But it would be nice to eat in a restaurant and walk on land. The end of any offshore passage always brought mixed feelings and this one was no different.

Ahead, Beth sat at the front of the cockpit, reading a book with her wild mane tamed in a ponytail. The only things she wore were her sunglasses and the ear buds that she listened through. George smiled…she was quite a woman.

Tova chose to spend her last day at sea on a towel ahead of the mast, soaking up the sun in an allover tan. The sisters might look alike, but Brigitta seldom took the time to savor life like that. Her skin had taken on the color of bronze.

George wished he had a novel to read, something to keep his mind occupied. Not far above the eastern horizon a United States Navy jet flew, heading south. Twice since dawn George had seen military aircraft.

To his left, Windy sat with a book open.

"How's the book?" he asked.

"All right," she answered, shutting it. "I have read better."

She had pulled her strawberry blonde hair back to make it behave in the wind, but an errant strand wandered across the gold rim of her sunglasses. She brushed it back to capture it behind an ear.

"How did you sleep last night?" he asked.

"Fine." She smiled. "Beth and I were laughing at your snoring. You were dead to the world."

Windy sat upright to look over the cabin top. Water whispered along the hull. She looked innocent enough, maybe her visit to his cabin had been a dream. From the safely behind his dark glasses, he looked at her curves and clearly remembered touching…so warm and soft.

He said, "I was tired."

"Any sign of land yet?"

"No," said George, then bringing the subject back, added, "I dreamt you snuck into my cabin and we made love."

Windy settled back and reached across to touch his arm. "Really? Was it good?"

"Heavenly."

"I dreamt something similar."

George smiled...she looked beautiful. Her white bikini bottom looked the size of a business card. A gold chain hung around her neck and gold hoops hung from her ears. He teased, "You are the most dressed woman on the boat."

She shrugged. "It's fun to dress up a little bit. You said freedom of the sea, so I guess that is freedom to wear nothing or something. I almost put on a sarong like Tova likes to wear, but decided on this instead."

He smiled. "You look lovely. Whatever works for you."

With a grin she grabbed the cuff of his shorts and gave them a tug, saying, "You are the most clothed person on board, all of the time. Why is that?"

George fidgeted and gave his standard answer. "I'm shy I guess."

The boat heeled a tad and surged ahead in a puff of wind. Water babbled along the hull. Windy faced into the wind and fussed with her ponytail, containing it with a shear scarf. The cloth waved at George.

Turning back, Windy said, "You heard from Brigitta today, didn't you?"

He nodded. "Yes. She wants to talk, maybe try to get back together."

"What do you want?"

He looked ahead, trying to see what wasn't there. Tortola still hid in the haze. "I was moving on," he said. "It felt like time."

"Are you still moving on?"

"I don't know."

"She hasn't treated you well. It's been all about her."

"I know."

A wave slapped against the port forward quarter, sending spray up into the air. For a moment the droplets sparkled like diamonds and seemed to freeze in the air, but then dropped into the sea with a hiss. Overhead, a lone commercial jet flew across the eastern sky, creating a long blemish in the expanse of blue. Silently, they watched it disappear to the south.

"What are you going to do?" asked Windy.

George wanted to take Windy in his arms, but he also knew that if Tova sat there he might want her in his arms. Or even Beth. Why couldn't his logical mind sort through the emotional clutter? The temptation? Was he that weak willed? Maybe the idea of the trip south with three women was a really bad one.

Windy opened her book and went back to reading.

At least he could talk to her. She enjoyed sailing for the sake of sailing. It was something they shared. Sea spray dusted George's sunglasses and he took them off to clean them.

Up on the cabin top, Tova looked like Brigitta, a Scandinavian goddess, though she certainly wasn't Brigitta. Brigitta would have been down inside the boat working at a computer, trying to solve some problem.

He looked at Beth, sitting at the front of the cockpit with her ear buds in, oblivious to George and Windy. Or was she? She knew Windy had a thing for him long before he did and guessed Tova to be trouble too. How did she perceive things so clearly that went right by him?

She had quickly sized up Brigitta and pointed out you always want most what you cannot have. He knew that. Was that the only reason he wanted Brigitta?

George looked at the empty horizon. Who would he want to be sailing alone with on an ocean passage?

"Windy, when we get to the Virgin Islands," he said, "Harold Habit wants to catch the rogue drone using an old wood boat as bait. He's asked me to sail it. Would you sail with me?"

Windy's face lit up. "Of course I would."

"The Navy would be there, Harold's boats too, so the danger would be minimal."

"What about Beth and Tova?"

"Do you think we need them?"

"No."

"Brigitta?"

He shook his head.

Beth looked up from her reading and smiled.

39

Sven Olson eased the main sheet a tad, squinted at the sail, and then surveyed the sparkling empty ocean around them. Life felt certainly grand. For twenty-nine days he and his family sailed their forty-six foot Colin Archer designed sailboat, *Fresh Air,* downwind from the Azores, having left Oslo the previous spring. The trip had been planned for years and finally his daughters, ages three, four, and six, were old enough. Somewhere to the south, just over the horizon, lay the Virgin Islands, but their landfall would be further west in Cuba.

The trip had been uneventful, except for the light wind. Boats of Colin Archer's design were known for their stoutness, not speed, so the trip had taken longer than initially planned, but that was of little concern. *Fresh Air* contained everything they needed.

Daily, Sven's wife, Leha, homeschooled their children, which took up most of the morning, then the family played games, read to the children, and sang while Sven played his guitar. Cooking and normal everyday chores took up a little bit of each day, but everything they did was turned into a learning experience for the children.

Onboard, they had plenty of water and food, and even grew lettuce in a box on the cabin top. Solar power kept the batteries charged to run a tiny refrigerator and lights. Purposely, they left with no long range radio communication, instead relying on short range VHF and a World Band Receiver to hear weather reports. Of course they had Emergency Position Indicating Radio Beacons in case of an emergency, both inside against a bulkhead and stowed in the eight-person life raft that sat securely on deck ahead of the mast. With a boat as strongly built as *Fresh Air*, Sven knew they never would need the life raft.

Sven watched the oldest, Elsa, carefully pour water on the lettuce. She stood atop the slowly swaying cabin as easily as one might stand on a concrete sidewalk. Elsa knew water was precious and she took great care to waste none.

Ebba, the youngest, sat on his wife's knee as she braided the young girl's thick sun-bleached hair. Ebba loved to wear a single braid down the middle of her back and would giggle wildly while she swung it about like a rope tail.

Down inside the boat the third child, Maja, played. She was different than the other two, content to play alone for hours. Sven would never admit it to anyone, but Maja was his favorite. When he did maintenance on the engine, Maja would watch and ask questions. She appeared to have an unusually strong mechanical aptitude.

The boat stopped with a thunk.

Sven jumped up and looked over the side, expecting to see a container fallen from a ship or maybe a large floating tree or even a piling. Instead, an enormous gray shape under the water backed away from *Fresh Air* until it nearly disappeared into the blue.

He leapt to the companionway. No water appeared to be leaking in. Leha shouted something. Elsa had fallen onto the starboard side deck. Sven carried her back to the cockpit.

Another thump jolted the boat upward several inches.

From a locker, Sven passed out life jackets. The children had been drilled in emergency preparedness and each silently put on their own.

Fresh Air went upward again, up and up, until she tipped to port. Ebba screamed, almost falling from the boat. Leha caught the young girl by the wrist.

Sven knew the boat had slid off the top of whatever it was that rammed them. Fearing another attack, he went forward to launch the life raft.

With a thunder-like crack, *Fresh Air* shook and tilted far to port. The sight of the mast hitting the water sickened Sven. Clinging to the nearly vertical deck, he pulled the release and kicked the life raft container into the sea. Immediately it inflated.

Water rushed in the companionway. *Fresh Air* was drowning.

Sven yanked the raft alongside their sinking home and tried to calm the children as they clambered along the leaning deck. One by one they stepped into the liferaft. Dashing back to the cockpit, he grabbed two five gallon containers of fresh water, then climbed into the raft himself, praying that whatever sunk *Fresh Air* would not go after the life raft.

The EPIRB aboard the life raft started transmitting their position to satellites.

With the large military presence in the area, their rescue happened within hours.

*

Nancy Atherson listened to the throaty growl of the twin inboard engines. Bob tossed the line onto the dock, spit over the side, and then climbed the ladder to the flying bridge. The boat looked far better than she imagined it would, with glistening white topsides and unblemished teak trim.

After reaching Red Hook on the ferry from St. John, Nancy had felt much safer, blending in with the throngs of cruise ship tourists visiting the island of St. Thomas. Sending off a text, she learned a Russian submarine hid twenty miles to the north, awaiting instructions. Coordinates were agreed on.

At a waterfront bar she had sat next to a slender man with his hair pulled back into a short ponytail. It turned out Bob owned a sport fishing boat and loved to talk about it and fishing. After a couple of drinks, she guessed enough about him to know he badly needed cash. She offered a thousand United Stated dollars to be taken offshore to a particular set of coordinates, never mentioning it would be a one way trip for her. Bob had been around long enough to know that anyone looking for a ride offshore to a particular location was probably picking up drugs dropped from an aircraft, so he had asked for five grand. Feigning reluctance, she had agreed.

Nancy followed Bob up to the bridge. "Your boat looks beautiful."

"Thanks. It's a Rybovich, built in 1954," he said. "It's mahogany planked. I rebuilt the engines myself." He pushed the throttles ahead and eased out of the slip. "She's forty-eight feet long and will do over thirty knots."

Nancy smiled. "We are in no hurry." Pulling out her phone, she sent one short text message.

Pillsbury Sound, between the east end of St. Thomas and the west end of St. John, sparkled. White sails poked across the sea and motorboats sped along. St. John appeared to be a lush tropical paradise, with white homes sprinkled on the steep hillsides. Beyond the point called Redhook, Bob gunned the engines. Within minutes they passed between Thatch Cay and Grass Cay, heading north out of the Caribbean Sea and into the Atlantic Ocean.

Bob grinned and pointed, "Those birds are called brown boobies," he said, laughing. "I like brown boobies."

I bet you do, thought Nancy, brown ones, white ones, and every color in between.

Two of the birds flew toward Grass Cay, then one dove into the sea only to pop up a few feet further on. High overhead, dark frigate birds made lazy circles, looking like lost kites.

Bob said, "Those frigate birds like to steal their meals from the boobies." He pushed the throttles further ahead and the engines hummed. White spray spit out either side of the boat.

Ahead, several islands broke up the horizon. Bob rattled off their names, but Nancy didn't pay attention. They would pass between the two largest, Great Tobago and Jost Van Dyke, and never be seen again.

The next day the United States Navy would pinpoint the location of their transmitting EPIRB, but a thorough search would only turn up pieces of mahogany floating on the surface.

*

Wilmoth Hollingshead nervously looked at the dark hillsides of St. John to starboard. Waves sloshed upward among the rocks along the shore, then settled down as if exhausted. Off the stern, the sun had set behind the island of St. Thomas, but it was too early to see bright lights on the hillsides. To port, a dark blue ferry pushed through the sea in the other direction, heading for Charlotte Amalie. Soon they would be turning east next to Whistling Cay and entering The Narrows.

The day before, Hollingshead had heard the warnings about a deranged mechanical sea monster attacking wood vessels. The idea sounded preposterous, but he did not ignore it. If he were going to be trapped in a marina somewhere, he preferred it to be in the British Virgin Islands. Late in the afternoon, he decided to move his classic old seventy-eight foot Trumpy motor yacht, *Mary*, to a slip at the Village Cay Marina in Road Town.

His captain and mate, a husband and wife team named Richard and Rachael Hob, had appeared hesitant, but agree to move the boat. Hollingshead sat on a leather stool next to the helm. Richard stood beside him in the wheel house, his hand on the wheel and ignoring the empty seat behind him. Hollingshead wasn't sure where Rachael was, but guessed she might be aft in the galley.

Hollingshead had owned *Mary* for twenty-two years, naming her after his late wife. *Mary* had been built in 1928 and meticulously maintained since then. The double-planked mahogany hull had recently been refastened and never leaked a drop. The shiny black topsides contrasted with the reddish-brown mahogany cabin. Richard and Rachael kept the bronze hardware gleaming and the varnish spotless. And once a year, Hollingshead brought in a professional varnishing team from Antigua to apply a fresh coat to be certain the varnish stayed flawless. Every five years the boat was hauled for a fresh coat of black Awlgrip on the topsides. He told himself it was done in memory of his deceased wife, but in reality she never liked boats.

The previous year Hollingshead slept aboard his boat two hundred and twenty nights. It was a number he certainly hoped to top. He glanced aft, hoping to see Rachael with her long lean legs. Someday he hoped to have a woman in his life again, but the years were slipping away.

The twin Detroit Diesels hummed below the deck, pushing the boat along at almost ten knots. He toyed with the end of his long white mustache. "How long until we are there?" he asked.

"Less than an hour," said Richard.

A white fiberglass sailboat motored in the other direction. Hollingshead turned to watch it pass, then said, "Those boats all look alike to me."

"Me too," said Richard, who had a habit of not disagreeing with his boss.

The sea surged upward between the dark bony ledges along Mary's Point to starboard, only to retreat a moment later. Tamarind trees covered Mary's Point up to the top, several hundred feet above the ocean and they could smell the land. Through the canyon-like cut between Whistling Cay and Mary's Point they could see Francis Bay, where three sailboats sat anchored. To port, the long narrow Great Thatch Cay walled in the north side of The Narrows. Ahead, small whitecaps nipped at the wave tops.

"Are you nervous?" asked Richard. He had never seen Hollingshead toy with the end of his mustache before. His usually bright blue eyes appeared a shade of gray.

"The whole idea is outrageous," he said. "A rogue mechanical monster attacking wood boats? It sounds like something out of a low budget science fiction movie."

The north side of Mary's Point rose vertically out of the sea, creating a formidable wall to starboard. Legend said escaped slaves jumped to their death off the point rather than be recaptured. Beyond, only empty forest covered the hillsides of St. John. Great Thatch, to the north, looked equally as uninhabited. Only the lights above the town of West End, a couple of miles ahead on the island of Tortola, showed signs of life.

"This looks like a perfect spot for an ambush," said Hollingshead. "We'll be abeam of Leinster Bay in a few minutes, duck in there. We'll anchor for the night where it is shallow."

"Are you sure?" asked Richard. "We'll be docked in well under an hour."

"All of my life I have run my businesses on gut feelings," said Hollingshead. "I have a bad feeling."

The impact took the entire bottom out of the old Trumpy, creating such a shock that the windows in front of the wheel house cracked in a million directions. A severed battery cable instantly killed everything electronic on board. The battery powered hand-held VHF fell from its wall-mount never to be seen again.

Richard initially fell to his knees, but then dashed aft, looking for Rachael. She was already at the tender, which hung from davits at the stern. By the time they had it launched and Hollingshead aboard, *Mary*'s decks were awash.

40

Mother lay on the sandy bottom in one hundred and eighty feet of water. In her months of traveling, she had never seen a place with so many small boats. Best of all, the warm water made communicating with her sharks easier. Under her instruction, the sharks poked through the dozens of bays and marinas searching out boats made of the unknown material.

Not many miles to the north, the bottom of the ocean dropped off into one of the deepest places on Earth. The deep water offered sanctuary if Mother were pursued. In the meantime, she waited silently.

*

Frihet's crew listened helplessly to the chatter on the VHF. A passing sailboat had spotted the sinking Trumpy and called the Coast Guard. Three boats reached the troubled vessel within a few minutes. With only the bow of *Mary* remaining above the water, a boat from the Virgin Islands National Park Police took the three people from their tender.

"They were lucky," said Beth.

George nodded his head. Tortola still lay six miles ahead, with pinpricks of light from scattered homes showing its mountainous silhouette. "We'll be anchored in a little over an hour," he said. "When we are a mile off of Tortola we'll run along the coast. It's deep water all the way."

Windy asked if anybody wanted anything, but nobody did. She disappeared inside the boat to come out a few minutes later wearing shorts and a baggy cotton shirt.

The day had been much like the others, with reading, sunning, or eating the main activities. But somehow things felt different, as each of them knew the trip was nearly over. Even before they heard the distress call, the somber mood surprised George. He had expected a bit of revelry. They had just finished eating a quiet dinner when the VHF came to life with chatter about the sinking Trumpy.

Beth came out of the boat wearing jeans and a tee shirt. George smiled, "Well, look at you. I don't recognize you in clothes."

The boat surged ahead in a puff of wind. "It almost feels good," said Beth. "Almost."

Tova said, "Are we supposed to be getting dressed?" She still wore only a tiny sarong tied around her hips.

"Whatever you want," said George.

Tova gave him a smile. "I am not getting dressed until I have to."

With the crew in the cockpit, George proceeded to tell them everything he knew about Harold Habit's plan to capture or stop the rogue under sea drone.

"Brigitta is going to be there?" said Tova, looking surprised.

"Yes," said George. "I am not sure what her part is in all of this."

"I was planning to leave when we got to St. Thomas," said Beth. "Do you mind if I stick around for a few days? I'd love to see this through."

George wondered if she wanted to see the drone stopped or the ongoing soap opera. "Of course it's all right," he said.

"Are you going to sail the wooden boat alone?" asked Beth.

"I asked Windy to sail with me. Two of us should be able to handle it. I know nothing more about the boat."

"Windy?" said Tova.

"She's proven herself in stressful sailing situations before," said George.

Tova turned to look ahead at Tortola.

About a mile off the beaches they steered west to run downwind along the dark shape of the island. With the drop in the apparent wind, they could hear steel pan music coming from one of the bars in Cane Garden Bay. Millions of stars made the night sky appear a shade of gray. They sailed past the Thatch Island Cut and the entrance to Sopers Hole. Off Great Thatch Cay's western end, they turned south, crossing The Narrows and into United States waters.

In the shadow of St. John, with the moon hidden behind its peaks, the night felt inky. To port, Mary's Point reached to the sky and blotted out the stars. Whistling Cay appeared a black shadow close to starboard. Radar guided them through and showed three boats anchored in Francis Bay, but none in Maho Bay a short distance beyond.

At a little after eleven o'clock, George walked up to the bow to free the anchor in twenty feet of water off Maho Point. With a slash it went down and the boat drifted back. The high mountains of St. John wrapped around the bay, creating a wind free oasis where the warm humid air smelled of the lush plants ashore. Stars overhead reflected on the glassy water and the only sound came from screaming coki frogs ashore.

Turning, he bumped into Tova's bare chest.

"I'm sorry," he blurted.

"No, I am sorry," she said. "I stood too close."

"I didn't know you were here." Her tan skin blended with the night, but her blonde hair almost blazed

"What a beautiful night," she said, reaching for his hand.

Her fingers felt tiny and warm and soft. George glanced aft and saw no one. "Shall we go to the cockpit and have a drink to celebrate?" he asked.

Her fingers squeezed his. "Can we spend some time sailing about the islands, I mean after all this mess with the drone is over?" She stood so close he felt her words on his face.

"I hope so," he said. "Let's go back to the cockpit." He saw Windy come out the companionway carrying a candle inside a hurricane shade. George slipped his hand from Tova's and placed it lightly on a bare shoulder. "Let's go aft."

As *Frihet* settled back on her anchor, he followed her into the cockpit. "Does anybody want a drink?"

"I opened a bottle of wine," said Beth, from inside.

"Scotch for me," said Windy, heading back down the companionway.

"Scotch for me too," chimed Tova.

Three tumblers and a bottle of Dalwhinnie appeared on the bridge deck, followed by a bottle of Hall Eighteen-Seventy-Three Cabernet and wine glasses. George poured a healthy inch in each of the tumblers, then started to open the wine. With a clunk, Windy dropped an ice cube into each of the scotches.

"Does anyone want music?" asked Windy.

"I'd rather just listen to the coki frogs," said George, sitting at the back of the cockpit with a tumbler in his hand.

"Me too," said Tova, sitting next to George. Under the bimini, the candle cast a soft yellow light, and beyond everything looked black, except the stars overhead and lights on St. Thomas in the distance to the west.

"It feels weird to not be moving," said Windy, noticing where Tova had sat. "And it is warm, sticky warm. Even when we had no wind out on the ocean, the boat's movement kept the air flowing." She pinched the cotton of her top to pull it away from her skin. "My clothes are sticking to me."

"How about a toast?" said George, raising his glass. "To one of the best crews I have ever sailed with, and certainly the best looking."

With a laugh they all took a drink.

Windy sat across from George. "How far is it to where we clear customs tomorrow?"

"It's only a few miles from here," said George.

A Coast Guard Securité message interrupted from the VHF radio, asking all wood boats to stay in port until further notice, and then went on to briefly explain the danger.

Beth, sitting at the front of the cockpit laughed. "It's about time they admitted the folly."

"It's going to cost Harold Habit a lot of money," said Windy, "between legal bills and replacing that drone."

"You think he'll replace it?" asked Tova. "I would give up and retire, if I had his money."

"I don't think he is that type," said George. "Money isn't what motivates him. He's an overachiever. His work is his passion.

"I'm dreaming about ice cream," said Beth, changing the subject. "Chocolate ice cream. That's what I'm looking forward to when I get to land."

"I've been thinking about steak," said George. "A big ribeye steak with a baked potato, maybe some red wine to go with it."

"I want to find somebody to do my nails," said Tova, laughing. "A manicure and a massage, that's what I am looking forward too. Then a trip to an empty beach."

Windy sipped her glass, then said, "I just want to sail among the islands."

The women asked questions about the various islands and George answered the best he could. Beth knew much about the British Virgins, having worked aboard boats out of Road Town, so she filled in some information. George offered more scotch, and Windy and Tova both held out their glasses. Beth's wine bottle was already more than half empty.

Tova asked how hard it was to learn to scuba dive, which brought on questions about dive spots and snorkeling.

"Speaking of water," said Beth, standing and pulling her jersey off over her head, "I'm going to slip into the water to float for a bit and cool off, then head to bed. It's late."

"Me too," said Windy. "A dip and a freshwater rinse. Who's up for a swim? I'll get towels."

George said nothing, but when Windy came back out of the boat she tossed a fourth towel at him.

In the dim candlelight, he watched the women shed their clothing, climb down to the swim platform, and then slip into the sea. Phosphorescence swirled around their hands and legs, making them giggle.

George stood up and said, "I'll see you in the morning." Then his cell phone rang.

41

George found the phone in a cubby beside the navigation station. The screen said wireless caller. He answered, "Hello?"

"George, we have you on satellite," came Brigitta's voice. "In the morning, clear in when the customs office opens at seven and come right over. We need to go over things with you."

They were watching George and his crew? Who were they? Harold? Harold and who? And no civil greeting…just down to business?

"We'll be there when we can," he said, then shut off the phone.

What was wrong with that woman? Could her rude conversation be related to the head injury she had the previous summer? Or was Tova right, Brigitta only focused on her own world?

He climbed the companionway stairs to find what was left of his scotch and downed it with one swallow. Tova floated on her back several feet behind the boat, with shards of phosphorescence clinging to her skin. Holding onto the swim platform, Windy and Beth talked about something while swirling platters of light danced between their feet.

George stepped out from under the bimini, dropped his shorts, then glanced defiantly up at the heavens before stepping down to the swim platform.

"Our fearless captain has gotten over his shyness," teased Beth. "You need to work on that tan, I thought the moon had come out."

Windy laughed, "In a way it did."

He dove in and popped up near Tova. The water felt good, clearing away the stickiness of the humidity and some of the fuzziness brought on by the alcohol.

"Did I hear your cell phone ring?" asked Beth, starting to swim towards him.

"Yeah."

"Who was it?"

He swam two strokes back toward the swim platform. "Nobody."

"Brigitta?" guessed Tova.

He nodded. "Yes. We're being watched by one of Harold's satellites."

"How much can they see," she asked.

Reaching for the swim platform, he said, "Well, enough to recognize our faces."

Windy asked, "Yikes. Can they tell we're skinny dipping?"

"Easily."

Windy laughed. "Oh my. Can we be arrested?"

"What did she want?" asked Beth.

"She told me to get through customs, first thing when they open, and then rush over to where she is, so we can be briefed."

"All business, that's my sister."

Over the top of St. John, the nearly full moon peeked, illuminating the Maho Bay in dim white light. The three sailboats anchored in Francis Bay glowed. Palm trees cast shadows on the silvery sandy beaches. Among whirls of phosphorescence, Tova swam toward the boat with her hair shining white.

"Let's give them something to really talk about," laughed Beth, moving closer to George's left.

Giggling, Windy boxed in George from his right, and said, "With the moon out they can really see us."

George started up the ladder, "I'm out of here."

*

The research vessel *Absent* sat anchored in fifty feet of water near the north end of Magen's Bay, a large bay on the north side of the island of St. Thomas. Her bow pointed into the light easterly breeze and, inside a room filled with electronic gear, three technicians listened. They had cracked the frequency and deciphered the language, letting them listen to the shark drones communication with the larger drone known as Mother.

Three miles to the north a United States Naval destroyer moved slowly to the east. The helicopter pad on the back was empty, as the aircraft flew almost continuous missions searching for the missing drone and also submarines from other countries that might try to intercept the vessel.

Just south of *Absent*, anchored further into Magen's Bay, a two hundred and twenty-three foot motor yacht named *Number One* hung on her anchor. Harold Habit had chartered *Number One* for three months at a discounted rate of $48,000 per week from a friend. The boat featured two helicopter pads over the aft deck, a feature Harold needed. Coming and going from the boat would be easier that way and also the aircraft would be used to locate and hopefully trap the fugitive drone.

Frihet dropped anchor just south of *Number One*. As she settled back on her anchor line, a large -inflatable pushed by three two hundred and fifty horsepower outboards came alongside.

"George," said Harold Habit, as the helmsman brought the tender abeam. "You are here early. We saw you arrive in Maho Bay late last night and I guessed we wouldn't see you until late."

"Brigitta called and said to get here ASAP," answered George.

Harold looked perplexed. "Called?"

"Yes, my cell phone." George laughed. "It was the first time it rang in ages."

"Well, come aboard and we'll take you over to *Number One*," said Harold. "All of you."

Earlier, the morning air had felt chilly as they motored by The Resort and along the white sand beaches. Clearing through Customs had been painless, even with a foggy heads caused by late night partying. In the light air they motored downwind across Pillsbury Sound, watching the ferries scurry between the islands and the sport fishing boats head for the fishing grounds of the North Drop.

Young crewmembers offered dock lines as the tender came alongside the open boarding port in the starboard side of *Number One*. George thought it looked like the entrance to a boat dealer's showroom, with everything sparkling clean inside and palm trees sprouting from teak pots. A long sleek dark blue motorboat, about thirty feet long and glistening, waited in a cradle for her chance in the water. Beyond, a twenty foot daysailor had her mast folded on deck and another large inflatable waited. Two smaller inflatables, each a dozen feet long, sat against a forward bulkhead. A parked forklift could move boats about or place them in the sea. Windsurfers and paddle boards stood along the wall beside dive gear.

"George," said Harold, "why don't you come with me. The rest of you can explore the boat. On the main deck you'll find they are still serving breakfast."

They walked to an elevator, where Tova, Beth, and Windy got off at the main deck, but George and Harold went up three decks, then walked forward, passing several young people along the way. Some dressed as crew, but most wore casual clothes and flip-flops or went bare foot.

"We have put together a team of experts," said Harold, slowing next to a flat teak door. "Some of the brightest minds in the world are aboard this boat right now."

"Is Brigitta here?"

Harold opened the door and they stepped inside. "She's on one of the Navy's ships at the moment," said Harold. "We are trying to work out triangulation to pinpoint where the missing drone is."

"Are we still going to need me sailing the wooden boat?"

"We think so. The drone is sitting on the bottom somewhere north of the big islands. If we can't pinpoint its location, we need to draw it out," said Harold. "Sit, please."

"So what is the plan?" asked George, dropping into a leather lined chair.

"We'll give it a day," said Harold. "They may find the drone. If not, we want you to sail between Red Hook, on the eastern end of St. Thomas, and Jost Van Dyke, in the British Virgin Islands. The Brits will go along with whatever we do in their waters."

George looked out a window at a desolate island to the northwest, which he recognized as Outer Brass Island. He knew the area well from years of running a daysail boat in the area. "I think my crew would like to go ashore somewhere."

"The boat we want you to sail is at Independent Boat Yard, around the south side of St. Thomas. Why don't you take your boat around to Red Hook? If we need you we'll be in touch and *Frihet* can stay there on anchor or in a slip. The Navy has a couple of young fellows that they would like to be your crew. We need Brigitta here."

"Brigitta?" said George, standing. "I didn't even consider sailing with her. And I'm not sailing with a couple of young Navy twerps that are just out of diapers. If I'm going to risk my neck it is with my people."

George's abrupt reaction surprised Harold. "George, calm down."

"Christ," said George. "You've created this monster that's destroying wood boats, and you expect me to…."

"God dammit George," said Harold. "The world is a dangerous place. Don't give me that shit."

"You've destroyed privacy," stammered George, flopping back into his chair and looking out the window. "There is no place a young couple can skinny-dip without someone's eyes watching. What has the world come to?"

"Religious terrorists, Russians, the Chinese, all competing for the same thing. There are too many people for the world's resources," said Harold. "We have to win, there is no second place."

George stared off at Outer Brass, wondering how long he could live on that empty island with no outside contact. Turning to Harold, he said, "Windy sails with me, and no one else."

Harold nodded. "Okay."

For the first time George noticed flecks of gray in Harold's hair. Around his eyes there were lines etched into his skin. The man had aged since George saw him last. Did he still love his work? He looked tired. What happened to the man's eternal optimism?

A phone on Harold's desk beeped and he picked it up. Setting it back, he said, "Brigitta is back and will be here shortly. Should I leave you two alone?"

George nodded.

A minute later the door opened and she stepped in. Harold made excuses and left. Brigitta looked like she always did, with her blonde hair back over her shoulders, the tiny dimples, and the flash of blue in her eyes…a Scandinavian jewel.

"How are you?" she started.

"Fine. And you?"

She nodded, then forced a smile. "Good. How was your trip?"

"Fucking fine," said George. "The love of my life ignored me, so I had the time of my life." He stood and walked to a window.

"I am sorry," she said. "I got wrapped up in work and before I knew it, you were…I don't know."

"Brigitta, I can't do this."

She started to sob.

"What is so important?" he asked. "More important than us? The world is a fucked up place and we are not going to change that. Let's just go sailing, you and me. Forget about all this crap."

She shook her head. "I can't."

"You have to."

"It's impossible. I can make a difference."

George took a deep breath. Maybe she could. He had never met anyone as smart as her. Was it wrong to just want to sail away? "I can't do it," he said. "I can't be your partner one minute and then a bystander the next, while you solve another of the world's great problems."

"Is it selfish of me?"

"No, it is selfish of me," he countered, wrapping his arms around her. "You want to save the world, I just want to save us."

Together they wept.

"Hey, let's go outside and get some air," said George, taking Brigitta by the hand.

Outside, neither said a word as the breeze dried what was left of their tears.

42

Bill Sanderlee could smell the land and flat light filtered in through the shades on the windows. Motionless, *A New Beginning* felt bolted to the bottom. Somewhere, a rooster crowed. His hand slid across the sheets to find a warm hip, but he didn't dare look.

The day before they had arrived in Great Harbour a half hour before customs on Jost Van Dyke closed. After clearing in, he offered to buy the crew dinner ashore at Foxy's Tamarind Bar. Randall insisted on staying aboard to be certain the boat remained safe, but Bill ordered him ashore with everyone else.

Not being yet tourist season, only about a dozen people were at Foxy's. *A New Beginning's* crew downed the first round of painkillers in no time, and soon were onto their third. While they ate a West Indian with broad shoulders appeared with a guitar and started to tell stories and strum a few songs. Foxy also made an appearance and told a tale or two, then disappeared. A second black man showed up with a drum and the tempo picked up. Two young couples, from one of the bare boats out in the harbor, started to dance. Another guitar player showed up with a bass. The broad shouldered West Indian removed his shirt between songs, revealing a muscular and hairless glossy chest. His smile almost glowed in the dim light. Almost immediately three couples from a big catamaran were out on the dance floor.

That was when Craig asked Trish to dance. Bill remembered Brook grabbed his hand to lead him out onto the floor. Betsy and Randall followed.

Another guitar player joined the band, then a man on the bongos. Even two young men with brass horns showed up. Soon everybody in the place danced, including the bar tender behind the bar.

Bill remembered dancing at various times with Brook, Betsy, and Trish, and then the whole crew as one. Slow songs and fast songs. The place started to feel very hot and he recalled sweat trickling down his sides. Betsy had looked sexy in a low cut top that left her middle bare above a very short skirt. During one particular salsa, he and Brook moved as if glued together and he remembered a kiss that lasted through one whole chorus.

Sometime, well after midnight, they returned to *A New Beginning*. Among much laughter and giggling a swim in the pool was suggested. Of course, after drinking so much alcohol, that meant skinny dipping. He couldn't remember getting out of the pool.

This wasn't the Bill Sanderlee that he had known for so many years. Staring up at the overhead, he wondered where this guy had been hiding, because the night before certainly had been fun. He wished they could stay there, and wondered what the Navy would want to ask him and how long it would take. When they got to St. Thomas, would the present crew want to stay on? He hoped so. Randall certainly appeared capable and the others did a great job.

Bill rolled and propped himself up. Brook's long brown hair spread over her pillow. He flopped back and the memories filled in.

The cool water of the pool had cleared away some of the alcohol and soon they paired off. Betsy had left with Randall, which caught him by surprise. Trish with Craig.

But Brook had been flirting with him all night and he certainly had enjoyed it. She came from north of Boston, an old money family with a long history of sailing out of Marblehead. Slender, with flashing blue eyes and silky brown hair, Brook had sophistication, grace, and one hell of a sexy body. Remembering that salsa still aroused him.

Bill slipped from the bed and headed for the shower. An hour later they were under way.

"Mr. Sanderlee," said Trish, "would you like another coffee?"

"No thanks," said Bill. "And please, call me Bill."

Randall stood next to the door of the pilot house, the wind filtering through his short blond hair. Craig sat in the chair in front of the helm, watching the instruments. On the leather couch in the back, Bill sat with his feet up on the table in front of him.

"Where's Betsy and Brook?" he asked.

"They're cleaning up," said Trish. "There were dirty towels by the pool and other laundry too. And the galley is a mess."

"When we get to St. Thomas we will add to the crew," said Bill. "Tell Betsy and Brook I want to talk to them. We'll all sit down and talk about this. I appreciate that all of you have stayed on and you will have a voice in how much crew we need and who we hire."

Three hours later they eased around Picara Point into Magen's Bay to anchor just south of *Frihet*.

"Now what do we do?" asked Randall.

"Wait," said Bill.

*

In Redhook, George brought *Frihet* alongside the end of B dock at American Yacht Harbor. Willing hands assisted with dock lines. When secure, Beth and Tova went ashore to find ice cream.

"You can change your mind at any time," said George. "I can sail the boat alone."

"No," said Windy. "I want to do this. What a story it is going to make."

"Let's go ashore for a drink."

As they started down the dock, Windy asked, "How was Brigitta?"

"She's okay. We both had a cry. It felt like somebody was dying."

"What is she going to do?"

"Save the world," said George. "And maybe she will. I can't be there while she is trying. Life is too short."

Glistening sport fishing boats filled most of the slips. At the shore end of the dock, they turned right. Windy asked, "When's the boat going to be ready?"

"Maybe tomorrow."

"What are they doing to it?"

"Brigitta said they are putting gear aboard that will entangle the drone's propeller and float it to the surface. They hope to recover it intact."

"How is it going to do that?"

"Canisters will come off our boat and burst to launch long armament fiber tentacles that will wrap around the drone's prop to stop it. They also will be buoyant and bring it to the surface."

"Do you think it will work?"

"My gut says no, but Brigitta is brilliant, so it may work."

They stopped at a shore side bar and slid onto two stools. "What will you have?" asked George.

"Actually, a gin and tonic. If I drink scotch this early I'll be useless before dinner."

"How about a margarita?"

"Great idea."

"Hey mate," said someone to George's left.

He turned to see Flake. "What the hell are you doing here?" he said, offering a hand.

"I just got in," he said. "*Raven* is on C dock."

"We're at the end of B dock."

"You hear about this craziness going on?" said Flake, sliding onto a stool next to George. "Some government undersea drone is out of control and whacking wooden sailboats?"

"Wooden boats," said George. "It appears it attacked two wood motor boats yesterday."

Flake ordered a rum and coke, then said, "That should thin out the day charter crowd some. I got no problem with that. My boat is fiberglass."

"Hopefully, it will all be resolved soon," said George, then turning to his right added, "You remember Windy."

"Most definitely," said Flake, raising his glass. "One of the prettiest women on the high seas. What happened to the rest of your crew?"

George laughed. "They are off looking for ice cream."

"Ah, you're a lucky man. I'm still lookin' for crew myself. The boat needs a good washing and the teak could use a bit of varnish."

George smiled. "If I hear of anybody looking, I'll let you know. We should be getting back to our boat."

"Thanks mate," said Flake.

Walking down the dock, Windy said, "Do you believe that guy?"

"There's lots like him down here," said George.

*

Six hours after the United States Navy personnel first boarded *A New Beginning*, they left. First, they asked the crew a series of questions as a group, then individually one at a time. When they finished that, they started over again, with different people asking the same questions. Notes were taken and recordings made. Bill and each of the crew had to answer questions about where they had grown up, gone to school, and lived, hopefully proving who they really were. By the time the Navy left, Bill wished he had never bought a boat.

"Can they accommodate us at American Yacht Harbor?" asked Bill, as his yacht rounded Redhook Point.

"No," said Randall. "They have no room. We are a bit large for their facilities."

"Let's anchor outside the harbor. We have all the amenities aboard."

"It's not the best anchorage."

"The weather is supposed to be good for the next few days. We'll be fine. Look at all the boats out here."

Around two dozen sailboats hung on anchors or moorings in Vessup Bay, the outermost part of Redhook Harbor. A white sandy beach curved along the shore from the west to the south, broken up by one dark rocky ledge in the middle before bending further to the east. Palm trees quivered over the sand and Hobie cats waited on the beach. Ashore at the northern end, cars parked in front of an island bar beside a broken up dock.

A New Beginning set her hook at the outermost part of Vessup Bay, where the beach ended and the bony cliffs started.

"What is next?" asked Randall.

"Let's get the tender in the water," said Bill. "I'll want to go ashore, as you probably want to too. Tell Trish to plan on dinner with four additional guests. She can buy whatever she needs, I'll give her a credit card. It can be something simple like hamburgers on the barbecue grill next to the pool. I'm going to call *Frihet* and get George and his crew to come over."

43

George eased their tender against the boarding platform at the stern of *A New Beginning*. Windy passed the painter to a waiting crewmember and George grabbed the edge of the platform.

"I'm glad you could make it," said Bill Sanderlee, coming down the stairs.

"Thank you for inviting us," said George.

Bill introduced his crew, then George and his bunch followed him up a flight to a second set of stairs and the pool area.

Flames danced over a large grill and torches illuminated the deck. Tables of hors d'oeuvres were lit by candles inside hurricane shades. Flickers of soft blue light wafted up from inside the pool. A long table against the back of the house contained every type of alcoholic beverage imaginable.

"You set quite a spread," commented George, watching Tova, Beth, and Windy mingle with Bill's crew.

"We are celebrating," said Bill. "It was quite a trip. Tell your crew to help themselves to anything they desire. This is a party for my crew, as well as yours, so nobody is really working."

For the next fifteen minutes, he filled George in on his trip to the islands.

"You are lucky to be alive," said George.

"I know. I still can't believe how I fell for Cynthia."

"She was a beautiful woman."

Bill nodded. "There are lots of beautiful women."

"It's a good thing that some of your crew stuck around."

"Randall wants to be my captain. What do you think?"

"Honesty is the most important thing. That, and he stayed around when the others ran away. He should be fine."

Brook stood beside the pool talking to Tova. Beyond them, Betsy, Randall, and Beth laughed about something. Windy and Trish chatted with Craig near the barbecue grill.

"Last night we got a little wild," said Bill, "over on Jost Van Dyke at Foxy's. I maybe crossed a line I shouldn't have."

George smiled. "Let me guess, you slept with one of your crew?"

Bill nodded. "Yeah, it was stupid of me."

"Rum and sun can make a man do crazy things," laughed George. "Do you like her?"

"Actually, I do. She's smart, loves being out on the water, and she's beautiful. But she's almost twenty years younger than I am."

"Be honest and follow your feelings. This is the Caribbean and nobody is going to judge you."

"What about you?" asked Bill. "How was your trip down? And when is Brigitta joining you?"

"It's a long story," said George. He went on with the highlights and tried to explain Brigitta's desire to chase her work.

Sizzling meat on the grill caused flames to flare. Windy used long tongs to flip the ribs. Craig stood next to her and said something that made her laugh. George felt a twinge of jealousy.

"So, can I convince you to teach me to sail?" asked Bill.

George smiled. Bill seemed like a nice guy and spending time with him would be fun. "I don't work cheap."

"I'll pay whatever you ask."

"Will it just be you, or will Brook be joining us?"

Bill glanced at Brook, then back at George. "How did you know?"

"I've been working on developing my intuition," smiled George. "Actually, it's the way she keeps glancing at you that gives it away."

"I'll talk to her about it. I think she already knows how to sail."

"We can do a sail together, just the four of us. It will be fun."

"Will Brigitta be joining us?"

George shook his head. "No."

"Dinner is ready," announced Windy.

*

Brigitta scrolled down the information on the computer screen. The numbers looked haphazard, but she kept going. There had to be a sequence that made sense.

A beep told her an email came from the testing facility in Maryland. She opened it to learn the aerial drone she had designed to mimic a falcon dove at almost one hundred and seventy-five miles an hour to pick a penny off of a table before ascending back to five hundred feet. The aeronautical engineers at NASA had sent along congratulations. A second test would be done the next morning.

She clicked back to the previous page. The missing underwater drone had been quiet for over twenty-four hours. None of the information made sense. Of course not, she thought. I have been thinking like a human, and the drone is a computer.

A knock on the door made her sit up. "Come in."

"Here are copies of the hard drives from Emil and Patrik's computers," said a young man. "They were the two spies aboard *Absent*."

"I know," said Brigitta, taking the thumb drives. "Thank you."

For the next hour she pawed through the files. Emil obviously was the smarter of the two. It appeared he actually communicated with the drone and possibly altered its software.

"Where is that drone?" she said to an empty room.

She walked to the door and stepped outside. Lights on the north side of St. Thomas punctured the dark shape of the island. The warm air felt thick and sticky and smelled of tropical plants from the shore. The enormous boat seemed empty, with everyone probably sleeping. Stopping next to the railing, she listened to the distant shrill of coki frogs.

Brigitta walked aft and then went up one set of stairs. *Number One* felt big enough to get lost on. Well aft, near the stern, two helicopters waited, but closer a swimming pool glowed a pale shade of blue. A large door caught her eye and she walked across to see what was inside. Just as she thought, there were stacks of white towels and she pulled one out.

She peeled her top off over her head and shook her hair back, trying to remember the last time she went swimming. It had to have been on the island of Nantucket the previous summer, when her family visited from Åland. Her shorts dropped to the deck and, laughing, she flipped them up onto the chair with her toe.

The gentle Caribbean breeze caressed her bare skin and she savored its gentle touch. What was it about being naked? It felt primal, a taste of freedom.

Taking a deep breath, some of the bottled up tension slipped away. Too many people counted on the things she did and often the thought overwhelmed her. She stepped to the edge of the deck to lean against the railing and looked at the moon reflecting on the water. What a night. It would be nice to share it with somebody. But who could understand her world?

The teak felt cool under her feet as she walked toward the pool. A pair of sliding doors at the forward end of the pool area caught her eye and she went over to look inside. She found a well-stocked bar. "Now this is perfect," she said to nobody.

Stepping behind the bar top, she looked for the selection of scotches. What was the one George had introduced her to that tasted so smooth? Brigitta recognized the bottle of Dalwhinnie and grabbed it by the neck. From an ice maker she put cubes in a tumbler, then nearly filled the glass.

Taking a sip, she couldn't help but think of George. "Thank you for this," she said.

Carrying the glass, she walked back towards the pool.

In the shallow end, she descended steps to sit with the water up to her shoulders. The scotch tasted silky, reminding her of orchards or honey. Sipping and staring at the stars, she tried to think of nothing. The water felt the same temperature as the air. Setting her glass on the side of the pool, she floated on her back, enjoying the weightlessness.

The undersea drone... she wished it would blow up so she could get on with the flying drones. Numbers and equations pranced through her head. Where could that drone be? Sitting again, she tried to force the thoughts from her head. Soon her glass was empty and she climbed from the pool to refill it.

A door on the starboard side clicked. Harold stood there. She blurted out in Swedish, "Herregud."

"I didn't know you were here," offered Harold.

"I'm sorry," said Brigitta, placing an arm across her chest and the glass at her crotch.

"I can leave and come back later."

"No. I mean, I can go get a bathing suit." She realized he had a towel wrapped around his waist and probably wore nothing else. Her own clothes were on the far side of the pool.

He smiled. "Don't do that. I was going to take a swim before going to bed. I do that whenever I can…and in the buff if possible."

She smiled and walked to her towel, which was only ten steps away. "I was just having a drink. Would you like one?"

"I think that is a perfect idea. There must be some scotch there."

With the towel wrapped around her torso, she stepped back behind the bar. "How do you like it?"

"Neat, no ice."

Brigitta poured an inch in a tumbler and handed it to him. "It feels like we have the whole boat to ourselves."

He took a sip and said, "It does. Everybody else must be asleep."

"Shall we look for shooting stars?" she asked, clicking her glass against his.

"Whatever you want," said Harold.

At the edge of the pool, they both set their towels aside and slipped quickly into the shallow end, sitting on steps with the water up to their shoulders. Overhead, they found satellites among the stars, but no shooting stars. They talked about the drone and politics in Washington. Harold laughed often, appearing unconcerned. Brigitta told him about the success she had with the imitation falcon and he seemed genuinely excited for her.

"I'm surprised George is running away to the islands," said Harold. "He would have made so much money working for me."

"We each have to follow our own dreams," said Brigitta.

"What are your dreams?"

She smiled. "I am not sure. Sometimes I want to bury myself in work, design the fastest of everything and bend the laws of physics, but other times I crave a quiet sunset with someone special."

Far away on the island, someone honked a car's horn. Listening closely, they could hear waves slipping between the rocks along the shore.

"What is Harold Habit going to be doing ten years from now?" asked Brigitta.

"I don't know. This is the only life I have known. Sometimes I try to slow things down, but I immediately get bored."

He held up his tumbler. "My glass is empty. Can I refill yours?"

"Let me," said Brigitta.

"No," insisted Harold. "Let me do this."

She watched him walk away and the twitching of his rear made her smile. For six or eight years older than her, he looked pretty good. Nobody would ever describe him as muscular, but he wasn't fat, more like a lean runner. As he returned carrying their two glasses, she looked away.

"Yikes," said Brigitta. "Are you trying to get me drunk?" The tumbler was filled to the brim.

Harold laughed. "I didn't want to have to fill them again for a while."

Brigitta set her glass on the edge of the pool and took a stroke into deep water. "So, where are all your hot girlfriends tonight?" she asked, turning to face Harold again. For years he had appeared at social events with either models or Hollywood actresses.

He laughed and settled down into the water. "None of them wanted to visit the Caribbean."

"None? What about Tara Tot?"

Tara had been a swimsuit model and then a successful actress. Frequently she had been seen attached to Harold's arm, particularly on Martha's Vineyard where they both owned homes.

"She's shooting a film somewhere in Europe," said Harold, swimming out into the deeper water too.

"So, she would have been here if not for that?"

"No. We haven't been in touch much lately. It was never really serious."

Brigitta slipped beneath the surface and swam underwater toward the far end of the pool. Never really serious? That wasn't what it had looked like to her.

Popping up, she asked, "Have you ever come close to getting married?"

"No, not really." Harold sat again in the shallow end with the water up to his chin. "I just never thought about it."

Brigitta swam back and sat close to his side. "You have never had someone in your life that you just had to have?"

Harold swallowed another gulp of scotch, obviously unused to such questions. "No. Work felt like play and I always just wanted to play. No relationship has ever felt serious."

"What about when work goes wrong? Our drone has killed people/"

"I know," said Harold. "It keeps me awake at night. But we must keep marching forward. It is work that needs to be done." He took another swallow of his scotch, then asked, "What have you heard from George?"

"He's ready to sail our wood boat."

Harold set his tumbler down and tried to float on his back, but became self-conscious.

"I can do it," said Brigitta, settling back and raising her legs to the surface. Her chest and toes poked above the surface.

He laughed and tried again. "I guess I can too."

When he arched his back, Brigitta shrieked, "Look at the sea snake."

They both giggled like children in the moonlight. He took a stroke into deeper water. She followed. He tried to float again, but then sunk under only to pop back up in the shallow end.

"You float better than I do," he said, sitting again and reaching for his glass. He swallowed another sip, then asked, "Is George…involved with your sister?"

Still treading water, Brigitta snapped, "I don't think so. What makes you ask that?"

"She looks so much like you, and they were alone together for a long time at sea. He could well be attracted to her." Brigitta looked upset, so he said, "I'm sorry, I thought you and George broke up."

She swam back. "We drifted apart. My life got too busy and our relationship sort of slipped away."

"Tova could be your twin."

"She isn't interested in him," she insisted, but wondered if it were a possibility. A bigger worry might be Windy. "Tova's just on a holiday."

Harold moved closer. "A holiday fling might be something they can't back out of."

"I know him, he wouldn't like her." She swallowed a mouthful of her drink. Or would he? And did she care? Her own relationship with George had certainly complicated things. Was it really over? Why was Harold asking all this? She swallowed more scotch.

Harold said nothing, but looked up at the stars. One satellite crossing to the right looked brighter than the others. When it finally disappeared, he said. "Too many people do not understand those of us that are driven by greater things."

Brigitta downed the last of her drink. "That is true," she said, holding the tumbler up so Harold would see it was empty.

"Let me refill that for you," he offered, standing to climb from the pool.

"Thanks. Ice please."

She leaned against the side of the pool and watched him put ice in both of their glasses, then pour the golden liquid. The moonlight created odd shadows and she noticed his distinct tan lines. As he walked back, she didn't look away.

"This is the best night I have had in a long time," he said. "I think we are well on our way to getting drunk."

Brigitta smiled. "I might already be there," she said, accepting her glass. "It's nice to have somebody to talk to." She watched Harold slide into the water. "Do you ever get lonely? I mean…for companionship, someone to cuddle with at night?"

Harold leaned back to look at the moon. "Yes, sometimes. Maybe I'm selfish. I can't put my own dreams aside, so someone else's could grow…I don't know. Somehow it seems pointless. I want people around me that are passionate about things, but those same people have little time for relationships."

"But isn't that what love is? Two people conceding some of their own dreams to forge a future together?"

Harold said nothing, but toyed with his tumbler, then said, "But what if one of their dreams is pointless, something frivolous, like living in a trailer in hokey-pokey New York?"

Brigitta wondered where that came from, they really were getting drunk. "They need to talk about it, or maybe one of them is simply the wrong person," said Brigitta. "Don't you believe in love?"

Harold said nothing, but swallowed another mouthful of scotch and then tried to float on his back again.

"I don't know what I believe," he said, giving up. "For long periods of time my life has been all about science and knowledge and moving forward. Human interaction in my life has only been about reaching some distant goal. I am told the world is in peril and we must save it. For days, weeks, years, we've buried ourselves in our work." He shook his head. "Nothing is said about love or families or…" Harold shut his eyes.

Brigitta had never seen Harold so emotional and reached to touch his shoulder. "It is all right."

His eyes opened and searched her face.

"We all choose our own path," said Brigitta.

Harold kissed her lips.

44

George stepped into the dockside bar and slid onto a stool at the end, then ordered a coffee. Three men sat in the center of the bar drinking coffee and reading newspapers. Flake sat at the far end with a bottle of Heineken in front of him. A pelican floated not fifteen feet from George, where the dock met the bar, and three dinghies were tied there waiting for their owners to return.

With caffeine entering his blood, George tried to remember the previous night. Bill Sanderlee had been a perfect host and his crew a happy bunch. The Caribbean was a new experience for all of them and the alcohol poured freely.

A grumbling ferry made George look to the east. On the horizon St. John looked dark green. One white sail reached to the north out beyond Cabrita Point. Nearer St. John three boats sailed to the south. It was like every other day in Red Hook.

The coffee scorched his lips, so George set it down. Bill had confided about what he feared was a blunder. The man would learn. Nobody could be as successful as him and not be a quick learner. George smiled, recalling the few minutes that he got to talk with Brook. She certainly was charming.

Knowing that the next day might be a big one, George had tried to round up his crew around eleven, but it was well after midnight by the time he pried them all out of *A New Beginning's* pool and headed for his own boat. It felt nice to be back in his cabin and tied along a dock.

The tradewinds rattled palm fronds over the roof and George turned to look down the dock. Windy and Beth had walked ashore and headed for the bar.

"Hi," said Windy sliding onto the stool beside him. "It's a beautiful morning."

"You got up early," said Beth, sitting beyond her.

"It is a nice morning," said George, looking at Windy. "You look great." She did, in shorts and a polo shirt that said *Frihet* over the left breast. "And I still don't recognize you in clothes," he said, looking at Beth.

Windy asked, "Have you heard anything? Are we sailing the bait boat today?"

"I haven't heard a thing." George motioned to the bar tender to bring two more coffees. "I was thinking about last night."

"It was fun" said Beth. "Sanderlee seems nice."

George told her how Sanderlee wanted to learn to sail and offered to hire *Frihet* for a whole week of private lessons.

"He'd learn quickly," said Windy.

"Bill thought Brook might come along too."

Windy said, "I talked to her for a while. She's done a lot of sailing. She grew up in Marblehead and her family belonged to the yacht club. But I think she's got a thing for Bill and I'm sure she'd love to come along just to be near him."

"I think so too," said George. "Bill is quite a catch, with all his money."

"Hey mate."

George turned to see Flake standing behind him holding a Heineken. "Morning, what's up?"

"I got me a gig taking out a young couple for a daysail, met them last night up at Duffy's Love Shack, you know, the bar across the street. They'd be newlyweds, been married only a couple of days and wanted the whole boat to themselves." Flake smiled and took a sip of his beer. "Me's been wondering if I could borrow one of your young women for the day, you know, to make sandwiches and stuff. It would be easy work and I'd reward her well."

"I don't think so," said George. "They're all busy with me."

"Awe, come on mate. It would only be for the day. Share and share equally, ain't that the pirate code?"

George shook his head. The man obviously had been drinking for quite a while. "I'm not a pirate. Why don't you ask up...."

'What's it pay?' asked Beth.

"One hundred for the day."

"Make it two and you got yourself a girl."

"One fifty," countered Flake, squinting with one eye.

"Three or nothing," said Beth.

Flake scratched at his chin. "That's a lot of money for a day's work, almost half of what I told them it would cost."

"Is the young bride a looker?" laughed Beth. "I'll have her topless before lunchtime or I'll work for free."

Flake beamed. "You're on mate." He elbowed George. "I like your crew, mate. They got the spirit of the Caribbean in their blood."

He pulled a wad of bills from his pocket and peeled off a hundred. "They're supposed to be at my boat on the end of C dock at ten. Here, get some stuff for lunch and be there before then."

Watching Flake walk away, George said, "You're really going to do it?"

"With him drinking this early in the day, I might be saving the newlywed's lives," laughed Beth. "You didn't need me today, did you?"

"No, do what you want. It might be easy money.

"Where's Tova?" he asked, changing the subject.

"Sleeping in. She drank an awful lot last night," said Beth, wearing a smirk. "I think something is bothering her."

"When will we know if we're sailing today?" asked Windy, changing the subject again.

George's phone vibrated and he answered it. A young male voice introduced himself and asked George to be at the main entrance to American Yacht Harbor at eight o'clock sharp, and to have his crew with him ready to sail.

*

Brigitta sipped black coffee and wondered if she had missed anything. Somewhere beyond the boat yard and across the road a rooster crowed. A motorboat idled its engines down on one of the docks. Across the other side of Bottoms Up's horseshoe shaped bar sat two pirates lost in the wrong century, with scraggy hair, gold earrings, and an abundance of tattoos on leathery tanned skin. Both appeared bleary eyed and she hoped they stayed on the far side of the bar.

The scruffy bar tender stepped out of the kitchen and she asked for another coffee. One of the men on the far side ordered a Heineken with a chaser of rum.

Earlier, she had taken one of *Number One's* tenders, with twin two hundred and fifty horse outboards, around the east end of St. Thomas. Zipping over the water, the wind pulled at her hair and cleared away some of the cobwebs created from the scotch consumed the night before. Through dark glasses she watched the sun peak over the horizon as she entered the narrow passage between the islands of Great Saint James and St. Thomas, called Current Cut. To port, a handful of sailboats had spent the night in the shelter of Christmas Cove and she wished she were on one, sleeping without a care in the world.

Inside Brenner Bay she entered the boat yard and tied the tender alongside the boat she hoped would lure Harold's drone to its capture. For the next hour she had double checked all of the boat's systems.

Sipping her coffee at the bar, she wondered what Harold's reaction was when he found her gone. Someone would have noticed the missing tender and guessed where it and she had gone.

What the hell had happened the night before?

She had never seen Harold like that, their relationship had always been just professional. Was it the alcohol? For a while he had seemed so…vulnerable. Did he have feelings for her? She had never considered him as….

A door slammed and she realized a taxi had stopped beside the bar. Harold stood beside it and watched it back away.

*

"Good morning," said Harold.

George nodded, watching the silver Range Rover, which had just dropped him and Windy off at Independent Boat Yard, drive away. Beyond, a half dozen West Indians waited for a bus in the shade of a giant genip tree. He answered, "Good morning." The day already felt sizzling hot.

"The boat is on the end of the dock," said Brigitta.

Her ponytail hung back onto bare shoulders. Hidden behind dark glasses, her eyes gave away no emotion. "What is the boat?" asked George. Her halter top said Fast Habit Yachts across the front in big tilted letters.

"She's a Sparkman and Stephens design, built in Germany in 1962," said Harold. "A pretty boat, 42 feet long, sloop rigged."

"Where did you find it?" asked Windy.

"It was here in the yard," said Harold. "The owner passed away and the family was eager to sell it. Two local boys were looking for work, so I had them freshen up the varnish while we were getting it ready."

"Do you have everything you need?" asked Brigitta.

George realized Brigitta had not turned to face Windy or even acknowledged her presence. What was that about? "I guess so," he answered. "I'm not sure what we need."

Harold started them down the dock. "We are hoping to lure the Mother out right away, so this may not take long. The Navy is getting impatient, as a lot of other people are too. I'm hoping she shows herself right away."

"I'll explain how the entangler works when we're on board," said Brigitta.

"The entangler?" said George. At the far end of the dock he could see the mahogany cabin and white topsides of the boat.

Brigitta ran her fingers back through her ponytail. "I hope we can trap the drone, ensnare it in Kevlar tentacles."

"So what is the plan?" asked George.

Harold stopped beside the boat, and said, "Take the boat around the east end of the island, through middle passage, and head for Jost Van Dyke. We think the drone is hiding somewhere between the islands. Our Navy and a British destroyer are in the area, along with an aircraft carrier ten miles to the north."

On the pinched mahogany transom, George read *Hope*. It seemed fitting.

The bronze ports had turned green, but the varnish on the mahogany cabin looked fresh. The bronze dorades had been polished and the spruce mast appeared perfect. "She looks nice," said George. The sail resting on the spruce boom looked new. On the headstay a roller furler held the genoa. A three eighths inch line tethered a ten foot rigid bottom inflatable to *Hope's* transom.

"The tender goes with you," continued Harold, "sort of a plan B. There are also inflatable life vests for you to wear and a life raft in the white canister ahead of the mast. We want both of you to be safe."

"It's a shame to wreck such a pretty boat," said George. "Why can't you just tow a wood barge and get the drone to attack that?"

"We've been doing that for three days now," said Harold. "It hasn't worked and we're not sure why. Almost all of the vessels attacked were sailboats, which is why we're trying this."

"Both have been planned for weeks," said Brigitta. "It was easy to get the barge up and working first."

"Tell me about the canisters on the deck," said George. There were four of them, two to a side, and each about ten feet long and the diameter of a barrel. Both ends were cone shaped and they sat in cradles that appeared made of teak.

"On impact," said Brigitta, "they launch over the side, or you can launch them manually by yanking the orange cable attached to each of them. In the water they are attracted to the largest mass of nearby steel, which will be the drone. Ten seconds after immersion, they bust, launching a thousand yards of Kevlar spaghetti-like tentacles that will ensnare the drone's propeller."

"What propels them?"

"Compressed air. It can't move them far, but we hope far enough."

George stepped aboard *Hope*. "Will the drone sink with its prop tangled?"

"The tentacles actually have a positive buoyancy," said Brigitta, beaming and pushing her sunglasses up onto the top of her head. "I figured out a way to do that."

George looked away from her eyes and tossed his duffle into the cabin. "I'm ready to go."

"I'll go with you," said Brigitta, stepping aboard too.

The startled look on Harold's face caught George's eye. "No," said George. "It's just Windy and me."

"If there is a problem with the canisters I might be able to fix it," said Brigitta.

George shook his head.

"We are heading back to *Number One*," said Harold, glaring at Brigitta. "George wants Windy to sail with him."

Windy stepped over the lifelines to board. "We'll be fine."

Brigitta uncleated the tender she had driven from *Number One* and climbed down into it. "I'll take the tender back."

"Is there anything else I have to know?" asked George.

"No," said Harold. "Just sail to Jost Van Dyke. The drone will find you on the way. Leave here about forty-five minutes from now, that will give us time to get back. When the drone strikes we will be all over you so fast you may not even get wet."

George forced a smile. "I hope we don't get wet."

Turning to Brigitta, Harold said, "One of the helicopters dropped me off at the National Guard base west of Red Hook and a taxi met me there. Can I ride back with you?"

George didn't recognize the look on her face. She said, "Of course."
Was she scared? Or angry?

45

"Let's get a cup of coffee," said George, watching the tender motor slowing out of the harbor. Brigitta was at the helm and Harold sat beside her saying something.

"What's up with Brigitta?" asked Windy. "She went out of her way to ignore me."

"I noticed."

"I think she isn't sure what she wants, her career or you."

"I've given up trying to understand her."

There were only two empty stools left at Bottoms Up, where most of the rag tag patrons sipped coffee while they read newspapers or watched the TV over the bar. George guessed they all worked in the yard somewhere.

"Are you scared?" asked Windy, as they waited.

George smiled. "Apprehensive is a better word. We'll be all right. Let's just stay on deck. The big danger would be getting trapped inside. Why don't we take the coffees back to the boat?"

"How did Harold talk you into this?"

"I don't know. He's done a lot for me and asked for this favor."

The heavy old boat hardly moved when they stepped aboard. George said, "I used to have a boat much like this when I did charters for The Resort. Those were good times."

He climbed down into the cabin. "These old boats don't have a lot of room in them, but I didn't need much."

The bulkhead and cabinets were all mahogany. The teak and holly sole showed wear at the bottom of the companionway ladder. The two burner stove indicated years of use and the galley sink had spots of rust. In the refrigerated box he found four one gallon containers of drinking water and a few groceries.

"At least Harold is taking care of us," he said.

"Where did your boat go?"

"I sold it. Sometimes I dream about her and wonder where she is." He set down his coffee. "Let's get out of here."

"Harold wanted us to wait."

"We'll stop for a quick swim to kill some time."

Windy smiled. "That sounds like a great idea. There's no breeze and its hot here in the boat yard."

The engine started right up. He asked, "Are we ready?"

Windy nodded and untied the last dock line, then stepped aboard. "Let's do it."

The stainless steel wheel at the helm felt small, compared to the one aboard *Frihet*. George turned it to starboard and pushed the transmission into gear. The boat inched forward.

A pelican floated near the end of the dock and lumbered into flight as they approached. Without a trace of a wake the boat slipped through the water, passing by the boats along the docks of Compass Point Marina.

*

"Why didn't you wake me?" asked Harold.

From behind her dark glasses, Brigitta watched a sailboat trying to anchor behind Happy Island. Beyond, a ferry motored toward Charlotte Amalie. Barely visible in the distance, St. Croix poked above the horizon. Riding with Harold was the last thing she wanted. Soon they would be out of the harbor and she could speed the boat up.

"I needed some time to think," said Brigitta. "And I wanted to go over the systems onboard *Hope*."

"A technician could have gone with you."

"I like to do some things alone."

Harold said, "Did what happened last night change our relationship?"

"You tell me? What did we do last night? We got drunk and had some pretty decent sex. Was it more than that?"

"We had been talking about how some people who are driven don't have time for normal relationships. I thought we were helping each other with…a need. Having a little fun."

What a geek, thought Brigitta. He doesn't understand what it is to be human, he's more like a machine, a computer…a fucking drone. "Is that what it was?"

"I'm sorry if I said things that made you think it was something more."

Brigitta pushed the throttles ahead. The engines roared and the boat jumped atop the waves.

"You didn't."

Over the rumble of the engines, Harold asked, "Why did you want to sail with George?"

Brigitta said nothing, but pushed the throttles to the max.

*

Outside of Benner Bay, Windy asked, "Are we going to raise the mainsail?"

"Sure. I'll give you a hand."

After bringing the bow up into the easterly breeze, he put the transmission into neutral. Windy already had the halyard attached to the head and the ties off the sail. Together they hoisted, winched, and then cleated it off.

"It's not like *Frihet*," he laughed.

Windy sheeted in the main and then freed up the genoa. "I like this."

"Me too. I'm spoiled though."

They sailed to the southeast, then tacked to the northeast twenty minutes later. In the southern end of Christmas Cove they doused the sails and dropped the anchor. *Hope* settled back on her rode with the transom in eight feet of water and not far from the rocky shore. George shortened up the dinghy's painter to keep its outboard well away from the rocks.

"We'll stay here a half hour," said George.

Four other boats were anchored in the cove and all but one were at the north end. They could hear the thunk thunk thunk of the anchor chain climbing up over the windlass of the nearest boat.

"This place is nice," said Windy.

"It's popular. You ready for a swim?"

"Yeah. Do you think Harold is watching us?" She climbed down into the boat and peeled her tee shirt off, exposing a bikini top.

"He's probably just getting back. He will be soon." George followed her in.

Slipping off her shorts, she asked, "Did you pack a bathing suit?"

"No, I only brought an extra pair of shorts and a shirt in a plastic bag, so they'd stay dry."

Windy laughed. "Are you going to swim bare ass?"

He tossed his shirt on a settee. "Are you up for it? There's a stack of clean towels in the head."

He stepped into the forward cabin and came out with a towel tied around his hips, only to find her dressed the same.

"You're getting into the Caribbean swing of things," he teased.

Twenty minutes later, he rinsed in the boat's cramped shower. "That felt great," he said, loud enough that Windy could hear in the main cabin.

"It did," she said.

He stepped out, drying himself off. "I wish we could stay about a week."

"Me too," said Windy, slipping by him and into the shower.

"There may not be much fresh water in the tanks, so go easy."

"I will," she said, over the running water.

George pulled on shorts and buttoned his shirt. Windy came out of the shower wrapped in a towel and her wet hair down on her shoulders.

"Don't forget sunscreen," said George. "This boat has no shade."

Windy smiled. "Can you put some on my back?"

With her holding the towel against her chest, he rubbed the lotion across her shoulders and down her back. "I think you can get the rest," he said.

She turned and said, "That felt heavenly, thanks."

George wrapped his arms around her. "I'm glad you are here." Her arms slid around his waist.

When he relaxed his hold, she looked up. And he kissed her.

"We should get going," he said, breaking it off.

"I know." Windy smiled, then turned her back to him to dress. "Do you think Harold saw us swimming bare ass?"

"I would bet money on it. Did you turn on the VHF radio?"

"I thought you did."

George smiled. "Let's wait a while. I left my phone back on *Frihet* so it wouldn't get wet. Harold must be bullshit that he can't reach us.

46

Mother had not moved for over twenty-four hours. She listened to the clicks and pings of her Autonomous Sharks. They were visiting all of the islands and harbors, cataloging every vessel made of wood. Periodically, one or two of the sharks would return to suckle on her titanium nipples and share volumes of information. Against a sand bottom and on her side to expose her nipples, Mother rested in one hundred and ten feet of water.

The number of wood vessels had surprised her. If a machine, driven by software, can feel excitement, Mother certainly did. For weeks she would hunt these dangerous vessels, and the warm water made communication with her sharks easier.

While waiting, Mother searched her memory for data on other islands or clusters of islands. There had to be more places where wood boats hid. She wanted to surface and connect via satellite to the World Wide Web to search for additional information, but that would be taking a huge risk. Instead, she sorted through stored information.

Mother knew the Navy waited not far to the north. Her sharks also tracked a Russian, a Chinese, and two American nuclear submarines, and one older diesel electric submarine from an unidentified country, probably South American. The sharks also spied on the research vessel and the yachts anchored at Magen's Bay, and the United States Navy ships to the west and British ship to the east. The aircraft carrier to the north worried Mother immensely because she had no way to keep track of her aircraft.

Several times each day, airplanes or helicopters dropped sonar buoys. It did not seem likely that they had located her, but she could never know for certain. If she waited long enough, she hoped they would lose interest and go away.

Earlier that morning, one of the sharks known as AS-11, noticed a large inflatable leaving the enormous yacht anchored at the outside of Magen's Bay. The shark poked its fin above the surface, exposing a miniscule camera, and there appeared to only be one person onboard. Due to the unusually early hour, the shark started to follow the boat, but it proved to be much too fast.

AS-11 swam back toward mother.

*

"Are you coming" asked Harold.

Brigitta's eyes flashed anger. "I'm coming."

"What is wrong?"

"Nothing," she said, looking back at the tender tied along the side of *Absent*.

"This way," said Harold.

They walked along the side deck and entered a steel door. Inside, a dozen technicians sat in front of computers, most staring at the screens and wearing blank expressions. Against the forward wall, two enormous displays showed satellite images of the Virgin Islands and one a nautical chart of the area.

Christine stood from a desk as they entered. Harold asked, "Do we have George on the screen?"

"The middle screen," she said. "He's anchored in Christmas Cove."

"What the hell is he doing there?"

"Having a swim."

"A swim? What the hell is he thinking? Zoom it in."

Christine said, "They're skinny dipping. I zoomed it out to give them some privacy."

"Where's a radio? I want to talk to him."

"I tried to call them," said Christine. "They mustn't have turned on their radio."

Harold glared at the screen.

Brigitta walked over to an empty seat in front of a computer and started to type. Rows of numbers appeared on the screen and she started to scroll down.

"What are you looking for?" asked Harold.

A young man handed a sheet of paper to Christine. "The sonar buoys have provided triangulation. We have coordinates of the most likely location of the drone."

"Mother?" asked Harold.

"Yes. She's at 18° 24' 46" north, 64° 47' 10" west, in a little over a hundred feet of water. The Navy is ready."

"They have to give us one shot at capturing the thing," said Harold. "Brigitta's got it all worked out."

Brigitta turned and headed for the door.

"What's up with her?" asked Christine.

"I don't know," said Harold.

*

On starboard tack, *Hope* sailed through narrow Current Cut into Pillsbury Sound. Ahead, the blue water sparkled from the morning sun and white puffy clouds hovered over the island of St. John to the east. A blue ferry plowed through the water toward St. Thomas and a white one motored toward The Resort on St. John.

"Would you like another coffee?" asked Windy.

"Sure, thanks," answered George.

A minute later Windy came back up the companionway carrying two mugs. "When do we have to start worrying?" she asked. "Do you think the drone will attack us here?"

"Not until we get north of Middle Passage," said George. "It's too confined in Pillsbury Sound. I'm sure it would be afraid of getting trapped." He wondered if he was giving the damn drone too much in the way of intelligence, but then decided he didn't care.

Windy sat on the port side of the cockpit with the sun on her face. "I'll be glad when this is over."

"Me too. Let's put on the inflatable floatation devices, just to be safe."

She smiled. "That's probably a good idea."

From a locker beneath a cockpit seat, she pulled out two of them. They fit like suspenders with a belt. "Not bad," said George, adding, "They'll give you funny tan lines."

Adjusting the fit of hers, Windy smiled. "I'm not going to have any tan lines a month from now. Maybe even two weeks from now." Beneath the device, she wore a pale blue bikini top with khaki shorts.

"A New England girl gone wild," laughed George. "I can't wait to see it."

"Hah! If you're lucky," she teased.

Overhead, three black frigate birds glided on the thermals. Close to the rocky shore of Water Point, several gray pelicans bobbed. Two sloops, with sails bright white in the morning sun, beat toward St. John and George guessed they were daysail boats filled with tourists.

Passing bony Cabrita Point, he pointed into Red Hook and said, "There's *A New Beginning*. She looks like she's coming out."

They eased the sheets and bore off the wind, heading just west of north and toward Middle Passage. Boat speed climbed to almost seven knots and, occasionally, waves slapped against the topsides to send sparkling spray into the air. Neither George nor Windy said a word.

Sailing near to the east end of Thatch Cay, they hardened up on the sails, pointing the boat toward Jost Van Dyke.

"I'll clean up," said Windy.

"Just put the mugs in the sink and turn on the VHF," said George. "I don't want you below deck."

"How far is it to Jost?"

"A little over seven miles," said George.

"What happens if nothing happens?"

"We just keep sailing, back and forth until something does happen."

"After dark?"

George shook his head. "I don't think it will take that long."

*

AS-11 nestled against Mother and latched on, absorbing electrical current and sharing megabytes of data. One interesting bit was the image of the blonde woman in the inflatable, which caused Mother to take notice. She recognized the woman as Brigitta Eriksson, the woman who had contributed to her creation and had been almost singularly responsible for her Autonomous Sharks ability to swim the way they did. In a way, she was Mother's mother, or at least the shark's grandmother.

Why was she there? And what was she doing? Could she be in danger? Was the high speed travel in the rigid inflatable some sort of escape?

Mother sent out a series of communications, asking an additional six sharks to investigate. Assisting Brigitta Eriksson would be more important than worrying about the Navy or the submarines or the boats made out of the mystery material.

*

"She did what?" asked Harold.

"Brigitta took one of the tenders," said the young man.

Harold shook his head. "That woman is crazy."

"There she is," said Christine, pointing at the middle screen in the front of the cabin. "She's headed for Red Hook." The speeding rigid bottom inflatable left a white wake. Zooming in, Brigitta's blonde hair blew in the wind.

Harold walked out of the cabin and onto the deck, then climbed a set of stairs to the wheel house. Stepping inside, he said, "Have you heard anything from the Navy?"

Captain Able shook his head. "No. We just have to be patient. They dropped six sonar buoys this morning, but apparently have picked up nothing new."

"That's what Christine said too."

Harold looked out through the big windows at the sparkling water. That was a lie. Christine gave the coordinates of where the drone was. How did the Navy not know that? "Can we see George from here?"

"No. He's passed north of Thatch Island now. We won't see him again."

"I'm going back to *Number One*," said Harold. "If anything happens, let me know."

*

Hope plowed through the sea to the northeast. A half dozen white sails shifted between the islands ahead of them. Aft, three sport fishing boats plowed north to fish along the edge of The North Drop. A half hour after passing through Middle Passage, George and Windy tacked to the southeast. Twenty minutes later, they could look down The Narrows and Sir Francis Drake Channel between the steep forested sides of St. John and Great Thatch Island. They tacked again. Neither had said a word, except when George had said, "Ready to tack."

A half hour later, Windy asked, "Is that Great Harbour?" More than two miles away, a dozen sailboats sat anchored against the side of Jost Van Dyke.

"It is. Ahead of us is Sandy Cay. It's the picture perfect Caribbean island, with a white sandy beach and palm trees, and nobody lives there."

"There are sailboats there."

"It's a popular spot," said George. "We'll have to go there sometime. It's the most fun first thing in the morning when we can have the whole island to ourselves."

Windy smiled for the first time since clearing Middle Passage. "Are you all right?" asked George.

She nodded. "It's just nerves."

"We'll be fine," assured George.

Soon they passed by Sandy Cay and then, fifteen minutes later, tacked toward Tortola. "That's Cane Garden Bay ahead of us," said George. "I've had some good times there."

About a mile from Tortola, they tacked to the north. "We'll run north for about twenty minutes, then bear off and sail along the north side of Sandy Cay to the east end of Jost Van Dyke. There's a tiny island there called Sandy Spit where we'll bear off to the south. I was hoping we'd be all done with this gig by now."

47

Tova felt *Frihet* move. "Who is there?"

"It is me, your sister," said Brigitta.

Tova climbed up the companionway. "How did you get here?" Brigitta's hair looked windblown and specks of dried salt spray dotted her sunglasses.

"It took a tender," said Brigitta. "It's over next to the dinghy dock." Tova wore very little, just a bikini bottom and a tiny shear tank top. "How was your trip down? Did you and George…get along all right?"

Tova smiled. "It was fun."

Brigitta tried to read her sister's face. "How much fun?" Tova looked about to cry. "Did you…seduce George? You stole every boyfriend I ever had."

"What is it to you? You are no longer interested in him."

"I never told you that."

"You hurt George, broke his heart."

"My work had me busy"

"Your work has always been the most important thing."

"You lured him on and then were going to fly home, leaving him broken," said Brigitta.

"It wasn't like that. Why are you here?" asked Tova. "I thought you were trying to catch that stupid drone."

Brigitta dropped onto a seat. "I was. We were. Harold…." She shook her head. "Harold is a shit."

Tova sat beside her sister and smiled. "Harold is a shit?"

"A shit. All he cares about is whatever he is working on."

"And you are not like that?" asked Tova, brushing a strand of her sister's hair back behind an ear.

"No," said Brigitta. "I am not that way."

"Of course you are. I have seen it since you were in school. You love a challenge, and science has been your challenge, particularly physics. Maybe if you were ugly men would have been more of a challenge and you would be married by now."

Brigitta looked at St. John to the east. Clouds stacked up around her summit, possibly threatening a shower. An arriving ferry rumbled toward the dock where a crowd waited and a pelican flew awkwardly along the shore. Could she be right?

"Where is Beth?" asked Brigitta.

"She is working on a daysail boat for the day."

"When will she be back?"

Tova shrugged. "I have no idea."

"Is George involved with Windy?"

Tova nodded. "I think so."

Brigitta stared across the harbor.

"Did you spy on us while we were sailing down from Bermuda?" asked Tova.

Brigitta shook her head. "No, I was busy working on the drones. Until recently I did not have access to Harold's satellites."

"You do now?"

Brigitta nodded. "Even through an app on my phone. I was given access to anything that might help find the undersea drone."

"Does it bother you, all this spying? What ever happened to privacy?"

"It does," said Brigitta. "Harold thinks it is so important. I am not so sure. There are people that want to give it to local police departments. If that happens everyone will have it."

"Brigitta Eriksson," said a voice on the dock. "Can I ask you a few questions?"

A young man about thirty stood with a note pad. Behind him a cameraman aimed a lens at them. It was easy to see they weren't sure which of them was Brigitta.

"Go away," said Brigitta.

"It won't take long," said the man, glancing between the two. "Is it true you helped design the submersible drone that has now gone amuck?"

Turning to Tova, Brigitta said, "Let's take this boat out of here. Undo the dock lines and I'll get the engine started."

As Tova stepped onto the dock, the man blocked her way. "It will only take a few minutes."

Tova stepped around him and uncleated the spring lines, then the bow line. Brigitta had the engine running and the bow thruster started to push the bow out.

"Which of you is Brigitta Eriksson?"

"Put that camera away," said Tova, reaching for the stern line.

After freeing it, she stepped aboard. The reporter did too. Before he could grab hold of anything, Tova shoved him backward. "You weren't invited."

Brigitta pushed the throttle ahead, leaving him swimming off the end of the dock. The smiling cameraman caught it all on video.

"Let's find someplace to hide," said Brigitta.

"Where are we going to do that?"

"Let's see if we can find George, or maybe Beth. They can't be too far away."

"The boat Beth is on is black and named *Raven*."

Outside the harbor they unfurled the sails and turned to the north. A light green ferry rumbled in their direction from St. John, followed by a cloud of blue smoke. Pelicans dove along the red rocks of Red Hook Point. Neither Brigitta nor Tova said a word, watching the island slip by.

People swam and sunned on Sapphire Beach. The white condominiums glistened on the hillside. Dozens of boats sat in the marina behind the beach. After clearing Shark Island, they steered for Middle Passage.

Away from St. Thomas, Tova peeled her tee shirt off and tossed it aside. "I've had enough of civilization for one day."

Brigitta smiled and did the same. "I'd forgotten how good the sun can feel and how much I love sailing."

They passed by the bony end of Thatch Cay and hardened up on the sails. Ahead lay Jost Van Dyke.

"I can get Harold's satellite images on the computer in the nav station," said Brigitta, setting the autopilot. "Maybe we can see *Raven* or *Hope*. Keep an eye on where we are going."

A few minutes later she said, "Come here."

Tova stepped down into the cabin and slid onto the seat beside Brigitta. On the computer screen *Hope* sailed lazily on a broad reach with the boom out and the genoa billowing.

"What is Windy doing?" asked Tova.

"I think she is throwing up over the side," said Brigitta, wearing a faint smile. "Either she is sea sick or being bait is too nerve racking for her."

Tova grinned. "Do you want George back?"

Brigitta nodded. "Yes. I want him back. What do you want? You aren't going to steal him away from me, are you?"

"You are my sister and he was your man. I will not get in your way, but if you ignore him to work on whatever you are designing, he will be mine."

*

Flake rounded *Raven* up into the wind and Beth pushed the anchor ahead in its roller, dumping it into the sea with a plop. The chain rattled out and the boat settled back. In ten feet of water, when forty feet of chain had tumbled out, Beth snubbed it off. The boat settled with the bow pointing easterly into the tradewinds. Beneath them, the turquoise water stretched to the empty shore.

"That there's Sandy Spit," said Flake, using his best pirate's voice and pointing to a tiny island ahead to starboard. "A man couldn't ask for a more perfect Caribbean Island. Look at that sand. You can see where the spit got her name." At the far end two sailboats had anchored.

The two honeymooners, William and Kathy, sat on the cabin top ahead of the mast, speechless. Beth had fed them each two bloody Marys and a rum punch by then. It had been a hot thirsty morning. To prime them into the mood, she had worn a tank top that said "SUN YOUR BUNS, SNORKEL NAKED". With the combination of sun and wind, the lovebirds were showing the effects of absorbed alcohol.

"It gets a might crowded sometimes," said Flake. "That's why I like anchoring here beside Little Jost Van Dyke. You do some snorkeling for a bit, then Beth here will feed you some lunch. After that the little beach tucked between them rocks is all yours for the afternoon. About three we'll start to sail back."

"It's a pretty spot," said Beth, watching Flake opening another beer back in the cockpit. "Some people call that beach Honeymoon Beach, because it is big enough for only one couple."

"It must be magical living here," said Kathy.

"It has its good points. Have either of you ever snorkeled before??" asked Beth. William looked like a college quarterback and Kathy might have been the head cheerleader.

"We both have," said William. "We brought our own gear."

"Great," said Beth. "I might do some snorkeling too. It is like we have the whole world to ourselves here."

William pulled his tee shirt off over his head.

Beth smiled and said, "You know, some of our guests discover snorkeling naked." She shrugged coyly, as if sharing a big secret. "It does make you feel close to nature, like being the first couple on the planet."

"We ought to try it," said William, setting his hand on Kathy's thigh.

Kathy glanced back at Flake.

"Don't mind him," said Beth. "Naked people are so common down here, he's liable to not even notice."

"Come on," said William, with an alcohol inspired smile.

Grinning at Kathy, Beth said, "I'd love to take my top off, would it bother you? I hate having tan lines."

Kathy laughed. "William would love it. And no tan lines does sound sexy."

Beth slipped her top off over her head, then shook her kinky blonde mane back.

"What the heck," said Kathy, reaching to untie her bikini's strings.

Beth glanced at Flake and thought, that bastard better pay up.

*

George sailed *Hope* on a broad reach, almost due north from Cane Garden Bay. Windy sat in the front of the cockpit, with her back against the cabin, watching Tortola grow distant. White sails poked along the shore of the island.

Windy wondered what lay along its shore to the east. Far away a long beach stretched to the horizon. Ahead of *Hope*'s bow, a dozen boats sailed toward Jost Van Dyke.

Time dragged.

Windy's sudden illness surprised George, but he couldn't fault her for it. The constant stress had tied a knot in his gut too. He tried to focus on the sound of the water hissing along the hull, but his mind kept wandering back…wondering when the crash would come.

He bore off the wind toward the east end of Jost Van Dyke. Sandy Cay lay to the west and the Atlantic Ocean to the north. A large naval aircraft flew east, about two miles ahead of them, and dropped a sonar buoy tethered to a parachute.

*

Mother blew water from her tanks to rise off the bottom, causing a cloud of silt and sand to rise. Silent batteries turned her propeller to push her east. Under her belly, only one shark still nursed. The remainder of her armada searched the harbors and bays in the surrounding islands, constantly sending back information in clicks, ticks, and clunks that blended with the underwater sounds of the ocean. Eight sharks searched for Brigitta.

*

Harold watched the six overhead screens in the main salon of *Number One*. Next to him, four technicians stared at computer screens and sorted through gathered data gathered by sonar buoys, satellites, drones, and the United States Navy.

He sat at an empty keyboard and typed a request for the location of Brigitta Eriksson. Twenty seconds later, on the center screen, he watched *Frihet* sailing north through Middle Passage. Zooming in, at the back of the bimini, Brigitta's blonde hair fluttered freely in the tradewinds. Or was it her sister? He picked up a VHF radio microphone and tried to call her, but received no answer. To no one, he said, "That woman is trouble."

Switching to a different satellite, he peaked under the corner of the bimini, where Tova's bare back leaned against the life lines. Brigitta sat behind the starboard wheel, at least he guessed that was her. The two looked identical in the satellite image, but facial recognition software said Brigitta sat to starboard. The wheel turned itself, so the autopilot had to be on. Still watching the two, into the microphone he said, "Sailing vessel *Hope*, sailing vessel *Hope*, this is *Number One*, come in please."

After a minute, he heard, "*Number One, this is Hope.*"

"Switch channel eight two."

George had never heard of using channel 82 and thought it was restricted to government use. He turned to it. ""What's up?"

*

"So tell me, what happened between you and Harold?" said Tova, sitting in the shade of the port side of the bimini.

Brigitta went through the highlights of the night before.

"Are you sure you don't want to chase him?" smiled Tova. "He's one of the richest men in the world."

Brigitta shook her head. "He does not know what love is. He has never been in love. It would be a cold life, spending it with him."

"Maybe he would like me," laughed Tova. "I look like you."

"All I did last night was relieve a need he had," said Brigitta. "To him I am a tool."

Grinning, Tova teased, "I would put up with that."

Brigitta said nothing, but instead shut off the autopilot to hand steer. The sea bubbled along the side of the hull and the tradewinds licked at her skin. To the east, white sails made little triangles along the side of Tortola. She wondered how anyone could be happy living with a man only because he was rich. There had to be more than that.

Away from the islands the wind backed more easterly. She had Tova harden up on the genoa and bring the boom to windward. *Frihet* charged along close to the wind. Brigitta wondered, how much faster the boat would go with a bendable keel? Could they point higher too? A wave slapped the starboard forward topsides, sending spray into the air. She did not notice the droplets sparkle before they dropped back into the sea. Could the boat be made so waves seldom spanked against its sides? It had to hurt boat speed. Maybe foils were the answer.

"What am I doing?" she said.

"What?"

"I am driving the boat and analyzing ways to improve it," said Brigitta. "I should be enjoying what we have, a boat that is like no other."

Tova smiled. "You cannot help where your brain wanders. You have always been restless."

48

"There's *Raven*," said Windy, pointing ahead.

Not far off of Little Jost Van Dyke, they could see the black boat anchored.

"Do you want to stop for lunch?" asked George.

"Can we?"

"It doesn't matter if Harold wants us too, we will. The break will be good for both of us."

Windy checked the genoa trim. Soon they reached the safety of shallow water. The drone could never attack with the water less than twenty feet deep. With *Raven* three boat lengths off to port, they rounded up, dropped the anchor, and doused the sails.

"Do you see Beth or Flake?" asked George.

"Beth waved," said Windy, stepping back into the cockpit. "I haven't seen anyone else."

"I'll make sandwiches."

"I'll help."

Without the tradewinds, the sun would have been unbearable. After applying additional sunscreen they made sandwiches and sat at the back of the cockpit to take advantage of the breeze. Little was said while they ate.

"I'd give anything for a beer," said George.

Windy smiled. "Me too. Do we have time for a swim?"

"We have time for anything you want."

*

Beth stood next to the companionway and looked out at Flake, who napped at the aft end of the cockpit. Since the anchor went down, the man had consumed four beers, and that was after sucking down a beer and sipping rum during their morning sail.

The two honeymooners, Kathy and William, had snorkeled in the morning, eaten lunch aboard, then swam to the island with towels held high over their heads to keep them dry. The last Beth had seen of them was when they disappeared behind a large boulder on the shore. It was easy to imagine what they were doing.

Flake should lose his captain's license, thought Beth. The man is useless. With his eyes still shut, he scratched at the stubble on his chin and moaned something unintelligible. She wondered if he even had a captain's license.

The flogging of sails made her look to starboard. Windy waving on the foredeck of *Hope* surprised her. Beth waved back and then slipped back inside *Raven's* cabin to escape the sun. In a few hours they would sail back to Red Hook and Flake would pay her.

"Hey," came a voice from the stern.

Beth climbed back to the cockpit and walked to the stern.

George treaded water. "Hi Beth, how's your day going?"

She looked down at him and then glanced at Flake. "Horribly," she said. "Flake is passed out drunk. But the guests are fine and happily humping ashore. I'll be glad when this day is over."

"Are you going to be alright?"

Beth nodded. "Yeah. We'll get through this. How are you doing?"

George glanced back at *Hope*. "Windy had a bout of nerves, but she seems to be doing okay. I was hoping this would be all over by now." He and Beth watched Windy swim toward them.

"I can't believe you are out there sailing and hoping to be sunk. It is crazy."

"You may be right."

Windy stopped beside George, wearing only a big smile. "Hi. How are you doing?"

"Okay," said Beth. "How about you?"

"I don't know," said Windy. "I'll tell you tomorrow."

"We should be getting back," said George. "I'm sure Harold is trying to call us again."

Swimming back, he thought about his last conversation with Harold. Harold had mentioned Brigitta taking *Frihet* with her sister. And there was no new information on the drone, which was a huge concern. Christine had it located, or thought she had, but then the damned thing moved. Neither the Navy nor Harold's people had heard anything new from the drone since then, only the usual undersea clicks and squeaks that are always heard under the sea. Their attempts at sonar triangulation had proved worthless. During the conversation, Harold had sounded terribly anxious. Was the usually cool calm Harold Habit getting rattled? And what could Brigitta be up to?

At the stern of *Hope,* he stopped to let Windy scurry up the swim ladder first, then followed.

Drying in the cockpit, he said, "Do you feel better?"

Windy nodded. "Yes. The swim really helped. I am sorry about this morning. It was nerves I guess."

George smiled. "It's fine, don't worry about it. The swim was fun."

Windy rubbed her head with a towel.

"You are beautiful," said George.

Windy snapped the towel and him and then wrapped it around her torso. "I'm learning to love skinny dipping. Who ever thought bathing suits were a good idea?"

"It's the only way to swim."

A few minutes later they hoisted the mainsail.

*

Autonomous Shark-09 latched onto a titanium nipple and shared a video with Mother. A blonde woman sailed to the northeast aboard a sleek boat. Mother recognized the woman as Brigitta Eriksson and adjusted her course more northerly, hoping to get near *Frihet,* the boat Brigitta sailed. Analyzing face identification data, Mother realized there were two Brigitta Eriksson's aboard *Frihet*. Cloning? Her processor sped through known information to see if that were possible.

*

Harold stopped at the stairs that led up to the helicopters and looked at his watch. The day was slipping away. The glistening white helicopter, Whirly One, and her pilot waited for orders on the starboard pad. Harold nodded to the pilot as he climbed aboard.

"Where to?" asked the pilot, handing Harold a set of headphones.

"Let's do a fly over of *Hope* and *Frihet*," said Harold.

The starter whined until the turbo started to fire. As the rumble increased, they lifted off.

Not a hundred feet above the sparkling blue ocean, they sped east. Harold pointed at the mountainous island of Jost Van Dyke in the distance and the pilot turned. The glistening water zipped beneath them. Approaching the white sandy beaches of Hans Lollik, they rose up and over the island's green hill, then dropped down to fly low over the sea again.

At the far end of Jost Van Dyke, *Hope* plowed through the water toward them. The copter sped past and turned to port over the black hulled *Raven* anchored in turquois water. Two honeymooners, entwined on a towel behind a boulder next to a tiny beach, went unnoticed. The aircraft completed the turn and sped to the southwest. Far ahead, Harold spotted *Frihet* sailing to the northeast.

Harold pointed toward the boat and then downward. The pilot dropped down to inches above the water and zipped past the boat, banked into a hasty turn, and then flew the craft alongside *Frihet*.

Harold picked up a VHF microphone. "*Frihet, Frihet, Frihet*, come in please."

The background noise almost made the conversation impossible, but Brigitta answered, "What do you want?"

"Please return to Red Hook. What do you think you are doing out here?"

"Trying to get away from the likes of you," said Brigitta, shutting off the VHF radio.

"Let's tack this baby over," she said.

Tova turned her back to the helicopter and prepared to release the genoa sheet.

As the boat turned away, the helicopter continued to the northeast, then made a U-turn to the left and disappeared to the west.

"Fuck him," said Brigitta. "I hate the man." She started to cry.

"Hey," said Tova, stepping aft to hug her sister. "Don't let that man get to you. Are you all right?"

Brigitta sobbed uncontrollably.

Tova looked about…the auto pilot steered and they were miles from anything to hit. She stayed beside Brigitta to console her. Something was definitely wrong with her sister.

"Come, let's enjoy this day," she said. "Teach me to sail this boat." She had never seen her sister cry like that.

Brigitta pushed her sunglasses up to wipe her eyes. "I am sorry."

"Don't be. Let's go find George."

Brigitta looked to the north, then said, "Come, hold the wheel, I'll see if I can find him on the computer."

*

Sailing on a broad reach, with the breeze over the port aft quarter, *Hope* plowed along at only a little over three knots. On that heading, the apparent wind dropped to near nothing and the day felt intolerably hot. Over Tortola and St. Thomas, white puffy clouds accumulated, but never promised rain or shade. Ahead, sport fishing boats headed back toward Red Hook.

"Do you have more sunscreen?" asked George.

Windy had put on a long-sleeved pale-blue shirt with her bikini bottom, along with a wide brimmed straw hat. "I put it on my legs," she said.

"We'll cook out here," said George. He also wore a long sleeve shirt with a cotton fedora. "By the time we reach Hans Lollik it will be almost five o'clock. I'm all for dropping the hook in the shallows between Hans and Little Hans islands and spending the night. I'm not keen on having this boat knocked out from beneath me in the dark."

Windy smiled. "I'll go along with that." She looked across the empty water toward St. Thomas and St. John. "You don't think the drone will attack today?"

Only two white sails poked along to the south. "I don't know what to think. I was hoping it would be all over this morning." Slightly to port of dead ahead, a sailboat beat directly toward them.

"Harold put plenty of food aboard the boat. He must have thought this might happen."

"We'll make the best of it," said George. "There is a bottle of wine. I didn't look in all the lockers, maybe there is something else too."

*

There could not be two Brigitta Erikssons. Mother accelerated. One had to be an imposter and possibly a threat.

49

"That's *Frihet*," said George. "She's coming right at us."

Windy peeked around the genoa. "What are they doing?"

"Damned if I know."

"She's going to pass on our portside."

"*Hope, Hope, Hope,* this is *Number One*, come in please." It was Harold's voice coming from the VHF Radio.

Frihet heeled to port with white water splitting at her bow.

"Do you want me to get the radio?" asked Windy.

George shook his head. "Shut it off."

Frihet passed within two boat lengths off the port side, bore off the wind behind *Hope*, and jibed over to catch up on *Hope's* starboard side.

"They are catching up fast," said Windy.

"This boat probably weighs half again what that one does, maybe more, and look how much sail they have."

They could hear the water parting on *Frihet's* bow. Soon, they could almost touch her bow pulpit. Brigitta stood behind the port helm, peering under the genoa.

"Did she ask to take your boat?" said Windy.

"It's as much hers as it is mine," said George.

Tova stood beside Brigitta. The topsides of *Frihet* were only a foot or two from *Hope's* aft quarter.

"As they go by us our sails will blanket theirs," said George. "They'll have trouble getting by."

Frihet crept by with not much more than an arm's length between the hulls.

"We have to talk," yelled Brigitta.

"This is not the time," answered George.

"Yes it is."

Crash!

Hope rose eight feet. Windy fell against the companionway. George's knees buckled, but his hands stayed locked onto the wheel.

"George!" screamed Brigitta.

Hope rolled to port and splashed back into the sea, causing George to lose his grip and fall against the port lifelines.

"Windy?" he yelled. "Are you okay?" She clutched the cockpit coaming with her feet dangling over the side.

To starboard the dark gray bow of Mother climbed like a missile rising from the sea. The rumble of a capitating propeller drummed in everyone's ears. Mother's bow pushed higher than *Hope*'s spreaders.

"The canisters," said George, forcing himself up.

All but one had launched themselves. Mother paused, then fell back onto the cabin of *Hope*, shattering the house and deck and nearly breaking the boat in two. The last canister disappeared under the sea as the boat slid out from under the massive drone. *Hope*'s mast tumbled to port.

Brigitta snapped the wheel to starboard and away from the drone, spinning *Frihet*, causing the boom to swing across in a jibe, and then the wind backed the sails, forcing a complete three-sixty. *Hope* lay shattered, her deck awash in the sea. As *Frihet*'s sails refilled, her bow started toward *Hope*'s transom.

Flaccid sails swirled in the water. Hope's bow settled beneath the surface. Her shattered mast submerged to port. Pieces of wood floated everywhere. The inflatable tender floated away attached to a chunk of the transom.

"George," screamed Brigitta. "Windy, climb aboard."

George tossed Windy onto *Frihet* as if she were a doll, then grabbed the pulpit.

The remains of *Hope* surged upward, pushed again by the drone, before slipping away. When Mother crashed down only splinters of *Hope* remained on the surface. Even the tender had disappeared.

Brigitta turned to starboard to jibe again.

"Head for Jost," said George, reaching the cockpit.

"I want to see if my canisters entangle the drone," said Brigitta.

"No! Let's get out of here."

From the west four gray helicopters approached.

"No." Brigitta spun *Frihet* back toward the boiling sea.

George pushed her aside and grabbed the wheel. "You can't endanger all of us."

"There it is," said Tova, pointing ahead.

Barely beneath the surface, the drone pushed up a wave as it raced toward them.

Like a clap of thunder, it slammed into *Frihet*'s hull under the cockpit, directly beneath where Tova stood next to the lifelines. The boat jumped upward and leaned to port, almost putting the rail underwater. Tova dropped to her knees and grabbed at a stanchion, barely staying aboard. With a rumble *Frihet*'s keel slid along the drone's top.

"The rudder," said George. "If it damages the rudder...."

Mother disappeared down into the sea on the starboard side. But the strings from the canisters tailed behind, obviously caught somehow on the drone. The tentacles slid under *Frihet* far enough beneath the surface that they did not entangle the keel or rudder. They appeared to be a hundred yards long in a spaghetti-like mass.

"It will work," said Brigitta. "My idea will work. Those strands are incredibly strong and will twist up around the propeller and force it to stop."

As the last of the cords disappeared, George adjusted the course toward Jost Van Dyke. Tova trimmed the sails.

"Let's hope the thing floats," said George, thinking it seemed like a long shot.

"Even if it doesn't," said Brigitta, "it is shallow enough here the Navy can easily retrieve the drone off the bottom."

Frihet accelerated, reaching at 7.1 knots. The breeze felt good and water whispered along the hull. Nobody spoke, which suited George's mood. He settled into the seat behind the port helm.

"What are they doing?" said Brigitta, looking back where they had come from.

The helicopters were dropping long slender tubes into the sea, two from each of the two helicopters.

"Those are torpedoes," said Brigitta, knowing the answer to her own question. "Why are they doing that? Why?"

George said nothing. It was obvious the Navy did not want to lose the drone again. Brigitta disappeared down the companionway. George guessed she would call Harold to find out what was happening.

Static on the VHF speaker next to the helm told him the radio had been turned on. "*Frihet, Frihet, Frihet,* this is the sailing vessel *Raven,* come in please." It sounded like Beth.

50

"Beth, is that you?" asked Brigitta, recognizing the accent as British.

"Yes. I heard you on the radio, and I hate to bother you. We're over in Great Harbour and need to be rescued."

"Rescued?"

Beth ran through an abbreviated account of how she and two tourists ended up spending the day with a quite drunk captain.

"Flake, the bloody fool, insisted on stopping here," said Beth. "He went ashore in the tender to clear customs and hasn't come back, and it has been over an hour. Can you come get us? I really am tempted to sail off in his boat, but the bloody bastard would most likely have us arrested."

George, listening in the cockpit, altered course, and asked Tova to harden up on the sheets. Great Harbour lay dead ahead.

Windy, leaning against the forward end of the cockpit, appeared dazed and her tan had paled. She had said little since *Hope* sunk beneath them.

"Of course," said Brigitta.

"What is happening out there?" asked Beth. "Has George found the drone?"

"He is onboard *Frihet* now. The drone sunk *Hope*," said Brigitta.

A waved smackped the forward starboard quarter, sending droplets aloft. To the south, something sounded like thunder and George wondered if a torpedo had found its mark. The helicopters remained in the area, he guessed probably searching for debris.

East of south and a half mile away, a hill of froth bubbled to the surface, followed by rumbles and another bulging mound of foam. The undersea explosions were not as dramatic as in the old movies.

Beth repeated, "Is he all right?"

"Yes. We'll be there in less than an hour," said Brigitta.

Brigitta climbed back out to the cockpit to sit at a forward corner. Her usual smile had faded. George wondered where she found the oversize sweatshirt she wore.

"Are you okay?" asked Tova.

"I just feel cold."

"Harold must have his reasons."

"He sent me a text," said Brigitta. "The Navy made the decision to destroy the drone. It was out of his hands."

They sailed without talking. The hour dragged, but clearing Dog Hole Point they picked out *Raven*'s black hull among the dozen white sailboats anchored in Great Harbour. When they were a hundred yards away, Beth stood on the side deck and waved. Beside her stood a young couple.

George sailed up behind *Raven*, easing the sails to slow *Frihet*. Coming alongside while barely making way, Beth passed two duffle bags to Tova, helped William and Kathy step aboard *Frihet*, and then followed. Turning away, *Frihet*'s sails filled with a pop and introductions were made.

"Where to?" asked George.

Beth smiled. "Someplace other than here, how about Little Harbour?"

"What about the honeymooners?"

"They don't have to be anywhere," said Beth.

"Nobody will miss us," said William, smiling. "This has been the most exciting day of our lives. Shanghaied by a drunken pirate, wait until our friends here this."

"You got a little sun today," said George. "You look like a lobster."

William smiled. "We'll live through it."

Beth smiled. "I took my pay out of his wallet, the full two hundred he promised. I don't know if he'll miss it when he gets back and sobers up."

"Brigitta, what do you want to do?" asked George.

"I do not want to go back. I do not want to see Harold again, ever."

Brigitta's reaction surprised George, particularly the anger in her eyes. He asked Tova to show Kathy and William around the boat and to put their things in his cabin. Stepping aside, he asked Beth to steer for a bit, then went to sit beside Windy.

"Are you all right?" he asked.

She nodded. "I'm fine."

"You look troubled."

"I thought we were going to die. I never felt so scared."

He noticed her hands shaking and slipped an arm around her shoulders in a hug. "We are fine, it is all over."

She nodded again and started to cry.

*

"Did they get it?" asked Captain Able.

Christine shook her head. "There is no way to know. I would think so."

In front of them, in the large cabin in the center of *Absent*'s belly, four technicians sat at computers, wearing headphones and staring at the screens. Sonar buoys sent data from a multitude of directions.

"We picked up something," said the one furthest away. On the screen in front of him a white line made regular waves. "I think it's the drone's prop."

The other technicians typed, trying to lock in on the sound too.

"Mother's?" asked Christine.

"Yes. I am quite sure. It must be dragging Brigitta's Kevlar strings and have some must have wrapped around the propeller. It is much louder than ever before."

"Can we triangulate?" asked Christine.

Fingers typed rapidly. Somewhere onboard a door shut with a thump.

"I got it," said a second technician. "She's near the bottom, moving northeast. Here are the coordinates." Latitude and longitude appeared on the screen overhead.

"How fast is it moving?"

"Not very, maybe one knot."

"Do you think the Navy hears it," asked Able.

Christine shook her head. "Our gear is much more sophisticated than theirs. They might have it, but I wouldn't bet on it."

"What about Harold?" asked Able. "Where is he?"

"He's aboard *Number One*. I should let him know his toy hasn't been destroyed."

"We still have another submarine about three miles to the east of Jost Van Dyke and just out of territorial waters," said the first technician.

"It's not one of ours. I believe it is Chinese. The Russian one seems to have disappeared north of Jost."

Able reached for a mug of coffee. "Are you going to call Harold?"

"I will. It would be nice if we could drop a sonar buoy or two to the north and maybe find that Russian boat."

*

The wash of Mother's propeller kicked up clouds of sand from the bottom. Her sensors said she made too much sound, but nothing could be done about it. The tangled web caused the props blades to turn out of balance, making her entire structure vibrate. And the buoyancy of the tentacles made moving ahead along the bottom difficult, simply staying submerged was a struggle.

When the torpedoes attacked, her sharks defended the only way they could, by swimming into the torpedoes and detonating them. Mother could not be sure how many she had lost, possibly more than half. Many had been out scouring the surrounding harbors and, until they returned, she could not be sure they were safe.

One of the sharks, AS-08, had seen the fake Brigitta clearly enough to know she was not the real Brigitta. In a hasty move, when the pretender stood near the lifelines, Mother had attempted to jar the boat, hoping to knock her into the sea. But by then the strands attached to Mother had worked their way around the propeller and caused her to slow. To save herself, she deliberately sunk to the bottom.

Four sharks had been sent out to find that boat with the imposter again. Three sharks stayed on the bottom with Mother and attempted untangling her. In a hundred and eighty feet of water, Mother settled on her side on the sandy bottom. Two sharks moved in to suckle on her belly while one started to nose at the strands.

*

"Harold is coming over in the tender," said Christine. "He's hoping the Navy thinks the drone is destroyed and goes home."

"Is that likely?" asked Captain Able.

"Not really." Christine sat at an empty computer and started to type. "Not unless they find some debris. Does anybody know where *Frihet* is? And has anybody heard anything from George."

"Not since before he stepped onto *Frihet*," said Able.

"Let's get him on the screen," said Christine, to the man sitting at her right. "Link into one of Harold's satellites."

51

George pushed the anchor off of its chocks and it slithered fifteen feet to the sandy bottom. The tradewinds settled *Frihet* back as he walked aft along the port deck. Beth shut off the auxiliary and stepped away from the port helm.

Earlier, soon after Beth, William, and Kathy had boarded back in Great Harbour, the celebration had started. A twelve pack of Heineken materialized from the refrigerator along with a bottle of Napa Valley Cabernet Sauvignon. Beth brought two bottles of Cruzan rum out. By the time they dropped the anchor near Diamond Cay off the east end of Jost Van Dyke, everyone had consumed a couple of drinks.

"Are you okay?" asked George, sitting beside Windy.

"I'm fine," she answered. "I guess my nerves are just rattled."

A "Yee-haw", followed by a splash let everyone know William had jumped off the boat.

"Hey," said Beth, "how about I take the tender ashore to find us some scotch? There's none left on the boat."

George smiled. "See what you can find. Maybe we'll go ashore later to get something to eat too. See what's available."

A second splash announced Tova had jumped into the sea too.

"I'll go with you," said Windy.

As they left, George stood on a cockpit seat to look at the swimmers. An arm slipped inside of his.

"Can we talk?" asked Brigitta.

"Is this the time?"

She nodded. "Ja."

"Inside?"

She shook her head yes and he followed her down the companionway steps.

"I am through with Harold," she said. "I will not work for a man who thinks he is God."

"He thinks he is God?"

"He believes he knows what is best for all of us. I cannot work for him."

George tried to read Brigitta's face, but saw only fear. "What does that mean?"

Brigitta said nothing, but raised a shoulder in a half-hearted shrug. Her eyes searched his face. "I am free of him. We can build a life together."

"A life together? What happens the next time you follow that inquisitive mind of yours to discover some unknown? Will our relationship be put on the back burner again?" George turned to look out the companionway. "I can't do it. I can't let myself be in love with you. I have been hurt too many times."

"Those days are over." Tears welled in her eyes.

George wrapped his arms around her. "Can we talk about this another time? You are the most beautiful and smartest woman I know, but I can't do it."

Her arms slipped around his waist. "Let me have a chance."

He gave her a squeeze. "Come out to the cockpit. Everyone is celebrating."

Kathy had joined William and Tova in the water. *Frihet*'s tender was pulled up on the beach and neither Beth nor Windy were in sight.

"Can I get you something to drink?" asked George.

"What do you have to mix with the rum?"

"Tonic."

"Just on the rocks then, assuming you have ice."

George laughed. It wasn't many years before that ice was a precious commodity on boats. "We have lots of ice. Would you like some lime juice? I think we were worried about scurvy when we bought them, because we bought ten of them."

Brigitta smiled. "Yes, lime would be nice. Det skulle vara trevligt, tack."

The spoken Swedish made George smile. Brigitta looked lovely. She had put on a pale blue lightweight jersey that was Tova's, and her hair was pulled back into a pony tail. When she forced a smile her eyes took on the color of her jersey.

As George handed her the drink, he said, "Tell me about the flying drones you were working on."

"The ones that fly like birds?"

He could see her excitement as he sat beside her. Near the beach, the tender headed back toward *Frihet*. Windy still didn't look to be in a partying mood. Tova climbed up the swim ladder to rinse with the shower hose. Soon, Kathy and William joined her with lots of laughing and giggling.

Brigitta went on about the possibilities of flight using the magnocellular plastics she had worked with. To George it all sounded like magic. Wearing a towel around her torso, Tova dropped onto the seat beside him to listen to Brigitta too.

Beth stopped the tender alongside and passed two bottles of twelve year old Macallan to George, then climbed aboard with Windy.

"We have an unwanted guest," said Beth, pointing at a black hull sloop rounding the east end of Jost Van Dyke. "It sure looks like *Raven* to me."

"How did Flake know we were here?" asked Tova.

"He must have seen us sailing east."

"Maybe he won't see us," said Brigitta.

"He's looking for his two hundred dollars," said George. "He'll see us."

The black boat eased her sheets to steer directly toward them.

"Skit," said Brigitta.

Beth laughed. "Skit?"

"That is shit in English," said Brigitta, smiling. "We do not need him, from what I heard he is an ass."

"How do you say ass in Swedish?" asked Beth.

"Röv."

"Okay, he's a röv."

Everyone laughed.

"We can certainly deal with a drunk," said George.

"Would you like a scotch?" asked Beth.

George smiled. "Why not"

"Isn't that *A New Beginning*?" asked Tova, pointing beyond *Raven*. The motor yacht had cleared the east end of the island.

"Bill Sanderlee's boat?" said George. "It sure looks like them."

*

"I have them on the screen," said Christine. "There's George, with Tova and Brigitta. Who's the other three?"

"The one with the blonde kinky hair is Beth Weatherington. She joined the boat in Bermuda," said Harold. "I have no idea who the other two are."

"What do you want to do?"

"Is Mother moving?"

"No. She's still is in the same place. Has the Navy made a move?"

"They haven't said a thing," said Harold. "That makes me think they know where it is too. Any sign of the Chinese or Russians?"

"No," said Christine. "If the Navy knows where it is, why don't they try to torpedo it again?"

Harold paced, obviously flustered. "I don't know. Maybe they are out of torpedoes, or maybe they don't want to admit they didn't get it the first time. They seem to suffer an inconceivable amount of pride."

"Why don't we go up there?" asked Captain Able. "We'll at least be closer to whatever happens."

"I can be there in five minutes on one of the helicopters," said Harold.

"And do what, you can't land on the water."

"All right, let's go," said Harold, dropping into an empty chair. "The Navy has a small research submarine on one of their boats. It may be in the water now looking for Mother. It could be looking at her now."

"And if they are?" asked Able.

"If the research sub is in the water we would hear it," said Christine. "Most of those aren't designed to be very quiet. Let's move up there. We'll be better able to hear what is going on, too."

*

Shark AS-07 raced back toward Mother. In Jost Van Dyke's East End Harbour she had seen Brigitta Eriksson and the imposter, both on the same boat. It was imperative that Mother know.

The little drone's sonar bounced off of a large steel object a mile to the east. Another submarine? Whose? First AS-07 must tell Mother about the phony Brigitta, and then she would investigate the vessel to the east beyond Sandy Cay.

*

Raven coasted up along *Frihet*'s starboard side, her sails flogging lazily. Flake wore a red bandana tied around his head and dark glasses hid his eyes.

"Hey buddy," he said. "I sees you got my mate on board. Me thinks the lady's got something of mine."

"You said the pay was a hundred for the day," said Beth, "double if I got your lady guest to take her top off. I did my end, so you owed me two hundred. While you were passed out drunk I helped myself."

"I was part of a wager?" laughed Kathy. "This day keeps getting better."

"How about we forget all about this," said George. "If you want to join us, we'll be having dinner ashore later."

Flake looked off to the south, then turned back and said, "I'm going to anchor up ahead. Maybe I'll join you ashore later. I hate to let the ladies down."

He turned *Raven* to starboard and drifted away. His sails finally filled and *Raven* accelerated.

"He's shit faced," said George. "He'll probably fall asleep and we won't see him until morning."

"I'm not afraid of him," said Beth, laughing. "Pour me a dab of that scotch."

A hundred yards away, Flake tacked to port to nuzzle his boat up into the shallows near Green Cay.

"*A New Beginning* is getting here fast," said Tova.

The large dark blue motor yacht headed directly towards them.

52

"They put their tender in the water," said Beth.

A New Beginning had anchored a hundred yards to the south, off *Frihet*'s starboard side. The big rigid-bottom inflatable motored toward them.

George poured another dram of scotch in his glass, then offered Tova some. She held her glass up, signaling yes. Windy's glass hadn't been touched.

"George," said Bill Sanderlee, coming alongside. "I made reservations ashore for my crew and yours. Please be my guests."

"We'd love it," said George. "What time?"

The conversation drifted to the day's events. Bill remained angry about the way the Navy had questioned his crew, as if they were suspects in a crime. George suggested Bill's crew visit *Frihet* for cocktails and soon the crews of both boats sat in the cockpit toasting all sorts of celebratory events.

A small helicopter flew over once, close enough they could recognize Harold Habit in the passenger seat, and they all waved. Harold didn't look happy and the aircraft disappeared around the corner of the hill on Jost Van Dyke.

George sat beside Beth and asked, "Where's Windy?"

"She's in her cabin."

"Is she all right?"

"She was pretty shook up by what happened today."

George excused himself and went inside the boat. The door to Windy's cabin was closed. He knocked. "Are you okay?"

"I'm fine," came from the inside.

"Can I come in?"

"Yes."

Windy sat on her bed against pillows stacked high. The red around her eyes said she had been crying.

"Why don't you come back outside?" asked George.

"I don't feel like it."

He sat beside her. "We're fine, the danger is over."

"I know." She wiped an errant tear from her cheek. "You know what the worst part was today? Knowing how upset my family would be if we were killed by that drone. They never liked me sailing offshore."

"We were not offshore. And sailing is safe, maybe as safe as walking down the street."

"I know, but they worry about me." Her face wrinkled up as if about to cry again. "I can't do this to them."

"Do what?"

"Make them worry. It isn't fair to them."

"You're not making sense. You can't give up sailing so they will stop worrying. That's nuts. Would they really want you to do that? Do they want you to stay on a couch somewhere so you'll be safe?"

"They would love me to stop sailing and settle down."

George shook his head. "Come here." He wrapped his arms around her. "We're going ashore in a half hour. Bill Sanderlee is taking us all to dinner. Come along with us."

Windy wiped an eye. "I don't know. I need a shower and some time to think."

"Is that a yes?"

Windy forced a smile. "A maybe."

George shut the door as he left her cabin.

William came down into the boat. "Can we shower?" he asked.

"Of course. Use the one on the swim platform," said George. "There's towels in the locker to starboard."

"Great. I have a clean shirt in my bag," said William. He looked to be having the time of his life.

At the aft end of the cockpit Tova, Brigitta, Kathy, and Betsy sat in a conversation about something. On the swim platform Beth rinsed suds from her hair. Bill and Brook sat on the cabin top laughing and talking. Randall and Trish leaned against the mast, looking toward Sandy Spit.

Beth came forward wrapped in a towel. "Is Windy okay?"

"Just rattled," said George. "She'll be okay."

"George," said Bill. "Come up here. We were wondering when we might get you to take us sailing."

Sitting next to them, George answered, "I haven't thought that far ahead. Can we talk about this in a couple of weeks? Things need to settle down."

"Sure. Is the drone dead?"

"I really don't know," offered George. "Either way, I think my part is done."

"George, look." It was Brigitta, standing and pointing to the east.

A dark shark fin slowly swam directly at them.

"Is that one of yours?"

Brigitta said, "Fan det, det är det. Och det finns en annan."

George understood none of the Swedish, so said, "You lost me babe."

"It is. And there is another one."

A second black fin sliced through the water only a few yards to the south of the first.

"Shit," said George.

Both of the fins slithered down out of sight.

"What are they doing?" asked George. By then everyone onboard stood to look at where the fins had been.

"They are searching, looking for something for Mother. Look over there." Brigitta pointed to the south. Another dark triangle cut through the water.

George walked aft to stand beside Brigitta. "What are they looking for?"

"I have no idea. Wood boats? Who knows?"

"How much input did you have in the designing of Mother?"

"Only the final tweaking. She had already been built when I got involved, but I helped with the fins, propeller, and shape of the bow."

"With her AI, or whatever it is they call its artificial intelligence, would the drone remember you?" asked George. "Harold said the drone was programmed to learn on its own. Maybe it is looking for you?"

"That's crazy," said Brigitta.

The sharks had disappeared and almost everyone was sitting again.

"Let's go ashore," said Bill.

A few needed a little more time to clean up, but twenty minutes later the tenders from *Frihet* and *A New Beginning* headed for the beach.

*

"The drone is moving again," said one of the technicians, as Harold entered the room.

"Can you tell where she is headed?"

"Northeast, toward the east end of Jost Van Dyke, She's a lot quieter than before, but still not as quiet as she once was." White lines danced across the screen in front of the technician. "Apparently it shed whatever caused it to vibrate before."

"This is bizarre," said Harold, watching a red X on another screen that depicted the location of the drone. A third screen looked down on George and the rest of his crew.

Christine pulled her phone from a pocket and looked at its display. Immediately she punched a number.

"What do you have?" she asked.

Two minutes later she said, "Get me Brigitta on the radio."

"They haven't been answering," said Harold. "What's up?"

"A man named Hanson, who was part of the team that programed Mother, sent me a text. He thinks the drone may be trying to protect Brigitta."

"What?"

"When she was working on the propeller and the fins, there was a certain amount of danger, because of the drone's autonomous nature. A moving fin or prop could easily crush a person. He programmed the drone to think of Brigitta as a mother figure, someone who created the drone, birthed her in a way. Hanson thinks that is why the drone crashed into *Frihet*. He watched it on a recorded satellite video and it hit directly below where Tova stood."

"That doesn't make sense," said Harold. "She looks exactly like Brigitta."

"Hanson thinks the drone sees the differences. It has the best in facial recognition technology that came from your company. It believes Tova as a threat," said Christine, sounding frustrated.

Harold looked out of a port to the south. "How long until this boat gets there?"

"The east end of Jost? Maybe an hour," said Captain Able.

"Keep trying to call them," said Harold.

*

Mother moved to the northeast, kicking up a cloud of silt off the bottom. If an autonomous machine with artificial intelligence can feel relief, she was glad to be free of the tentacles that had entangled her propeller. Six of her sharks moved with her and more swam ahead. It created a feeling of security and power.

One shark reported on Brigitta's location and also that of the imposter. A second one confirmed it. Mother knew what she had to do.

53

George's cell phone vibrated, but he ignored it. The band cavorted through another Calypso song and a dozen sweaty people moved to its rhythm on the dance floor. By that time George worked on his fifth scotch and focusing taxed his abilities. Warm sticky air that smelled of tropical foliage filtered through the place, but beneath his bare feet the sand felt cool. If it weren't for the mosquitoes chomping on his shins....

Dinner had been excellent, with spiny lobsters all around and drinks aplenty. Bill Sanderlee had ordered for everyone. Rum flowed as if it were free. The music had gone on nonstop, starting shortly after they sat. Two couples from charter boats were the first on the dance floor, but the crews of *A New Beginning* and *Frihet* kept the place hopping.

Shortly after the meal, Tova grabbed George's hand to lead him onto the dance floor. By then a multitude of couples were dancing and George found himself dancing first with Brigitta and then Beth, as well as Betsy and finally Trish from *A New Beginning*. The band never quit between songs, but slid from one into the next. The dance floor felt increasingly hot, somewhere between a furnace and a sauna. Sweat trickled down inside George's shirt. Finally, in a lull, George escaped back to his table.

"Where's Windy?" asked George, dropping into a chair beside Beth.

"She walked out the back."

"I'm going to see if I can find her."

George slipped out the back of the bar into much cooler air. Coki frogs screamed and stars pierced the sky. The air felt heavy and smelled of greenery. To the right, dim lights shined inside a small home a hundred feet away. Closer to the left, the silhouette of an unlit building stood against the starlit sky. George walked that direction.

Passing the building, he headed toward the beach and turned away from the loud music. Waves tickled onto the sand and phosphorescence flickered where the water kissed the shore. Hobie cats were pulled up onto the beach with their masts pointed skyward. The dark silhouette of a young woman sat on the furthest one.

"Windy?" said George.

"George?"

"I was wondering where you went."

"I needed time to think."

"Can I join you?" asked George.

"Of course."

He slipped up onto the Hobie's trampoline beside her. "Are you all right?"

"I'm fine. What a beautiful night."

"It is. There's lots of them down here."

Little waves licked the sand near their feet. Far to the south lights flickered on the island of Tortola.

Windy set her hand on George's. "George, I'm going to fly back home."

"To Cape Cod? To stay?"

"Yes." In the dark he couldn't see her face, but he sensed her smile. "I want to be near my family. This has been great fun, but I am a New England girl and that is where I need to be."

"I can understand," said George, wishing he could see her face. "You are a special woman and I am glad to know you. This living on a boat isn't for everybody."

Her hand squeezed his. "I know. Now let's go back inside and dance. I may never get to dance to Calypso again."

*

"Their boat looks dark," said Christine. "*A New Beginning,* too. There's hardly a light on."

"I think everyone is ashore," said Captain Able. "I'll have the crew launch the work boats."

Absent settled back on her anchor chain a hundred feet south of *A New Beginning.* Only a few lights showed ashore, punching holes in the dark silhouette of Jost Van Dyke. Music drifted across the water from the bar and the bass guitar pounded like a heartbeat. About a dozen sailboats shared the anchorage.

"What is Harold doing?" asked Able.

The whispers of waves kissing the beach drifted in the pilothouse door. Land lights reflected off the water, along with pinpricks from the stars.

"He is in a video call with the programmer Hanson. Maybe they can come up with a plan."

"Let's hope so," said Able. He picked up a phone to speak with the crew setting the workboats in the water, then set it down a minute later.

"Would you like to go ashore?" he asked.

Christine smiled. "Can we dance to at least one song?"

Able smiled. "Of course. Let me see who else wants to go."

*

George glanced at his Rolex. Other than being on watch when sailing offshore, he hadn't been up that late in years. An hour earlier, he spotted *Absent*'s lights as she anchored south of his boat. About a half hour later, one of her workboat's came ashore.

Harold sat across from him at the picnic table, wide awake and alert, as though his day had just started. Inside the dimly lit bar, the tempo hadn't slowed and the dance floor looked crowded. A light breeze slipped around the back of the building, cooling George and Harold in the darkness.

"So, you really think the drone will take the bait?" asked George.

"Hanson seems to think so," said Harold. "This artificial intelligence stuff is a new ball game, and nobody is sure how these things will learn. Hanson thinks the drone has learned maternal instincts, which is why she caters to her sharks like a protective mother. And Hanson thinks it has tried to protect Brigitta."

"What do you think?"

"I don't know what to think. My new ideas ran out when I built the satellites."

"So when are we going to try it?"

"Tomorrow afternoon. With everyone up this late, tomorrow morning could be a disaster."

Looking inside the murky bar, Windy danced with Bill from *A New Beginning*. The stab of jealousy surprised George.

"Do you really think you can get Brigitta to go along?" asked George.

*

Mother crept along the bottom, listening to her sharks. A half dozen were reporting at once. She sorted through the information…Brigitta's location, the imposter's whereabouts, the boat they sailed on, other vessels around them, and the troubling position of the Navy and submarines.

Shark AS-07 reported another vessel listening also, and appearing to shadow Brigitta. A small ship. On the side of the boat's bow the word *Absent* meant nothing to Mother. Her stored data could find nothing about it, its owner, nor its purpose. But the vessel's silhouette looked much like a retired Russian research vessel and that caused concern. Somewhere in her memory it had been planted to never trust a Russian.

Conflicting concepts flicked through Mother's processor. One moment she needed to dash to Brigitta's rescue, then the next save herself and the drones. The urges clashed and disordered her normally organized processer.

54

Off the transom, Jost Van Dyke woke to the gray light of dawn. Ahead of the boat, to the east, the sun had yet to appear, yet the sky glowed in shades of white. Tortola looked like a dark hulk to the southeast and a sooty cloud hung near her peak. George stretched to straighten out sore muscles and tasted the air. The night had been spent on a cockpit seat, while the newlywed couple slept in his cabin.

The group had returned to the boat a little after one in the morning. Someone had said something about another drink and, thankfully, nobody seconded the motion. As the crew disappeared into the cabin, George had stretched out on a cockpit seat.

Earlier, when he woke and went inside to make the coffee, Tova and Brigitta had slept among tussled sheets on the settees, one to port and the other to starboard. He purposely had not looked long enough to figure out who was who.

A Navy MH-60R helicopter hummed eastward a few miles to the south. A long black and white cylinder hung from a cable beneath its belly. George guessed that meant they didn't know the location of the drone and they were still looking for it. Sipping his coffee, he watched the copter turn to the north and disappear over the horizon a few minutes later.

"God morgon, hur är kaffet?" said Brigitta, coming up the companionway and carrying a steaming mug.

"Fine," said George. "You are up early."

She looked sleepy and wore a pale blue tee shirt that hung down over her hips. A breath of wind lifted a strand of her hair across her face.

She pushed it back behind an ear and sat next to him. She asked, "Did Harold talk to you?"

George nodded his head and said, "Yes." Brigitta's eyes picked up the color of her tee shirt and he almost forgot the question. He ached to wrap his arms around her, but feared the pain she had caused. He blurted out, "Did he convince you to go along?"

"Ja. It is the only way to save the drone."

George sipped from his mug and watched a distant frigate bird. "I thought you were mad at him."

Brigitta swallowed a mouthful of her coffee, then set down the mug to pull her hair back into a ponytail. "I am, but the drone was difficult to create. I hate to see it all lost."

A laughing gull flew by, inspecting the boat for possible food to steal, then veered toward the land to search for scraps outside the bar. Feeble waves swished up onto the beach and the palm trees stood rock still. Far to the east, a lone sailboat motored downwind along the coast north of Tortola.

"Let's take the dinghy ashore," said George, "and find someplace for a swim."

Brigitta smiled. "That would be fun. I will find us some towels."

Well away from the boat, George gunned the dinghy and it popped up onto a plane. Five minutes later they approached the sands of an empty beach on the island of Little Jost Van Dyke. When George killed the engine and stood to tilt it forward, Brigitta slipped over the bow with the painter in her hand. Together they pulled the boat up onto the beach.

"There's a goat path that goes to the top of the hill," said George. "Let's go up and watch the sun come up over Tortola."

He took her hand to lead the way, but soon the path narrowed, so he walked in front. Prickly cactus lined the way and loose stones rolled under their feet, but they reached the rocky top as the sun peered over Tortola. Instantly the air felt warmer.

"What a way to start the day," said Brigitta.

George sat on a weather worn ledge. The air smelled of dried leaves and a few leaves rustled from a breath of wind. Far to the east, white sails from a distant schooner headed south. The rising sun felt hot on George's bare shoulders and he wished he had worn more than just canvas shorts. "It sure is."

"Look," said Brigitta, pointing to the east. A British destroyer appeared over the horizon and motored toward Tortola.

"They are still looking for the drone," said George.

Brigitta sat beside him, looking down at her feet where a hermit crab peeked out from its shell. Touching it with her toe, it disappeared inside its shell and rolled three feet down the hill. Turning to George, she asked, "Can we have another chance?"

A gentle tradewind breeze gently tugged at her hair and the morning sun reflected in her eyes. Neither of them had thought to bring sunglasses and the light made her to squint. George forced a smile and said, "What are our chances? Fifty-fifty?"

"No. I am through working for Harold Habit. My life will be my own. We will make it. I want to be with you."

Brigitta's eyes looked the color of the sea around them. George asked, "What about Tomorrow's Yachts? Didn't they want you to design a bunch of boats?"

"I'll do it on my terms, when I want and where I want. I can work from a computer anywhere. There is already more money in my bank account than I ever imagined. We can have the time of our lives."

Below them, pelicans dove over the bright blue shallows between Green Cay and Little Jost Van Dyke. For a moment they both watched, then Brigitta pointed at a frigate bird soaring overhead like a kite.

"Look at the way they fly," she said. "They can soar for days. We were working on drones that looked just like them and could do the same thing."

Higher, two more frigate birds ascended on rising air currents. George asked, "How do we know those are not drones?"

She laughed. "We don't. I suppose they could be."

Brigitta's eyes stayed on the birds. The lower one dropped down, then plunged still lower, almost to the surface of the sea, before climbing again. Brigitta stood to watch, mesmerized. Whatever the bird sought had escaped and it had to search again.

"You liked working on the aerial drones, didn't you?" said George.

"It was fun," said Brigitta, still watching.

Her eyes never left the bird. When it dropped toward the sea again, she flinched, as if diving too. George wondered if she memorized the bird's every move.

He said, "It's hot. Let's go back to the beach for a swim."

Stepping from the path onto the sand, George wondered if anyone else aboard *Frihet* was awake. The sand still felt cool beneath his feet and the rocks along the shore blocked the breeze. "Did you bring a bathing suit?" he asked.

"No. I didn't have one."

George smiled. "Me either."

He dropped his shorts, stepped out of them, then walked into the water to swim out. Stopping well away from shore, where his feet barely touched the bottom, he looked back. Brigitta swam out after him.

"It feels good," she said.

"It does." George slipped under the water to swim to the east. Popping up, Brigitta had followed.

"I should swim every morning," he said. "It clears my head and the exercise is great."

Brigitta beamed. "We can make it a daily ritual."

George dunked down to wrap his arms around her waist and lift her up. She squealed and he dropped her back into the sea. Laughing, he said, "Only if you swim with me."

"I promise."

"Come on," he said, starting for the shore.

When he swam into the sandy bottom, he turned to sit and watched Brigitta swimming in. She stopped beside him, sitting in chest deep water. "That was fun," she said. Pushing her hair back lifted breasts clear of the water.

George tried not to look, and said, "It felt good."

She reached for his hand. "Are we going to give it, and by that I mean our relationship, a try?"

"We have to," said George. "I can't get you out of my head. Every day I think of you."

"Jag älskar dig och jag vill ha dig."

"I love you too." George squeezed her hand and pulled her in for a kiss. Breaking it off, he said, "Let's get today over with."

She smiled. "Then we can go sailing?"

He nodded. "Yes. We need some time alone."

Dressing, he tried to sort out what he felt. Brigitta had been mesmerized by the soaring frigate bird. That was worrisome. Was she still interested in the aerial drone project? Would she run off to see it to its completion? And their little skinny-dip...it didn't feel...he wasn't sure. Was the magic gone? Or was he being overly cautious, just so he wouldn't get hurt again?

She pulled the pale blue jersey over her head then flipped her hair out of the collar. A smile flashed his way, but the magnetic attraction he used to feel had disappeared.

Why had he said the things he did? Was it only because he knew that was what she wanted to hear?

55

George had the satellite feed on the large computer in *Frihet*'s nav station. Before Brigitta had left she set it up for him. Zooming in, he counted six shark drones in the water between Sandy Spit and his boat. One swam lazy circles around *Frihet*, four milled around off the beach of Sandy Spit, and the sixth drifted along the eastern shore of Jost Van Dyke. Obviously they were watching events.

Somewhere to the south, in water much deeper, Mother sat waiting, probably listening to the sharks reporting what they were seeing. The last triangulation attempt had narrowed her position down to a one square mile area, but so far the Navy had not intervened.

Brigitta and Tova stood on the white sand beach of Sandy Spit beneath a cluster of palm trees that quivered in the strengthening tradewinds. It was hard to imagine two non-twins looking more alike anywhere on Earth. Both had dressed in khaki shorts and tank tops.

At one o'clock they were supposed to act as if arguing, to the point where physical violence seemed eminent. If nothing happened, they were to climb into the wood skiff and head into the cove created by Jost Van Dyke, Little Jost, and Green Cay, dramatically arguing all the way. Hopefully the drone would be drawn out into shallow water and show herself.

*

"So what do you want to argue about?" asked Tova, trying to lighten the mood. Brigitta had not smiled since she had first seen her that morning.

"I feel like cry."

"Why?"

"George doesn't love me anymore."

Tova picked up a tiny white shell and tossed it into the sea. "He was yours to lose. What did you think would happen? You spent all your time working."

"You tried to steal him from me, didn't you?"

"No, I never tried to steal him from you. You lost him. Only when I thought the two of you were done did I try to...."

"You did! You seduced him," shouted Brigitta, with tears running down her cheeks.

"No. George is a good man."

"You tried to take him from me."

"No I did not. He was crazy for you, but you ignored him."

"I did not." Brigitta started to sob uncontrollably.

Tova watched the Navy helicopter flying along the islands to the south. "He is a nice man. I would love to spend time with him. Was your work so important?"

Brigitta dropped to her knees, appearing about to vomit.

"We are supposed to argue, fight," said Tova, kneeling beside her and setting her hand on her sister's shoulder. "We want the drone to try and rescue you. This is too much."

Brigitta brushed her sister away and screamed, "You are a shit. Have you no scruples?"

*

Watching the two women on the satellite feed, George sipped an iced coffee and assumed the conflict was all an act. Beth and Windy stood next to him also watching, but neither said a word. The four shark drones still cruised off of Sandy Spit's beach and another circled their boat. The sixth drone had disappeared. Up on the foredeck, William and Kathy chatted, oblivious to the rest of the world.

Aboard *Absent*, Harold, Christine, and Captain Able watched the scene from inside the cavernous cabin in the center of the research vessel. Around them, technicians continually attempted to pinpoint Mother's location and decipher what the sharks were saying.

Two United States Navy MH-60R helicopters flew low over the water five miles to the north, hidden by the island of Little Jost Van Dike. Each was armed with two air to subsurface Mark 54 acoustic torpedoes.

North of Tortola, the British frigate HMS Dragon waited. Her surface to subsurface missiles ready if needed. Deep inside the vessel a team of technicians tried to unravel the location of Mother before the American team did, if only for pride.

Hidden by the northern horizon, the United States aircraft carrier *USS Dwight D. Eisenhower* launched aircraft armed with missiles and torpedoes on a rotating basis. The aircraft remained hidden over the horizon or at extreme altitude.

George sipped his iced coffee and wished for a scotch.

*

"Should we get in the skiff?" asked Tova.

"Stay away from me," yelled Brigitta, standing to swing a fist at her sister.

Tova stepped back out of the way. "Are you alright?"

"I am fine!" Brigitta ran for the boat to push it free of the beach.

Tova caught up just as the boat started to float. "You are not yourself."

Sobbing, Brigitta said, "Leave me alone. Stay here. Just let me go away."

"It is the head injury," said Tova. "You have been working too hard."

"I am fine," screamed Brigitta, pushing Tova back. "I swim…you run…boats suck, all boats suck, Harold sucks, winter is coming. Where is our mom? I want my mother…."

"You don't make sense, listen to yourself."

Brigitta climbed into the boat and tilted the outboard down into the water. As she pulled the starter rope, Tova clambered aboard and said, "You need to go home. You are not well."

The motor barked on the second pull and roared as Brigitta backed the boat away from the beach.

"Shut the thing off," yelled Tova. "We need to get you to a doctor."

With a twist of the throttle, the boat jumped ahead.

Tova fell against a seat.

*

Through transmissions from her sharks, Mother took it all in. Grave danger threatened Brigitta in the shape of an almost identical blonde woman. Mother had to do something about it. She lifted from the bottom to accelerate northward. Traveling at more than thirty knots and hugging the bottom, she closed the distance rapidly.

The water under Brigitta's boat was only twenty feet deep, but soon would pass to where the bottom dropped to sixty feet.

Images of the two women bickering came from the sharks. Mother's sensors showed a narrow stretch of deeper water ahead of the two women. She adjusted her course to intercept them there. Artificial Intelligence does not panic, only becomes determined. Saving Brigitta became paramount.

But rather than travel where the bottom dropped off, Brigitta steered northward and followed the three fathom contour, following the edge of Little Jost Van Dyke.

*

As the water beneath them turned from turquoise to blue, Brigitta spotted the drone speeding in their direction. Traveling only a few feet beneath the surface, it pushed up an enormous bulging bow wave that towered like a rolling hill. She snapped the tiller over to port and twisted the throttle, heading for shallower water. Mother accelerated in desperation.

Seeing the wall of water get close, Tova jumped from the boat.

The water lightened from indigo to turquoise as the bow wave rolled the skiff to starboard.

Mother's bow crashed hard into the bottom, pushing her hull upward on the sand. The firm sea bottom held Mother half out of the sea with her propeller slashing at the surface.

"Brigitta!" yelled Tova.

A black helicopter appeared over Little Jost Van Dyke and zipped low over the water. Men in black wet suits started dropping out of its bottom and into the sea.

A second chopper appeared. Men dropped onto the drone.

"Brigitta," cried Tova.

*

When the skiff pulled away from Sandy Spit, George headed for the inflatable tied to the stern of *Frihet*. Beth jumped into it with him and Windy stayed behind to man the radio if needed. They zipped across the clear water as Mother pushed the hill of water across in front of them. When Mother collided with Brigitta's boat, they were still two hundred yards away.

Then the helicopters appeared. A moment later men were jumping from helicopters onto the drone and into the sea.

Over the hum of the outboard, George heard what sounded like muffled gunshots. Later he would learn the Navy SEALs came equipped with bang sticks designed for protection against real sharks, and they worked equally as well on shark drones.

Beth spotted Tova in the water fifty yards behind the drone. They turned to grab her.

Over the back of the grounded drone and Brigitta's skiff, a Navy SEAL helicopter hovered while three divers worked in the water. A dangling cable became taught and lifted Brigitta along with one diver from the water. George slowed the inflatable to watch.

"Are you okay?" asked Beth, setting a hand on George's shoulder.

"Yeah. I hope she is too."

Tova sat ahead of them on the floor at the front of the boat, with her arms wrapped across her chest and wet hair draped down onto her shoulders. She shivered with tears running down her cheeks.

"Are you alright?" asked George.

Tova nodded and said, "Yag mår bra."

The helicopter with Brigitta aboard lifted skyward and headed north. George turned back toward *Frihet,* leaving the carnage behind. Passing *Raven,* Flake tried to catch their attention, but they ignored him.

A third chopper came over the island to hover over the gray steel island created by Harold Habit's enormous beached drone. Waves lapped at its eastern side and its twisted propeller still turned in a jerky motion. It was hard to imagine something so large having remained hidden for so long.

George brought the tender alongside *Frihet* and grabbed the gunnel. Tova crawled aboard first, wet and somber. As Beth climbed up, a massive explosion shook the air.

Thick black smoke rose from the aft end of the drone and the last helicopter lifted away. Around the end of Sandy Spit, two big black inflatables approached with additional SEAL teams.

"Harold is going to be pissed," said George. "He wanted to save the drone."

"Brigitta will be too," said Tova, still dripping. "She is not well. This will not be good for her."

56

George sat in the aft end of the cockpit and watched the trail of smoke drifting up from the aft end of Mother. It was obvious the Navy SEALs wanted to disable the drone permanently and blew her propeller to hell. Artificial Intelligence out of control was a serious worry for many people. Two helicopters hovered overhead and four large inflatables milled around the dark carcass of the disabled drone.

"Do you want a drink?" asked Beth.

"What time is it?" asked George.

"A little after three. Does it matter?"

One of the helicopters left to the north and the inflatables started to come alongside the drone.

He said, "Sure." His cell phone vibrated in his pocket, so he glanced at the display. Harold Habit. He tossed it up on the cabin top under the dodger.

"I need to go see my sister," said Tova, coming up the companionway. She had pulled on a baggy tee shirt along with dry shorts. Her eyes looked like she had been crying.

"Ask Beth to call Harold for you," said George. "I'm through with this whole mess."

While the two of them disappeared inside the boat, he watched another helicopter come in, hover over the broken drone, and then lower a man onto the top of the disabled hulk. George took a big swallow from his tumbler.

"George," said Tova, sticking her hear up the companionway. "Harold has a boat coming over to pick me up."

"Fine."

A minute later Tova came back up the companionway carrying large duffle. "I had fun," she said. "I did not want our trip to end this way."

George tried to force a smile and think up something clever to say as the inflatable came along side, but could only come up with, "Me either."

Tova stepped aboard, turned back to face George, then gave a little wave.

Coming aft along the starboard deck, William asked, "When can we go back to our hotel room?"

57

George rounded *Frihet* up into the wind in the shelter of the southernmost end of Christmas Cove. Beth freed the mainsail while Windy pushed the anchor overboard. As it plummeted to the bottom, both flaked the mainsail, then secured it with ties. Windy's cleating off of the anchor line brought the bow back into the wind and the stern settled back to within twenty feet of the rocky shore.

"What a day," said George, dropping onto a seat as the rode became taught.

Beth smiled. "Another drink?"

"I want a swim and a shower first," said George.

"That sounds like a good idea," said Windy. "Let me grab some towels."

West of them, a bright green ferry plowed through Current Cut, headed for Charlotte Amalia. Off the yacht club, more than a mile away on the east end of St. Thomas, two dozen little white sails fought to be first around the windward mark. Puffy white clouds hung over the top of St. Thomas in an otherwise bright blue sky.

Harold Habit's work boat had taken William and Kathy back to the island. They promised to stay in touch, but George had heard that enough in the past to know it was unlikely. After they had left, he, Windy, and Beth hoisted the anchor and sailed southwest toward the east end of St. Thomas. Little had been said along the way, with each lost in their own private thoughts. It felt good to be anchored someplace quiet.

George slipped off his shorts and dove off the transom.

Popping up, he turned to look back. Both Windy and Beth followed his example. Swimming toward the shore, the cool water cleared his mind. Where would Brigitta and Tova go? Back to the Åland Islands? It was beyond his control, so he struggled to let it go. And Windy? Did the drone really scare her that badly?

Swimming with his head underwater, he could hear the buzz of the ferry's engines and tasted saltiness on his lips. This was the present and he was among the islands that he loved. Between two large boulders on the sandy shore, he turned to sit on the sand with the water up over his waist. Both Beth and Windy swam towards him, heads bobbing and arms flailing. The scent of frangipani drifted from the hill behind him.

"Hey," said Beth, slowing a few feet away. "The water feels great."

"Hi," said Windy, her head popping clear of the sea.

"I needed this," said George.

"We all did," said Beth, turning to sit to George's left.

"This is one of my favorite places," said George. "Especially when I can anchor down this end. There's a bit of privacy here."

"I can see that," said Beth, sitting with her breasts awash.

Windy stopped to his right. "There is no place back home like this."

A pale green ferry raced to the west as a distant cruise ship poked southward, coming out of Charlotte Amalie Harbor. Two faraway sailboats motored toward them with mainsails up and headsails furled. A jet flew behind the peak of St. Thomas, leaving a long contrail and probably headed for the North American continent.

"I'm glad to be back here," said George. "It feels like I've been gone more than one winter."

"How often did you come to this cove?" asked Windy.

"Every chance I could get. Usually once or twice a month. It was an easy stop when I previsioned on St. Thomas, and it was a great place to just sit and work on my boat."

Two pelicans jumped up from the water next to tiny Fish Cay in the middle of the cove, their big wings struggling to lift them into the air. One banked to the left and crashed into the sea, followed almost immediately by the other. The two sat squeezing seawater out of the pouches beneath their bills to strain out a meal.

"What a spot," said Windy. Giggling, she tried to float on her back. "I could stay here forever."

George became very aware of Windy's nakedness. Turning to Beth, he asked, "Have you found any more boats for sale?"

She grinned at his discomfort. "I really haven't had time to look. There's just been too many distractions." She took a deep breath, which teasingly lifted her chest above the water.

"What are we doing tonight for dinner?" asked Windy, sitting again next to George. "I think we should celebrate. The drone is dead."

"There are lots of things in the freezer," offered George.

"Are there any lobsters around here?" asked Beth.

George sat up. "I used to find them on the reef that runs off the southwestern corner of this island."

"Let's give it a try."

Fifteen minutes later, the three snorkeled away from the boat and island, following the rocky reef into deeper water.

Windy had never experienced anything like it. The water caressed her skin, feeling neither warm nor cold…more like floating on air. Beneath her, bright yellow and black fish darted among the rocks and fingers of coral. Purple fan-like corals waved in the currents. Fish with scales the size of thumbnails and colored like a carnival troupe chomped on the rocks and coral. She could actually hear the crunching. Sea anemones, little fan-like blossoms, disappeared as fast as the speed of light when she tried to touch them. A charcoal gray fish with yellow stripes, she guessed to be some sort of angle fish, hung almost motionless against an enormous stag horn coral.

Beth slipped downward often, peeking into the dark crevasses, only to shake her head and then ascend slowly the surface. Bubbles trailed and sparkled. Windy watched and soon learned to do the same, kicking slowly downward before peering into the dark holes. The two women mesmerized George, with their lean muscles working the dive fins and then their peaceful ascents to the surface. Mermaids…beautiful mermaids.

He dove often to swim beside them and searched too, but sometimes followed, not to look for lobsters but just to watch the way they swam. Beth looked as home in the sea as a fish, but Windy seemed to be learning quickly.

Near the end of the reef, Beth looked up from forty feet down to give the thumbs up, then signified a large lobster by placing her hands three feet apart. Even with the snorkel in her mouth, it was easy to see her smile, and at that depth, she had looked very small.

George lifted his fins above the surface, to let their weight along with the weight of his legs push him downward, then kicked slowly toward the bottom. Kick, kick, kick, kick, kick, concentrating on relaxing and streamlining his body to conserve oxygen...then looking into the dark crevasse. It was the largest lobster he had seen in years. He glanced upward, where Windy and Beth looked tiny on the silvery surface. His lungs felt about to explode, so he drifted up.

Bursting above the water, he said, "That's a monster."

Beth laughed. "It will feed us all."

George nodded his head, adjusted his mask, and then gulped air. Giving Beth the thumbs up, he headed downward again.

Far below, Windy already looked into the hole where the lobster lurked. That shy New England girl was snorkeling naked and forty feet down. George found it hard to believe she was the same young woman he had left Cape Cod with. Was she really ready to give all this up for a life along the chilly New England coast?

He stopped beside her and she pointed in. A second smaller lobster stood behind the larger one. Through the glass of her dive mask, her eyes glowed with excitement.

George carefully slipped the snare behind the bigger one, then brought it forward and pulled the snare wire tight. The big crustacean fought valiantly, but it was no match for a hundred and seventy pound human.

58

George climbed up to the cockpit, squinting in the flat morning light. The mug of coffee in his hand promised waking and the air felt cool. Off to port, *Absent* sat anchored. She must have come in after dark. Ahead of the bow, to the north, the same sailboats were anchored as the day before. He settled against the stern pulpit and tried to remember the night before.

After snorkeling, cleaning up, and dressing, they had opened a bottle of Jura Tastival 2016 single malt and poured healthy drams into three tumblers. While George prepared the lobster, Windy and Beth started rice and made a salad. It had felt like a night to celebrate and all were in a good mood.

A second scotch had followed the first and then they sipped a third while the lobster cooked on the grill. While George divvied up the lobster, Beth opened a bottle of Renteria 2011 Cabernet Sauvignon and poured three glasses. By that time St. Thomas glowed from a thousand lit homes and only the faintest tinge of orange remained over the western horizon.

George remembered lingering in the cockpit. None of them had said much, the day had defied words, but they watched the night close in as a brightly lit cruise ship eased toward Charlotte Amalie. He had wondered about Brigitta and Tova. And what was Harold's next move? Could they save any of the drone or was it a total loss?

Finally, Beth had said something about going to bed and Windy seconded the motion. After the two disappeared inside the boat, George sat and watched the lights start to go out on St. Thomas. It felt good to be back in the Caribbean.

The rumble of a ferry passing through Current Cut brought him back to the present. He dropped back into the cabin and to check emails in the nav station. The first came from Tova.

George,
I am taking Brigitta home. She is not well and appears to be having some sort of breakdown. Harold's doctor gave her a sedative and she is resting peacefully, but when she is awake the things she says do not make sense. She needs a long period of quiet time. Harold offered the use of his jet.

I had fun sailing with you. It is too bad we did not have time to sail in the islands and get to know each other better. Taking care of my sister is the most important thing now.

Tova

In disbelief, George read it a second time. Brigitta was flying back to Åland. Would she be gone forever? In a panic, he promised himself he would write to Tova later.

The second email came from Harold. The first part mentioned Brigitta flying back to Scandinavia, but then he thanked George for his help recovering the drone.

"Hey," said Windy, stepping barefoot from her cabin. "Is there more of that coffee?"

George pointed at the coffee maker, "Help yourself."

"Emails?" she asked pouring.

George nodded. "Brigitta and Tova are on their way home."

"For good?"

"I guess," said George. Windy wore a short halter dress the color of mangoes with her hair back in a thick ponytail. Catching himself staring, he turned back to the computer.

The last email came from Elbridge Chapman, the CEO of Tomorrow's Yacht.

George,
I have exciting news. There are customers lining up to inquire about the TY50. In three weeks a young professional couple is flying to St.

Martin for a two week vacation and would like to spend a day or two sailing with you. Let me know your schedule and I will arrange timing. And then in mid-December a young man, who will be vacationing on Virgin Gorda, would like a day sailing with you. Both of these potential customers are serious and I hope you can accommodate them. Let me know your plans.

    Sincerely,
    Eldridge

George shut off the computer and climbed back to the cockpit where Windy stood facing into the breeze.

"The air smells nice," she said.

George stopped beside her and took a deep breath…something sweet blossomed on the shore. "It feels good to be back in the Caribbean," he said. Near a large shoreside boulder a pelican lifted skyward, banked hard, then plummeted like a stone. "Are you sure you want to leave?"

Windy forced a smile. "If my family knew what happened yesterday they would have died. I hate to make them worry."

George smiled and reached for her hand. "They didn't know, so they didn't worry."

Windy feebly shrugged one shoulder. "It was fun snorkeling yesterday."

"It's my favorite exercise," said George. "I try to swim every day."

Beth was up inside the boat, finding a mug and pouring coffee, then came up the companionway. Her hair appeared to explode in every direction and she wore not a stitch of clothing. Sitting with her back against the cabin, she asked, "When did they get here?" she asked, motioning toward *Absent*.

"Sometime in the night," said George.

Beth sipped her coffee. "This is a beautiful spot. I'll have to come here again."

Windy said something about checking emails and disappeared inside the boat. George leaned against the stern pulpit, wishing he had worn his dark glasses.

"So what are your plans?" he asked. "Have you found a boat to buy?"

"There are two boats on St. Thomas I want to look at, and one up on Virgin Gorda."

"If you're not in a hurry, I'm going to be needing a mate. There's a couple of potential customers that want to go for a sail."

Beth smiled and slid down to George's end of the cockpit. "What happened to all your young ladies?"

George ran through an abbreviated version of what had transpired with Tova, Brigitta, and Windy.

"You have had some bad luck," laughed Beth. "I will think about it. How soon do you have to know?"

"The sooner the better."

"I feel like a morning swim," said Beth. "Are you interested?"

"We have company coming," said George, pointing at a large orange inflatable approaching from *Absent*.

Beth disappeared inside the boat and George stood to greet the guests. When the big tender came alongside, Christine offered its painter.

"Come aboard for coffee," said George, taking the offered line.

Shutting off the outboards, Captain Able said, "We were going to invite you over."

"There is plenty of coffee already made," said George. "I insist."

Captain Able and Christine looked like tourists, in shorts and tee shirts. Beth came back on deck wearing a bikini bottom with a tank top, followed by Windy.

"When did you get here?" asked George, herding everyone toward the cockpit.

"Late last night about midnight," said Christine. "We saw you anchored here on the satellite image."

"Spying on us," laughed George.

"I'm afraid so," said Able, sitting in the cockpit.

"What's Harold up to?" asked George.

"He's working with the Navy to salvage his drone. They had the CPU out of it before dark last night," said Christine. "Our part in this is done, so he told us to take a few days off. Anchoring over here looked like a good place to get away from everything."

"That's what we thought too," said Beth.

Windy started to fill mugs with coffee.

"Several of my team want to fly back to the States as soon as possible," said Christine, "they've been away from home a long time. Later today we will take them to Charlotte Amalia where they can take a taxi to the airport." She smiled and set her hand on Able's. "After that we may visit a few of the other islands before heading home."

"We are going to do a little sailing too," said Windy, glancing at George.

"How are they going to move the drone?" asked George.

"The Navy has a big tug coming down. They'll tow it to Norfolk, Virginia," said Able. He also mentioned that the Russian and Chinese subs, which had been shadowing the operation, had disappeared right after the drone ran aground.

"We should be going," said Able, setting down his empty mug.

"One thing," said George. "Why did Harold name that boat *Absent*?"

Captain Able shook his head. "I am not really sure. When we were rigging the boat out to hunt the drone, he wanted it out on the sea, not in port. He wanted it absent."

"The man does have an odd sense of humor," said George.

"And an odd sense of right and wrong," said Beth.

George agreed with her inwardly, while glancing at the captain and Christine and wondering what they thought. Harold signed their paychecks every month.

59

Turning the helm, she rounded *Frihet* up into the wind as George freed the mainsail halyard. The white sail slithered downward to pile up on the boom. He walked forward to free the anchor and with a plop the hook plummeted down through the crystal clear water to hit the sandy bottom. The bow settled off to starboard. The tradewinds tugged at a strand of her hair and pulled at a corner of her tee shirt. Together, they muscled the mainsail into ties and then cleated off the anchor line.

Turquoise water stretched to the beach and the breeze cooled the air. Faraway off the stern, boats sailed toward Norman Island and, still further away, white sails poked along the eastern shore of St. John. Near Roger's Point at the end of the beach, two pelicans bobbed in the surf, looking quite content. White puffy clouds littered the sky and three distant frigate birds made lazy circles overhead. In less than an hour the sun would slip behind the southeast corner of St. John, basking all the Windward Islands in the shadow of nightfall. Small waves quietly kissed the sandy shore.

"What a spot," she said, stepping back into the cockpit. A puff of wind dragged a strand of her hair across her sunglasses and she pushed it aside. "It is the loveliest beach I have ever seen."

"And there is nobody else here," said George. "It is all ours."

She stopped to peer over the cabin top at the beach again. The sand sloped up to sea grape trees and an occasional coconut palm leaned toward the water. Craggy rocks marked each end of the beach, but between the sand looked white and unblemished.

"It's so peaceful. The last four days on St. Thomas were awful, waiting for the government people and their bullshit. I'm glad to be away from there."

"Would you like to go ashore?"

One palm tree leaned far out toward the water and its fronds rattled in the wind. Among the green leaves, behind it stood the remains of an old brick and stone building, one of the few remaining remnants of the sugar plantations. A fat silvery log had washed up close to the top of the white beach and would have made a lovely seat. Sea grapes grew in a cluster and hung out over the sand, creating a natural canopy to provide shade.

"It will be there in the morning. Can we spend some time there tomorrow?"

"Of course. We're in no hurry. We can spend the whole day here if you want." He pointed toward the island. "There is a path that will take us to the top of the hill if we want. The view is spectacular."

"That would be fun. Can we watch the sunrise from up there?"

George laughed. "Will you be up that early?"

With a grin, she said, "I don't know. Maybe."

"My first gig is in St. Martin and it isn't for two weeks," said George. "We can do whatever we want until then."

"What is the first job?"

"Just a daysail to show off this boat and maybe sell another one like it. You'll love the island, we'll eat out on the French side. The food is incredible. After that we take Bill Sanderlee and Brook out so Bill can learn to sail. That might take a week or whatever he wants."

She pushed her hair back, then grabbed the back of her tank top to pull it off over her head. Shaking her hair free, she tossed the shirt aside before straightening her sunglasses.

George laughed. "I see you really have gotten over your inhibitions."

"It is just you and me here, and I know you do not mind."

"I don't think anyone could mind," said George.

"Sailing with Brook and Bill will be fun. I like her, both of them actually,"

"Me too," said George.

"Where will we take them?"

"Wherever they want, maybe St. Martin or St. Barts."

"What's up after that?"

"One more daysail to sell a boat, that time leaving from Virgin Gorda. If we do sell a second boat, we don't have to really work again all winter. Or maybe even the next year."

Facing into the tradewinds, the breeze blew her hair back. George watched her wrestle it back into an unruly ponytail. They said nothing. She looked at the beach and along the shore running to the east.

He wondered what she was thinking. The figureheads beneath the bowsprits on old New England sailing vessels could have been modeled after her. The woman certainly had changed.

George settled into the center of the cockpit, where the air felt warmer. He asked, "Did I tell you Captain Moore is going to have another boat built?"

"No." She sat beside him. "His insurance will cover it?"

"No. Harold is paying for the whole thing. A yard up in Brooklyn, Maine is going to build it. It will be identical to his old boat, except brand new."

"That's incredible."

A frigate bird overhead caught their eyes and silently they watched it disappear to the north over the island. Waves soundlessly licked the beach and white clouds drifted to the west.

"Steaks later?" asked George, breaking the mood.

"That sounds perfect."

"It's warm. How about a swim first?"

The smile lit her face. "Sure, the sun is still warm. A quick one and then a shower before cocktails."

With her back to George, the bikini bottom slipped off and she giggled like a mischievous child.

"I see you've gotten completely over your shyness," laughed George.

"This feels so naughty," she said, stepping to the side of the boat, then glancing back added, "And incredibly nice." She sliced into the water with barely a splash.

George hurried to follow, taking three strokes under the water to pop up beside her.

"Wow."

Treading water, she smiled and said, "This feels heavenly."

"It does."

Starting a slow side-stroke back toward the boat, she asked, "Do you think Beth will buy that boat on St. Thomas?"

George smiled, "The price is right and it looked good to me."

She grabbed the swim ladder and dunked under to swish her hair back. "She would be crazy not to buy it. Sailing is her dream."

Catching up, George asked, "Sailing was your dream too. Have you decided to stay the whole winter?"

Windy beamed and nodded her head. "You couldn't chase me away."

The End

Jerry Allen grew up in eastern Massachusetts as the landscape changed from rural to suburban. With an abundance of woods to play in around his home and summers spent boating on Cape Cod, he naturally developed a love for the outdoors and adventure.

During his twenties Jerry lived in northern New Hampshire and earned his living as a logger. Eventually, he moved back to Massachusetts to help his father run a tree care business.

When the family business was sold, Jerry moved aboard a sailboat with his wife and infant daughter to sail down the coast to Florida. The following spring he cruised the Bahamas and then up the East coast again to work at a colorful old fashioned boat yard on Cape Cod. That fall he sailed south to the Caribbean, which Jerry would call home for over ten years.

All of his life Jerry has loved to write and, while living aboard, he finally found the time. After having several magazine articles published, he started writing novels. The characters Jerry lived and worked with gave him all the inspiration he needed.

The call of his New England roots was strong and pulled him back to the island of Martha's Vineyard, where he has unpacked his things and built a successful woodworking shop. But eventually the carnival atmosphere of the island chased him away to the quiet of the North Woods.

Along the way he crossed paths with a woman he had met twenty-five years earlier in the Virgin Islands. Discovering they shared much more than just a love for sailing, he married the woman and now they hike, fly fish, and run their two German wirehaired pointers in the Great North Woods. When the weather is lousy Jerry stays in and writes a bit.

Novels by Jerry Allen

Force of Habit
Winter of the Swan
Power Lies
Cast and Blast
Break a Bad Habit
Bad Habit
The Resort